SO-BAH-921

SALT

APR 2 1 2016

FIC Barne

Barnes, C.
Salt.

PRICE: $22.57 (3559/he   )

ALSO BY COLIN F. BARNES

Soil

Code Breakers: Alpha

Code Breakers: Beta

Code Breakers: Gamma

Code Breakers: Delta

WRITING AS WEARMOUTH & BARNES

Critical Dawn

Critical Path

Critical Strike

Sequence

COLIN F. BARNES

SALT

47NORTH

This is a work of fiction. Names, characters, organizations, places, events, and incidents are either products of the author's imagination or are used fictitiously.

Text copyright © 2015 Colin F. Barnes

All rights reserved.

No part of this book may be reproduced, or stored in a retrieval system, or transmitted in any form or by any means, electronic, mechanical, photocopying, recording, or otherwise, without express written permission of the publisher.

Published by 47North, Seattle

www.apub.com

Amazon, the Amazon logo, and 47North are trademarks of Amazon.com, Inc., or its affiliates.

ISBN-13: 978-1503948211
ISBN-10: 1503948218

Cover design by Jason Blackburn

Printed in the United States of America

SALT

SALT

CHAPTER ONE

I t took just a few weeks for the world to end.

Before the solar storms melted the ice and set off the earthquakes, releasing massive quantities of water trapped in the Earth's crust, Eva had lived every day with verve and optimism. Even with a positive approach to things, she could still hear the radio broadcasts by panicked geologists and climatologists as they struggled to piece together the data.

It turned out some of them were correct about how much trapped water there actually was, compacted and held within miles and miles of rock.

The barrage of solar storms instigated a domino effect of catastrophic disasters, bursting open the crusts with the movement of the plates. The internal heat and pressure pushed up the trapped water, both heating and adding to the volume in the seas by an order of magnitude that no one could have predicted.

Despite such a monumental natural disaster, Eva had tried to stay optimistic. Humanity was highly adaptive – she held on to that. It was all she truly had now that Mike was leaving.

Eva, along with the rest of the residents of the flotilla, stationed by the Pico de Orizaba Mountain in Mexico, hadn't expected anyone to leave so soon after the last one.

Each time a member of the flotilla took the fateful journey outward, to find resources, survivors, and land, it always felt too soon. With their numbers down to just one hundred and twenty-five, each lost soul had that much more impact on the group dynamic, the loss more keenly felt.

For Eva, this one cut deeper than the rest.

For two years she had lived on the flotilla, after spending a year post-disaster floating around the seas on various vessels barely staying alive. Yet as difficult as that period had been, knowing Mike was leaving was worse.

She pulled her windbreaker close around her neck, tasted salt on her lips from a salt mask that she and everyone else wore when outside to help keep the infection at bay. She ignored her hair as it blew in front of her eyes. She didn't want to see his face, his expression.

She'd break, and then the guilt would spill out, bringing the truth with it.

In the grey light of the afternoon, Mike Nelson turned his back on the flotilla and sorted through the meagre supplies on the deck of the small fishing boat. There, with the tip of the mountain, the Pico de Orizaba, jutting out from the single, world-spanning ocean, the small boat appeared in the weak midday sun as indefatigable as driftwood. And when the storms returned after this rare, calm break, she feared the boat would be nothing more than wreckage.

All volunteers were given a month's food and water, and enough fuel to last two days. If the harsh waves from the storms didn't kill them, they'd have to survive on their own with whatever they could find. So far, in thirteen months, none of the twelve volunteers had returned.

That meant no other survivors found, no other landmass . . . no answers.

'It's too soon,' Jean cried. Jean – Mike's wife, Eva's best friend. Eva placed an arm around Jean's shoulder, unable to give her verbal support for fear the truth of her feelings for the woman's husband would suddenly tumble out, cajoled by shame and guilt.

If Mike weren't to return, it would be better to let Jean think he loved her. Eva couldn't wound her with the truth on a day like this. If Jean felt only half of what Eva did, she couldn't put her through that pain.

Mike would leave as a loyal husband and doting father, a true hero in times of great need. That the odds of him returning were short only made his sacrifice that much greater, especially as he'd agreed to leave two weeks earlier than scheduled, on account of the sudden change in weather. Not that that fact had assuaged the anger of the crowd.

They had gathered on the deck of the British naval destroyer, the HMS *Bravo*. The flotilla captain, Jim Reynolds – captain of a cruise ship which made up the centrepiece of the flotilla – and his son and vice-captain, Duncan, stood by the winch and lowered down the last of Mike's promised supplies. It seemed the rest of the crew were still below decks, no doubt working on their duties.

The remaining crowd, gathered on the bow of the destroyer, stared towards Jim, their silent majority making it clear what they thought of his decision. They only remained quiet for Mike's sake. But Eva could feel the tension increase with every passing minute.

They blamed Jim for the loss of the volunteers. Each family who lost a loved one would focus their grief and hatred on Jim, as if it were his hands that killed them. But Eva knew he was just doing his best. The residents had elected him due to his previous captain's role on the *Alonsa*, but many wouldn't let him get on with the job of helping to hold the flotilla together.

Not that this issue was the only cause of a split amongst the survivors.

Standing clear of the group of bystanders, her long brown hair blowing against her white robes, Susan Faust, the leader of a cabal of religious fundamentalists, held her arms aloft, flung her head back, and spoke in a babble of tongues, her German accent punctuating each syllable. Her flock of twenty-five believers, seemingly understanding the garbled words, bowed their heads to their chests and murmured 'Amen.'

Eva had seen this ritual with each volunteer that had left. She would gather her congregation and suggest that the volunteer's fate was in God's hands, and that the reason why no one left was that those not in her influence were bringing doom upon the group, inciting God's wrath.

'Bloody lunatic,' one of the onlookers whispered to Eva, nodding her shaved head towards Faust. Her words were muffled behind her salt mask. 'Her and her lot took the Kiwis' food right from their table yesterday. They think they can get away with anything with their so-called God on their side. They make me sick.'

Eva sighed. She heard many such complaints, but nothing could be proven – yet. Eva wanted to avoid getting involved with rumours and accusations. She didn't want to have to deal with mob justice.

She wished Faust's lot would just get involved more and work with the others on the flotilla. Instead, Faust sought division, keeping her flock outside of the community's responsibilities. You'd never see one of Faust's followers volunteer to go out and find more resources or survivors. Eva had never seen one of them help with the fishing duties, the sorting of drift for useful items, or any number of jobs that were required to keep life viable on the flotilla.

Individuals would perish in this new, drowned world.

Beside Susan's group, Marcus Graves looked on. He wore his usual long, black coat, its collar protecting his ears from the chilling Mexican winds. The solar storms that had instigated the drowning had continued to rage, sending the Earth's climate into a chaotic tailspin.

There were no recognisable seasons anymore; just day after day of heavy clouds, rain and high winds.

Eva caught Graves' attention. He flashed her a wolfish grin. Although 'grin' was generous. It was more a baring of teeth. Marcus fancied himself a leader. But unlike Susan, he did not have the charisma or religious fervour to attract larger support outside of his immediate family. His group numbered just four, all from his own family, or 'firm' as he called them in his east London accent. He kept his eyes firmly on Eva. She ignored him and looked away.

She wondered if he knew about her and Mike, the latter having worked for Marcus on a number of jobs recently. She ignored the knotting in her stomach at the thought of that scumbag having something on her. If there was one character among this motley crew who'd use such knowledge for personal gain, it was he.

If she was being entirely honest with herself, it wasn't just the secret of her affair coming out that she worried about so much; it was the exposing of the guilt she felt about betraying her friend – and the inevitable time when she would have to confess to Jean.

It made her feel sick just thinking of it. It wasn't as if she meant anything to happen, neither of them did, but then that was perhaps her just trying to rationalise it away; she had seen it many times herself on the force – people cheating on each other for no other reason than that it just happened. At the time she had never believed them, thought it was just an easy cover for their lies and guilt, but now being on the other side of things, she had more empathy with them.

Eva moved through the crowd, wanting to get some distance between her and Graves. At least that was what she told herself. Being farther away from Jean was just a coincidence. *Right.*

An unsettled murmuring broke out amongst the crowd as Jim brought up the empty winch. The time was approaching fast. Everyone on the flotilla had their unique ritual when it came to these events. Eva's was to grip the railing of the *Bravo* and try not to be sick with hope. Hope that, somehow, this one would be the one to find help, other survivors . . . or . . . she didn't know what. She just hoped.

Otherwise they were just sending these people, these survivors, to their watery doom. Maybe that's why they volunteered, she thought – to get it over and done with?

Life on the flotilla was getting harder each week. The hulls rusted and decayed, their makeshift wind turbines became less efficient, which made the fact Jim had decided to bring forward a launch that much more galling. Two days' fuel for the boat could have gone to the running of the flotilla. Given the grumbles of the crowd, it seemed she wasn't the only one who had figured that one out.

'Why Mike, Eva? Why now?' Ade said as he stepped beside her, his voice carrying the characteristic South African pinched vowels. He looked alien to Eva then. Any time Ade wasn't flashing his great white smile seemed like an abhorrent time. The old engineer had seemed to thrive since he came to the flotilla, half dead, dehydrated, on the wreckage of a South African military lifeboat. 'He was one of the best here, ya know?'

'I know,' Eva said. She watched Mike strap the last of his supplies down and enter the small, half-open cabin of the boat. 'I know too well.'

The small craft was less a boat, more a floating coffin, she thought. They should have given him one of the larger vessels chained to the vast floating city of ships. They could have spared it. The flotilla stretched for nearly three-quarters of a mile edge to edge, and a half-mile deep. Hundreds of vessels and wrecks conjoined to form the last, as far as she knew, vestige of humanity.

The family who'd lived on the one he'd been given, the *Tracer*, had gone overboard the week before in a joint suicide pact during their fishing shift. She didn't like the idea of Mike taking it. Felt like inviting unnecessary bad juju. She tried to ignore the image of Mike splashing into the water like the fisherman and his wife.

Fishing was one of the few things that had prospered since the world drowned. Seven billion humans meant a lot of food for fish, including predators: eels, sharks, whales. Eva knew there was some irony in there somewhere, but couldn't bring herself to finish the thought.

Jean was crying, her voice the only one heard among the group now that Faust had finally finished her sermon. Even the wind had died.

Eva had never seen it so calm.

The boats no longer rocked or rolled like before. It made her uneasy after spending the last two years used to getting around the vast surface of the floating ships in the near-endless storms.

Mike looked up to the group. Eva watched him out of the corner of her eye and gripped the railing so hard she thought her knuckles would split out of her skin. Her tears retreated.

From inside the cabin, Mike waved. For a moment, Eva released her grip, ready to wave back, but as she turned her head, she saw it was Jean whom Mike was waving to.

A husband to the very last.

He caught Eva's eye for a moment before she could look away. His expression said everything, and her chest tightened. When she looked back, he had turned away and started the engines.

A spluttering of diesel smoke hovered by the stern as the boat's prop churned the water. At first it didn't look like he was moving, but when Eva finally blinked, she saw the whitewater trail bobbing behind him as he headed towards the mountain peak.

He'd go round the east side and head north to Alaska, where Mount McKinley would be above water level, and where Jim and the others believed he might find survivors, it being higher than Pico de Orizaba, around which the flotilla was built. The other alternative was to go south to Aconcagua, a mountain in Argentina.

The last two volunteers had gone south.

The fuel wouldn't last long enough anyway, everyone knew, but still they volunteered. Hope was a powerful motivator.

But not for Mike. He wouldn't do this unless there was something else going on.

Eva wasn't naive enough to believe his love for her would keep him from leaving. He'd have stayed because he was loyal to Jean and his six-year-old son, Danny. Even though his feelings for Eva were clear, and vice versa, he had never betrayed Jean, was never unfaithful.

The *Tracer* approached the craggy peak and disappeared beyond it. When the trail of wake had dissolved into the ocean, the crowd seemed to take a breath and come to life. An explosion of emotion poured out. Eva turned to see Jean holding Danny close to her, his face buried against her waist. Tears tracked down Jean's face. Yet more drips in the ocean. Her grief wouldn't bring him back.

'I'll miss him,' Ade said, rubbing his hand across his dark-skinned forehead. He smelled of grease and diesel. His overalls hung off his wiry frame and whipped in the wind that had seemed to pause during Mike's progress before returning to batter the flotilla as it had always done. The ripple of waves increased, each one cresting that bit higher. White spray splashed against the peak and the hull of the *Bravo* that had run aground against the mountain's ridges.

Ade turned from Eva and loped across the deck of the *Bravo*, then hopped down onto the next level, a Chinese container ship carrying a multitude of now-empty containers.

The ones that had anything in them had long since been emptied, the items repurposed for use on the flotilla to grow food, set up fish farms and produce drinking water from the ocean. Some of the survivors made their homes in the containers, the rigid metal boxes providing good shelter from the harsh weather.

With nearly a hundred ships lashed together, most of them run aground on the Orizaba's various ridges, the survivors had set up a desalination system using both natural and fuel-assisted means: the latter would be no good within weeks, once the carefully rationed fuel eventually ran out. Only time and tight controls would tell whether natural evaporation-based desalination would be enough to sustain the current number of survivors.

Beyond the container ship lay a rolling city of smaller craft: fishing vessels, yachts, life rafts, a tug, and even a competition-level racing catamaran. She watched Ade expertly navigate the streets made from boards and pieces of wreckage. A maze of paths wove a complicated pattern throughout the flotilla, which seemed to grow and change organically as new pathways were found and sections of the place came into the possession of different people.

That was Graves' ambition: to grab segments of the flotilla when someone died, left or committed suicide. He and his family dominated a fifth of the deck space, threatening anyone else who dared to lay claim – not that there were many; space wasn't a huge issue when there were so few people left, making Graves' ambitions petty and futile. She'd seen it all the time on the streets, minor drug dealers and gangsters vying over some corner that had no great influence in the scheme of things.

Ade ducked below the makeshift streets at the corner of *Sweet Mary*, a trawler, and the *Slice of Life*, a leisure boat. That was central

Graves territory. Ade usually worked out of Jim's cruise ship, the *Alonsa*, in the engineering department. They had set up workshops there to repurpose and salvage what they could. A minute later, Graves and his firm followed the African engineer, making Eva wonder what Ade was up to with that lot.

Yet another question on a day that seemed full of them.

Eva was about to return to her cabin on the cruise ship when she heard a few people shout behind her. Someone – pushing through the crowd, running towards Jim and Duncan, who were tying off the winch – brushed past her, nearly knocking her off her feet.

A hand grabbed her, stopped her from falling.

'Careful,' Jean said, letting go of Eva's hand as she righted herself. Jean's face was puffy and wet, her eyes red. She looked at Eva as if she could see right through her. 'I know,' she added. 'Mike told me . . . before he . . .'

Eva's mouth dropped open, the shock and confusion stealing her words. One of Faust's followers screamed as he was slammed against the railing. Eva spun away from Jean, saw a hooded man rush towards Jim, a gaff hook in his right hand.

Before Eva realised what she was doing, her cop instincts kicked in, and she sprinted after him. She launched herself forward, tackling the man around his waist.

The momentum pushed him hard against the *Bravo*'s main six-inch-gun turret, now rusted and useless.

The impact winded Eva, and she lost her footing, taking the man to the deck with her. The gaff hook clattered beside her. The man reached out for it, but a foot stamped on his forearm. A pair of hands reached beneath Eva's arms and lifted her up. She turned to face Duncan. He flashed a smile at her through his great red beard.

Jim's face was the complete opposite, despite the genetic similarity.

His foot pressed harder against the man's arm, making him scream with pain. Reaching down, Jim grabbed the man by the collar and lifted him to his feet, slamming him against the side of the gun's turret section.

'Nicely done,' Duncan said in his curious half-Scottish, half-English accent. 'If you hadn't tackled him in time, my old man would have taken that in his back.' He pointed to the hook with his foot.

The crowd had gathered round, wondering who the man was.

Despite his hooded face, Eva knew he was one of Graves' firm.

Jim said something to him that Eva couldn't hear.

'Really, thanks,' Duncan said before helping his father lead the man away towards the bridge of the ship.

'You're welcome,' Eva said as they walked away. She rubbed her ribs, clearing the pain from her fall.

Before Jim ducked inside, he turned to the others and glared. 'I think you've had your fill of drama today. Get back to work. This flotilla won't survive on its own.' He gave a curt nod of thanks to Eva. She returned the gesture.

The crowd mumbled their responses before dispersing to their various vessels and responsibilities. The question of the man's motives became a fevered topic among the group. The citizens shared various wild and fanciful theories.

Eva had no ideas beyond an obvious assassination ploy, but wondered if it was part of something bigger – perhaps something to do with Graves.

But would he really be so stupid as to try to take out Jim like that? Sure, Jim wasn't Mr Popular these days with his hardline stance on strict maintenance work and the sending of volunteers, but he still had the support of a good number of the group and most of the crew from the *Bravo*. She put the mystery to the back of her mind for now. The full details would no doubt come out via the grapevine soon enough. She would keep her ears and eyes open for anything that might seem related. One never knew when a random association would bring that spark of inspiration.

Besides, secrets never lasted long on the flotilla.

Eva headed towards the *Alonsa*, found herself in step with Jean, and remembered the woman's confession just minutes before.

'Look, it's . . . I'm . . .' Eva began to say, speaking through her mask, but the words wouldn't come.

Jean just shook her head and placed an arm around Eva's waist; her other arm gripped Danny. 'Don't say anything. We both loved him. That's all that matters. Let's just look out for each other from now on. We need you, Danny and I.'

Choking on her long-held tears, Eva nodded and returned Jean's hug, all the while trying not to break apart with guilt. She focused on the southern horizon. A gathering formation of slate-grey clouds conspired together; their secrets flashed white and yellow, lighting up their insides, X-rays of bad intentions. A storm was brewing and had the flotilla within its sights.

Just keep going, Mike. Just keep going.

CHAPTER TWO

J im heard a commotion coming from out on the *Bravo*'s deck as he passed through the narrow passage below the steps. Two men were shouting at each other; not an isolated case these days, he thought wearily as he dashed up the steps and out onto the deck, pulling his salt mask over his mouth.

The corners of his lips were cracked and sore from the salt. He licked his lips and wished he had kept his hip flask of rum with him. The salt, Dr Singh had said, was what kept the infection at bay: the bacterium at fault lay dormant in a salt solution. Only when the salt content went down would the bacteria come alive and start to replicate again.

A few metres away, two men had each other by the lapels and were staggering about the deck.

They were two of the *Bravo* maintenance crew. Jim had noticed them arguing the day before. He rushed over and forced himself between them, pushing them aside with his arms. To the smaller, older man, Jim said, 'What the hell is going on?'

'This fool was adjusting the food provisions,' the man said, his voice muffled through his tattered white and grey facemask. Jim turned to the taller man and asked if it was true.

'The old swine's a liar,' the taller man said. 'I was doing a stocktake, is all. He had no right being down there in the stores, anyway. What were you up to, you old fool? Thought *you* could steal extra rations?'

'That's enough! Both of you,' Jim snapped, his patience wearing thin. 'I'm sick of all this bickering. We need to stay united. We need to show the rest of the flotilla that we're in control of things, that we're capable of surviving. I don't care who was doing what: it stops now. Understood?'

The younger, taller man gave Jim an 'Or what?' look, to which Jim responded, 'If you don't like it on the crew, you can always leave and go live with the other residents – that goes for both of you. We're elected to serve the needs of the people, not sneak away with extra food. You want me to put this out to the public?'

Both men dropped their heads and sighed, their masks crinkling as they inhaled and then exhaled. Jim felt the faint drops of rain and shivered beneath his thick coat. 'The rain's coming,' he said. 'You better get inside; no need to stand out here risking infection, not since Karel was diagnosed yesterday. I can't keep losing crew.' And he couldn't. With the flu-like infection seemingly getting worse as the flotilla struggled to contain it, they'd get to a point where there would be too few people to maintain the desalinators, the farms and the fishing schedules.

The two men grumbled something that resembled an apology and headed into the doorway and down the steps into the *Bravo*. Jim followed, his arms and legs trembling slightly with the cold. He needed a break today, and some rum. All three men stopped at the salt bath – a large bucket – and washed their hands, drying them on a towel hung on a hook above.

Jim sat heavily at the desk. He lit a whale-oil candle and leaned back in his chair. The dull off-white decor of the *Bravo*'s captain's office seemed to suck the light into shadow, reflecting his own mood. Despite what the residents thought, these days were harder on him than they could imagine.

He didn't enjoy sending people away, but their survival depended on it.

If they just stayed where they were, they'd slowly go mad and turn on each other. He'd already seen it start to happen, fractures within the society growing wider, spreading like a cancer. Hell, even his own crew was now fighting amongst each other.

Duncan hobbled into the office, carrying a flask, and slumped in the chair opposite. 'Studying the charts again, Dad?'

Duncan's right leg was permanently crooked after he had capsized during the early settlement of the flotilla. One of the smaller boats had broken away and been toppled by a freak wave. Despite a broken leg, Duncan had managed to save the crew and bring the boat back to the safety of the other ships. But Dr Singh had only been able to splint it. She'd said it really needed a plate and screws, but their medical facilities were not up to that level of operation.

Still, Duncan was young enough to work around it.

'Just plotting Mike's likely route.'

Jim traced his fingers across the well-worn chart stretched across the desk, repaired by sticky tape at various points. He wanted to remind Duncan that he was his captain, not his father, when on shift, but what did it matter now? His position was growing weaker by the day. He wouldn't be captain for much longer if things carried on the way they were.

'Frank in the brig now?' Jim asked.

'Yeah, the crew got him settled. He won't cause any issues now.'

'I want him questioned, but don't let them get too rough. We're not at war here, you understand? Graves isn't stupid; there's more to this than it seems at first sight. Let's play it safe, and don't do anything rash.'

Duncan nodded. 'Sure.' He removed the cap from the flask, took out two inner cups, placed them on the desk and filled each with a healthy measure of flotilla-grog: three parts water, one part rum.

'How much do we have left?' Jim asked as he lifted the cup to his lips.

'Two more flasks after this.'

Jim grunted his disappointment but knew that wasn't entirely true. They had managed to salvage a few crates of cheap, Chinese knock-off rum when the container ship had drifted by. They'd cut it so thin with water to make it last that getting drunk took considerable commitment. Still, Jim took a deep gulp, enjoying the nasty burn it brought.

One of the crates remained in Jim's possession. Uncut. Just for emergencies.

'It's a reminder, son.'

'What is?' Duncan wiped his mouth with the back of his hand.

'The burn. A reminder we're still alive, despite everything. We're still here.'

'Much to Faust's chagrin, eh? She's real pissed that she and her delusional followers weren't taken up in the rapture.'

'This ain't a biblical apocalypse. Maybe one day the crazy bitch will be right, but now it's just science and nature, and we're caught up in the middle of it. But we're still drinking rum and riding the waves, and if there's sufficient luck or fortune or whatever else you want to call it, that poor bastard Mike will make it.'

Duncan held up his cup in a toast. 'To Mike.'

Jim finished his cup and made to refill it but stopped himself.

After a silence, Duncan said, 'He's not, though, is he, Dad? Going to make it, I mean. None of the others have – no radio comms, no returns. The only thing that ever came back was Aadi's boat wreckage.'

Jim shrugged. 'Ionosphere's still screwed by the solar storms, so I doubt we'll get another radio signal any time soon. The planet's hostile to us now. We've just got to find a way, somehow. But you're getting me maudlin here. What was it you wanted to talk to me about before we saw Mike off?'

Duncan leaned forward now and looked over his shoulder to the closed door. 'The sabotage has stepped up. I took a measurement of fuel stocks after sorting out Mike's share.'

'I'm not going to like this, am I?'

'No. We should have had enough reserve stocks for at least three months of running some of the generators and the desalinators, but when I calculated it, it appears we've enough for less than a week at current usage.'

Jim took a moment to think of the consequences. With no fuel to run the desalination units, they'd have to rely on the manual evaporation methods. Would there be enough water generated to sustain the current levels?

They'd been stockpiling rainwater in some of the containers, but with the bacteria spreading, Dr Singh had advised them to use only boiled desalinated water. The flu-like symptoms seemed to mutate when water evaporated off the ocean and returned as rain.

Dr Singh had proved that the salt kept the bacteria in a spore mode, which stopped it from mutating into its deadlier form – one that turned rational human beings into vegetables.

The quarantine section, set up in the medical rooms of the *Alonsa*, had fifteen people within it now. New diagnoses had gone from monthly to weekly. The doctor and her young assistant, Annette, took weekly samples and tested them for the bacteria.

Ideally, they would test every day, but they just didn't have the time or resources.

So far, they had discovered no cure. Every dwelling within the collection of boats and ships had salt baths by its doors. People were encouraged to continually wash their hands in these in order to keep the spread of the bacteria at bay.

'We're going to need to figure out a system of boiling the rain stocks,' Jim said. 'Without fuel.'

'We could dismantle some of the smaller vessels, perhaps trawl for wreckage and driftwood.'

Given that the world had drowned, all of its cities lay beneath the water, creating tonnes of debris. The waves often brought miles and miles of plastic and wood . . . and bodies. Jim considered for a brief moment using the bodies for fuel but was too sickened by himself to take that thought any further.

They'd have to start sorting through all the trash and debris on the flotilla, gather material for burning, and not just the personal quantities that everyone used for their day-to-day needs. They'd need to be more organised, set up a proper system of boiling and allocation.

'How're the hydro and wind turbines doing? Our battery levels?'

'I've got Ade and his team working on the wind turbines, as they're generating just ten percent of what they normally should. Hydros . . . well, it's not looking good.'

Jim reached for the flask, poured another cup and downed it in one. He focused on the burn, reminding himself that he was still alive.

'What did you want me to do?' Duncan asked.

'Ade's compromised. Get him off the job, send some of our crew down to the workshops to help Stanic and see if they can't get the hydro and wind turbines back up to full capacity. In the meantime, I'll order a brown-out.'

'Are you sure? I mean, you saw the crowd today, the levels of hate towards us—'

'Me, Dunc. They hate *me* – for sending the volunteers away. But I don't care how much they hate me. I'll be damned if I'm going to let this place descend into chaos. We need order and structure. They can wish I'm dead for all I care, but power is to be shut off within the hour. You understand?'

'Aye, Captain, I understand.' Duncan stood and saluted.

'Go. I'll inform the flotilla over the PA. Cut all power and generators until I tell you to put them back on. In the meantime, get the crew to get some answers from Frank; find out what the hell Graves is up to, if it's even anything to do with him.'

Duncan nodded and left the office, leaving the flask of rum behind on the table, the cups empty and waiting.

Although it wouldn't help much, Jim finished the grog before moving to the radio PA system. He took the transmitter off the hook and informed the flotilla that all power would be cut until further notice.

Even as he was saying the words, he could feel a shift in the air as though the very place had altered its psychology. He knew this wouldn't be welcomed so soon after Mike's departure.

But they, and Duncan, were wrong. Mike would find survival, just not where the others thought.

And it would be for their own damned good.

CHAPTER THREE

Eva and Jean, standing either side of Danny, took his hands and helped him across the narrow planks that led from a group of African fishing vessels, roped together like an island within the flotilla, to the half-sunk hull of the once-grand cruiser, *Alonsa*.

Their progress to Jean's cabin was soundtracked by the first grumbles of thunder. One day's calm weather was all they'd got. Eva had wished for more, hoping that this day would prove to be a tipping point, the moment when the Earth's weather settled and improved. Fine rain tickled the bare skin of her neck as she lifted Danny across to Jean standing within the *Alonsa*, her arms out.

Today would not be the tipping point.

The jagged wound in the hull, where it had first struck the rocks of the Orizaba, provided easy access to the ship's lower levels. Only the lowest two had flooded. The rest were converted into various workshops, Dr Kyra Singh's quarantine and lab, and general stores. Eva's cabin, next to Jean and Mike's, lay two levels above.

Sometimes at night she'd hear Ade and members of Jim's crew working on some contraption or other. They had dismantled the engines and other damaged parts of the ship to reuse elsewhere.

No words were spoken as Eva followed Jean and Danny through the tight passageways towards the central staircase. The elevator had long since stopped working. Even if it did, they could never justify the power usage. The ship looked like an internal version of the flotilla's exterior.

Throughout the corridors and rooms, sheet metal, old doors, pieces of furniture and whatever wreckage could be used had been repurposed to create new floors and room partitions. The *Alonsa* tilted fifteen or so degrees to its port side, the side facing the Orizaba peak.

At the lowest level, one could see the rock piercing through the bottom of the hull.

Eva ascended the stairs, gripping on to a thick rope that had been tied to the top to help combat this tilt. The floor of the narrow wood-panelled corridor that led to her cabin had been wedged to counteract the tilt. Even though she only stood five-and-a-half feet tall, she had to duck. The level above had collapsed during a fire. Burnt-out timbers and iron girders hung down like the guts of a whale.

'Eva, will you come in for tea?' Jean said as she and Danny reached their cabin.

Although Eva didn't want to, she knew she was in the woman's debt, and the way Jean looked at Eva told her that she really didn't want to be alone. In truth, neither did Eva.

'Sure,' she said. 'Thanks.'

'We got extra provisions,' Danny said. 'For Daddy's mission.'

'That's good, Dan.'

She felt for the kid. At his age, how could anyone truly explain the situation? That he thought his father had left on a mission was probably the least horrible lie. And in some ways, Mike *was* on a mission, but for survival rather than discovery.

Before Eva entered Jean's cabin, a group of Chinese teenagers ran past her, nearly knocking into her. One of the smaller kids, wearing what would have been highly desirable designer sneakers, led the others, chattering excited words.

It made her realise how resilient kids were.

Even after the near-extinction of their race and in their desperate situation, they still found joy in things. She'd seen this particular group take a small boat on one of the calmer days to scale the Orizaba. Once at the top, they had pinned a makeshift flag to the summit: a Chinese flag made from the red and yellow fabric from a life raft. Jim hadn't been happy that he and some of his crew had had to rescue them.

The flag had lasted less than an hour before the storms tore it away.

Eva closed the door behind her and sat on a cushioned sofa.

Jean and Mike had made their cabin – two knocked together – a cosy and comfortable living space. Open plan, it featured two beds on the far side beneath a porthole, its glass covered with algae. A kitchenette made from packing crates lined the opposite wall. In the middle were a narrow sofa and a small table that Mike had made from driftwood.

She'd once seen a table like that in her native Idaho.

A designer-furniture store selling bespoke, handcrafted pieces had had a table just like it for five thousand dollars. Authentic, they said.

Value had a different meaning on the flotilla.

Jean handed her a lukewarm cup of tea. A blend cut with dried seaweed. The container ship was full of tea, but like everything, the initial rationing had expanded and their stocks had diminished faster than they had hoped.

It seemed everything was cut with something now.

Soon, they'd be entirely reliant on the ocean.

The tea didn't help. It tasted foul. She could normally tolerate it. She choked it down regardless, not wanting to look at Jean from across the table. Danny had taken to his bed, where he had a collection of books and comics that he'd found in one of the other ship's cabins.

After the *Alonsa* had come aground, a fire had broken out through a section of the cabins. Eva could never get the sight of all those burned bodies out of her mind. She had removed four of them from her own cabin. The detritus of their lives was left behind, a reminder to her that so many who had perished were real people and not just numbers.

'Jean, look, I have to say this.'

'No, you don't. I get it. Mike and I talked about trying for another baby.'

Both women lowered their voices so Danny couldn't hear. The increasing patter of rain against the hull provided a cover of sound. He wouldn't hear anyway once he got absorbed in his stories.

'Until I came along?' Eva said. 'You know I never planned for any of this to happen. I never wanted to betray our friendship. I never even knew what I felt until . . .'

'Go on,' Jean prompted. 'Tell me. We've nothing to hide anymore.'

'I was out on fishing duty one day a few months ago. I slipped pulling in the nets; they got snagged on something. I nearly went over. Mike was there. He grabbed me, stopped me from going in while others stood by and watched. There was just something in that moment that I knew. Like I said, I didn't plan it. I wish I could have changed my feelings. But we never . . . you know?'

'I know. He told me everything this morning. It seems neither of us got to really love Mike.'

'You didn't try for the baby, then?' Eva asked, hating herself for putting her friend through the heartache of this conversation.

Jean just shook her head before turning to look at Danny, his knees up by his chest, the comic flat against his legs. She turned back and said, 'If anything happens to me, would you look out for him?'

'Of course, but what do you mean, if anything happens to you? You're not thinking of—'

'Suicide? No, absolutely not. What if Mike comes back? I know his love for me is different, but I couldn't do that to him. Couldn't let him return to find Danny orphaned.'

Eva reached out and took Jean's hand to stop it from shaking. Her hand was cold and clammy. 'I'll look out for him, I promise. But don't go doing anything stupid. I need you too. There's a bad feeling about this place these days. We need to stick together.'

Jean squeezed Eva's hand. 'Thank you. This might sound strange, given you're effectively my husband's mistress, but we've a spare berth here now. I'd like it if you would join us. I don't like the idea of either of us being alone.'

Before Eva could respond, a pair of long shadows appeared beneath the door. Someone knocked. The door handle turned, and it opened. Two of Graves' firm, wearing brand-new salt masks made from dampened white fabric, stood in the doorway.

'Well, well. You two ladies are lookin' cosy, ain't ya?'

Eva stood, took two strides across the room and blocked their ingress.

She recognised them instantly. Graves' cousins: Shaley and Tyson. The latter was essentially Marcus's enforcer. His right eye had been taken out with a hot poker. Some dispute with another London gang back in the day. Shaley was his brother, the brightest of the pair, but still not exactly the sharpest tool in the box.

'What do you two want?' Eva said, adjusting her weight onto her left foot and twisting her hips slightly, ready to kick out with her right if she needed to.

Shaley stuck his head in farther and looked either side, nodding his approval. 'Nice digs you got 'ere, love. Shame Mike had to go and lose his claim to it, what with his volunteering and all. But you know how this goes down. We won't be complete bastards about it. Marcus has said to give you a hand clearing out. We're gentlemen like that, you see. Old-fashioned manners, innit?'

This part of the flotilla wasn't in the usual areas Graves and his lot were interested in. Eva wondered what it was about these quarters that made them so eager. She was about to ask when Jean joined her and said, 'Get the hell out of here. He's not been gone an hour and you're already sniffing around. Well, you're out of luck. You're not having this place.'

Tyson pulled his mask down, exposing salt-damaged lips, and scowled.

Shaley continued, 'Temper, temper, love. I don't make the rules. We're just following Marcus's orders. Just doin' my job, ain't I? It's not like you ain't got anywhere to go, is it? There's always the containers. I'm sure you and Eva here can make it warm and welcoming, eh?'

'What does Marcus want with this place? Something to do with Mike?'

'Like I said, you best speak to Marcus. I'm just doing as he asked. Don't make this any more difficult than it needs to be, darlin'.'

Eva stepped forward, bringing her face within inches of Shaley's, and stared into his dark, hooded eyes. 'Listen to me real close. You leave Jean alone. You and your stupid brother can go hassle someone else. You're not bullying anyone here, you understand? If you don't like that, I suggest you go running back to your feckless cousin.'

At first, Shaley didn't blink or move, but as Eva remained steadfast, blocking their access, he eventually let out a breath, smiled and stepped back. He cast a look at Jean before glancing back to Eva. 'I can see why Mike fancied this one; bitch's got fire in her belly. I bet she's a real goer in the sack too.'

Tyson chuckled and brought his single green eye to look over Eva, devouring her body as if seeing a woman for the first time. His scowl turned to a lustful grin.

Eva's skin prickled. A blanket of heat flashed across her face and neck. She drove her shinbone into his crotch.

He sucked in his breath and fell to his knees.

Shaley spun to reach for his brother.

Eva thrust out a palm strike, catching him in the throat.

He stumbled forward, choking for air.

Eva pushed him back into the corridor, where he collapsed next to Tyson.

She stood over him, gripped the lapels of his smartly cut but tatty suit jacket, and yelled into his face. 'I'm telling you once more out of courtesy. Leave this woman alone. If you have an issue, you come to me. And you can pass that onto Marcus. You understand?'

The choking man nodded his head, tried to say something but wheezed, struggling for air as he scrambled to his feet. Groaning and clutching his balls, Tyson stood, and together the cousins stumbled back down the corridor.

Eva stood in the doorway until they had disappeared from view.

Jean stared at her, pale and shaking. 'What did they want?' she said, her voice warbling.

'I have no idea. But I'm sure we'll figure it out. Here, sit down. Have some more tea,' Eva said, helping her friend to the sofa. Danny had come to his mother's side.

'What did those men want?' he said. 'Are they friends of Daddy?'

'No, Dan, they're not. But don't worry about them, okay? You just look after your mom. She's not feeling well.'

Eva sat beside Jean, poured a cup of seaweed tea and handed it to her. She thought about Marcus and Mike, wondering what they had been up to and why the former had sent his goons here. Maybe they were looking for something? Eva filed it away as yet another question to deal with.

Jean took the cup. It shook in her hand. 'I can't believe you did that. Stood up to them, I mean . . .'

'Working as a cop gives you certain skills, especially in Baltimore.'

'I thought you were a homicide detective?' Jean said.

'Yeah, but a decade before that I was a cop on the streets. You get to deal with worse people than those assholes, trust me. I'll pay a visit to Graves later. But in the meantime, I'd find somewhere safe for your valuables and essentials. Look, I'm going to have to leave in a moment. I'm on patrol tonight, and Flick will be waiting for me to take over her shift. If you don't feel safe, I've got a lock box in my cabin.' She handed Jean a key. 'Use that to store anything precious to you, okay? I'll check by later on my rounds. Graves' expansion plans have been stepped up lately. Wouldn't surprise me if he's got a bunch of people running errands for him.'

She thought of Ade then. Perhaps on her patrol tonight, she'd take a walk over to the other side of the container ship and see what Ade had been up to earlier. If she met up with Graves, all the better.

Jean took the key into her fist and hugged Eva. 'Thanks, for everything.'

'Least I can do.' And she meant it.

Eva stood and was headed to the door when the PA sounded its familiar crackle.

This is your captain, Jim. I'm afraid I've some bad news. I know this is the worst possible time, what with Mike leaving us, but it's come to my attention that our fuel and power stocks have been compromised. My crew will work around the clock to get things back to normal, but in the meantime I've decided to cut power until we can get to the bottom of this.

That means no radio, lights or heating. Conserve what fuel or wood you might have personally. I'll arrange a flotilla meeting in the next day or so. Once I have more information. Please support each other. Together we can make this work, but only together.

Captain, out.

Jean slumped against the sofa and dropped her head.

Eva sighed and tried not to get caught up with the bad news, but it didn't stop the tingle inside her head from bothering her, nagging her like it used to back in the force. Something bad was going down. And now without the power, she'd have to run her patrol in the dark, with just her wind-up torch. The two possible explanations could be that someone was either stealing the fuel or using it in ways that burned it too quickly. She thought of Faust and her group, the rumours of them stealing and stockpiling their own resources.

She would make sure she would pass Faust's area of the flotilla during the patrol and see if she could spot anything to help confirm or deny the hunch.

To sum up her feelings, a fork of lightning flashed against the Orizaba's rock face, lighting up the porthole, casting green light through the algae. A crash of thunder immediately followed, directly above. The hull of the ship seemed to groan and voice her unease.

It's going to be a long night.

CHAPTER FOUR

J im entered the wheelhouse of the *Bravo*, heading for the brig to find Duncan, but his son was already making his way to him.

'You got something from Frank?' Jim said.

Duncan grinned. 'Yeah, we got something all right. And it didn't require much to get him talking. He's shit scared.'

'Of what?'

'You mean who.'

'Go on. What did he say?' Jim leaned against the wheel of the ship. The steering had seized up since it had run aground on the range three years ago. Jim remembered the sight of the *Bravo* – stuck at nearly at a forty-five degree angle on the rocks. He had done the very same thing with the *Alonsa*. It had taken months of work, but eventually he'd organised them so that they made up the bulk of the flotilla. The two ships provided the backbone for all the others to join like ribs.

Duncan closed the door behind him, shutting off any would-be eavesdroppers.

'He said someone paid him a visit last night, threatened his family if he didn't make the attempt on your life. Had to be today when the crowd were gathered for Mike's departure.'

'They wanted it to be public, then . . . Did he say who coerced him to do this?'

'No, he didn't know him. The person wore a hood and a mask, visited him early this morning while Frank was still in his bunk. But he did say he had a US military pistol. Frank's a gun nut apparently and recognised it instantly. The guy had already taken Frank's wife and used her life as payment for this job.'

Jim sighed, rubbing his chin. When they'd first set up the flotilla, they had a strict no firearms policy, for the safety of everyone. All guns were tossed over the side, and any new boats or ships that joined the flotilla were checked. Still, it wasn't beyond the realm of possibility that someone had decided to keep one for personal safety.

'Other than the US sub here, there are no other American military vessels. And those on the sub were all dead. All weapons were tossed. I was there when we brought it in and swept it for resources.'

'Could have found it on a yacht or one of the pleasure craft. There's a whole bunch of American ones on the west side. What's to say one of the owners of those wasn't military? Perhaps on leave or retired, and whoever this is found it?'

'Aye, it's possible. The last thing we need at this time is a nutter with a gun. But that brings up the question – if they're armed and obviously not a little crazy, why get Frank to try and take me down with a gaff hook? Surely it'd be easier to shoot me if this guy really wanted me dead.'

'So you think this was designed to fail? A distraction, or a warning or something?'

'Maybe.' Jim thought about it. That someone wanted him dead wasn't exactly startling news. His decisions were never popular, but then everyone else wasn't in his position, trying to keep the community together. That it was likely to be a diversion or distraction seemed the most obvious choice. But for what?

'The other issue is whether Frank's telling the truth. This could be a load of bollocks to cover for Marcus,' Jim said.

'I don't think so. He even asked that we keep him locked up, for his own safety. He's so scared at this stage, he doesn't even care that this guy, whoever he is, has his wife. He says he'll be dead within hours of leaving here.'

'And he said nothing else about this man? Nothing else about what he wanted. What his accent was. Any weird smells or something that could identify him?'

'Just said he was American. Couldn't tell what state or accent. Frank's only ever been out of the UK once, and lucky for him, it was the day he was on a boat with Marcus; otherwise he'd have drowned with everyone else.'

'There are at least thirty Americans on board. We can't just round them up.' Jim yawned, the effects of the rum and the stress of the day catching up with him. He needed someone who knew investigation. *Eva.* She'd be on patrol tonight. 'Okay,' he said. 'We need help with this. You fancy a stroll out in the storm with your old man?'

'But what if *he's* out there waiting?'

'In this weather? I can imagine him being a little crazy, but he doesn't sound stupid. Besides, there's nothing stopping him from just coming in here and gunning me down. No, there's something else going on here. And like or loathe Graves' lot, we can't just ignore the fact Frank's wife has been taken.'

'Would buy you some favour with Graves too, I imagine.'

'Unlikely, but possible.'

The wind gusted across Jim's face and mask, bringing with it a cloud of sea spray. The sun had gone down, and the black clouds, full of menace, hid the moon. Brief flashes of lightning, followed by deafening thunder, lit up the flotilla erratically, each split-second flash burning the image into Jim's vision and helping him find his way through the maze of wreckage paths.

'Eva will be on patrol for a few hours yet,' Jim shouted over the din of the weather to Duncan, who had his waterproof fishing jacket done up tight around his chin. His hat blew at all angles with each gust of wind. Only his eyes were visible over his white mask.

'Reminds me of the old days on the trawler,' Duncan said as a wave crashed between the *Bravo* and the mountain, sending an avalanche of chilled water over the side of the ship and running off down the sides.

Jim leaned into the wind, lighting his way with a rechargeable torch, and headed to the bow of the ship, where a rope ladder led down to what he called the fish-maze: a group of some thirty-odd fishing boats, tiny and large, cobbled together with chains and ropes and netting.

Large sections of white fibreglass hull from some dead millionaire's yacht had been cut into long pieces, creating a network of planks across the decks of the various boats. Holes had been cut into the ends of each one, and ropes looped through to keep everything together while allowing them to move with the rise and fall of the tide.

Tonight was particularly wild.

Since the oceans had risen to cover all but the tallest mountains, the tidal system had been strange and erratic. Some days, despite the storms, the sea remained level, and other times, like tonight, it felt like there were entirely unnatural forces at work beneath the water.

Various people, their faces illuminated by flickering candles, looked out of their cabin windows and portholes as Jim and Duncan

continued through the maze and headed for the west side: Graves'
territory.

None of them returned Jim's smile or wave of acknowledgement. Quite the opposite: they shook their heads at him, mouthed
various obscenities of discontent.

'You've gone too far this time, Jim,' one old-timer said from
behind an opened porthole. 'I've said it once, I'll say it again –
you're pushing us too hard. Now a brown-out? Too much, Jim. Too
much. With that the old man snuffed out a candle and disappeared
into the gloom.

'Ignore them, Dad,' Duncan said. 'They'll get used to it by
tomorrow morning.'

'They've got no choice. If I don't instigate this, then who will
make sure we've enough fuel stocks to use? If those fools want to
ignore me and do what they want, then so be it. But I'll continue
to do what I can.'

Jim slipped when he reached the end of the fish-maze. He tried
to leap across the gap to the lower part of the container ship – all
red rusted metal and square edges – but his foot lost its grip on an
algae-covered board, and he fell backwards.

Duncan was there. He caught him by the waist. 'Easy, Dad.
You're not a young buck anymore. Watch your step.'

Jim shrugged him off. 'I might be at the end of middle age, but
I'm not a cripple yet.'

He adjusted his stance and jumped the gap, landing on the
deck of the container ship. As he landed, the torch slipped from
his hand. He reached out for it, the grip just bouncing off his
fingertips, sending it rolling away over the edge and into the sea.
The float device, attached to the end of the grip, was no help. As the
boats rose and fell on the waves, the two hulls crushed it, the light
winking out in the gloom of the water.

'Goddamnit.'

'Don't worry about it,' Duncan said from the other side. 'I brought a spare.'

Jim helped his son across. 'Eva should be around here somewhere,' Jim said. 'She's covering this and most of Graves' spot.' It pained him to refer to the west side of the flotilla as Marcus Graves', but that was the truth. He and his firm had tight control of it, threatening anyone who dared claim it back. One day someone would stand up to him, and he'd be sorry.

To make matters worse, some of the containers in his area held the stockpiled fuel and other resources, such as fresh water and canned goods.

'Oh, crap,' Duncan said.

'What is it?'

'Battery's dead in mine.' He tapped the side of the flashlight against his palm. Nothing happened.

A crash of thunder covered his words, but when it dissipated, Jim pointed between rows of containers.

Duncan leaned in, whispering, 'What is it?'

'I saw movement there. The lightning reflected off a dark coat. Someone's heading for the northern section.'

'The stockpiles?' Duncan asked, but really it was more of a statement. 'And it wasn't Eva?'

'No,' Jim said. 'Come on. This might be our saboteur.'

Like predators stalking their prey, Jim and Duncan followed the dark shape through the rows of containers. They passed a few semi-open units, the dull amber light of candles glowing inside.

Each flash of lightning gave them a fix on their quarry.

'Wait,' Jim said as he ducked in behind a blue double-height container. Duncan slipped into a row opposite. Jim pointed forward to the series of locked units, the very ones that held their reserve fuel stocks.

Jim watched as their target worried at the iron padlock and chains. It occurred to Jim then that whoever it was, they weren't professional. They had a steel bar and were trying to prise the lock off. It'd never be opened that way. Still, the person worked, their dark waterproof coat flapping in the wind.

Stepping slowly and quietly, Jim moved out from his position and approached the thief. He took a gutting knife from his belt and crept closer. Duncan stepped out from behind Jim and took the left side, wielding the flashlight like a weapon. Jim took the right side.

When the last crash of thunder passed, he called out, 'Put your hands where we can see them, and step away from the container.'

The person dropped the bar, visibly startled at the command. They spun round and nearly slipped on the wet deck. Duncan rushed forward, pushing the figure against the steel doors, and pulled its hood back.

Jim leaned forward as a flash of lightning revealed a face.

'Susan?' Jim said, taken completely off guard. 'What the hell are *you* doing?' He had been expecting one of Marcus's goons.

Duncan lowered his flashlight and stepped back.

The woman looked scared out of her skin. Jim didn't blame her; Duncan was an imposing figure, especially with his thick ginger beard hiding most of his face and his long hair giving him the look of a Viking.

Susan remained quiet, her face growing defiant.

Jim moved closer. 'I asked you a question, Faust. What do you think you're doing? Why are you trying to get to the supplies? You working for Graves now, eh?'

She lowered her mask and spat on the deck. 'Like I'd work for that scum,' she said in her strong German accent.

'So you're working for someone, then?' Duncan asked.

'I work only for *Him*, and for my people. The way you walk about here, thinking you're the one in control, making decisions for the rest of us! I answer to a higher power, Captain.'

'What? You're telling me this is God's work? God tell you to steal from your own people, did he?' Jim said.

'I owe you no explanation.' Susan crossed her arms. 'I explain my actions to no man. Especially not the likes of you.'

'Well, explanations or not, Faust, you've earned yourself a berth in the brig.'

Duncan grabbed the woman, spinning her around, and brought her arms behind her back. He reached into his coat, pulled out a set of plastic ties and bound her wrists.

'Get your filthy hands off me,' she cried.

'If you start talking . . .' Jim said.

She spat at his face, but the wind whipped it away. Her face twisted into a grimace. How a woman filled with such hate could lead a growing congregation of converts, Jim just couldn't understand. 'No? Fine, let's take her back to the *Bravo*, Dunc. We'll catch up with Eva later towards the end of her shift.'

'Righto,' Duncan said, pushing Susan Faust ahead of him.

As they made their way back to the *Bravo*, forcing Faust up the ladder to the ship's bow, Jim heard a scream from the stern of the ship.

Beyond the stern of the *Bravo* was one of the main fishing trawlers used by the community to bring in the nets from the edge of the flotilla, but there shouldn't be anyone on the trawler tonight; they weren't due for netting for another two days.

'Did you hear that?' Jim said as Duncan continued to push Faust ahead.

'What's that?'

The sounds of rain and the grumble of thunder made it difficult to speak, so Jim had to shout. As he did, another scream came on the air, and all three of them stopped and looked in the same direction. A few seconds later Jim saw a dark shape running towards the trawler across the various boats lashed together off the *Bravo's* starboard side. A flashlight's beam bounced ahead of the runner.

'It's Eva,' Jim shouted. 'You take Faust to the brig, find out what else she might have stolen. I'll see what the matter is.'

Before Duncan could speak, Jim set off, running towards the trawler, trying to catch up with Eva. She seemed to move like a stop-frame motion picture, her image jumping forward with each flash of lightning.

Eventually he caught up with her. She leaned over the side of the trawler, her hands covered in blood. She looked out to the roiling sea and screamed, 'Jean!'

CHAPTER FIVE

E va swept her flashlight across the surface of the water. The waves crashed against the boat, covering her face in salt water. Her mask dangled down around her neck. She blinked away the spray and continued to train the beam of light on the water's surface. 'Jean,' she screamed. 'Jean!'

A dark spot appeared beneath her light, disappeared, and then appeared again. A weak yell came to her on the wind. Jean was there. Then Eva saw two arms shoot out from the water. Jean stretched her head back and screamed before she went under the water again.

Blood shone like oil around her as the water thrashed. Then Eva knew why Jean was screaming. It was the thing she feared the most: *sharks.*

Eva turned away from the edge and sprinted across the trawler's wooden deck, grabbing on to fishing crates and netting to prevent falling over. Her heart pounded, and her chest tightened against her straining lungs as she smashed open the cabin door and crashed in. She found the harpoon gun and made sure it was cocked and ready for use.

Back at the rail, she held the flashlight in her mouth.

She saw the blood and thrashing in the water and sighted down the harpoon's length, hoping against hope that she wouldn't accidentally hit Jean.

The thick, ancient form of a great white was visible beneath the water as it circled Jean's position. Her body was limp on the surface now, but if there was a chance . . .

The shark straightened. With a flick of its tail fin, it brought its nose up out of the water. Its mouth opened; its teeth gleamed beneath Eva's light. Its dark eye seemed to blink.

Holding her breath, Eva pulled the trigger.

The harpoon fired out of the gun and struck the shark just behind its mouth, slicing through its gills. It turned away with the hit. The rope, coiled behind her, burned her arm as it ran out. She dropped the gun, gripped the rope and tied it to a bollard on the trawler's deck.

Once the slack had run out, the boat jerked with each pull as the shark tried to get free, but the barb was hooked too deep. It wouldn't get free now.

'Jesus, Eva, what's going on?'

She spun at the voice, raising her flashlight ready to strike someone down. A hand gripped her wrist.

'It's me, Jim.'

'Jean's gone over. Please help me.'

Jim looked down at the rope and the emptied harpoon gun. A confused expression came over his tired face, but his bright blue eyes sharpened, as he too knew the truth. 'A shark?'

'Quick, help me get her in.'

With Jim's help, Eva grabbed a weighted net and managed to throw it over Jean's body and drag her in. They used a couple of long boat hooks to catch Jean under the arms and lift her up.

For a moment she moved as if she might still be alive.

'Jean, it's okay. We've got you,' Eva said.

But as they lifted her clear of the water, Eva had to hold back the impulse to throw up. Jean's legs were in tatters; blood dripped from her wounds.

They brought her remains into the boat and covered her ravaged body with a tarp.

The rope went limp.

Eva cast her flashlight across the waters and saw a dozen fins piercing the surface, lured by Jean's blood, but with no body, the predators would have no easy meal tonight. She cut away the rope, letting it fall from the side of the boat, hoping the one she'd shot was dead.

She turned to Jean's body.

Jim was standing over her, checking her neck and wrist for a pulse. Her eyes were shut, and her mouth hung open. Jim shook his head before pulling the tarp over her face.

'I'm so sorry. She's gone,' he said, his voice barely audible over the storm and the pounding of blood rushing through Eva's head.

Seeing dead bodies wasn't usually a big deal to her, thanks to her previous job and the last few years of seeing corpses on boats and ships, but the suddenness of this, and the fact it was Jean, hit her hard. She lost her balance and fell backward.

Jim grabbed her, steadying her before leading her into the trawler's cabin.

'You need to tell me what happened,' Jim said as he busied himself making a pot of tea on the small gas stove. Outside, the rattle of rigging and a ship's bell acted like a hypnotic song, helping to slow her heartbeat down.

'Why would Jean go over?' Jim asked. 'Grief for Mike?'

Eva closed her eyes, concentrating on the events before the sharks . . . 'No. This was not suicide. Someone did this. Someone killed her by throwing her over. This is murder, Jim. Cold-blooded murder.'

'It wouldn't be the first time the spouse of a volunteer has gone over with grief. We have to see that as a possibility.'

'You're not listening to me. I saw someone on my patrol. I was on my way to speak with Graves—' Eva stopped, not wanting to go into detail about what she'd done to Shaley and Tyson. Knowing how Jim felt about Marcus, it'd only cause more upset and more aggravation. She didn't want anything to get in the way of finding out who had killed Jean.

Jim caught her stopping herself and raised an eyebrow. 'To see Graves about what?'

'Just some stupid trivial thing. It doesn't matter. I didn't go anyway. I was heading back to start my route properly when I saw a light here on the trawler. When I got closer, I must have spooked them.'

'Did you get a look at them?' Jim handed her a cup of tea and sat down again.

'No. I just saw Jean hit the water, but heard someone running off across the boards. What is it with you Brits and tea?'

'Calms the nerves, helps you think clearly.'

'It tastes like shit, and I don't need calm nerves. I know what I damn well saw. Hell, you can even see the footprint in the blood on the deck. And half of Jean's coat is torn on the railing that's nearly coming away. That's what we call a sign of struggle.'

'Okay, I get it. I'm sorry. Let's just think things through. Who would want her dead? You mentioned something about Graves. Do you think he's involved?'

Eva tipped the tea out of an open porthole, unable to stand its awful stench a moment longer. 'I doubt it. There was . . . an altercation earlier when Shaley and Tyson turned up to claim Mike's possessions. I persuaded them that it wasn't such a good idea, but it was nothing that would make him kill Jean. Graves is many things, but he's not so stupid as to kill someone like this.'

'I don't know what you thought of coincidences when you were in the force,' Jim said, 'but I've got Frank in the brig. That puts Marcus Graves at the centre of two incidents in the same day.'

'What did Frank have to say about his pathetic attempt? You're not really taking that seriously, are you? Seems to me it was all for show.'

Jim sat back, scrutinising her, not answering her question.

'You don't think you can trust me?' Eva said. 'Is it something to do with Jean?'

'No, quite the opposite, but listen. I was out tonight because I wanted to find you. And after this, I think it's even more important.'

'What is?'

'Mike, he came to me specifically to request volunteer status, and when the weather broke, it was him that wanted to get away. Said it was safer for everyone concerned.'

Eva thought about that. She had spoken with Mike that very morning, and he hadn't mentioned any of this. Could Jim be lying? If so, what would his motivation be? To take the responsibility off his shoulders, perhaps? But then surely, he'd make sure the whole community knew it wasn't his decision. It wasn't like he needed the extra hassle.

'Mike did some work for Graves recently,' Eva said. 'And I noticed Ade going to Graves' place this morning. Do you know anything about that?'

'I don't, but Mike was really eager to leave when I spoke with him. I thought that perhaps he'd upset Marcus over something.'

'None of this makes any sense,' Eva said. She leant back against the cabin wall, feeling its smooth wooden surface against her skull. She wondered how many fishermen or women had sat against this very spot, rubbing it smooth, thinking over their problems, their grief.

'You said you were looking for me,' she said wearily, the weight of sorrow sinking into her guts. 'What is it you wanted?'

'Someone put Frank up to it. Took his wife as a bargaining chip.'

'Man, this is getting messed up. Look, I'm sorry Frank tried to come at you like that – I know it can't be easy being everyone's target because of the shitty conditions of this place – but what's his wife got to do with any of this? Are you suggesting it might be linked to Jean's . . . murder?'

'Frank mentioned the guy had a pistol. I'll get you all the details, but kidnapping, assassination and murder in the same day . . . If that's not a coincidence worth investigating, I don't know what is. Will you take this on, like you would a case?'

'Only if I do it my way.'

Jim shrugged. 'Do what you want; it's your investigation.'

'On one condition,' Eva said, leaning forward over the table.

'Name it.'

'You make sure Danny has a safe place. Before I came out, Jean asked me to look out for him if anything happened to her. It seems she knew something was up after all. I betrayed her friendship with Mike; I'm not going to betray my promise to her now.'

'We'll bring him into the *Bravo* right away. I'll send Duncan and some of the crew. In the meantime, you can set up in the ops room; use that as a base of operations. It's secure.'

He handed her a key. She pocketed it.

'So, you in?' He held out his hand.

She shook it, gripping hard. 'I'm in. But I will be judge, jury and executioner on this one.'

'You gotta do what you gotta do.'

Eva let go of Jim's hand, stood and walked out of the cabin. She stopped at the tarp, pulled it back and looked down at Jean's face one last time.

Pain was etched into every salted skin cell.

'I'll get them, Jean, I promise you that.' *I owe you at least that much.*

She accompanied Jim back to the *Bravo*.

Duncan and two crewmen were already setting out to retrieve Danny. That poor kid. Losing two parents in the same day. Too damned cruel. But then she thought back to her family, her child, the one she'd left at home while she agreed to take a boat trip on some smuggling operation.

It was days like these that made her wish she'd stayed behind with her daughter. Together in death was better than separated in life.

CHAPTER SIX

Eva had decided to start the investigation with Frank straight away, even before the sun had come up. Although she doubted he had anything to do with Jean's murder, she did promise Jim she would look into it, and there was always an outside chance something would be connected, especially given Marcus's interest in Jean's quarters.

She had made her way down to the brig of the *Bravo*, washing her hands in the salt bath as she went and scrubbing away a few remaining flecks of blood.

Patrice, a Frenchman and a member of the crew who used to work on the *Alonsa* was standing guard at the steel door. He yawned before smiling at Eva. 'Bonjour, mon amie. Come to question Frank?'

'Jim told you?'

'Oui. Wasn't expecting you until later. Must be eager.'

Eva looked down at her feet and shrugged, not wanting to explain that she just wanted this over and done with so she could hurry up and get on with finding Jean's murderer. She felt bad about trivialising an attempt on Jim's life, but Jean had to take priority. This was driven as much by guilt as it was by justice. She still felt terrible about her betrayal with Mike. Even though Jean had understood, it didn't make it any easier.

'You better go in, then. Ignore Susan; she's been ranting since she was locked up, though she's asleep right now. Hopefully she'll stay that way for a while.'

'Thanks, Patrice.'

'Oh, and I'm very sorry to hear about Jean. I hope you find out what happened.'

She just gave him a quick nod. A lump of grief bubbled up in her throat. Any words spoken threatened to let all her emotion come spilling out in an ugly torrent. She worried that if she started, she wouldn't be able to stop.

The Frenchman turned and opened the thick steel door. It creaked on its hinges, metal scraping on metal. It reminded her of her days working at the station. That clang of barred doors, the clunk of the lock . . . Those sounds had embedded themselves into her subconscious.

When she stepped inside the small brig with its half dozen cells, she was transported back to Baltimore on her first day of the job. That was before her precious daughter was born, when she was still dating a young officer and enjoying her first experience on the force.

She missed those early days of camaraderie.

The brig smelled of grease and body sweat, just as it did back then. A faint stench of stale urine hung cloyingly in the air. She pulled her salt mask up and approached Frank's cell. Both he and Susan were asleep and snoring heavily in their cots. At least they had a mattress and a working toilet, she thought; that was more than some of the flotilla residents had when camping out in the containers.

Patrice appeared behind her, his hot breath tickling the back of her neck. She jumped and spun round.

'I'm sorry,' he said. 'I didn't meant to startle you. I wanted to know if you wanted me to . . . how you say . . . back you up?'

'That's kind of you, Patrice, but no, I'll be fine. I'm just questioning him. I won't need to enter the cell.' She smiled behind her mask and waited for him to get the idea and leave. After a moment he did just that, spinning on his heel and leaving her alone in the brig. He kept the door ajar, the dark silhouette of his body visible through the gap.

With the reassurance of him being there if needed, she leaned forward and gripped the bars of Frank's cell. His cot was on the left side and placed vertically down the cell, with his head near the door. Eva leant down and tapped him on the head a few times until he woke with a tired spluttering.

'Hey, Frank, wake up. I've got some questions for you,' Eva said.

He groggily turned onto his side before hauling his large frame up with a moan. His eyes were narrow and his hair stuck up at odd angles. He turned to her and squinted. 'Who the fuck's that?' he said, his words sounding like damp gravel running down a metal roof.

'Eva. I need to talk to you about what you tried to do yesterday – among other things.'

Frank leaned forward onto his knees and coughed up phlegm, which he spat into the open bowl of the toilet on the other side of the six-foot-wide cell.

'I told Duncan everything. Nothing else to say.'

'Yeah, well, I disagree.'

'You're stronger than you look,' Frank said with a sly smile, rubbing his ribs. 'You'd have made a good rugby player with a tackle like that.'

Eva shrugged off his bullshit and continued to question him as Susan remained asleep, snoring loudly. 'You said you were blackmailed into this, and that your wife was kidnapped.'

Frank stared right at her. She saw a few micro-expressions at the corners of his eyes as he spoke. 'Shouldn't you or Jim be out there trying to find her?'

'I think it's a waste of time and resources,' Eva said, noting that this didn't get a rise from him as she'd expected. 'I think you're bullshitting about your wife, and this guy forcing you to do this. You see, Frank, it just doesn't stack up.'

'How so?' he said, glancing away from her.

'If I wanted Jim dead and I had a pistol, I'd have just shot him. Would have been easier. Secondly, if I were to blackmail some- one into doing it for me, I wouldn't choose an ex-junkie screw-up like you. Literally any one of your family here would have been a better choice and I'm sure Marcus wouldn't have needed too much encouragement to get rid of Jim, considering how they hate each other.'

'Like I said,' Frank continued, keeping his face in shadow, 'some American guy said if I didn't do it, my wife would be in trouble.'

'Didn't you think of asking why?'

'Of course, but I didn't get much of an answer. I don't know why you're bugging me about this; you should be trying to find this bloke before he strikes again.'

'What's he after?' Eva pressed. 'Did he give you any indication at all of what all this was about?'

Now Frank did turn to her and moved forward into the pale light so Eva could see his face, clear down to each individual wrinkle and crevice. His face looked like the end of a chopping block, with scars and pockmarks giving his skin a cratered appearance.

'He did say something about not letting people know. I didn't quite catch all of it. Naturally, I was scared for my life – and my wife's, of course.' That last phrase Eva noticed was tacked on like an afterthought.

The first part, however, seemed genuine to her. She'd questioned enough scumbags in her time to notice when their bravado dropped and they said something with sincerity and truth.

Eva continued to question Frank for another ten minutes until Susan woke. She felt she had got all she would out of him as he started to repeat himself – which she made sure of to ensure that his story was consistent. And it was, lies and all.

She came away from the questioning not believing that his wife had actually been kidnapped, but she was almost certain someone had threatened him. The only rational reason she could come up with was that it had all been some kind of elaborate distraction for something else . . .

What, exactly, she didn't know – yet.

Tiredness threatened to dull her thoughts completely so she headed back to her cabin in the *Alonsa* to let sleep take away the pain, even if only temporarily. Tomorrow would be the start of a new day, a new investigation and a new journey, the destination of which she didn't yet know.

With the dawn breaking over the horizon and amber light shining into Danny's cabin, Jim handed him one of his books. 'Here you go, son. That'll keep you busy for a while.'

The boy wiped his face. It was clear he'd been crying.

Duncan sat down on the bunk next to him. 'You'll be safe here, mate. You'll have me and the crew in the next cabins. Anything you want, just ask. And if you want, we'll let you tag along with some of the engineers. How'd you like to learn metalworking?'

Danny shrugged, holding the book in his hands. 'I suppose that would be fun.'

'No rush, son. You just get yourself settled. We'll bring you some breakfast in a bit.'

'Thanks,' Danny said. He sat back on his bunk, just staring at the book. Poor kid looked shell-shocked. At least Eva had managed to calm him down. It would take a while for him to come to terms with things, but he was young and resilient. The crew would make sure he stayed occupied. And *Grimm's Fairy Tales* would take him a while to work his way through.

'Okay, son, you stay there. One of the crew will be along shortly. Dunc, if you wouldn't mind.' Jim nodded to the open door.

Duncan patted Danny on the shoulder.

It was the most affection Jim had ever seen Duncan give a child; it didn't come naturally to him. Probably explained why he and his wife had never had kids, and why he spent so much time on the boats. Duncan was a true man of the sea. He coped better out here than anyone Jim had known.

They closed the door to Danny's cabin and moved down the narrow, grey-walled corridor towards the destroyer's brig section, ducking under the small hatches as they went.

They arrived at the small makeshift brig in what used to be senior-rates cabins: just six cells, three a side, metal bars welded in place of the wooden doors.

Frank faced Faust through the bars.

Jim thought he saw something between them, some acknowledgement or understanding. Did that mean they were working together? He considered that Frank's attempt might have been a distraction for Susan's sabotage . . . or perhaps this was some plan devised by Marcus. Frank had been known for his drug addiction before the flotilla; there was a possibility that his brains were just addled. Probably better to keep him locked up anyway – especially as it meant one fewer goon for Marcus to order about for whatever he was up to.

When Jim and Duncan came into view, Frank pressed his face against the bars and eagerly said, 'Any news of my wife? Did you find the guy?'

'We're working on it,' Jim said. 'We've allocated resources, and we're investigating a few leads.'

'Is that it? What the hell, man? She could have been butchered by now.'

Duncan moved directly in front of Frank. 'Have some damn respect. You're lucky I've not thrown you to the sharks for attempted murder.'

'Tell me, Frank,' Jim said, 'why'd you tip us off about the stocks going missing?' He dropped the bluff to see if that would make him open up about what was really going on.

'What?' Frank said. 'I never said anything about—'

Jim saw Susan's face suddenly sharpen as she stared at Frank. Jim focused on her. 'Oh, that makes sense now.'

'What does?' she said.

'You're both in on it. You seem a little pissed off at dear Frank here for dropping you in it, Miss Faust. That not part of the plan, eh?'

'I never said anything about that,' Frank protested.

Susan sneered at him, turning her attention to Jim. 'I've nothing to do with Frank. Stupid. That's not it at all.'

'Oh? Tell me, then, what did you want the stockpiles for? Planning a little party for you and your flock? It's not like that would be the first time, now, would it?'

Her silence was damning. For months now, Susan had increasingly separated herself and her group from the rest of the residents. Only last week he had needed to break up a fight between Dietmar, one of her most loyal acolytes, and Henzo, a fisherman. Dietmar had apparently stolen his day's catch and threatened Henzo.

Despite going to see Faust and her flock, Jim couldn't find any evidence. The residents were putting more pressure on him to take action, but what could he really do? He was already taking a risk by bringing Faust here. He wouldn't be surprised if her followers would be coming to see him at any moment once they had decided on their course of action.

Jim turned to Frank.

'Right, you two. I've run out of patience. This place is on the verge of self-destruction, so your two lives mean nothing to me. Honestly, you're a hassle I could do without. And if you both happened to go missing, you'd make my job here a hell of a lot easier. So here's the deal: you start talking, telling me what the hell is going on, or I'll leave Dunc here to do as he wishes.'

Frank laughed, but as he looked at Duncan's fierce gaze, the sound died in his throat.

Susan remained silent, clearly working out her next move.

Jim gave them a minute before turning his back and heading for the door. 'They're all yours, Dunc. If you want to feed them to the sharks, go for it. I'm sick of this bullshit. Or perhaps you could just let Frank out, give his American friend a chance to catch up with him.'

He got two steps down the corridor when Frank yelled, 'Okay, okay! Wait – we can work something out.'

Jim smiled to himself. There were some benefits of having an ex–rugby-playing son who looked like Thor and the threat of death. 'You ready to talk, then, Frank? Because if not . . .'

'Yes, yes, come on, let's work this out. I'll tell you whatever you want.'

All the time he was jabbering on, Jim noticed Susan trying to hide in the shadows of the cell. Although Jim wasn't an expert on such matters, he could tell she was as guilty as sin. The holiest often were, he thought. He stood with his back to her, blocking her view of Frank, but he still wanted her to hear everything.

'First of all, Frank, tell me, who is responsible for the theft of the resources and the sabotage of the hydro and wind turbines. Is it Marcus?'

'No. Marcus ain't into all that. You don't shit on your own doorstep, you know?'

'Don't give me all that gang member loyalty crap. Marcus is scum.'

'Hey, that's my family. Tone it down a bit.'

'I'm getting real tired here, Frank. Spill.'

'Fine. Fuck's sake, it was her.' He pointed across the cell to Faust. 'The whole thing – the theft and the sabotage. Marcus figured it out a day ago. That Turkish kid spotted her and Meredith snooping about one of the wind turbines and he passed the info on to Marcus.'

Faust lost all control of herself, flying into a rage, grabbing the bars and screaming at Frank in her weird garbled language. Duncan and Jim stood back, watching her launch an unintelligible tirade at Frank as if she were possessed.

Her body bucked and her hair flew all about her.

Frank just looked at Jim as if to say, 'See? The woman's nuts and totally guilty.'

When she finally stopped screaming in tongues, she said, 'You'll burn in hell, Frank! You'll burn in hell!'

'Easy, Susan. Hit a nerve, did he?' Jim asked.

She turned her head to look at him, every muscle contorted in hate. 'God despises you. All of you. *He* spoke to me.' She spat on the ground by Jim's feet.

'Really? What did *He* say?' Jim prompted.

'You'll all burn. Especially you.' She pointed at Jim through the bars. 'Your lies will be exposed, and everyone will know the truth of what you've done. You're gonna burn for all eternity.'

'Shut your mouth. How dare you? You risk the lives of all in this community, for your own twisted view of the world. It's you who will burn, Faust. I'll see to it myself if I have to.'

'Dad, relax.' Duncan gripped Jim's shoulders, but the rage within him burned, and he threw his son off. Turning to Frank, who was now laughing, Jim reached through the bars, gripped him by the throat and pulled him close so his face was squashed against the cell door.

'You think this is funny, eh? A poor kid was orphaned last night. You know anything about that? One of your scumbag family thought they'd get Jean out of the way to claim her husband's property? Who was it, Frank?'

Duncan gripped Jim's forearms and pulled him away. 'That's enough, Dad. For God's sake, what's got into you?'

Faust was grinning through the bars now.

'Truth hurts, doesn't it, Captain Jim? It's nothing compared to the hell that awaits you.'

Frank eventually spoke up. 'Honest, Jim, I know nothing about Jean. I already told Eva this. I swear!'

Jim could tell he was being sincere. Having one's windpipe nearly crushed could do that to a man. And it did corroborate what he had told Eva. 'Screw you both. You can rot for all I care.'

Jim shrugged out of Duncan's grip and stormed down the corridor.

Duncan tried to follow, but Jim spun around. 'Son, I want you to find and help Eva. Find this killer and the man who put Frank up to this. For the sake of Jean and Mike, find him, and when you do, send him over to the damned sharks.'

'Dad, what's wrong? Faust is just a nutter; don't let her get to you. She's just nicking stuff for her poxy congregation. We'll get the hydro and wind turbines up and running in no time.'

Jim's heart was still racing, his jaw clenching and unclenching. 'Please just do as I ask you for once.' He turned his back on his son and headed for his own cabin. 'And make sure that kid gets a meal.'

◆

Jim locked the thick metal door behind him and then sat down on his bunk, dropping his head into his hands. His head pulsed with an oncoming migraine. His chest hurt. For the briefest moment he questioned his role. Was he doing the right thing? Faust's words had hurt. He wondered if she truly knew or was just talking her usual hatred. If she did know, he'd have to do something about it. She was already a cancer in the community; he couldn't let her poison people's hope with her narrow-minded pseudo-religious nonsense. But could he really do it? If it came to it . . .

He guessed he could. *If it came to it.*

Double-checking that the door was locked, he pressed his ear against it to make sure no one was passing by outside before lifting up his bunk. He used a stick to hold it in place, and with his fishing knife, he prised out a series of rivets holding a plate to the wall.

Reaching in, he pulled out a metal container the size of a shoebox.

Taking out a key attached to a wire around his neck, hidden beneath his shirt, he turned it in the lock and entered a code on the five-digit tumbler.

The lid popped open, revealing a silver hip flask and a handheld radio with a tape printer attached to the side. The last item was a small leather-bound notebook.

Still being careful not to make any noise, he brought the bunk back down and placed the box on the mattress. He took two swigs of uncut rum, breathing it in, allowing the alcohol to work its way down into his stomach. He grimaced slightly at the pure burn and swigged another two shots before the feeling dissipated.

He checked his watch. It was time.

Stopping for another moment to ensure no one was outside, he switched on the modified radio, took the spool of wire from the back and reached it up to a pipe running along the cabin.

From a casual look it appeared the same as any pipe, but when twisted, it revealed an antenna wire inside. He attached the two wires and confirmed the signal. It was weak, but it would be enough for a small data burst.

Taking the notebook, he flipped to the last updated page, marked by a ribbon. He entered a message, using the encryption model in the notebook to obscure the text. The message when unencrypted at the other end would read:

Jim-11877687-Last Message R/d. Confirm receipt of resource. End.

The modified radio scrambled the message into information packets and, using just battery power, sent a one-second data burst. Three seconds later a black square flashed twice on the pale green screen to indicate it had reached its destination.

Jim breathed out, took another snap of rum and waited.

It only took two minutes for the reply. The black square flashed twice. The paper edged out of the printer digit by digit. He used the code in the notebook to transpose the encrypted message. It read:

Clare-11877688-Last Message R/d. Can confirm resource. Mike is with us. Project Update: breakthrough. Need another volunteer. Three days. This could be it. End.

His heart seemed to miss a beat at the word *breakthrough*. Could it really be? Then the dread set in: another volunteer. His list was empty. Mike was the last. He couldn't get another one in just three days. It was too soon after Mike and now the power issues. He thought about sending Frank or Susan, but he couldn't do it as a public spectacle like the usual volunteer set-up.

How the hell could he get someone out without anyone else seeing them?

Somehow he'd have to figure it out, though.

A breakthrough!

CHAPTER SEVEN

*E*va's *daughter, Emily, is running across the family's farm. She has a smear of dirt on her face, just above her dimple. Her plaited hair swings behind her, her laugh lilting on the air. She reaches her arms out.*

Eva's standing there, her arms wide, ready to receive her daughter, but no matter how long she waits, she can't reach her. Emily's face twists. Tears spill from her eyes. The crying sounds like it's coming from some place far off, somewhere familiar. Beneath the crying is the sound of water . . . no, rain. The sound of rain.

The crying doesn't sound like her daughter anymore. The image of the farm dissipates, replaced by the familiar sight of the beige wood-panelled cabin walls.

Eva snapped her eyes open. She felt hung over, her soul still entrenched in the dream world while her corporeal body woke into reality. The two existences clashing, obfuscating what was real.

The sound of a child sobbing was still there amid the confusion. Emily was a ghost now, but the sound was so real.

Blinking, Eva sat up from her bed, rubbing the spectres from her eyes. In bare feet and wearing a long shirt, she made her way through into the kitchen area of her cabin. There, huddling into the corner, hugging his knees, Danny sobbed.

'Danny? I thought you were on the *Bravo*. Are you okay? Where's Duncan?'

She knelt down and reached out for the boy, pulling his arms away from his face. 'Hey, it's just me,' she said, trying to get him to look up. 'I was going to come see you later. Looks like you beat me to it, eh?'

Her attempts at reaching him felt awkward. Had she always been this terrible at communicating with children? She thought back to Emily. *No*, she thought. She wasn't always this awkward, but unlike Danny, Emily didn't have both of her parents leave her within twenty-four hours. *No, she just had one . . . Me.*

Eventually, Danny looked up. His blue eyes, so like his father's, were rimmed with red.

'Danny, do Duncan and Jim know you're here?'

He shook his head.

'They were arguing,' he said as if that explained everything. 'So I came here. I miss . . .' The tears grew glossy in his eyes as he choked on the words.

With a hug, she brought him close to her, feeling the poor kid shake in her embrace. 'I know, Dan, I know.' Despite his very real grief, all she could do was imagine Emily in his place, feeling the same way when Eva had left her behind, before the drowning.

'You won't have to stay on the *Bravo*,' Eva said. 'It was just temporary while we work a few things out. I was going to come and get you later today, remember? You know I'm here for you, don't you?'

'I know. I . . . I don't like it there. Can I stay here with you?'

'Soon, Dan. Right now things aren't safe here. I've got a job to do, but I promise it'll only be temporary. The *Bravo* is the best place right now. Besides, they have the best food there. Did you have breakfast?'

'No, I sneaked out while Duncan was going to get me something. Will he be mad at me?'

'I doubt it. He'll probably eat the breakfast himself anyway. A guy that large has a big appetite. But we should let them know you're okay in case they get worried. The storm's getting up, and we don't want them thinking you've . . .' She was about to joke about going over the side, but let her words drift off as she thought about Jean.

'Why did Dad have to go?' Danny asked, wiping his eyes, gaining composure.

'We all have to go at some point,' Eva said before she could stop herself. 'I mean, we all have to do something for each other. Together we're stronger, and your dad, he's one of the strongest. He's gone out to find help. Eventually we won't have to live here on the boats.'

'We can go home?' Dan said, his eyes wide with hope and optimism.

What could she say to that? Tell the truth, crush him, or lie and give him false hope? She took the easy way out. 'Maybe one day.'

'Will he come back soon? I miss him.'

'We hope so, Dan. *I* hope so.'

Eva stood and pulled Dan to his feet.

'Let's get you a change of clothes,' Eva said, 'and some of your comics. We'll both go back and deal with Duncan, let him know you're safe. I'll stay with you at the *Bravo* tonight, how's that?'

He smiled and just nodded.

As she led him out of her kitchen and turned to Mike and Jean's – soon to be Marcus's – cabin, she heard movement inside.

'You just stay here. Don't move, okay?' Eva left Danny in the doorway of her cabin. She stalked into the corridor and approached the door, trying to ascertain how many there were in Jean's cabin. She could see movement through the crack of the door and counted at least two distinct people. Their voices were low, indecipherable. She wished she'd brought a weapon.

She leaned forward, trying to get a better angle. A hand grabbed her by the back of her neck, pulled her into the room with a hard yank and threw her to the floor.

Standing in front of her was Marcus Graves, grim-faced, his hands in the pockets of his long, black coat. His dark hair stuck to his face, wet with the rain from the storm. A puddle dripped around his booted feet.

Behind him, Ade was bent over the storage section of the bed.

The mattress had been pushed up and he was rooting around inside, throwing Mike's and Jean's possessions out onto the floor.

Danny screamed out behind her.

She turned her head.

Shaley had Danny by the shoulders. She realised then it was Tyson who'd pulled her into the room. He stood over her, his legs as wide as his sick grin.

'What is this, Graves?' Eva said, getting to her knees.

Tyson's hands on her shoulders stopped her from getting to her feet, forcing her to look up to Graves' smug face.

'Where's the memory stick, love?' Graves said, his voice upbeat despite the veiled sense of violence beneath his voice.

'What memory stick?'

'Oh, come, come. Don't play coy with me now. Don't make this harder than it needs to be. Not a good thing for a kid to witness all this unpleasantness.'

She tried again to stand, but Tyson pushed his considerable weight down onto her shoulders, gripping her with his meaty fingers, making her yell with pain.

She fell forward and splayed her legs, knocking Tyson off balance. Grabbing his wrists, she twisted hard, breaking his grip. Ducking her head and pulling his arms forward, she slipped back through his legs. Before he could rebalance, she stood and kicked out, crunching her foot into his balls for the second time.

He made no noise beyond a gasp of breath as he grabbed the offending area and fell forward in a heap.

Marcus raised a hand. 'Jesus, Eva, give the guy a break. He'll never father kids again at this rate.'

'Good. Who'd want that animal to breed?'

Danny grabbed her from the side, having escaped Shaley's grip. She turned in time to see a fist coming her way; she ducked and caught a harmless, glancing blow on her shoulder.

Marcus stepped forward and caught Shaley before he fell off balance. Ade was still throwing things out of the bed's storage area. Marcus turned back to Eva.

Raising his voice, Marcus said, 'Can everyone stop being a fucking muppet for one second? I'm just trying to sort this mess out.'

'What mess? And what memory stick?' Eva said.

As he moved close to her, Marcus's body language relaxed. Shaley and Tyson stood behind him, not looking particularly happy but respecting Graves' control.

Staring directly into her eyes, Marcus said slowly and clearly, 'Now, are you telling me, straight up, with no word of a lie, that you've not seen a memory stick belonging to Mike? He didn't leave anything with you before his little voyage?'

'No. I've no damned clue what the hell all this is about.' Eva stared at him, refusing to back down beneath his assertiveness. She'd dealt with scumbags way worse than him; she'd be damned if she'd let him intimidate her, especially in front of Danny. He needed to know she could look out for him as promised.

'Well, then, we're up shit creek without a paddle,' Marcus said, turning his back on Eva. 'Ade, you got anything?'

'Not yet, man. Still looking.'

'So what's so important about this memory stick? And why didn't you just ask Jean for it?' Eva said, ignoring Tyson, whose face was dark with rage. Even just saying her name brought back that awful image of her body in the water . . .

'Need-to-know basis, love. Jean didn't know anything about it, and all you need to know is that it's important to me.'

'Important enough to kill for?' She felt awful saying that with Danny beside her, but he wasn't stupid. He knew what had happened to his mother.

'Now look here. I might be many things, but I ain't a callous son of a bitch. I wouldn't do that to her. Besides, I spoke to her a few hours before that. She didn't know anything about it either.'

'So where's all this coming from, then? Why do you need this memory stick? It's not like you can do much with computers out here, is it?'

They only had a couple of working computers: one in engineering and the other on the *Bravo*. Neither was much use beyond tracking supplies.

Marcus rubbed his chin and seemed to be trying to work out how much to tell her. 'Mike and I . . . worked together on a project, you see. He did a bit of work for me here and there. Nothing dodgy like; just some engineering stuff. Well, one day he comes to me with something he found – mentioned a memory stick. The next minute I know he's in a boat heading for Atlantis or wherever. I figured he left whatever he found with his lovely wife.'

Eva mulled it over. Despite herself, she couldn't help but believe him. It all added up: Mike had been working with Graves; she'd seen that herself. And then there was this sudden volunteering and disappearance as soon as the weather changed. In addition to all that, he just hadn't seemed himself on the day he left.

'Say I believe you, and there is this memory stick floating about, would someone else be prepared to kill for it?'

'Hell knows. Maybe. All I know is that Mike was freaking out the last time I spoke with him. Didn't want to work for me anymore, said he'd learned too much. All cryptic stuff.' Graves turned to Danny, who stuck to Eva like a limpet, unable to comprehend everything that was going on around him. 'Look, son, I'm real sorry about your mum and dad. It's real rough, but we'll figure something out. All this is connected, you see. You just be a brave soldier and stick with Eva, okay?'

Danny just nodded and hugged Eva tighter.

'Hey, man, I got something,' Ade said, unfolding his lanky frame from the bed. He brought out a five-inch-square wooden box. He moved between Shaley and Tyson and placed it on the small dining table. Inside were some old Polaroid photos and a key attached to a small floating ball.

'Interesting,' Marcus said, taking it.

Danny rushed forward. 'Hey, that's my dad's!'

Marcus held the key up out of Danny's reach while placing a hand on the boy's shoulder. 'It's okay, son. We're just looking. You say it's your dad's . . . What's it a key to?'

'His quiet place,' Danny said. 'Now give it back. It's not yours.'

'Quiet place?' Marcus said. 'Where's that, then?'

Danny shrugged. Eva put her hand on the boy's shoulders. 'How often did Mike go to his quiet place, Dan?'

The boy looked at her with uncertainty. She smiled at him. 'It's okay. You can tell me. I'm trying to help, remember? Me and you are a team, right?'

'Maybe every few days. It was usually after my bedtime. Said he was going to read and work on a surprise.'

'That's all he said?'

'Yeah.'

'And he used to take that key with him?'

Danny nodded.

Marcus took Eva's arm gently and whispered, 'Come outside with me. We need to talk without the kid. No funny business.'

'Danny, you stay here for a moment with Ade. I just need to talk with Mr Graves, okay? I'll just be outside here.'

The boy looked concerned, but she left him with Ade, all the while watching Tyson and Shaley. There was something about this whole situation that set off her gut-feeling spidey-sense. It was all too much of a coincidence. There was some connection here, some story waiting to be told. The fact that Mike apparently had some secret place to visit in addition to Graves' concerns told her that Jean had known something worth killing for, something that Mike had known, too – and neither of them had told Marcus. If she could figure that out, it'd take her closer to Jean's murderer.

Once outside, they dropped their voices. Graves started. 'Look, Eva, I know what you think of me, I've seen the way you look at me, but you've got to listen now and know I'm telling you the truth, okay?'

'You talk, and I'll tell you if I think you're full of shit.'

'Fine. First of all, I know about your and Mike's little relationship. He told me everything the day before he left. The day he told me he was done on the project I had set him.'

'What project?'

'None of your business. Listen, I knew something was wrong with him that day. Now Mike's a tough guy, he don't scare easily, but there was something that he discovered that scared him witless. He said that if he stayed around, his family would be in danger.'

'His going hasn't changed that much, has it?'

'Sadly, no, but you've got to believe me, I had nothing to do with Jean. I sent the boys round to find the memory stick and remove Jean while we searched. I had every intention of leaving her alone after that.'

'Yeah, now you're triggering my bullshit detector.'

He shrugged, not committing or defending one way or another. She didn't doubt he was looking for the memory stick, but certainly doubted he would have left Jean alone. It was a nice section of the ship, all things considered. He'd no doubt want it for himself if he could get it.

'Cut to the chase, Graves. What's so important about the memory stick?'

'I don't know . . . yet. But someone wants it real bad. And if someone is willing to kill for it, it means it's worth something. Besides, like you, I want to find the bastard and feed them to the fish. It's clear to me, and probably to you too, that Jean's death is tied up with all this.'

Eva thought he was right on that. Jean had no other enemies to speak of, and she had little to do with Faust's lot, so there was no other motive. If what Mike had found had scared him so much that he'd volunteered to leave the flotilla to protect his family, then it wasn't a huge stretch of the imagination to guess that if someone had known about this and was after what Mike had found, Jean would become a target.

'And you know for certain Mike had this memory stick?' Eva asked.

'Yeah. He found it one day while exploring some of the newer boats. Found a cache in a safe.'

'And let me guess – you cracked the safe?'

'I can't confirm or deny that. Either way, he kept the loot; I thought nothing of it. It looked like a pack of old rags to me. But there was this stick, you see, and some papers. Mike said they were encrypted, couldn't read a word of them.'

'Wait, why are you telling me all this? If this thing, whatever it is, is worth something, why get me involved? You know exactly what I think of you, and that opinion isn't changing any time soon.'

Marcus gave her a sly smile. She had to give him credit: he had a certain charisma, despite being a complete arsehole.

'Here's the deal, love. I know what you were; know what you're capable of. I want you to work for me, find this memory stick, find out what's on those papers and what scared Mike so much he abandoned his family.'

'And what's in it for me?'

'A nice yacht in my manor; extra resources. This place is going down the shitter. Stuff's breaking down, things are going missing. How long do you think Jim's decisions are going to be tolerated? There's mutiny afoot. And you know as well as I do what'll happen if complete anarchy breaks out in this place: we'll all be screwed. You help me solve this little riddle, you get the killer, and Danny gets a safe place with people capable of looking after him. And that extends to you too.'

'Tell me one thing first,' Eva said.

'What?'

'That stupid business with Frank. What the hell was that all about?'

He shrugged. 'Nothing to do with me.'

'And you know about his wife?'

'I don't believe that story. He came to me an hour before going after Jim. You know Frank's an ex-crack addict, right? His brains are scrambled; fuck knows what goes on in there half the time.'

'So you've seen her, then, his wife?'

'I don't keep tabs on everyone.'

'That's exactly what you do.'

The sly grin again.

'She's fine. She was out working the compost bins last night. Frank's talking shit. If someone put him up to take out ol' Jim, they didn't have his wife. He tried it for some other reason. But really, I couldn't give a crap about the reasons behind it. Jim's a dead man walking these days. If Frank didn't take him out, one of Faust's nutters will. She's been riling them up lately.'

'So that sack of shit was lying after all!' Eva said, thinking back to what Frank had told her earlier. She berated herself for not seeing through his lies, but she reminded herself that it had been a long, torturous time since she had questioned anyone like that. Skills dull over time, but the thought of her insight and intuition also being blunted brought a sense of dread. How was she going to catch the killer if she couldn't even tell when a scumbag like Frank was lying?

'You really think Faust's lot are capable of splitting the flotilla like that? Most of us just view them as loonies, clinging on to some misguided sense of faith as a way of surviving. I know they've been a pain lately, but they've not been actively dangerous.

'I've seen it before,' Marcus said. 'Back in the East End. You think these groups are just whackos, but over time they gain numbers and start a feedback loop of madness to the point where they believe their own bullshit.'

'That's worrying, which is just what we don't need on top of everything else,' Eva said with a sigh. Then, focusing her mind on the task at hand, she said, 'Getting back to your earlier point, what exactly is it you think I can do for you?'

'Investigation, love. I want you to find out where this key goes, and recover the stuff that Mike found before he buggered off. Before whoever killed Jean gets it. And besides, who the hell wants a killer running loose about the place? You're an ex-copper; that's kind of your thing, ain't it? Better than fishing and being a general dogsbody, right? You find the gear, you'll likely find the killer. It's not like you've got anything else to go on.'

She hated to admit it, but he was right; she didn't have any other leads.

He handed her the key.

'Here. See? You can trust me. Take it, find out where it leads, and come speak to me when you've got something to share. If we're to find the memory stick and figure out what scared Mike so bad, we're going to need to know where that key leads. It seems to me that wherever it takes us is where we'll find the memory stick and discover just what the killer was after. In the meantime, I'll make sure Shaley and Tyson aren't on your case. Hell, you can use them for your investigations if you want. They make good guard dogs.'

'No, they don't,' Eva said.

Marcus chuckled. 'Well, not against you, obviously, but they're not all bad. We'll also make sure the kid stays safe. You saw how easily Jim and Duncan let him out of their care. Poor kid. I'll make sure I've got eyes on him at all times until you find the killer.'

She couldn't deny that Marcus's influence covered a large area of the flotilla. He had people all over the place, keeping an eye on developments. If Danny was to remain safe while she was investigating Jean's murder – and figuring out what Frank was lying about – it made sense to have Marcus's resources backing her up.

She held out a hand. 'Why do I feel like I'm doing a deal with the devil?'

Marcus bowed, took her hand and kissed the backs of her fingers.

'Maybe you are, love, but better the devil you know, right?'

CHAPTER EIGHT

J im put the last rivet back in place and sat on his bed. The sound of waves battering the side of the *Bravo* echoed into the small room, the steel amplifying the water's kisses. Thunder roared in the distance. If the weather kept up, it would be even more difficult to send a 'volunteer'.

He thought about visiting Frank, getting him to take Faust, but that would require too much trust. He couldn't afford for Frank to come back to the flotilla with the truth.

A knock on the door made him start.

'Captain? Are you in there? It's Duncan.'

Jim stood, looked around him to make sure he hadn't left anything out and unlocked the door. Duncan's large frame filled the open space. Worry etched waves into his forehead beneath his long, wild hair. More a Viking as every day passed, Jim thought.

'What is it, Dunc?'

'Just wanted to give you a progress update. The hydro should be back on in a few days. The engineering boys have figured out the problem. Someone smashed up the transformer. They're putting together a new one.'

'That's good. With the way the storm's coming in, that should generate enough power to recharge the batteries. What about the wind turbines?'

'The main one took a real battering. Most of the gears and fins are damaged beyond repair. The guys say they can fabricate new parts, but it's going to take a while.'

'At least it's something. That bitch Faust's plans won't stop us all just yet.'

Duncan's worry seemed to deepen.

'What is it, son?'

'We discovered that the powered desalinators were destroyed last night. Even if we get the power back on, they're beyond repair. Need parts that we just don't have. We're down to natural evaporation. We've got enough water stocks for about three days before we're out.'

'Faust's people?'

Duncan shrugged his hefty shoulders. 'Hard to tell, but after her reaction this morning, I wouldn't rule it out.'

'This is not good,' Jim said, rubbing his face, all the while thinking of sending Faust to the sharks as a warning to her congregation. 'You think this could be part of her plans for mutiny?'

'Unless her idea of mutiny is to kill off most of the population, I don't think so. It seems more calculated. You saw what she was like this morning. The woman's nuts.'

'But she's clever,' Jim added. 'Don't underestimate the intellect behind the fury. She knows what she's doing. Her flock grows bigger every day as people cling to any meaning to all this. We've got to keep this place together, Dunc. United, we're safe.'

'I know, Dad. I know.'

'How's Danny getting on?'

'Oh, crap. I forgot to take the kid his breakfast.'

'Do that now, son. That poor kid is probably scared and over-whelmed with grief. You see that he's okay. After that, let Stanic know I want a word with him. There must be some way those desalinators can be fixed.'

'On it,' Duncan said as he dashed off down the corridor, ducking beneath the low beams and runs of pipes.

Jim left his room and was about to head towards the brig when he heard commotion coming from outside. Putting on his water-proof coat and hood, he headed out.

Surrounding the bow and standing in a group on a number of smaller boats lashed to the *Bravo*'s railings, Faust's congregation were calling for her release. At least half of the flotilla had come out of their boats and storage containers to watch the proceedings.

Jim approached the group. They grew quiet. A single person stepped forward, a pale-skinned, sick-looking woman in her late sixties. She lowered her salt mask. 'You have to release Susan right this minute, Jim. You're holding her unjustly. We can't allow that to happen.'

The politeness was a front; he'd seen this woman, Meredith, act as crazy as Faust once before, in one of their many rituals.

'I can't do that,' Jim said, squinting against the rain as it splashed into his face. The wind whipped it almost at right angles. 'She tried to steal the flotilla's stocks.'

'The divine will not allow it! *He* has spoken to her. She does *His* work.'

'Look, divine entity or not, there's no stealing of resources on this flotilla. You know it, she knows it and everyone else knows it. I'm doing the will of the people. That supersedes any voices Susan may have heard in her head.'

That was the wrong thing to say. Meredith's face twisted into a mask of hate. The rest of her group shouted and yelled, every word incomprehensible. As one, they moved from the smaller boats until they reached the ladders and steps that led up to the deck.

Jim stood his ground. 'I'm telling you people to stand back. I've done nothing wrong here.'

That only appeared to encourage them as they started to climb onto the deck, forcing Jim to retreat. They gathered pace and number; at least thirty of them had climbed over the bow and were heading for him angrily, as though they were ready to lynch him. He had no doubt they would do it, too. Driven by their mad priestess, these people could be stirred up to do almost anything in *His* name.

They continued to stalk Jim. He scrambled up to the bridge section. He couldn't let them get in. They'd overrun the ship. But he was just one man. He stopped a few yards from the door.

When it seemed like they would rush him, Duncan and three of his crew stepped out and stood by Jim's side. Duncan held a gaff hook. 'You lot, back up,' he shouted over their heads. 'You're out of order.'

They stopped for a brief moment and then surged forward, roaring with fury. Two younger men rushed up and tried to disarm Duncan, but he was too quick: he swung the blunt end of the pike, catching one of them on the side of the head, sending him slipping to the deck.

'Stop!' Jim shouted over the wind and rain. 'This is madness.'

The words fell on deaf ears.

'Kill him!' Meredith screamed, pointing her finger at Duncan.

A smaller group of five men and women broke off from the pack and dashed towards Duncan. Jim and the crew members stood by him, braced for the impact. As they tangled in a melee of flying fists and kicks, Jim saw more people approach from one of the old fishing vessels to the side.

Marcus Graves and three of his goons clambered over the railings and systematically dispersed the crowd, mostly by throwing them over the side of the railings onto the boats beneath. Once they had cleared nearly half the group, Meredith and her mad allies backed off, screaming obscenities.

Eventually they retreated fully.

Graves and Jim pushed them all the way to the edge of the bow and stood guard as they lowered themselves down onto the next level. 'You lot, fuck off,' Graves said. 'And don't come back. Otherwise there'll be a world of trouble even your God won't protect you from, you hear me?'

Meredith looked up from the bottom of the ladder and spat at the ground. 'You'll regret this, Graves,' she said. 'You'll burn in hell with him.' She pointed to Jim.

'Bloody hell. What's with all the burning?' Graves said.

Together they watched Faust's group disperse.

'You're bleeding, old man,' Graves said, pointing to Jim's cheek.

Jim dabbed a hand at it and winced. Someone had scratched him deep.

Duncan approached, still carrying the gaff hook. 'You okay, Dad?'

'I'm fine. Just need to clean this up. Let's get inside.'

'Good idea, Captain,' Graves said. 'I need to have a word with you.'

Shaley and Tyson, grinning from the fight, stayed outside and kept watch like obedient dogs.

'I'm telling you for the final time, Graves, Frank's going nowhere. Attempted murder isn't something I can easily forget. Besides, he's scared out of his tiny mind. He doesn't want to leave.'

Jim stood opposite Marcus Graves in his bridge office. Marcus had taken Jim's seat as though the office were his. Jim remained standing, not wanting to be at the other's level. He pushed against the plaster across his cheek. The cut was sore but had stopped bleeding.

'That's all crap, about his wife,' Graves said. 'There's no American threatening him.'

'So why else did he come after me? On your orders, perhaps?'

'Don't be a twat, Jim. You think I'd send an idiot like Frank after you? If I wanted you dead, I'd do it myself.'

Jim flinched at the threat. He was starting to get more than a little pissed off with people thinking he was expendable. 'If it wasn't for me, this flotilla would have self-destructed months ago. I've kept this place together, given us all a life. And in case you've forgotten, I was elected to this position.'

'Who are you trying to convince here, eh? You or me?'

'What is it you want? I've got better things to do than waste my time with the likes of you.'

'Easy, sunshine. Let's keep things respectful, shall we? No need to get all excited. Think of your heart. Take a seat.'

'Like I said. Just tell me what you want.'

'I want Frank back.'

'Why? You said yourself you chucked him out of your little gang.'

Marcus smiled at the taunt. 'My *little gang* has need of him for something, but it doesn't need to trouble you. Here's the deal. You give me Frank, and I'll make sure Faust is . . . dealt with. She and her flock will no longer be an issue here.'

'And why would you do that? It's certainly not for saving my arse,' Jim said, scrutinising Graves, trying to figure out the man's motivations. The way he lounged back all casual on Jim's chair made Jim want to kick the legs out from beneath him.

'Mutiny is in the air, Jim. That fracas today, that's just the beginning. Both you and I, despite being polar opposites, know

76

that if we're all to survive, this flotilla has to function. It has to stay united . . . even if it means making a few sacrifices along the way.'

'That's not how it should be done,' Jim said.

'You don't think it's worth crushing a few bad apples for the greater good?'

Jim's first reaction was to say no, but then he thought back to each of those volunteers that had been sent away. He'd sacrificed them for the greater good. What was so wrong with doing the same with Faust and the troublemakers? Hadn't he already set a precedent in his own mind as to what was acceptable?

'You know it is,' Graves said as though he could read Jim's mind.

Jim sat down and sighed. 'So what do you have in mind?'

'I suggest that you accidentally leave the brig unattended one night, the key at hand, and my boys will remove Frank to a safe place and Faust . . . to a not-so-safe place.'

Jim mulled it over. Letting Frank out seemed crazy, considering the guy had attempted to murder him. 'I need some answers and assurances,' Jim said.

'That's fair enough. What you got in mind?'

'I need to know what was behind Frank's assassination attempt. If you're saying this American figure isn't real and you didn't order the hit, then why the hell did Frank try to put a gaff hook into my back?'

'Okay,' Graves said, leaning forward, clasping his hands together, locking his fingers and tapping his thumbs. 'Here's the deal. We spring Frank to somewhere safe where we can all have a chat. I'll make sure we get the truth out of him. Then we deal with Faust.'

'If I agree to this, I want Faust removed my way.'

Graves shrugged. 'Sure. No skin off my nose. You say how, and it'll be done. But not until Frank's handed over.' Graves unclasped his hands and held out his right hand, palm open. 'We got a deal?'

Jim considered it for a moment, but saw no other way out of the mess. He just wanted it sorted one way or another. 'Fine, you've got a deal,' Jim said, shaking his hand.

CHAPTER NINE

Eva took a sip from her flask and washed down the starchy potato soup. She admired the ingenuity of the men and women who had managed to dredge for dirt and make it suitable for growing vegetables. They had found boxes of seeds on one of the container ships. So far, they'd managed to grow potatoes and tomatoes, and in the hull of a shipwrecked trawler they'd even grown mushrooms. Made a nice change from fish. Although from now on she'd take great delight in eating the pan-fried shark steak.

Danny finished his meal and sat on the bed with his head buried in a comic.

Ade sat opposite Eva, his long arms resting on the dining table. 'He's not coming,' he said.

'He'll come. Just relax.' At first, Eva had considered that perhaps Ade was in on all this – whatever *this* was – but she had confirmed with his bunkmate that he had been asleep at the time of Jean's death. Despite his working with Graves, there was nothing about Ade that would cause any other suspicion. He and Mike were good friends, anyway; she couldn't imagine him suddenly throwing that away and killing his friend's wife.

Like Ade, Duncan was one of the few people she had learned she could rely on. He was the rock of that place. Hardly ever fazed or fussed, he just got on with things, full of optimism. She could really do with a dose of that right now.

She squeezed the flotation ball attached to the key, wondering where on this floating city it would take her. The key was thick and strong with a square edge. Modern-looking, she thought. Perhaps a safe or some expensive padlock. If anyone knew where the key would fit, it was Duncan. He'd been here since day one, along with Jim, building the flotilla, capturing boats that drifted by, pulling them in with ropes and hooks.

'Hey, you wanted to see me?'

She saw his great beard before his face as Duncan leaned in through the door.

'I've got something for you, Dan,' Duncan said, walking across the cabin until he towered over the boy. He passed him a small cardboard box. Danny opened the lid. The succulent, spicy smell of barbecued gull wafted around the room, making her potato soup suddenly seem unfulfilling.

'Wow, thanks, Duncan,' Danny said, grabbing the bird and biting a section off the breast. Grease dripped down his chin as he devoured the meat.

'Sorry I didn't get back to you in time before you left. You scared the hell out of me,' Duncan said. 'Here, take this. If you ever go for a walk, stay in touch.' He handed Danny a two-way radio. 'You know how to use one of these?'

Danny nodded.

'Good lad, keep it on channel nineteen, okay?'

Duncan took a seat at the head of the dining table, dwarfing it with his great chest and thick arms. He turned to face Eva and Ade. 'So,' he said, his voice low, 'what's this all about?'

The South African said, 'We found something. We need your expertise.'

Duncan's bushy eyebrows rose. 'Oh?'

Eva opened her hand and showed him the key. 'We need to know what this is for. Do you recognise it?'

Duncan took the key, examined it closely and ran his fingers across the surface. 'Where'd you get this?'

Ade was about to say something when Eva cut him off, 'I found it. It's not really important where or how. I just need to know if you know what it is and where it might belong.'

Duncan breathed out long and slow before inhaling noisily and letting out another long breath. 'I don't know how you got hold of this, but I know exactly what it is and exactly where it goes.'

Eva waited, but he didn't follow up.

'Well,' Ade prompted, 'what is it, man?'

Staring at Eva with that intense look of his, Duncan said, 'It opens the sub.'

It was Eva's turn to show surprise. She wasn't expecting that. 'Are you sure? The submarine, as in the nuclear sub, the one here under the flotilla? The one that no one's been into since the day it arrived?'

'Yeah, the very same.'

'No way, man, it can't be,' Ade said, grinning with surprise and confusion, then lowering his voice. 'Why would the kid's old man want to go in there, eh? I heard the reactor got damaged when it turned up here. Isn't it full of radiation by now?'

Eva took the key back before Duncan could refuse to give it back. He looked irritated.

'Duncan, I need a favour from you,' Eva said.

'No, that's not going to happen.'

'You didn't even let me ask you.'

'I know what you want, and there's no way Jim would allow it.'

'I'm sure you could think of something.'

'You want me to betray my own father?'

'If it means bringing Jean's killer to justice, yes.'

'Why don't I just ask him first?'

'He'll say no.'

'He might not.'

Ade was looking confused, his head turning from Eva to Duncan like he was watching a tennis match.

'Jim doesn't need to know. You're wearing your big-boy pants now, Dunc. You don't need his permission. Besides, you're doing this as a personal favour to me. The woman who's helped you out of a few issues lately. You remember the rigging problem? Who was it who climbed up there in a shitty storm and fixed it before it came away and damaged your little sweetheart's yacht?'

'She wasn't, and isn't, my sweetheart,' Duncan said. 'You volunteered to fix it anyway. I didn't make you do it against your wishes.'

'Don't matter, Dunc. We're still buds, right? Buds help each other out. You might do things differently back in England, but in America, we help each other, stand up for one another. Think of Jean. Think of Danny.'

'You sure this has something to do with Jean's death?' Duncan asked with a whisper.

'It might do, but I won't know unless you do me this favour.'

Having had enough, unable to read between the lines, Ade butted in. 'What are you guys talking about? What is it you want, Eva?'

'Scuba gear,' Duncan said.

'And you're gonna get it for me, aren't you, Dunc?' Eva gave him the sweetest smile she could manage.

Shaking his head and sighing, Duncan stood up. 'Okay, I'll do it, but if you damage it, you're the ones to speak to my dad. He'll hit the roof. We've got only three sets left and not a lot of air in the tanks. I won't take the rap for this, you understand?'

'It's all right, Dunc. We won't need a lot of air to get to the sub and back.'

'Fine, but it'll have to be later tonight. I won't be able to get it out of the storage during the day – too many of the crew milling about. And I'll need the key from Dad. He won't just give it to me.'

'Call Ade on the two-way when you have it. I want to go first thing in the morning and see what Mike was up to.'

Eva couldn't imagine what Mike would have been doing going to and from the sub. It meant he had had his own scuba gear. But why the sub at all? It had been shut up for the last two years. It was then that she started to get that sense that something bad was going on. Encrypted documents, memory sticks, murders, and now a US nuclear sub. Plus the stuff with Frank.

Bad juju, she thought. *This is swimming in bad juju.*

Eva woke from her nap and stepped towards the kitchen area. She stubbed her toe against the edge of a cabinet, swore loudly, then remembered Danny and swore under her breath. The room was in darkness. She'd napped for longer than expected, the exhaustion and emotional ride of the last few days having sapped her energy.

Her watch face glowed in the dark and said it was just gone 8:00 p.m.

She wondered if Duncan had got the key from Jim yet. She stumbled across to the kitchenette, groping for the kettle, remembered they didn't have any generated power and moved to the dining room area, where Mike and Jean kept a stock of kindling to light the small wood-burning stove.

As she was feeding the pieces of driftwood in, she called out for Danny. No answer. Her eyes had adapted to the dark now, and she noticed he wasn't in his bed. Dropping the kindling to the floor, she rushed to her nightstand and picked up her two-way.

'Danny, this is Eva. Are you getting this?'

No answer – just static. Her heart raced. He was supposed to have stayed with her until she took him back to the *Bravo*. She pressed the button again. 'Danny, this is Eva. Where are you?'

'Eva, this is Stanic. I saw Danny go past the *Slice of Life* a few moments ago, heading for the fish-maze.'

'Thanks. I'm on my way. If you see him, tell him to use his radio and call me.'

'Will do. Wrap up warm; the storm's nasty out there tonight. Wouldn't want another going-over.'

'Roger that,' she said.

The ship swayed heavily, buffeted by the waves, as they squeezed through the gap between the Orizaba and the *Alonsa*. If Danny got too close, a wave could . . . *No.* She banished the thought, put on her wet-weather suit and mask and rushed out of her cabin. She had an idea of where he might be heading.

She left the safety of the cruise liner. As she ducked through the ragged aperture in the hull, the wind nearly blew her onto her back as it gusted, picking up power as it roared through the narrow confines of the floating city. She always thought 'city' was too grand. It was more like a shantytown.

She jumped across onto the main section of the flotilla and took a shortcut. Instead of going through the container ships and then the maze, she jumped over the railing of a ferry until she landed on a small fishing boat.

The smaller craft lined the edge of the flotilla as it faced the Orizaba. Bow to stern, they created a buffer, allowing people on fishing duty to easily reach deeper waters without going too far, especially when they were line fishing or net casting.

Movement from the cabin pulled her up short. She steadied herself, moving her hand towards her belt where she kept a knife. The shadows shifted further and a squat man wearing his mask and yellow jacket poked his head out of the doorway.

'Eva? What you doin'?' the man said, squinting his wrinkled leathery eyelids.

'Nolberto . . . Sorry, I didn't expect anyone to be here. I was just . . . It doesn't matter. I need to get going. I'm sorry for disturbing you.'

'Getting bad, isn't it?' he said in broken English, accented heavily with his native Peruvian tones. He dropped his eyes and rubbed a rag across them before adjusting his mask back into place. 'They took Saywa to quarantine this morning.'

'Oh, I'm so sorry to hear that,' Eva said, reaching out her hand to grip him by the shoulder. 'She's a strong kid,' Eva added. 'I'm sure she'll fight it. Doctor Singh will look after her.'

Nolberto nodded his head rapidly a few times, still rubbing his eyes before turning away and heading back into his cabin. Eva wanted to say something else to comfort him, but she had to make Danny her priority. She mumbled her best wishes and climbed over the cabin towards the string of other craft, trying to put the worry of the infection to the back of her mind. More people getting the disease really wasn't what the flotilla needed at the moment – or any moment.

She clambered from one boat to the next, all the while bracing herself each time a wave crashed against the boats, drenching her in a wall of spray.

On the final boat, she moved to the edge and looked up. A great anchor chain hung from the bow of the *Bravo* and disappeared into the roiling sea beneath, its rusted iron bleeding a dark orange trail down the ship's battleship-grey skin.

The beam of her flashlight caught the reflective yellow of a fisherman's coat.

'Danny!'

His face appeared over the edge. 'Eva?'

'Stay where you are.'

Eva leaned forward to grab the chain. Using the huge links as foot- and handholds, she quickly ascended until she reached the railing. She pulled herself up and over, slipping on the deck as she landed awkwardly, blown off course by a gust of wind.

Her hood covered her face. She pushed it up and saw Danny, swamped inside his dad's coat, running to her.

'You've got to stop going out on your own,' Eva said. 'Where's your radio?'

He shrugged, hanging his head. 'I'm sorry,' he said, his voice muffled by his mask, which was far too large for his small face. The container in which they had found the masks hadn't had any sized for a child.

She pulled him close, shielding him from the storm.

'It's okay. You're safe. Let's get you inside.'

Even though she shook with a mixture of fear and anger, she couldn't take it out on him. He knew what he'd done was wrong, but the poor kid was grieving, wasn't thinking straight.

Eva started to lead Danny to the bridge when something in the distance, just beyond the Orizaba, caught her attention. Thinking it was distant lightning, she paid it no attention, but then Danny pulled on her hand.

'Look, Eva, he's come back. I knew he would!'

'What?'

Eva turned. There, riding the waves and coming towards the flotilla, was the *Tracer*. Mike was indeed coming back.

CHAPTER TEN

A curious energy manifested itself within the *Bravo*. Crew members were shouting, their voices echoing against the metal walls. Jim sat up in his bunk and poked his head out of his cabin.

'What's the problem?' he asked Jason, one of the young kids who worked in Jim's crew.

'He's back. We've finally got one back.' The kid beamed a grin of amazement.

'Wait, what?'

'Mike's back. The *Tracer's* coming.'

Jason rushed off as three other crew dashed down the narrow corridor.

Shit. That was not supposed to happen.

Jim ducked back inside his cabin. His chest tightened as he tried to think of what to do. He considered radioing the others to find out why they had returned Mike, but then he thought about what Mike would say. He'd surely expose Jim's lies and secrets.

Jim had to get there first.

Taking a swig of the watered-down rum from his flask, he stepped out and headed for the upper deck, putting on his water-proof suit and mask as he went.

When he got to the deck, Eva and Danny were standing at the edge, accompanied by five crew members and a gathering of twenty or so flotilla citizens.

Still a hundred and fifty feet or so away, the *Tracer* rode up and down the waves, inching ever closer, its lights bouncing around in the dark.

Lightning lit up the dark clouds off in the distance beyond the Orizaba.

Rain lashed at an oblique angle, soaking his hood and mask.

'Okay, everyone, clear the deck. I'm bringing him in.' He pushed his way through the group of onlookers, trying to ignore the tumult of questions, rumours and gossip. He looked to his right, over the fish-maze and the container ship, and across to the *Alonsa*.

It seemed everyone had heard the news and had come out of their cabins to see if it were true.

Jim lowered a rope ladder to the line of fishing vessels bordering the port side. As he descended the last rung and landed on the deck of a fishing boat, he noticed Eva preparing to follow him.

'Eva, stay there,' he shouted. He had to yell to make himself heard over the sound of the waves, the wind and the rain. 'I'll need you to tie us up when I bring him in. And make sure Danny doesn't do anything stupid.'

A rumble of thunder swallowed Eva's words, but she remained on deck.

Jim ducked into the fishing boat's wheelhouse and turned the key. The diesel engines spluttered and came to life. Most of these boats had had their fuel siphoned and stored to ration it for as long as possible, but they always left a few gallons in for emergency uses.

Pushing the throttle lever halfway and spinning the wheel, Jim turned away and headed north, pushing the thirty-foot boat against the tide, increasing the throttle as he crested each wave, gaining speed as he rushed down the other side so that he had the momentum to ride up the next wave. It reminded him of when he had taken Duncan to Coney Island one summer and ridden the roller coaster.

That was the last summer with Morag, his wife.

Jim got closer to the *Tracer*'s position. He couldn't help but feel numb, the memory of his wife draining him of motivation, but he reminded himself that she would have wanted him to carry on, even if it were only for Duncan's sake.

A few minutes later Jim was approaching the starboard side of Mike's boat. Although the main lights were on, he couldn't see Mike at the wheel. He pulled his boat up to its side and, tying off the wheel, cut the engines and ran onto the deck, grabbing a rope as he went. Waiting for the right moment, when the two boats got close enough, he looped the rope around the bollards of both boats, lashing them together.

He repeated the procedure twice more.

'Mike, you in there?' he called out, leaning over to see into the cabin. No one stirred.

He waited for a calm moment between waves, climbed aboard and entered the cabin. Mike was there, lying beneath an old tarp, his face swollen and feverish.

Jim stood back, poking him with a foot. 'Mike, you hear me?' He couldn't tell if Mike was still alive, the movement of the boats making it hard to tell if his chest was rising and falling.

Mike opened his lids, revealing milky white eyes, like an advanced form of cataracts. He blinked, and those terrible eyes turned to regard Jim. Mike's lips were badly cracked and bloated. They quivered as he spoke wheezing, incoherent words.

'What did you see, Mike?' Jim asked, trying to figure out if Mike had reached the destination.

Mike said nothing, just kept mumbling random sounds. His body shook and sweat poured from his forehead, making him look waxy beneath the cabin's amber light.

'Mike, it's me, Jim. Remember?'

No response. Mike was completely catatonic. Fearful that this was an advanced form of the infection, Jim backed off and climbed into his own boat. He got his radio and called for Dr Singh on the emergency medical channel.

'Doctor Singh, this is Jim. Do you read me? Over.'

The doctor's words eventually came through after a period of static. 'I read you, Jim. What's happening? I heard Mike's back.'

'I've got him here. He's sick, real sick. Can you meet me by the *Alonsa*? I'll bring him there, away from the crowds.'

'I'll be right there, Jim. Over.'

Using the tide to his advantage, Jim pulsed the engine on his boat to drag the *Tracer* down the edge of the flotilla, away from the *Bravo*. He passed the ragtag collection of rafts, wrecks and smaller boats and approached his old ship, his pride and joy, the *Alonsa*. She made up the northern edge of the flotilla, providing protection from the harsh waves that filtered between the floating city and the Orizaba. A wooden bridge spanned a five-foot gap between the ragged entry point in the *Alonsa*'s hull and the main part of the flotilla.

Dr Singh stood on the bridge, wearing a facemask and gloves beneath her waterproofs. She waved to Jim, and he waved back to acknowledge her position.

He gunned the engine until the diesel ran out.

The momentum and the power of the tide pushed his boat and the *Tracer* towards the bridge. He spun the wheel to face the make-shift dock that he and Stanic's team of engineers had built in the early days. Dr Singh moved from the bridge to stand by the dock. When they were close enough, Jim threw her a rope. She tied it expertly off onto a bollard, tightening it as Jim navigated the pair of boats closer in.

Jim shouted his thanks over the storm as he jumped up onto the dock and tied a second rope to secure the two boats.

'He's in there,' Jim said, explaining the symptoms.

Dr Singh climbed aboard and went in to assess Mike's condition.

A dozen flotilla citizens were approaching.

'Is it him? Is it Mike?' Charles, one of the elderly skippers, said.

'What did he find?' That was Chun, one of the surviving crew of the Chinese container ship.

Darren, one of the entertainers from the *Alonsa,* added, 'He found something, didn't he, Jim? He must have done.'

Behind the gathering, Eva and Danny approached.

He couldn't let the kid see Mike in this condition, but he had to tell him something. Moving through the crowd, Jim stopped Eva and Danny and held his palms up. 'Look, I'm sorry, but you can't go any farther.'

'Why?' Eva asked. 'What's going on?'

Jim looked at Danny and thought he would just go with the truth. 'I'm sorry, son, but your dad's sick. It's nothing to worry about just yet, but we have to get him to Dr Singh's medical room to make sure he's okay.'

'I want to see him,' Eva said.

'I can't allow that, Eva. I'm sorry.' Jim tried to keep his voice calm. 'He might be contagious, and we can't afford an outbreak. Let Doctor Singh see to him first, make sure he's okay, and we'll go from there. Take Danny back to the *Bravo*. I'll be right over with more information as soon as I know anything else.'

Eva didn't look convinced, but Jim didn't move, just waited until she gave in and agreed. 'I'm coming to see him later, Jim, whatever the case may be.'

'Sure. But just give us time for now. I'll explain more later.'

Eva nodded, clearly trusting Jim. 'Come on, Danny. We'll let the doctor make sure your dad is okay and see him later.' Despite the boy's obvious disappointment and confusion, she led him away.

Keeping Mike wrapped in the tarp and breathing through one of Dr Singh's facemasks, Jim helped the doctor take Mike to the medical rooms. A cruise ship of that size didn't have a fully equipped hospital, but it did have decent enough facilities that they had managed to create a set of quarantine rooms to help manage the spread of the bacterium.

They carried Mike into the last empty one and laid him on a bed. The patients in the other rooms peered through the windows set in the wooden doors. Jim nodded his acknowledgement to them, but they just stared out at him blankly. *Poor bastards,* he thought. Some of them had been in there for over ten months waiting for a cure, gradually growing weaker.

Dr Singh gave Jim some salt-washed antibacterial wipes to clean his hands when they left the quarantine zone and moved back into Singh's office.

'So what do you think?' Jim asked. Mike was gibbering weird sounds, his eyes focusing on something no one else could see.

'Catatonic, high temperature, bloating. I'd say it's the results of the infection on first look. Or possibly a more advanced form. Where has he been?'

Jim shrugged his shoulders. 'No idea. Will he ever come out of the catatonia and be able to speak?'

'At this stage, it's impossible to say. If the bacterium has mutated, there's no real way of knowing what the symptoms will be. I'll have to do some tests and observe him.'

'Will you call me first, before anyone else, if he starts to talk? If he found something out there, I need to know first. We can't let the flotilla panic over something until we know the full situation.'

'Of course, Jim. And if you feel ill at any time, come to me straight away. Although the bacterium hasn't shown any signs of transmission through touch or air, we can't rule out that this could still happen.'

'I'll speak to you straight away, Doc. But call me as soon as anything happens.'

Jim shook her hand and left, heading for the *Bravo*. He had to send a message, find out why Mike had come back. They had confirmed his arrival, so why was he here? Jim balanced on a razor's edge of anxiety as he thought about what response he would get and what it meant for everyone.

This wasn't supposed to happen. This wasn't planned for. It hadn't even been considered in the contingencies.

No one should have come back.

CHAPTER ELEVEN

Eva knelt to face Danny. He sat on the edge of the bunk, rubbing the tears from his face.

'I know, Dan, but they're doing the right thing. I'm sure your dad will be fine. It's just a precaution. You want him to be okay, don't you?'

'But I just want to see him. I don't understand.'

'We don't know where he's been or what's happened to him. We just want to make sure he's okay. Listen, I'll go speak with the doctor and find out when you can visit, okay? But you've got to stay here and relax. Everything will be fine.'

'You promise?'

She hated when kids demanded that. How could she promise anything? If she didn't, though, Danny would just fear the worst. Even with Emily, Eva had been made to feel like a liar when her promises hadn't been kept. Lying to a child was a necessary evil to protect them, allow them time to learn the truth in their own time. Eva just hoped that her promises and false hope would come true, and she could be spared the grief of Danny knowing she had lied to them.

She held his hand between hers. 'I promise. But you've got to promise me something in return. You have to promise me you'll stay here; don't go running off anywhere, okay?'

'Okay, I guess,' he said.

'There's a good lad. It's getting late. You try to get some sleep, and hopefully we'll go and see your dad in the morning. I'm sure he must be very tired after his adventure. The sooner you sleep, the sooner you'll get to see him.'

'Like Christmas,' Danny said. 'Dad always said to go to sleep quickly so we would get our presents sooner.'

'Exactly like that.'

Eva kissed him on the head and pulled the blankets over him. 'I'll see you in the morning. If you need anything, Duncan and Jim are just in the next cabins.'

'Where will you be?'

'I'll be back here later, Dan. I just have to take care of a few things.'

After they'd said their goodnights, she closed the cabin door behind her and headed out to the *Alonsa*. She wanted to see Mike, find out what the situation was.

'Hey,' Duncan said, coming out of a narrow corridor, his great bulk filling up the space. 'I've got it.'

'Got what?' Eva said, her head full of thoughts and her memory failing.

Duncan pulled her into the corridor and looked around before placing a key in her palm. He leant in close and whispered, 'The key to the scuba storage, as promised.'

Of course, she thought, the case suddenly rushing back to her.

'Be quick, while my dad's preoccupied. They're kept in the hold. Everyone is too busy gossiping to pay attention. You should be able to get there and out without anyone seeing you. But if you're caught, I didn't give you the key, okay?'

'Won't Jim know they're gone?'

'Probably not. He's freaking out over this Mike thing. People are going to be bugging him for hours.'

'Thanks,' Eva said, giving Duncan a quick hug, but as she made to move away, Duncan squeezed her close.

'Be careful,' he said before releasing her.

'I . . . will.' She turned away, hiding her blush, and set off. She still intended to see Mike first. She could come back and get the scuba gear a little later. By then everyone would be back on their respective boats gossiping about the news.

Eva made her way through the tight corridors. Ducting, cables and tubes ran overhead; along the sides were stacks of cardboard boxes of supplies and piles of driftwood drying for use as fuel.

Every footstep rang out, echoing. Shadows gathered at every turn. She didn't understand why Jim and the others, elected to oversee the running of the flotilla, had chosen this old destroyer instead of the more comfortable surroundings of the *Alonsa*. She'd hate to live in the tight confines of this vessel. All the grey decor and sparse, militaristic styling reminded her of the time before the drowning: all those unnecessary wars. Perhaps what they had now was better. As soon as she thought that, she admonished herself. For all she knew, those on the flotilla were the only ones left. That much death was never preferable in any circumstance.

Humanity wasn't perfect, but that didn't mean it was better that she and the remaining survivors didn't exist at all.

She climbed the metal steps to the upper decks and bumped into Jim along the way. He looked distracted, his attention flitting this way and that. Heavy bags hung beneath his eyes and worry lines were etched deeply into his forehead.

'Sorry,' Eva said. 'I didn't see you there.'

Jim backed up to let her by, mumbled something, but then reached out and grabbed her arm. She spun round. 'What is it?'

He gestured to a low, open doorway leading into the wheelhouse. She went in and he followed behind her. He closed the door.

'Jim?'

'You've got to stay away from Mike,' Jim said, the wrinkles getting deeper and his nostrils flaring.

'Why? What's going on? What are you hiding from us?'

Jim closed his eyes and took a deep breath. 'Why does everyone have to question everything? I'm telling you, stay away from Mike. He's sick. Really sick.'

'The bacterium?'

'Worse. Far worse. We don't know what it is. But he can't talk, and he looks real bad. Singh's running what tests she can to figure it out, but he's in quarantine until we know more. We have no idea what he found out there. I can't afford to let anyone else near him. Do you understand what I'm telling you?'

Eva took a step back, not liking Jim's expression. She knew he was under a lot of pressure, but for the most part he handled it like the true captain he was. But now, it was as though she were looking at someone else completely.

'Okay, I get it. Did he say anything at all?'

'No. He can't talk.' Jim's shoulders relaxed as he exhaled and slumped against the door. He rubbed his face and seemed to age a decade. 'God knows what we're gonna tell his kid. It's not looking good. Mike's just murmuring a load of gibberish. It's like his body is alive but no one's at home.'

Eva reached out and touched Jim's shoulder. 'I understand. You're looking tired. Why don't you get some sleep? We don't want you getting ill too. Who else is going to hold us all together, huh?'

Jim looked at her, opened his mouth and seemed about to speak but gave her a wan smile instead and nodded. 'You're right. I'll head off now. Give me time, and I'll make sure you're one of the first to see Mike when Singh gives me the go-ahead. But please, Eva, trust me on this.'

'I trust you. Now, go get some rest.'

Jim nodded, turned and opened the door. Together they left the wheelhouse. Jim headed down to the cabins. When he was out of view, Eva turned the other way and headed for the hold storage in the lower decks. She'd stay away from Mike for now, but she would still take advantage of this opportunity to grab the scuba gear and take a look inside the sub.

She didn't like to distrust Jim, but she suspected there was more to it than just sickness. Perhaps it was tied into all this stuff about the key and the memory stick. Her intuition might be dulled, but she was getting more than a hint of subterfuge from Jim, which in itself was enough to cause worry; he'd never struck her as the type to hide anything before.

Eva took the scuba gear from the locker, placed it inside one of the storage sacks and left the ship, her hand automatically lifting the salt mask into place. Once on the upper deck, she headed to Marcus's yacht.

When she arrived, she glanced through the window. Marcus and his family were sitting with Ade around a table, playing cards. She tapped on the window and Ade came out.

'You get the gear, girl?'

'Yeah, Duncan came through. You ever scuba-dived before?'

'Like a fish.'

'Come on, then. Let's go check it out.'

The rain ran off Ade's face. His wide grin seemed to catch the moonlight through the parting clouds. Eva shivered at the thought of diving down into the dark.

Although the sub wasn't very far from the flotilla, just fifty feet off the rearmost vessel and thirty feet below the surface, the thought of spending any time in the water at all without seeing what was swimming around them almost made her change her mind. But then she remembered Jean. She didn't know for certain if Mike's activities were definitely connected to her murder, but it was the only thing she had to go on; she was determined to find out Mike's secret and see where it took her. One way or another, she had to see it through.

CHAPTER TWELVE

J im locked the door behind him and performed his ritual
with the practised movements of a junkie preparing his next
fix: bunk up, panel off, box out, bunk down, radio on and
send. He watched the little black square on the screen, waiting
for it to flash twice to indicate that the message had got through.
Nothing. No one home.

He disconnected the antenna and slammed the radio back into
the box, spilling the papers and notebook onto the bunk. His hands
shook, and he became light-headed with a thousand unanswered
questions. If *they* weren't answering, then it would likely mean *she*
wasn't there anymore. This was his one guiding light, his one focus
that had kept him believing they would eventually find a future, a
home. And worse, there was nothing he could do to find out, not
without leaving the flotilla, not without leaving his only son behind.

Gathering the dozens of paper messages with the encrypted
text, he folded them neatly and placed them back in the box.
The notebook with the last agreed encryption key went into his
shirt pocket.

Placing the box back behind the panel, Jim collapsed onto
the bunk and forced himself to think things through, find a way

forward out of this mess. That Mike wasn't talking gave him time, but how long that would last, he couldn't tell.

The plan to send Susan Faust was of no use now. Although, as he considered it again, it seemed like a rash idea anyway. There was no way she would willingly sail the boat out beyond the horizon to where the others would pick her up. He closed his eyes and pictured his wife on their wedding day – how splendid she'd looked in her white dress, her blonde hair piled high, exposing her elegant neck. He breathed in, then out, steadying his thoughts, trying to bring himself back to a position of focus. He was making bad choices right now.

If he was going to sort this out, he'd need to think more clearly. With Mike back, there was no way he could justify sending anyone, let alone an unwilling participant. However, he still had to make up his mind what to do with Susan.

Although he still suspected her and her group of acolytes of sabotaging the hydro and wind turbines, perhaps antagonising them would only make things worse. There was the option of releasing her, and trying to make peace with them. If they wanted to live separately from the other residents, that could be arranged. There was enough space on the flotilla. If having their own place to live meant they'd stop hassling the others, then all the better.

He'd rather that than having to take matters to their logical conclusion.

But then there was Frank – Graves would still want him out, and it wasn't really clear what had motivated the attack. Jim shook his head, unable to see a clear route through this mess.

The weight of responsibility threatened to crush his chest as his breathing became shallow again, despite his meditation attempt.

He pictured himself before the world had drowned, captaining the *Alonsa* on her maiden voyage. A nice cruise around South America. He pictured the warm weather, the beaches that he'd managed to enjoy for a few snatched hours during stops. He pictured the guests on board enjoying the ship's roster of entertainment and how they would all greet him with smiles and admiration.

In those days, his leadership had been something to respect, and he'd worked hard to live up to those standards. But here, on the flotilla, things had a chaotic nature that he was increasingly finding difficult to cope with. Burdened by indecision, he left to pay Mike another visit, just in case those murmurings turned to words, and those words turned to accusations and revelations.

Jim took the route through the containers. He might as well check on the stocks and storage while he was out and about. It was another opportunity to make sure none of Faust's congregation was trying to steal any more fuel, water or food.

The rain had stopped, thankfully, but the wind still cut a cold edge, attacking his extremities with a ruthless prejudice. He pulled his hat down lower over his ears and pulled his collar and mask up, but still the winds bit deep.

He navigated his way through the dark tunnels created by the containers and passed a number of flotilla citizens huddled around their small driftwood fires, the smoke twisting out through the open doorways of their container homes. He moved quickly to avoid recognition. They'd only bug him about Mike.

Throughout his walk, as he passed through the maze of paths, he heard the same questions over and over within the boat's cabins:

'What do you think Mike saw?'

'Is it true he found someone?'

'Will we be saved, finally?'

'I heard he's sick; has he brought a new bacterium back with him?'

On and on, endless conspiracy theories, conjecture and rumour.

By the time morning came around, the information would have mixed with speculation and the truth would be obscured by fantasy. But that wasn't something Jim could worry about now. He just had to make sure Mike's return remained a mystery, one way or another.

He came to the container that Faust had earlier tried to break into. To Jim's satisfaction, the chains and locks were still in place. He tested them just to make sure. Still solid, secure. Although their drinking-water stocks might be in peril, individuals would be able to boil the seawater and gather the condensation. It would be tough, but they could survive for a while like that, at least until the desalination units were up and running again.

Coming to the edge of the Chinese carrier ship, Jim prepared to climb down to the lower level created by a number of damaged pleasure craft that were lashed together with boards and sheet metal, fibreglass and sails. He turned around to grip the rail. A dark figure appeared in front of him, making him jump. He let out a surprised breath.

'Jim, old son, need a hand?'

'Marcus, you scared me for a moment there. What are you doing?'

'Just having a lovely stroll about. Nice night for it, innit?'

'It's cold,' Jim replied, his voice tightening. Graves wasn't the kind of man he wanted to bump into on a dark night.

Graves didn't say anything, just stood there, looking grim.

'About our deal,' Jim said, thinking he should just get it over and done with while he had the chance. 'It's off. There's no need to . . . deal with Faust now.'

Marcus raised an eyebrow and said nothing, waiting for Jim to continue.

'You see, things have changed. I'm going to release her, make things right with her people. Work out a peaceful solution to this.'

'Oh, peaceful, huh? Yeah, that's not going to work. That lot are beyond peace. They pose a threat that needs dealing with. Besides, Jim, you're forgetting that I want Frank out.'

'He tried to kill me,' Jim said.

Graves shrugged as though that had no meaning.

'He stays inside until I figure out what the attack was all about,' Jim said.

'Jim, my old son.' Graves gripped Jim's shoulder, pulling him close. 'I don't think you fully understand the situation here. You made a deal, and we're sticking by it. There's no negotiation on this now. You understand? It's done. I thought you were a man of honour, Jim. A man of your word. Or is Faust right? Are you a liar and a betrayer? Are you a sinner, Jim?'

'We're all sinners here,' Jim said, pushing Graves' hand off his shoulder.

Graves grabbed Jim by his coat and pushed him back until his feet started to slip on the edge. Jim tried to push out with his arms, but the jacket material had bunched beneath them, restricting his movement.

'I'll make this real simple for you,' Marcus said as he pitched Jim towards the edge. 'If you don't release Frank by the morning, we'll take him by force, and you and I will have some serious words. You understand that?'

Anger bloomed inside Jim, and all he wanted to do then was smash Graves in the face and send him over, but he had no choice but to nod and agree.

'Say you understand,' Graves said.

'Fine. I understand.'

Marcus smiled and pulled Jim from the edge, letting him go.

Jim had to throw his arms and body forward to prevent himself from losing his balance and toppling backwards off the container ship's deck. He steadied himself, bunched a fist ready to strike out, but when he looked up, Graves was already walking away into the dark passages between the containers, replacing his mask as though he had just had a friendly chat with an ally.

Jim kicked out with frustration and stifled a shout. It seemed wherever he turned, trouble waited for him, and Marcus wasn't the kind of trouble he wanted. He took a moment to gather his cool, and slowly, with shaking hands, made his way down to the lower level and headed for Singh's medical facility, all the while concocting murderous scenarios of how to deal with Marcus, Frank and Susan Faust.

I'm not the murderer here, he reminded himself, banishing his violent thoughts.

CHAPTER THIRTEEN

Eva and Ade trod water, holding on to each other's arms. They had their breathing masks on, regulators in. Ade had brought along a high-powered diving light to help illuminate their way, while Eva had her diving knife clipped to her belt. Neither wore a full wetsuit. There just wasn't time. Ade was used to the temperatures, but Eva wore a suit covering her top half and arms. They would only be in the water for a short while, with any luck.

She checked the pouch clipped to the arms of her buoyancy control backpack. Inside was the key to the lock that would give them access to the sub. She made the okay sign by forming a circle with her thumb and forefinger. Ade returned it. He pointed down with his thumb, and Eva nodded. With that, the South African dived down into the water, his body slipping through the darkness.

The diving light created a wide bloom of illumination, making it easy for Eva to dive in and catch up with Ade. She followed him as he gracefully kicked his flippered feet and propelled himself towards the long, dark shape hanging under the water.

Eva's muscles tightened with cold and the terrible suspense of expecting a shark to suddenly appear out of the gloom. She and Ade had surveyed the surface while they got ready, and with the aid of the moon, they had concluded there were no fins apparent.

It didn't mean they weren't there, though, waiting in the dark.

Ade's light bounced off a tall angular shape: the sub's sail.

Eva could make out the two black fins, or planes, sticking out either side like wings.

Within a few more feet, Eva could make out the links of heavy chain wrapped around the sail and through the handles that opened into the lockout trunk.

They drew nearer. All the while Eva scanned her periphery, waiting for something to come darting out of the shadows, but all she saw were small, frenzied schools of young mackerel.

A graceful ray glided far below her, reminding her of a stealth plane as it cut through the water, its fins undulating with unseen currents.

Ade kicked his legs harder and approached the sub's sail. He gripped the chain and turned to give Eva the okay sign again.

She kicked harder and caught up, placing her feet on the hull of the craft.

It seemed strange to be standing on top of a submarine out here, she thought. But she remembered why she was here. Using the illumination of Ade's diving light, she found the heavy-duty lock holding the chains together. It was fastened through the two large metal handles on the escape hatch, holding it closed.

Taking the key from the pouch, she fitted it into the lock and turned it. Although she couldn't hear it, she felt the mechanism click into place and the chains loosen. It was her turn to give the okay sign as she removed the key, replaced it in the secure pouch and pulled the chains from the lock.

The hatch opened slowly as the chains fell aside. Ade went first, holding the light in front of him as he dove down into the dark of the escape tube.

He had told Eva earlier, at the surface, how it would work.

They would enter a separate chamber with its own pressure. It would be full of water if someone had recently left it. Inside the chamber, the submarine had controls to expel the water and pressurise it, meaning they could open a second hatch into the main submarine compartment.

The lockout trunk was exactly as Ade had said, full of water, but he was already scanning the controls on the bulkhead and lighting his way around.

Eva gripped the handles of the interior hatch that led to the submarine to hold herself in place as she waited. At least in here she didn't have to worry about sharks.

Something slid against her leg and she yelled out with surprise, sending a column of air bubbles upwards. She kicked out as something brushed her leg again, as though whatever it might be was inspecting her, testing whether she was food or not.

Ade swung round, shone his light.

Eva's heart raced. She had the urge to just kick out and get the hell out of there. With both her and Ade in the tight confines of the lockout trunk, with no other lights, she felt trapped. She spun round, trying to see what had touched her, and briefly felt something tap against her flipper.

Ade questioned her with the okay signal, and she shook her head. He swam closer, placed his hand on her arm and shone the light down into the dark water. Something quickly swam away, but as Ade tracked it, she saw it.

An eel. Just a harmless eel.

Eva controlled her breathing, felt her heart rate drop.

Ade grinned behind his mask before turning to examine the controls once more.

A few minutes later Eva sensed something start to shift and move as though the submarine had woken from its slumber. Lights came on, making the water glow.

A deep rumble stirred the water before forcing it out through pressurised jets. Eva clung to the handles of the interior hatch as the water level dropped and the pressure increased. She spotted the eel thrashing in the movement and descending to near her feet.

She feared for it then, worried that the water would fully drain, leaving it to gasp and thrash in the open air. She kicked gently with her flipper towards one of the jets and watched with relief as the eel righted itself and headed out into the sea beyond.

A small mercy, a small act of kindness . . . She hoped it would bring her some karma for whatever might lay ahead, even though she had never believed in such a thing. She had seen hundreds of examples of why it didn't exist in her time on the force. Plenty of good people who had dedicated their lives to helping others would find themselves shot, stabbed, beaten or robbed. And in many of the murders she investigated, the victims turned out to be some of the most generous and loving people she had known, and yet karma had deserted them, and they'd fallen prey to some malevolent force. Paid a price on a debt they did not owe.

But then we all pay for each other's debts, she thought, *whether that's fair or not.*

When the water level dropped to chest height, Ade removed his regulator and took a breath.

'It's okay,' he said. 'You can breathe normally now. Save your tanks.'

She pulled the regulator from her mouth, enjoying the sensation of being free from it. The air was stale, dry compared to the mix in the tanks, but it was air. She wiped her hair back and removed her mask, letting it hang around her neck. She tucked the regulator under the straps to her buoyancy pack to prevent it from snagging.

'That feels good,' Eva said. 'I know it's not long, but I'm not a natural scuba diver.' She'd done some in her previous life. When she was younger, she'd held ambitions to be a Marine and spent some of her teenage summers in Hawaii learning to scuba dive and snorkel, but unlike Ade, who moved like a fish, she had never felt entirely comfortable being under the water. Didn't enjoy the idea of all the weight pressing down on her. She carried enough guilt already and didn't need the extra burden.

'You're doing fine, Eva. Let's get inside and take a look around. Mike must have come here for a reason.'

'And there's no radiation risk from the damaged reactor?'

'No, I don't think so. I was with Stanic and the other engineers when Jim first brought the sub in. The power was off, but there was no radiation leak. We tried to run it, thinking the reactor could power the flotilla, but Stanic couldn't find a way. Said it'd be too dangerous to try to run, but in its current state, it's fine.'

'I hope you're right. I don't fancy growing an extra head or something.'

'Nah, man, you'll get sick first.'

'Yeah, thanks, Ade. I was trying to lighten the mood.'

'Ah, sorry. Okay, the water is low enough, and the pressure is okay. See? The hatch has closed. When we leave, we do the opposite, and the hatch will open. Ladies first?'

It was at that point she wished she had a firearm. She felt naked entering an unknown place without her police-issue pistol in her hands. But she remembered her knife: she unclipped it from her belt and held it out with a sure grip in her right hand.

With her left, she pulled on the interior hatch. She realised she'd been holding a long breath in her lungs, and exhaled loudly after nothing came rushing out of the blackness.

'Can I have your light, Ade?'

He handed it to her. She shone it ahead of her and stepped inside the main compartment. For a moment she felt like the characters in the *Alien* film, the crew of the *Nostromo* as they explored the dark corridors of the abandoned facility. Only she didn't have a maze to negotiate or a bleeping radar to put her on the edge of suspense; instead, she had a tight, unfamiliar tube to investigate.

'It's like a tomb,' Ade said, following behind her, 'only one where the bodies have been taken away. It's creepy, man.'

'And you're making it creepier, Ade. Cut it out.'

The light shone off metal surfaces in all directions as they ducked through the bulkheads to reach the deeper parts of the sub. 'The mess hall,' Eva said as she stepped between tables and chairs lined up in a narrow section. To the left of the tables, an equally narrow galley with a food-serving area lined the opposite side.

There were some plates still on the tables. Some of the food, perhaps potatoes, had dissolved into a mouldy gloop within the serving trays.

Eva remembered something Jim had said about when they'd first boarded the sub: the entire crew were found dead. She pictured a corpse sitting at the table, the knife and fork still in his hands.

She slid on the floor and slipped backwards before Ade grabbed her by the tanks.

'Easy,' he said.

When Eva looked down, she saw the floor was wet. Someone had been here recently after all. The hairs on her arms rose, and she shivered as she considered that someone might be in here, right at that moment, hiding in the shadows, like the sharks outside.

'Mike must have definitely been here recently,' she said, point-ing to the wet prints – none of which matched the one she had seen on the fishing boat, which she'd memorised before the rain had washed it away.

Using the diving light, they followed the prints through the mess hall until they arrived at the bunks. Three high on each side, they didn't leave a lot of room for each submariner. She felt another tinge of claustrophobia grip her, thinking about squeezing into one of these bunks. How they could spend any length of time down here, she would never know.

'Check the bunks,' Eva said as she placed the light on the floor to light up the area as best as possible. Running her hands through the dark spaces, she tried to ignore the fear that something lurking beneath the sheets would grab her hand.

Eva and Ade went from bunk to bunk, investigating, won-dering if Mike had stashed the memory stick here. All they found was the detritus of lives previously lived: photographs of smiling families before the drowning. Families smiling with a mixture of pride and fear.

Despite herself, with each photo she saw, she pictured her own family, her daughter. She had had a similar photo in her locker at the police station. Her mom and pop, hardy farmer types, waving at her from the porch of their old house, bewildered as to why she'd give up a good honest, Idaho farming life for the violent, corrupt wilds of Baltimore.

'I want to make a difference to people's lives,' she had explained at the time. Growing potatoes wouldn't bring closure or justice to a widow whose husband had been murdered. There, though, among the filth and dregs of society, she could make a difference, even though at times she felt it wasn't enough. One could never turn back the tide alone. The Earth had taught her that one, time and time again.

'Nothing here,' Ade said.

'Ditto.'

'There's one place he's likely to have used,' Ade said, pointing forward. This time, he took the light and led the way.

Eva followed as they continued to slip through the narrow accesses, passing great machines that would create oxygen from the water and others that scrubbed the recycled air. They stood like goliaths within the sub, their fascias an amalgam of dials, switches and levers, answering to a secret physical operating language that only a few would know.

Ade disappeared into a side cabin, taking the light with him and plunging the rest of the sub into darkness. She stumbled, holding out her hands to find her way.

'Ade, what the hell are you doing?'

'Sorry, man. Here.' He pointed the light out of the room to guide her.

This cabin was as narrow as any other, but was clearly the captain's room. A single bunk was a luxury here. A console with a computer unit and screen lined the main room, and next to it stood a desk and a switchboard. He could run the craft from here if he needed to, it seemed.

Eva inspected the floor and, like in the rest of the sub, found wet patches. They stopped at the bunk. Eva moved across and searched through the nooks and spaces, checking under the bed and in every dark space. Ade did likewise at the other end, searching above and below the desk, behind the console.

After what seemed like a lifetime of disappointments, Eva found nothing and was about to turn to Ade to say they should move on when she noticed a crack in the floor, the edge of which caught the light.

Eva knelt down and prised the edge up with her knife. It moved.

'Ade, I've got something. Bring the light over, will you?'

He spun and shone the light down on Eva's position.

With two solid pushes, a half-foot section of the floor came up to reveal a plastic zip-lock bag, within which were what looked like a number of files and—

'It's the stick,' Ade said. 'You found it!'

Eva pulled out the bag and held it to the light. Indeed, within the bag was a small clear plastic box holding a memory stick. The files, in plain manila envelopes, were half an inch thick. She unzipped the bag and took them out, leafing through the papers. They were encrypted into some kind of code. Presumably, the encryption key was on the USB.

Ade took the USB stick and placed it within a waterproof pouch attached to his backpack straps.

Eva put the files back into the waterproof bag and secured it before tucking it into her belt.

'Let's get the hell out of here,' Eva said. 'This place gives me the creeps something bad.'

'I hear you, man,' Ade said. 'We'll need to go out via the lockout.'

'Lead the way.'

On their way back, Eva couldn't help but feel a sense of growing satisfaction. It was like the old buzz from before when she'd find some crucial piece of evidence that led to an arrest. She felt close. Wouldn't be long now before she found some answers, and hopefully a clue to the murderer's identity – still assuming that this was all connected, though she did have that tingle of intuition that told her it was more than likely.

* * *

They left the sub as they'd found it, exited via the lockout and swam slowly up to the surface. When they were about twenty feet away,

Eva noticed a string of bubbles around her. She slowed, and a shape swam past in her extreme peripheral vision. She spun round but couldn't quite see what it was. That's when she noticed Ade was not behind or below her.

Panicked, she brought the light round, trying to illuminate the water to find him. She couldn't see him, but in his place there was a cloud of blood. Through the cloud, something moved, knocking the light from her hand.

Eva reached out to grab it, but she couldn't move fast enough, and instead she grabbed uselessly at the water as the light fell through the swirling blood, shining as though it had a life of its own. When the light dropped low enough, she caught a glimpse of Ade's body sinking, his arms and legs limp.

Something grabbed her tanks and yanked at them; she flailed her arms and spat her regulator out as she tried to scream. With one hand over her head to fend off her attacker and the other trying to grab her regulator, she fought like a wildcat, kicking out and spinning – anything to free herself.

She struck out with a kick and her foot connected with something firm.

It had her flipper and was pulling her closer.

With bubbles rising from her mouth and her lungs straining, she pulled the knife from her belt and thrust out into the dark.

Her flipper came free as her knife bit into something meaty.

She kicked away, managed to grab her regulator and took a deep breath of air as she aimed for the surface. But her hope was short-lived: no air left . . . Whatever had attacked her must have punctured or disconnected the tanks.

Her lungs burned; adrenalin flooded her system. She kicked hard for the surface, all the while wondering who or what had attacked her and whether it was even now chasing her down.

Without the light she couldn't tell, and she didn't want to stop and take a look around.

She breached the surface and inhaled a mixture of air and spray, making her cough and choke. The image of Ade's bleeding body sinking to the bottom came to her.

She couldn't help him now, had to get to safety.

Looking around, getting her bearings, she saw a few amber lights from within the cabins of the flotilla. Fixing the position, she kicked out and swam as hard as she could. With each stroke she felt a pain in her ribs.

She stopped, dabbed at her ribs and cried out. Blood covered her hand.

A cut ran deep; she must have been injured in the struggle. Had she done it herself, with her own knife? She felt light-headed and thought she was going to vomit, but she sucked in a deep breath and continued to the flotilla. It was no more than fifty feet away, but each stroke required everything she had just to keep going.

Only once she looked back and thought she saw a fin break the surface.

For all she knew, it could have been a panic-induced hallucination, but it didn't matter; the panic and fear were still real. She tried to block out the image of Jean being ripped apart by a shark and focused on getting to the flotilla.

Don't look back; just keep going.

She said it over and over in her mind, a survival mantra. With all the effort she could muster, she kicked and swam, every breath laboured and painful, every second expecting something to take her down, drag her below the water. Her vision dimmed with each stroke, the world growing darker.

The pain no longer registered, and she forgot for a moment why she had to swim. Where was she going? The tiredness overwhelmed her. She just needed to rest . . .

Eva lost consciousness before she reached the flotilla; her last waking memory was of someone standing on a raft lashed to the edge, screaming her name.

CHAPTER FOURTEEN

J im stood mesmerised at the door to Mike's quarantine room. A sheet of plastic had been fixed across the door, an extra precaution because of his condition.

The way Mike's milky eyes turned to stare at him through the small, square window gave Jim a cold shiver. *He must recognise me*, Jim thought. Did he know that Jim had sent him to the other place on purpose? Did he know that he was a 'resource'?

Odd sounds and words continued to emerge from Mike's mouth. It was as though he had discovered a new language. For a brief moment it reminded Jim of Faust and her wild, gibberish outbursts spoken in 'tongues'. He tried to discern a pattern in Mike's words, but they were too random, too . . . different. The murmurings of a madman.

Just what had he seen to turn him into this? Was everyone over there like this now? Without any response via the radio, Jim had nothing to go on. He considered taking a boat and going out there himself, but feared what he might find, feared that he would end up like Mike.

Jim dragged his attention away from Mike's eyes and left the quarantine room. 'He's still not saying anything.'

'You should get some rest, Jim,' said Dr Singh from behind her desk. 'I'll let you know as soon as there's any progress.'

He regarded the doctor. 'Have you any idea of what this is?'

'Early tests seem to indicate this is similar to the current bacterium. It reacts the same way to the salt tests, but it's far more aggressive. I'll know more in the next few days.'

'Transmission?'

'Hard to tell right now. If it were airborne, both you and I would be showing symptoms. How are you feeling?'

He shrugged. 'Okay, kind of.'

'Oh? Something playing on your mind?'

'No, nothing more than usual.'

'I know stocks are low, but I could prescribe something to help you rest.'

'I'm fine, thanks.'

'I'm worried about you, Jim. You look run-down, stressed. We need you fighting fit.'

He held his hand up in an apology at his sharp tone. 'I'm sorry, I'm just a little stressed lately. Murders, sabotage, and . . .' He looked round the makeshift quarantine, noting how the numbers had swelled over the last few days with at least four new cases of infection discovered. They'd soon run out of space for new cases.

Dr Singh watched him as he assessed the room. 'I know,' she said. 'The frequency of the infected cases is increasing faster than it's ever done, but I'm working on it as best I can.'

'I know you are, Doc. It's just worrying that it might be mutating, getting out of control. What if the salt baths and masks aren't enough anymore?'

The two of them just stared at each other, silent, both keeping the horror of that eventuality unspoken.

'I should go,' Jim said, suddenly feeling exposed. 'If he says anything, you contact me first, right?'

'Of course, Jim.'

Duncan burst into the medial area, carrying Eva in his arms, her head and legs hanging limply. He sidestepped through the narrow corridor towards Singh's clinic room.

Blood covered Duncan's hands. It stained a dark patch on the front of his white *Alonsa* crew shirt. A bandage hastily made from one of his sleeves was wrapped around Eva's ribs.

'Duncan, what's happened?' Jim said.

'She's cut, unconscious. Help me.'

Singh helped Duncan take Eva into a room on the left. Inside was a small theatre of sorts.

She had Duncan lay Eva on the bed.

'Son, tell us – what happened?' Jim said, trying to control a rising panic within him.

'I . . . I . . . don't know. I just found her like this. She's been badly cut about her ribs. I don't know how much blood she's lost. She was unconscious when I found her.'

Jim clenched his fist again, turned his back and suppressed a yell of anger and frustration. If there was one person on this godforsaken flotilla he didn't want to lose, it was Eva. She was one of the few capable, good people left.

'It has to be the same person who killed Jean,' Duncan said.

Jim didn't think he sounded too convinced.

'You two, leave me to it,' Singh said as she pushed them aside. 'You're just getting in my way.'

She urged them out of the room and returned her attentions to Eva's unconscious body. Jim caught a glimpse of the ragged wound as Singh removed the makeshift bandage.

With the door now closed, Jim turned to his son and raised an eyebrow. 'You tell me the truth. What happened to her?'

'I'm telling you the truth,' Duncan said, glowering.

'Where did you find her?'

'On the west side. She'd slipped between that old catamaran and the tug. Someone must have stabbed her and left her there to die.'

'And you just happened to find her?'

Duncan's brow furrowed. 'What are you saying? You think I'm lying about this? Why would I?'

Jim shrugged; he knew Duncan was holding something back, but he didn't know what. And, surprisingly, he realised he just didn't care anymore. When not even his own son could be honest with him, he knew his time on the flotilla was rapidly coming to an end.

'Have you seen Stanic this evening?' Jim asked.

'What? No, why? How's that important right now?'

'I need to speak with him, about the repairs.'

'Eva's in there, probably dying, and you're more concerned about some goddamned repairs?'

'The repairs are important. I want you to go find him and get me a progress report on the hydro and wind turbines. We need those desalination units up and running as soon as possible. As for Eva, are you going to tell me the truth?'

'It's like I told you,' Duncan said, slowly and clearly, as if Jim were getting old and needed things explained to him more carefully, 'I found her in the water with a stab wound. What do you want me to say?'

'If that's what you're going to stick with, then I guess that's that. I still need that progress report. Do your duty first, and then you can check on Eva. The flotilla comes first. You understand me, boy?'

Duncan glared at Jim, his nostrils flaring. Jim stood his ground, waiting for his response.

'Fine,' Duncan said, storming off towards the door. 'But if anything happens to her while I'm away, that's all on you . . . Captain.'

Jim turned away and watched as Dr Singh cleaned the wound and began to stitch Eva up. *She'll be okay*, Jim thought. Singh was as good a doctor as he had met. But even so, he didn't buy Duncan's explanation. That left the question of what had actually happened. He'd wait until Singh was done and then question her.

If there was something going down on this flotilla, it was his business to know.

———◆———

Jim yawned and jolted in his chair, nearly toppling out of it. He blinked, realising he had dozed off for a while. The smell of coffee made his stomach tighten.

Dr Singh placed a steaming mug on the desk in front of him. She sat opposite and cradled a mug in her hands. She had changed out of her blue uniform and was wearing an old shirt and jeans.

'I didn't want to wake you,' Singh said. 'You clearly needed the rest.'

'But?'

'Eva's awake. I thought you might want to talk with her.'

He nodded. 'Thanks for the coffee. There can't be much left now?'

'A personal stash,' she said with a smile. 'I've been saving my rations for emergencies.'

He took a sip of the hot, bitter liquid and sighed. 'I'm sorry for the way I acted earlier. It's just . . . this place, you know? It's . . . getting fractured.'

'You can confide in me, take some of the strain off. We've been friends long enough, Jim. I know you. I'm on your side.'

He knew she was right. She had been the doctor assigned to the *Alonsa* when he first took charge of the ship. She, along with Duncan, had been a constant source of support.

Support or not, he couldn't tell her the truth; not yet. No one could know what he knew. It would split the flotilla, make all their chances of survival that much slimmer. Not to mention that if the truth got out, he would likely be exiled or, worse, killed.

They wouldn't react too well to the fact that the so-called volunteers had no idea where they were going or what was waiting for them. Hell, Jim wasn't even completely sure.

'Thanks,' Jim said. 'I appreciate it.'

He stood and entered Singh's theatre. Eva sat up in the bed, her ribs bandaged and wrapped, and forced a smile in greeting. Jim offered her his mug of coffee.

'Need a brew?'

She shook her head. 'No, thank you. I'm okay with water. Where's Duncan?'

'He had to attend to other duties. But I'll let him know you're awake. What happened?'

'I don't really know, or at least, things happened too quick, so it was hard to tell.'

'Well, remember what you can and tell me.' Jim kept his voice low and calm, a mask for the anxiety and anger he felt, both for her condition and Duncan's lies. He didn't expect Eva to be entirely honest, but perhaps between the two of them he could read between the lines, discover a thread of truth.

'I saw someone scoping out Mike and Jean's cabin, so I followed. I tracked them into the west end when I lost sight of them. The next thing I know, I'm in the water, bleeding, losing consciousness. I vaguely remember Duncan pulling me out. Beyond that, there's not much else to say.'

'Did you get a look at this person?'

'No, they were wearing dark overalls or perhaps waders. I must have spooked them when they ran off. It was too dark to see much else beyond that.'

'You think they were Jean's killer?'

'Perhaps, but it's hard to tell.'

Eva kept her arms crossed over her body, and her eyes darted about the room before settling on him with a glare. Her voice was terse and he got the hint of defensiveness from her; perhaps she was not being completely truthful. He thought about pushing her, but didn't want her to completely clam up. He'd figure it out sooner or later.

'Well,' he said, 'I'm glad Duncan found you in time. The doc says you should be fine. It's just a flesh wound.'

'I'll continue my investigation as soon as I can,' Eva said. 'I want to catch this bastard, even if it's the last thing I do.'

'Let's hope it doesn't come to that. You just take it easy for now. I'll have some of the crew take watch over Jean's cabin in case they decide to come back. You think they were looking for something?'

'It's possible. But what, I have no idea.'

'Must be something valuable if they're willing to kill for it.'

'I guess so. Oh, by the way, how's Danny? Is he being looked after?'

'Yeah, he's with the crew on the *Bravo*. They're teaching him how to play poker.'

'Good, good. Listen, don't tell him about this. I don't want him to worry.'

'Sure.' Jim placed his hand on the door handle. Turning back to face Eva, he added, 'If you remember anything, let me know, won't you?'

'Sure thing, Jim.'

Jim headed out into the cold night with a maelstrom of thoughts in his head. He was quickly losing the will to care about all the various threads hanging and decided that when he got back to the *Bravo*, he would just release Frank and Susan and let whatever was going to happen.

Why should he bother trying to hold these people together when they didn't trust him?

As far as anyone knew, they were the only humans left: everyone else had drowned or died of starvation and disease. If this lot wanted to end humanity, then who was he to stop them? Was there any reason to go on anyway?

Living aboard a floating collection of junk was no real life. And even this small number of people couldn't agree on how best to live. Perhaps it was a sign that humanity's time was up.

Perhaps, he thought. *Perhaps it is.*

CHAPTER FIFTEEN

Eva woke to excited voices. Each syllable caused a stab-bing pain in her head. She rolled over and winced, cry-ing out. It all came back to her then: Ade, the wound in her side, Duncan, Dr Singh . . . She felt her stomach cramp as her head spun.

'Marcus, she's awake.'

Shaley's familiar face looked in from a low doorway. It dawned on her then where she was: Marcus's yacht. The fine wood-panelled berth with the roof-mounted lights and plush furnishings reminded her of when she had first been here at Marcus's request. That was one of her first days on the flotilla. It was also the day she learned that Marcus was a thoroughbred scumbag. That she was here, in his bed, made her want to vomit.

'Give me some privacy,' she said to Shaley as he ogled her from the door.

She noticed she was almost naked beneath the sheets, wearing just her panties and the wrappings around her ribs.

Had they undressed her? The thought of them seeing her naked made her skin crawl.

'I said get the hell out.' She threw a pillow at Shaley. It struck him and fell to the floor. He gave her a sly grin before closing the door.

Creep!

'Leave her alone, Shal,' Marcus called out from the living quarters. 'Eva, there's some clean clothes on the nightstand. I hope they fit; they were all I could find at short notice.'

On the nightstand she found a pair of wool socks, jeans, a woman's T-shirt and a large, baggy blue sweater. She lifted them off the nightstand, smelled them, expecting rank sweat, but to her surprise they were freshly laundered.

It took her fifteen minutes to put on the clothes, feeling a stabbing pain in her ribs every time she twisted or bent over. Sweat covered her arms and face by the time she had finished. She sat back on the bed and rested her head in her hands, waiting for the pain to subside.

A knock came from beyond the door.

'You okay in there, love?'

'Yeah, Marcus, I'll be right out. Just give me a few moments.'

'Sure thing.'

Although she was likely drugged with antibiotics and pain meds – which were clearly wearing off by now – she could have sworn that Marcus was actually sincere in trying to help her. She wondered then if he knew about Ade and the lost USB drive. Was this just his way of softening her up before interrogating her, demanding to know where the key was? Would he lose his cool and take the loss out on her? Losing Jean had been bad enough, and now Ade was gone too. Although people died frequently on the flotilla, Ade's loss would be especially hard once all this was over. He was one of the few genuinely good guys she'd ever met, and he'd died working for Marcus.

Suddenly she felt exposed, at risk, wondering again what was so important about the memory stick and what Marcus would do once he knew it was lost. Would he get physical this time? She'd seen him get tough with a few flotilla members before, but never a woman: though that didn't mean he wasn't capable.

She looked around for a weapon, wincing as she bent down to check inside the small cupboard space beneath the bed and the drawers of the nightstand. She found a pen and a small pewter ornament of a yacht. That was no good. But the pen could be useful. She'd once stabbed a member of Baltimore's leading crime family in the neck with one when he had tried to overpower her in an alley.

If her aim was right, she could hit an artery.

She hid the pen up the sleeve of the sweater.

Marcus, along with Shaley, Tyson and Shaley's wife, Catherine – or Caff as they called her – sat on cream-covered settees around a large table, playing cards. Small plates of fried seaweed and sushi sat next to mugs of tea. The sun was shining brightly through the yacht's windows, a light drizzle of rain tapping out a steady rhythm on the glass.

'Here she is,' Marcus said. 'The survivor. Glad to have you back, love.'

'You look like shit,' Tyson said before turning away with disinterest.

Marcus cuffed him across the face. 'Have some damned respect, Ty. You're on my boat. We keep it civil. Understand?'

'Not where that bitch is concerned.'

'Get over it, Ty. Your balls will heal soon enough.' The group laughed.

Jesus, Eva thought. *Why'd I have to wake up to this lot?*

'Why am I here?' she said as she sat in the space next to Marcus, which he indicated with a tap of his hand and a welcoming smile.

The smile of a shark just before it's about to kill something, she thought.

'I happened to stumble upon Duncan last night and heard you weren't well. Decided to bring you someplace comfortable. You'd only catch something you don't want in Singh's place.'

'That all?'

'Well, now that you mention it, there are a few things we need to discuss.'

'About Ade,' she said, uncomfortable with the 'family' staring at her. Catherine, or Caff, hadn't said a word, just glared at Eva like she was a piece of dirt. 'He . . .'

'Yeah, we know, love. Poor bastard's fish food. We'll miss him for sure.'

'I'm sorry. I tried, but it happened so fast . . . I couldn't . . .' She hung her head and took a deep breath.

Marcus put an arm around her shoulders. She recoiled, pushing him away, but he held on and hugged her anyway. Speaking into her ear, he said, 'I know you did your best. It must have been awful; I understand, okay?' He let her go, and they locked eyes.

Was there sincerity there or subterfuge? Her instinct told her not to trust him, but his actions thus far had told her the opposite. Her dad had always told her to take people at face value, give the benefit of the doubt, but then he'd mostly dealt with cows and fields of potatoes. Much easier to take that attitude when you weren't running down crime bosses and murderers, or stuck on a flotilla with some wannabe gangsters.

'What now?' she asked. 'Ade had the drive in his pouch . . . I panicked and swam for the surface. It's lost now, again, and we won't be able to find out what scared Mike away.'

Caff spoke first, surprising Eva. Her fierce expression had softened. She brushed the long blonde hair from her face and brought out the files Eva had recovered. She pushed across a couple of pages from one of the manila folders. 'They're the only ones not encrypted,' she began. 'I went through each page and found these among them. They're like journal entries of some sort.'

'From the submarine's second in command,' Marcus said. 'And get this: the submarine weren't no ghost ship when it turned up. There were two survivors.'

'Wait, what? No way,' Eva said. 'Jim has always said it arrived with the crew dead. He wouldn't lie about that.'

'I don't think old Jim's as squeaky clean as he'd like everyone to believe,' Marcus said.

'But,' Caff interjected, 'from the notes, it appears Jim might not even have realised. Do you remember the first volunteer that left us?'

Eva shook her head. 'I came after the second had left.'

'Well, I do,' Marcus said. 'Worked in engineering. Ran the place before Stanic turned up. And, crucially for this little mystery, worked with Mike.'

'So, what does that mean?' Eva asked.

'Before Mike left,' Marcus said, 'he came to me, as I explained previously, but he got wind of these files from this first volunteer guy; his name escapes me now. Anyway, he told Mike about his journal and how it went missing, and he wanted to recover it. Said it had important information in it. So Mike, being the curious sort, searched for it and found this package here, along with the USB drive, in a safe on one of the yachts – and later stashed it back in the sub where you found it.'

'So Mike has sat on this information for over a year?'

'Nah, he didn't find it until recently. When he left, the first volunteer gave him a piece of paper with a code on it. Mike has been trying to figure it out ever since. The volunteer said it was crucial Mike found the journal and drive.'

Eva looked at the files spread across the table. She pieced together the events so far, realised that when Mike had found this cache, the killer, whoever it was, had also found out and was trying to recover the information.

'So we've got someone who has killed two people already because of what we're looking at here,' Eva said. 'I doubt they'll stop now. They've probably got the USB drive from Ade, which means we can't decrypt all this lot. I'm guessing that the drive has the decryption key on it. This means Mike must have known what was in these files.'

'We might still be able to crack the code without the drive,' Marcus said, though Eva wasn't so sure.

She looked at the group, suppressing her indignation. Marcus had street smarts, sure, but none of them around the table had the kind of mind capable of decrypting top-secret documents.

'No offence, but I don't think that's going to be possible. Look at the paper; it's official US government letterhead, from the sub. Military. I doubt they'd use anything that could so easily be decoded. There's a reason this person has killed two people already.'

'And we can assume they have the key. They'll want this next,' Marcus said, jabbing a finger on the files. He had a glint in his eye that Eva didn't like.

'You're not thinking of using them as bait, are you?'

'Why not? This shit's got to be important. I want that USB drive. I want to know what's so important about these files that both the volunteer and Mike abandoned this place and someone else is willing to kill for it. Despite what you think, Mike was my friend too, and it don't take a genius to put two and two together and figure out that the person after all this stuff was probably also the one who killed Jean. I want justice for my friend as much as you do. If it means baiting the killer, I'll do it.'

'And you could be next,' Eva said.

He shrugged. 'Not if we get them first.'

'What do you have in mind?'

'Well, let's think about this logically. If it's the same guy that blackmailed Frank, we know he's American. We also know the key to the sub was copied, so it's likely someone who knows how to work metal, perhaps someone in engineering.'

'Wait,' Eva said. 'If you're suggesting the killer made the key, how did Mike get it?'

'It was with the stash Mike found in the safe.'

'Well, if we're only going by the evidence,' Eva said, 'we're potentially looking at one of five men in engineering.'

Caff chimed in, 'Are we discounting the women there?'

'Yes,' Eva said. 'The footprints on the trawler were definitely men's.'

'So,' Marcus said. 'All we need to do is work out which one it is.'

'Unless they find us first,' Caff said. 'I don't like the idea that they know we've got this. It's not safe. I don't want anything to do with it. We've survived this long; I don't want to get thrown overboard by some nutter.'

Marcus took her hand in his. 'You'll be perfectly safe, Caff. Trust me. Have I ever done you or the family wrong?'

'Plenty of times. You're a reckless bastard.'

'But that's why you love me, right?'

Eva got up and fetched a glass of water from the jug on the side. All Graves' family crap was making her feel queasy, and not a little sad from the grief of losing her own family. Did he even know how privileged he was to still have most of his family with him?

It seemed especially cruel to her that they were only still together because they had been smuggling goods on a boat at the time of the drowning.

Whoever said crime doesn't pay clearly didn't live in the real world. She'd seen it pay so much of the time. You only had to look at the banking industry executives who always got away with their crimes, their bonuses afterwards bigger than ever. Grimly she thought that with the drowning, there had been a whole lot of justice dispensed along with the tragedy. But justice or not, she'd turn back time in an instant if she could.

The world was a better place with people in it, even if some of them were no good.

'Right, I'm gonna go get Frank,' Marcus said, checking his watch. 'You lot keep all this safe. Eva, you need anything?'

'No, I'm okay. Thanks for the clothes and the water.'

'My pleasure, love. Make yourself at home. You're welcome here as long as you want.'

Eva wanted to tell him thanks but no thanks, but despite the hideous company, she didn't feel capable of leaving the confines of the yacht. It was a great deal more comfortable than her cabin, and at least here she had other people around her in case the killer decided to pay her a visit while she was incapacitated.

But then she thought of Danny.

'There's one thing you could do for me,' Eva said.

Marcus raised an eyebrow. 'What is it?'

'While you're on the *Bravo*, can you check in on Danny? Make sure Duncan and the others are looking after him. He's lost his radio, so . . .'

'Sure. I'll let him know you're still looking out for him.'

'Thanks.'

Marcus gave her a wink and left the cabin.

Tyson followed behind him, leaving Eva alone with Shaley and Caff.

The atmosphere changed instantly. Caff gave her an awkward smile before her face returned to its usual scowl. Eva didn't think they would try anything while Marcus was gone, but she didn't know for certain. She made sure the pen in her right sleeve was in place, letting it drop into her palm.

CHAPTER SIXTEEN

J im stared at the radio's screen. Still no response. His hand trembled. He'd been up all night trying to send a message, but nothing had arrived and nothing had come back.

A sob broke from his throat. He dropped the radio to his bunk and lay down.

Their only hope had gone. *His* only hope.

'Why me?' he said into his pillow, muffling the words. 'Why us?'

He didn't know why he was questioning it.

Since the drowning, nothing really made sense anymore, despite the illusion of order, hope and survival. How had he even come to be in this position? Why had the people of the flotilla voted for him? He was a hollow man, after all, incapable of the role – a pretender.

Perhaps Frank had been right to try to take him out with that gaff hook. Perhaps he deserved it. He thought about Graves' ultimatum and saw that it was already morning.

For the first time since he had come back during the night, he noticed the sun shining outside the porthole, making the tips of the waves glow white and yellow.

Floating trash caught the light and sparkled like gifts, but they were just remnants of a bygone era. It was the usual stuff: sports balls of various kinds, boxes, timbers from broken houses and plastic. Always so much plastic.

It seemed humanity's legacy didn't amount to much. All that time and energy to make useless plastic crap.

Wars fought to control access to oil reserves so developing countries could build factories and make more pointless plastic rubbish for the *consumers.*

He blinked and looked away from the sea of trash and gathered his radio together, hiding it back behind the secret panel, replacing the false rivets with his knife. He stood up, looked at the knife in his hand and thought about Graves and Frank and Faust.

Barely remembering how he'd got there, or whom he had passed along the way, Jim found himself standing outside the cells.

Both Frank and Faust were asleep on their cots. *Just slit their throats where they sleep. They won't even know . . .*

Two problems gone, like the cities and the homes.

Just more trash dealt with and thrown out. Two thorns cut from the branch and disposed of. Just two cuts . . .

Frank's head was inches away from the bars. Jim could just reach in and finish him right there with one single cut. Jim approached closer and gripped a bar with his left hand, the knife shaking in his right. He focused on Frank's exposed neck, mentally pictured the cut, the futile struggle and the end of one of his problems.

Somewhere in the real world, Jim vaguely recognised Duncan's voice.

He turned round to see Duncan facing Tyson and Marcus.

Duncan said something and tried to hold his arms out, but Tyson threw a vicious overhand right hook, catching Duncan on the chin, sending him crumpling to the floor with a heavy thud that rumbled up Jim's feet.

The two thugs were on Jim in seconds, but not before Jim had placed the knife inside the holder on his belt to hide his guilt.

Marcus stalked close, his faces just inches from Jim's, his breath smelling of fish and seaweed. Tyson glared at Jim from over Marcus's shoulder.

'Frank's still in the cell,' Graves said, his voice low and dangerous. 'It's morning, Jim.'

Jim backed off and thought about reaching for his knife again. They'd be on him too quickly, but seeing Duncan in a crumpled heap made his hand shake with fury.

'You want to go, do you, Jim?' Marcus said. 'All het up and want to throw a few fists?'

'Screw you, Graves. Screw you and all your family.'

'Language, Jim, let's keep this civil; people are sleeping.'

'Frank's not going anywhere,' Jim said, placing his hand on the knife handle.

'You forgetting our deal in your old age?'

Whispering, Jim replied, 'I told you last night, I've changed my mind. Frank stays.' Why were these words coming out of his mouth now? Only last night he had come to the decision that he'd just let Frank go. Perhaps it was Marcus's face that angered Jim so much; perhaps he'd done it just to spite him.

Graves stroked his chin and watched as Frank stirred in his bunk, and then he turned to Susan's cell. 'We can work something out where none of us sheds any blood today.'

It was a full minute before he spoke again, and by that time Duncan had come round and got to his feet. He looked groggy but okay. He rubbed at his chin. Squinting, he focused on Tyson and stepped forward.

'Dunc, wait,' Jim said.

Tyson spun round and brought his fists up, but Duncan stepped back, waiting.

'Chill, Ty. Everyone just chill,' Marcus said.

Both Tyson and Duncan stepped back, eyeing each other, but they waited.

Marcus stepped closer to Jim and dropped his voice. 'You want Faust gone, but not like before. I get it. I'll do you a deal. You get off my case and let Frank go without me taking him by force, and I'll arrange for Faust to be dealt with as you please. You can't say fairer than that, Jim.' Marcus moved back to give Jim room. 'Well?'

Faust was quiet on her bunk, but Jim sensed she wasn't sleeping. She was probably analysing everything that was going on, but she wouldn't have heard the last exchange. He wondered if he could actually do away with her with his own hands. Although he had never been a violent man, this place had a way of twisting people.

'We're imperfect,' Jim said. 'All of us. We're not who we're supposed to be.'

'What?' Graves said.

'Never mind.' Jim sighed, deciding he'd just get this over and done with. 'Look, I'm too tired to argue any longer. Take Frank and deliver on your promise; otherwise I'll come for you, Graves, is that clear? I'll come for you and your family.'

Marcus held out his hand. Jim shook it, trying to crush his grip. Marcus just smiled.

Jim let go and reached for his keys, but they weren't in his breast pocket.

'My keys . . . I don't know . . .'

'Got them here,' Duncan said. 'I found them earlier; it was why I was coming down this way . . . until these turned up, that is.'

Duncan inched past Tyson and handed Jim the set of keys. 'Dad, you don't have to do this.'

'It's for the best.' Jim took the keys and unlocked the cell door. Frank had sat up and was smiling, his expression one of smug self-satisfaction. 'Come on,' Jim beckoned. 'Get the hell out of my cell.'

Frank dusted himself off and left the cell, embracing Marcus and Tyson as he went.

'Well, that wasn't so hard, was it, Jim?' Marcus said. 'I'll be in touch about my favour to you later. But trust me, it'll be done.'

'Going so soon?' Susan Faust had risen and was standing with her back against the rear wall of the cell, shrouding herself in shadows. 'I'll miss all this sparkling conversation.'

Jim ignored her and addressed Marcus. 'Now get off my ship. You've got what you want.'

'That I do, Jim, that I do. And yes, we'll be on our merry way. But before I do, I promised Eva I'd ask after Danny. How's he doing?'

'He's doing fine,' Duncan said. 'Where's Eva? You've been to see her?'

'She's with me. She's in good spirits. Must be my charming personality. Never fails to cheer everyone up. Well, gents, I'll bid you all a good fucking day. I've got business to handle.'

'So long, Jim. Thanks for the hospitality,' Frank said.

'Go fuck yourself, Frank,' Jim said, as he watched the three of them leave. Duncan stood aside, watching Tyson closely. After they'd left, he turned to Jim, but Jim held up his hand. 'I don't want to hear a word about all this, okay? I've got bigger issues to deal with. Did you find Stanic last night?'

'Yeah. Reckons he's found a way to fix the desalinators. Should be done within a few days.'

'Good.'

'Well, if that's all?' Duncan said.

Jim nodded but didn't look at his son. The thought that he had lied to him last night about Eva still jabbed at him. He and Duncan had always been so close, the best of friends and allies, but something had happened along the way. *The way of all people*, Jim thought. Even family.

Duncan left, not saying a word. Jim thought about saying something, calling him back, but hesitated, and then it was too late.

'Well, just you and me, Captain,' Faust said. 'Why don't you come inside and keep me company, eh? I've seen the way you look at me. I bet you even watch me when I sleep, don't you?'

Jim thought about taking up his knife again and dealing with her there and then, but the crew were already moving about the ship. It wouldn't take a genius to work out what had happened, and even though they were 'his' crew, he couldn't trust anyone not to blab, not even his own son.

Still, he stepped closer to the cell. 'What is it you actually want, Susan? I mean, all this act aside, deep down, what is it you want?'

She brushed her wild hair from her face and bit on her finger as she thought, thrusting her lip out and pouting as though she were a schoolgirl. 'For starters, to see you fall. I want to watch you hit rock bottom. I want to see you beg for forgiveness. Then' – Faust stepped closer, gripping the bars – 'I want to see you burn for your lies.'

Jim's hand shook by his side. He could just reach out, grab her by the neck and choke the life from her. He took a deep breath to calm his racing heart. 'People like you have no value to humanity. You want nothing but destruction.'

'And you don't, Captain? I can see your struggle. I can see how hard it is for you to resist destroying me. It's man's way, is it not? Destroy things you don't understand. How long is it since you've been with a woman?'

'If there is a hell,' Jim said, 'we'll both be there. You want to see us all burn? You'll be right there with us. There is no rapture for you. Or any of us.'

'I guess we'll both find out, won't we?'

'Perhaps sooner than you think.'

CHAPTER SEVENTEEN

E va winced as she leant over the table to grab another file
from the cache of documents.

'Here,' Caff said, 'let me help.'

'It's fine. I can reach it.'

'Look, I know our reputation, and I know what you think of
us. But I'm trying to help you here. Genuinely, I've got no grudge
against you. I don't understand your hostility.'

Eva had to admit Caff had a point, although she couldn't extend
that to all of Graves' business doings. He'd been blackmailing,
threatening and claiming possession of the flotilla for as long as
she could remember. Just because he was playing nice now didn't
make him what they'd call a 'stand-up guy'. But Caff certainly
had done nothing towards Eva to warrant her hostility. She'd give
her that.

'I'm sorry. This is weird, me being here, working with you and
Shaley.'

'I can't say I'm thrilled about it either,' Shaley said. 'But we've
got a common goal, so might as well make the best of a bad situation, right?'

'Fair enough,' Eva said. 'Can you pass me that file, please?'

Caff, sitting to Eva's right, reached over and handed Eva the file. 'What have you found out?'

'Nothing much yet. Just snippets from Mike's and the first volunteer's notes. Just trying to piece together what this could be about. Perhaps see if there's anything that can help decode the text.'

'You know, this is probably about the bacterium,' Caff said, pouring another cup of tea.

'Governments are always fucking with that kind of thing, aren't they?' Shaley added. He was seated on the starboard side of the yacht, lounging with his legs up on one of the settees.

'You're suggesting it's manmade?'

'Could be,' Caff said. 'I heard Mike's in a bad way with an advanced form of it. Who knows what he found out there? Could be that the government is behind it.'

'The governments are gone with the rest of the world. No one has heard from anyone of any authority since the drowning. It doesn't make sense.'

'Well,' Shaley said, sitting up and leaning forward, his elbows on his knees. 'It's got to be some big secret, some conspiracy, ain't it? Otherwise, what would be worth killing for? It seems to me that this killer is either trying to cover something up, whatever is written in those documents, or he's trying to use the information for his own good.'

'Yeah,' Caff added. 'Think about it. There's nothing left, right? We've been on the radios since the damned apocalypse, and who have we found? A few survivors here and there. If there's nothing else out there, why would someone on this flotilla be so interested in these documents?'

Eva felt like there could be something in that. It did make sense. What was there to gain from top-secret documents now that this flotilla was all that there was? It wouldn't matter either way.

Even if the infection was manmade and part of some government conspiracy, so what? It wasn't as if it would change anything now.

'I don't know. There's something else going on here. But either way, we won't know that until we decode this stuff, and I'm making no headway. I sometimes think I've identified words, maybe similar ones throughout the text, but they don't match any kind of sentence structure. I think without that USB drive we'll never know.'

'What do Mike's notes say?' Caff asked, pointing to the scraps of notebook paper among the files.

'Not much, just talking about the first survivor and his experiences of tracking the files down to a safe in a yacht. Beyond that, there's nothing else. Hopefully, Doctor Singh can help him and we'll be able to question him directly. I'm sure he must know more than what he has written down here.'

'There's also the engineer guy who left first,' Shaley said. 'No one seems to remember his name. But if we ask around, perhaps someone will remember him and give us a new clue or direction.'

'That's possible,' Eva said, but she doubted it. It was a long time ago, and many people on the flotilla had died since then. Three years of post-drowning living were far more difficult to recall than regular life, with an almost daily struggle to keep things going. 'One thing that would be interesting to find out: why both he and Mike wanted to leave the flotilla after finding this stuff. There's something we're not seeing. And that doesn't sit well with me.'

Shaley stretched out and shrugged. 'We could probably just wait until the killer turns up and ask them.'

'Yeah, no,' Eva said. 'I'm not going to wait to be killed. He's going to pay for what he's done, and I'd rather find him before he comes after us.'

Eva knew at that point that the killer probably knew who she was and where she was. After all, she had been there with Ade when he attacked. He must know, too, where the files were being held.

Probably all the more reason to stay with Graves, she thought. Strength in numbers. Also, by staying away from Duncan and Danny, it meant they were unlikely to be put in harm's way unnecessarily. She didn't like it one bit, but had to admit to herself that it was the safest bet.

'Look who's back,' Caff said, smiling and moving towards the steps that led onto the main deck.

Oh, great, Eva thought. Frank. As if she wasn't feeling awkward enough.

Marcus, Tyson and Frank came below deck and quickly filled up the yacht's lounge area. Shaley stood and shook Frank's hand. 'Glad to have you back, you old crazy bastard.'

'How's me wife?' Frank said. 'Where is she?'

'She's fine,' Shaley said. 'Over in your boat. You wanna pay a conjugal visit?'

'Nah, poor woman's suffered enough,' Frank said as everyone laughed.

'Wait a minute,' Eva said, breaking up the chat as she stood suddenly 'You told me and Jim that she was kidnapped. I knew you were lying. Perhaps now that you've conned your way out of the brig, you'll explain yourself.' Eva's scalp tingled with the outburst. Her face flushed and her ribs screamed with pain, but she didn't let on.

Frank turned towards her, the smile easing off his face. 'How's the ribs? I heard the news about you and Ade. Terrible business that, he was a good one.'

'I'll live, unlike Ade. You better start talking, Frank. Tell me what the hell is going on with you and this business with Jim. It's all related, isn't it? The killings, the files, the memory stick, your pathetic attempt.'

Sitting opposite Eva on the plush settee of the yacht, Frank sighed heavily and looked her in the eye as he said, 'Sure, I covered the truth with the whole kidnapping thing; it was easier that way, and besides, it was all I could think of in the moment.'

Eva leaned forward. 'Spill it.'

'Here's something that might help things,' Frank said, reaching into his jacket. He pulled out a key and passed it to Eva.

'What's this?'

'Looks like a key to me,' Marcus said with a smirk.

'Funny guy,' Eva said. 'I mean, why is it important, and what does it have to do with my question?'

Frank sat down at the table and leaned his elbows on the surface. 'Well, the chap who blackmailed me to have a go at Jim gave me that key as payment. It's a key to one of the flotilla's storage units. The one where a lot of the tinned food, seed and water stocks is kept. I'll just say right now, though, that I wasn't going to kill Jim. I was just . . . making it look like it so in case this guy was watching, he wouldn't suspect anything was up. Jim's a fool, but I ain't into just killing people on a whim, no matter how desperate some people think I am.'

'Why get you to take Jim out in the first place?' Eva said. 'It doesn't make any sense, especially as the killer could have just done it himself, like he did Jean and presumably Ade.'

Frank shrugged his rounded shoulders. 'He talked about a strategy. I didn't really get what he was saying. I ain't that kind of clever, you know? Now, I ain't Sherlock Holmes or anything, but I'd say he wanted Jim taken out for a distraction while he went about his business, whatever that might be.'

Eva considered Frank's words. She took a leap of faith and assumed for the purposes of her thought experiment that Frank was telling the truth. It did make sense that if this killer was after Mike, or at least what Mike knew, then removing Jim would cause enough of a distraction that the flotilla's fragile calm would splinter.

She had seen it before in a gang's turf wars: they often caused trouble just to stir things up, make it harder to work out what was really going on underneath it all. Frank's words came back to her, though, regarding the stocks. 'You stole precious reserves from the flotilla with this key?' she said.

'Hey now,' Frank said, holding his palms up. 'I didn't do no such thing. We might not be whiter than white, but we ain't stupid. We wouldn't steal food from our own gaff.'

'She's doing her job, aren't you, love?' Marcus said.

Eva looked Marcus right in the eyes. 'You call me love one more time and it won't just be Tyson who'll have bruised balls for a week. My name's Eva. Use it.'

Caff smirked. The others went silent, expectant.

Eva thought she might have let her temper take her too far. But Marcus grinned and let out a belly laugh. 'You're precious, Eva, I'll give you that. And fair enough, let's all be civil, on both sides, right?'

'Right,' she said, unable to decide if he was being genuine or mocking her.

'So anyway,' Frank said, 'the key is a copy made from sheet metal. Who do we know who uses sheet metal and has the tools and equipment to make such an intricate copy?'

'Someone in engineering,' Eva said. 'We already guessed that, but this only adds to that theory.'

'We'll need a manifest of everyone who's taken shifts there in the last couple of years,' Marcus said. 'And who do we know who has such a document?'

'Jim's got it,' Eva said, 'and if anyone is going to get it, it'll be me. I know you guys have issues. He's under a lot of strain at the moment. Let me handle it.'

Marcus sucked in his breath and thought for a moment. 'That might be best. Okay, we'll keep the documents in my safe here. Shal, Ty, you mind staying behind and guarding it with Caff here?'

'I ain't going nowhere either,' Frank said. 'The nutter will probably do me in for not going after Jim properly.'

'Bring the wife over,' Marcus added. 'We've got room if we squeeze together.' He eyed Eva as he spoke, and her skin crawled at the thought. That was her cue to leave the yacht. But before seeing Jim, she wanted to pay Mike a visit.

When she'd eased her way out onto the deck, Marcus followed her up and shut the door behind him.

'Hey, Eva, wait up.'

'What is it?'

'I'm not happy about you just wandering around on your own. It's not safe for a—'

'A woman? Were you really going to say a woman?'

'Ha ha, no, of course not, I was going to say an *injured* woman.'

'It's sweet of you, but I think I'll be fine. This guy doesn't seem to take unnecessary risks.' She looked around and pointed to the flotilla citizens around them, busy with their various tasks. Kids were running between boats while their parents were tightening ropes and making condensation boxes for manual desalination.

Whenever the wind dropped and the sun shone, it brought everyone out.

'Let me send one of the boys with you at least, just to make sure.'

Eva cocked her head, analysing this weird man in front of her. Clearly he was the biggest, sleaziest perp among all the survivors, yet here he was again, being all charming and caring. She couldn't help but wonder what was in it for him.

'I'm fine,' she said.

He shrugged. 'You can't say I didn't offer.'

'Nope, and I appreciate it, but if I don't move about, this wound will just keep me laid up for ages. Better to walk it off.'

'We'll keep an eye out,' Marcus said as he returned to the cabin door. 'Just in case.'

'Appreciated.'

Eva had visions of Shaley or Tyson clumsily following her about the flotilla, making themselves entirely conspicuous. Still, she had to admit it didn't hurt to have an extra pair of eyes on her while she headed to the *Alonsa*. After all, Singh's medical bay wasn't far from engineering . . . Perhaps she could scope it out, see if anyone reacted. She'd often used the same tactic to flush out a crim.

The human body has a terrible way of signalling guilt.

Eva winced as she headed out, but it felt good to breathe the fresh air. Even the light drizzle was refreshing. But under her good mood lurked an anxiety that gripped her stomach as if she were a kid waiting to go to prom.

She would finally get a chance to see Mike again – whatever condition he might be in.

CHAPTER EIGHTEEN

I t wasn't yet afternoon and Jim had finished another bottle of the reserve rum. A full bottle, gone. He could barely remember drinking it, just wanted the solace of the burn and the fog. His brain buzzed and spun. The radio dropped from his hands to the cabin floor.

'No response,' he mumbled to himself. 'I've been sacrificed.'

He laughed at the thought of those who had sworn him to secrecy just upping and going, leaving him behind like some jilted teenage lover. Only this time there wasn't going to be another sweetheart to come along.

This was the end.

He bent over to grab the radio and nearly fell off his bunk, only managing to keep himself from hitting the deck by landing on his forearms.

He swept the radio under the bunk, not even bothering to hide it behind the panel. 'Fuck it,' he grumbled and sat heavily against the ship's hull, his head resting against the porthole.

Through his blurred vision he saw the pictures of himself and his wife taped to the back of the cabin door. In another, he and Duncan were waving from the deck of Duncan's first boat: a small two-man sailing boat that he'd used to teach Duncan how to sail. His son was only twelve in that picture, but already he was almost as tall as Jim. Kid Mountain they called him. 'Growing like a weed,' his wife would say. 'Good genes,' Jim would retort. He was, of course, talking about Morag, the light of his and Duncan's lives.

Or at least Duncan's first sixteen years.

Cancer, he thought, the biggest scourge of the day.

Still, it had nothing on what had come after.

What he wouldn't give to have helped her, or even to have had the tumour himself. She deserved life more. Even now, he'd give anything to spend one more day with her.

Tears streaked down his face, but he wiped them away and focused on a holiday snap. It had been taken when he and Morag visited Egypt. They'd both got severe sunburn on the second day. Two pasty-white Scots didn't stand a chance in forty-degree temperatures, but Morag had always wanted to see the sphinxes and the pyramids.

At least she got to see them before the cancer, he thought. At least there was that.

Faust was right in one sense about the way he looked at her, but he was seeing past her visage, picturing his wife. What cruel aspect of fate decreed that a vicious, evil harpy like Faust could survive while his wife had to surrender her life?

Was that Faust's God? If it was, Jim hoped he had a chance to meet Him one day. He'd tell the fucker what he thought of Him. He slumped onto his side, waiting to black out.

The door to the cabin opened. Duncan's shadow stretched across the floor until it covered the bunk. He just stood there, waiting.

'Man Mountain,' Jim said, his words slurring. 'Growed like a weed. All the genes.'

'Dad? What's wrong?'

'Hah. Everything . . . Haven't you seen the world, son?'

Duncan ducked under the doorframe and stepped inside, making Jim feel like a bug looking up at a giant as he lay on his back.

'Are you drunk?'

'Why the hell not? Not like being sober and responssissible's done me any favours.'

Duncan knelt down and lifted Jim until he was sitting up, his back against the ship's hull. Jim could feel the waves getting heavier, and he let his body and mind roll with them, enjoying the swaying, spinning sensation. Duncan looked like a wild bear with his hair and beard obscuring his face.

'How'd you get so damned hairy?'

'Like that's important now.'

'Ah, what? There's news, eh? Good, bad . . . lemme guess. Itsa a bad 'un, right?'

'I spoke with Stanic again. There's been a setback with the repairs. Also, the new parts fabricated for the wind turbines have been stolen.'

'Who cares anymore, eh? You? Faust? Marcus . . . How about Mike? Said anything, he has? Mumble gibber, mumble . . . God knows what anyone cares about now, eh?'

'Get a grip of yourself, Dad. You're supposed to be the captain of this place. We all need you. Stay there. I'm going to get my stash of coffee, get you sobered up. This ain't you.'

'If only you knew, Bear, what would you think, eh? You'd forgive ya old man, ha! Not likely, eh? . . . Not likely.'

Before Duncan had a chance to speak, Jim stood on unsteady legs, grabbing his son to hold himself up. He pushed him back out of the cabin. 'Go, leave me. I've got memories to forget.'

'Dad, wait.'

'Leave me alone, goddamnit. Go!'

Jim kicked the cabin door closed and fumbled for the lock. He couldn't quite get the latch closed. He swore and returned to his bunk, waving an arm underneath to fish for the radio. He randomly pressed the buttons, hoping for some response on the screen, each press of 'send' bringing another sob, more tears.

He kept trying until the excess of alcohol took over and darkness enveloped him.

CHAPTER NINETEEN

Eva reached for the door handle to Dr Singh's medical room, smelling disinfectant. It reminded her of the hospital where she had given birth to Emily. She remembered the long labour. Ironic that Emily had taken so long to come into the world. Once she was out, she lived life as if she had it on short-term loan. They all did, but still, for Emily it had been too short.

She drew a breath as the pain from her wound flared, making her pull her arm back. Her ribs ached and the stab wound throbbed, a pulsing reminder of her task. She had both Ade and Jean to avenge; she wasn't going to let a flesh wound stop her. She'd use the pain as motivation.

'Here, let me.' An arm, a man's, reached around her to open the door, allowing the hospital smell to waft out more strongly.

She took a step inside, turned and realised it was Stanic. He smiled his curious shy smile. The weather-stroked skin folded at the corners of his brown eyes. Windswept hair, black with flecks of silver, was brushed back behind his ears.

'Hey,' Eva said, 'thanks.'

'I heard you had a fall,' Stanic said, pointing to her ribs. 'How you doing?'

'It's okay. I can get about – to a degree. Just heading in to see the doc, get it checked out. How're the repairs coming along?'

A shadow came over the engineer's face. 'They're problematic. Things go missing here, things get broken. It's like I'm working against the tide.'

'I'm sure you'll figure it out. You usually do.'

'Hah. Thanks for the vote of confidence.'

Eva wanted to approach the subject of someone using the engineering department for making keys, but she couldn't quite frame it without having him asking more questions. So far, no one had been told about Ade's death, and Jean's was mostly considered an accident by those outside of the circle of truth.

Stanic made to turn but must have read something in her face. 'Was there something else?'

'Yeah, erm, no . . . Just . . . Who do you think is sabotaging the equipment? Anything strange going on in engineering lately?'

'No idea. There's been rumours it's one of Faust's lot, but I don't buy it, personally. Probably someone working with Graves, but to what end, I don't know. Engineering is fine; the men and women there are decent people. We're all just trying to keep things going, you know?'

'Yeah, I hear you. If you notice anything odd, you'll come tell me, won't you?'

'Putting your old skills to use, are you? Should I call you Detective Morgan from now on?' Stanic flashed her a quick smile.

'Ha ha, no, Eva'll be fine, but you know, I'm just professionally curious, I suppose. Life on this old wreck will be much easier if we can keep the power and desalinators going.'

'I'll let you know. Would be nice not to keep having to repair the repairs. I'll see you around, Eva. Watch your step.'

'I will, Stanic. Thanks.'

She watched as he walked off down the narrow corridor, then closed the door behind her and headed towards the main office of the medical facility. *Facility* always sounded too grand for what was really a couple of doctors' examination rooms, repurposed storage units and a retrofitted theatre. The quarantine section was situated behind this area, in what had been, in their former life on the *Alonsa*, a series of function rooms.

Dr Singh, in her familiar blue medical shift, sat at her desk filling out some paperwork. She dropped her pen when Eva hobbled towards her.

'Hey, Eva, you surprised me there.'

'Sorry, am I interrupting?' Eva leaned against the desk, her hand flat on its surface to take the pressure off her ribs.

Singh sighed and sat back in her chair, rubbing the tiredness from her eyes. 'No, I should take a break. I've been up all night, running tests on Mike.'

'How is he?'

'Still catatonic, still uttering gibberish. I'm at a loss really, but I'll figure something out, I'm sure. How are you, by the way? You shouldn't be moving around.'

'I can't just sit around. It's really not that bad. You did a great job of stitching me up, and the painkillers really helped.'

'Hopefully that'll still be the case when they wear off. Our stocks are pretty low these days. Come here. Let me take a look at it, make sure it's healing okay.'

Singh eased herself out of the chair, came round the desk and lifted Eva's sweater to reveal the bandage wrap. Undoing the adhesive pad at the edge, she lifted just enough to expose the wound beneath.

'The wound's looking good. Stitches are holding up, no sign of tearing or infection. Come back again tomorrow so I can keep an eye on it, but it seems to be moving in the right direction.' Singh reapplied the bandage and pulled Eva's sweater back in place.

'Thanks, Doc.'

'You're welcome.'

'You're looking really tired. Why don't you get some sleep?'

'I can't right now, not with the extra cases coming in lately. Besides, it's approaching visiting hour for the quarantined patients. When that's over, I'll get a few Zs. By then, my assistant should have the results of Mike's test.'

'Can I see him?' Eva said.

The doctor hesitated for a moment, then nodded. 'Sure. But I'll warn you, it's not a pleasant sight.'

'Don't worry about me, Doc. I've seen far worse, I'm sure.'

Dr Singh helped Eva through two doors until she came to the adapted function rooms. Each door along the passage, ten either side, had clear plastic taped to its exterior. Through the round windows, Eva saw the various patients lying on their cots or standing against the door looking out.

Some mouthed what looked like hello.

Eva recognised every person. At one time they had been kind and useful members of the flotilla, but one by one they had succumbed to the infection and ended up here.

Although the bacterium didn't seem to transfer easily from one person to the next, it was deemed too dangerous to take the chance. Most of them understood that, but there were always a few who didn't and who wanted out. Eva waved and nodded at the ones by the doors, giving them the respect they deserved.

How cruel, she thought, to have survived everything the world had thrown at them, only to be rewarded with a sickness that slowly killed them without any hope of a cure.

They reached Mike's room at the rear of the quarantine zone. It was through a second set of doors for added protection. Dr Singh held back the plastic and allowed Eva inside.

'I'll wait outside,' Singh said. 'Are you okay?'

'Sure.'

When the doctor left her on her own, Eva shuffled to the door and looked in. Her heart seemed to skip a beat when she saw him, sitting cross-legged in the corner of his room, his arms hanging limp by his side.

He gazed off into the far distance, his lips moving in those strange patterns of his. Drool covered his chin. His eyes looked like someone had painted them on, or carved them from chalk. She had expected him to maybe notice her.

A hopeful part of her thought that her being there might have woken him from his catatonia. A friendly face, a face that he had once declared his love for, but no, he wouldn't look her way, couldn't see her. Just what was it that he *did* see out there?

Ten minutes went by as Eva stared in, wondering that very question.

Behind her came the noise of visitors arriving to see their sick family members. She realised she'd been crying and wiped the tears away with the sleeve of Graves' sweater. As though thinking of him had the power to summon him, Marcus appeared behind her, his hand resting on her shoulder.

'He don't look good, does he? Poor sod. I'm sorry, Eva. I know how much you meant to him.'

'It's the not knowing that hurts the most,' Eva replied, turning away. 'What are you doing here?'

'I said I'd keep an eye out for you. When you didn't come out for a while, I came to make sure you were okay. So, are you?'

Eva thought about it for a while: was anyone okay, really? At what point did being okay happen when all around them there was only loss?

She didn't answer. Instead, she made to leave the quarantine room, steeling herself against the grief of having to leave behind the one she loved for the second time. In addition, it brought back that one memory, the one that would never die: the one where Eva left Emily behind and doomed her to die alone.

Marcus helped her through the doors until she came to the main section, where the visitors, much like Eva a few minutes previously, were standing outside the various doors, looking in. The difference was, they could talk with their family members. Not that much was being said. What could be said other than 'love you', 'get well soon', 'don't give up'?

They were just reactions now. Just something you said to avoid the cold silence.

Both Eva and Marcus quietly greeted the visitors as they walked through. Everyone knew everyone on the flotilla, which made these situations worse. For Eva, anyway. She had always been accused by her police chief of having too much empathy. Of taking too much interest in people's lives. But the way she figured it, so few people did anymore; she could at least make a difference, albeit a small and insignificant one. Most of the cops in her district did it for the money and pension; they couldn't understand that she did it for justice.

She did it for the victims.

Dr Singh emptied her mug of tea in a single gulp and stifled another yawn. She handed Eva a piece of paper with an annotation of Mike's gibberish on it. 'Take it. Perhaps it might make sense one day.'

'Thanks,' Eva said, taking it and folding it up into quarters. 'You will let me know if Mike does say anything, won't you? I'd like to be the first when he does.'

'Jim asked me the same thing last night. He was quite insistent. I've never seen him so . . . intense. What is so important about what Mike knows?'

'Jim's under a lot of strain,' Marcus said.

'I guess we're just curious about what happened,' Eva said, as she wondered what could be so important to Jim.

'There's more going on than we realise,' Singh said. 'I've known Jim a long time, and that wasn't him last night. I fear he's losing it. With the nonsense about your Frank going after him, Marcus, and Faust's group being a pain in the arse, it's too much pressure for anyone to handle. Not to mention the increase in the frequency of infection.'

'Hey, I had nothing to do with Frank. Besides, that's not why Jim's freaking out. I'm sure it'll all come out in the wash.'

Eva stepped away from Marcus and headed for the exit. 'I'll come back tomorrow if Mike hasn't changed in the meantime, Doc,' Eva said. 'Thanks for letting me see him.'

'Take care, and don't do anything stupid. That wound needs time and rest to heal.'

Eva waved to the doc without turning back and then reached out for the door, but Marcus got there first, opening it and standing back for her to walk through.

She muttered her thanks.

Once outside, she turned to him. 'You've got to go easy on Jim. He's a good man.'

'Hey, I know, but he's not infallible, you know.'

'You fancy taking over, do you? You see all this chaos as an opportunity?'

'Every day is an opportunity, love.'

'You really think you'll be able to do a better job than Jim's done? Will the other residents get behind you if you seize control? I don't. Faust's lot won't support you. It's not like you've earned a good reputation here.'

Marcus shrugged. 'I guess time will tell. Maybe I'll be better than you think. Maybe the other residents are fed up with Jim and will just be happy with a new face in charge, making better decisions.'

'You're a cocky one,' Eva said, shaking her head. 'Many people think they can lead . . . but then it's easier to say that when you're on the sidelines. Being in the firing line is a different matter.'

'I guess we'll see, then.' Marcus smiled at her and walked off down the corridor. Instead of turning right to head out, however, he turned left towards the main staircase.

'Hey, where are you going?' Eva said.

'Engineering,' he called back. 'I need to have a word with Stanic about Ade. And we can see if anything crops up to help us with our little problem.'

'Let me know if you discover anything.'

He stopped then and turned back to face her. 'Wait, what? You not coming after all, then?'

'No, you go. I've got something else I want to follow up.'

'I'll come with you, then.'

'No,' Eva said. 'I'll go on my own. Don't even dare to follow. I appreciate you looking out for me, but nothing's going to happen in broad daylight with everyone out doing their business. Besides, I've got a manifest to get.'

'If that's what you want, love. It's your life. Don't say I didn't try.' With that, he turned on his heel and walked off, his long black coat flapping out behind him.

Eva couldn't tell if he was an arsehole naturally or whether he had to work on it. Whatever, she wanted to check on Danny, and while she was there, she wanted to drop in on Jim, maybe get some answers about his reaction to Mike, or at the very least the manifest.

CHAPTER TWENTY

Jim woke and threw up on the floor as he tried to get off his bunk. His head pounded and his guts churned. He swayed and fell back, hitting his head against a shelf, which sent him sprawling on his arse. He clenched his jaw and held his breath as pain shot up his spine.

'Motherfucker.' His skull seemed on fire inside and out, thanks to the rum, and to hitting his head on the shelf. He put his hands on his knees and leaned forward, trying to stop his vision from swirling. His throat burned, and he spat out the rum-laced saliva. Wiping his face with the blanket from his bunk, he stumbled to his feet, resting his hands against the door to regain his balance.

The cabin was lit by weak moonlight. The wind had got up, making it harder for him to remain standing. Waves smashed against the hull. They might as well have been smashing against his head.

Jim's family picture stared back at him, reminding him of the man he had been, judging him for the man he had become. With a flash of fury, he swiped the pictures from the door and ripped them up, throwing them to the floor.

'That's not me,' he slurred. 'Was never me.' He didn't recognise his old self anymore. It didn't just seem like a lifetime ago; it seemed like someone else's lifetime ago.

Falling back onto the bunk, he sat on the radio. He'd been cradling it all afternoon, hoping for a response, hoping for something to just make some fucking sense. He raised his arm, ready to throw the radio against the wall, smash it to pieces to replicate his life. But he couldn't do it; his fate was still tethered to that little screen. All he wanted was to see his message received, to know they were still there.

He let the radio fall safely from his hands onto the bunk as he collapsed onto his side.

Jim's breath came long and slow. His heart rate dropped, and as though they were connected, the waves seemed to calm. But his mind still raged. He thought about Faust.

Her sneering face mocked him. She knew, he thought. The way she kept going on about his lies, she must know. It was too late now for the truth to come out. There was nothing to say anymore. Besides, if Mike ever managed to speak again, he'd tell everyone what he saw, who he saw. They'd put it together and realise Jim had known all along.

They would revolt. Rebel. It would tear the place apart.

Did he care? Beneath it all, he still did. Even if he couldn't go on, he wanted to give the others a chance. Faust had to be dealt with as a priority. He remembered Graves saying it would be dealt with, but she was still there, alive, a ticking time bomb.

Sitting up, Jim reached to his nightstand and picked up his regular two-way radio. Switching to Marcus's private channel, he depressed the switch and said, 'Graves, you there? It's Jim. Come in.'

He knew he sounded drunk, didn't care.

Again he tried, 'Graves, pick up. I don't have all day.'

The radio squelched with static. The EM field remained messed up by the solar storms, but the two-ways should still work within the small distance of the flotilla. The bastard was ignoring him. He was about to press the button again when Graves' voice came through the tinny speaker.

'Jim, what's going on? What do you want?'

'It's not done. We had an agreement.'

'We do, and it will be done, but on my schedule.'

'I warned you before, Graves.'

The signal was cut. This time, Jim didn't stop himself. He threw the two-way against the opposite wall of his cabin with as much force as he could muster. It shattered into pieces. Bits of plastic flew in all directions, and the circuit board broke in half. The remnants clattered to the floor. Jim stood, grabbed his knife and left the cabin. If Graves wouldn't uphold the deal, he'd sort it himself.

———◆———

Faust was leaning against the bars, looking bored, when Jim approached. She looked up and stretched a sneering smile across her vicious face, although her expression faltered when Jim locked eyes with her.

Perhaps it was a natural reaction to a threat, he thought. Something about his intentions translated to her and knocked her down a peg. But still, she puffed herself up, held out her chin and started to spew a tangle of profanities.

'Had second thoughts, Captain?' she said. 'Want some company, after all, huh?'

She spat in Jim's face and he reached out and grabbed her scrawny throat with his right hand, crushing her windpipe, watching as her face turned a dark shade of purple.

She kicked uselessly, scratched at his face, but he continued to squeeze, pulling her face into the bars. Ignoring her pathetic attacks, he leaned his face in like a lover going in for a kiss.

'You tell me now, what the hell do you think you know about me?' He could smell his own foul breath as he slurred out the words with heavy breaths. 'Enough for me to end you right here?'

She choked; her eyes bulged.

He eased his grip slightly.

'I'm waiting. What do you know? You've got five seconds.'

'I . . . I . . .'

'Jim? What the hell?'

Jim let Faust go and staggered back, dropping his knife to the floor. 'Eva? It's not what you think.'

Eva gazed at Faust, then back to Jim, her eyes wide, her mouth open, trying to form words. Jim stumbled towards her and gripped her arms. He tried to talk, but the words intermingled with his sobs. Eva pushed him away but held on to his jacket to stop him from falling over. 'You're drunk,' she said. 'Where's Duncan?'

Jim just shrugged.

'Come with me. Let's get you settled.'

On the way back through the corridors and up the stairs to the cabin quarters, a number of crew members stopped and asked if Jim was all right. Eva had managed to avoid most questioning by saying he was ill. And he guessed he was. Not just drunk, but sick to the core.

He looked at his right hand and saw the redness from where he'd gripped Susan Faust's neck. Was he really going to do it? Was he really going to kill someone with his bare hand? 'I've fallen so far,' he said, dragging his feet as Eva propped him up. 'I'm not a good man.'

'Are any of us good?' Eva said.

'You, you're good. Always were. Me, I'm a liar and a coward.'

'You're just drunk, Jim. You'll see things differently when you sober up.'

'I would have killed her if you didn't come.'

'You don't know that,' Eva said, but Jim could tell by her voice that she didn't believe it.

It was pretty clear to anyone watching him what he would have done.

He took a breath and steadied himself as they approached his open cabin.

CHAPTER TWENTY-ONE

Eva stepped into Jim's cabin and gagged at the smell. She avoided stepping into a pool of vomit. A bottle of rum, empty, lay on its side by the smashed remains of a two-way radio. Old photos, ripped like confetti, littered the floor and the bunk.

'Christ, Jim, you did a number in here, didn't you?'

He slumped onto the bunk, dropping his head to his chest. As he did so, the momentum of his weight knocked something off the bunk. A radio thudded to the floor.

Eva picked up the radio. It wasn't a two-way; it looked like some kind of military VHF unit. A wire from the radio snaked up past the porthole, and she saw it was coming from one of the pipes. The wire must be an antenna, she thought.

Jim raised his head and opened his eyes. When he saw Eva holding the radio, his face dropped. 'I can explain . . . It's not what you think . . .'

That was when she noticed dozens of long, thin pieces of paper, curled like shavings of wood, scattered across the bed sheets. 'What the hell is this?' Eva said, picking up one of the fragments. Coded text was printed on one side, and she realised it had come from a small printer on the edge of the radio. The screen was blank, but the power was on.

'Who have you been talking to?' Eva said, her voice high and taut, her face flushing with anger and confusion. Jim reached out but fell back. Eva turned and closed the door, locking the latch. Leaning into Jim, she shook the radio in front of his face. 'Tell me, Jim,' she shouted. 'What's all this code? Where's this from? This is connected with the volunteers, isn't it? Is this why you were so eager to know what Mike was trying to say?'

Her heart pounded in her chest, and her hand shook. It felt like the day she'd realised the world as she knew it was coming to an end. Another huge, unimaginable shock to the system. Here was this man, one of the few she trusted, and he appeared to be the same as everyone else: a duplicitous coward.

For a minute they both stared at each other. Eva refused to back off, waiting patiently for the truth to come out. As it would. She knew. She'd been in enough interrogations to know that once a person was confronted, it was only a matter of time.

Jim's first thoughts would be about self-preservation. He'd think of ways he could explain this away, like a husband caught cheating on his wife. 'I can explain' were usually the first words out of someone's mouth. They'd go through a few rounds of that before trying to blame someone else. Only here, Jim had no one else to blame. This mess was all his, and there was no escape. No way out. The only course of action left was the truth.

'I can explain,' Jim said.

Eva said nothing, waiting for the process to begin.

Another minute passed, then another. Finally, wiping his face, and perhaps sobering up enough to realise the situation, Jim said, 'You're right.'

'About what?'

'This is everything to do with the volunteers and Mike. I've been lying to you since day one. Before, even. And the same goes for everyone on the flotilla. No one knows the truth. Perhaps Mike does, but well, you saw him.'

'What's on these papers?'

'Messages. Encoded messages.'

'Who from?'

Jim squirmed and scrunched up his face, reacting to some inner pain.

'Sit down,' Jim said. 'It's easier if I explain from the start.'

He leaned over and opened the porthole. The fresh salt wind brought swift relief from the stench in the cabin. He threw a pillow over the pool of vomit and sprayed a few squirts of deodorant to help mask the acrid scent. He threw the bottle of rum out of the porthole, watching as it drifted away on the tide.

Eva waited patiently as he fell to his knees and gathered together the confetti of his past life. When he was finished, he sat back on the opposite edge of the bunk and rested his back and head against the grey steel bulkhead. With a deep breath, he looked Eva directly in the eyes and said, 'It was always about survival. Secrecy was paramount.'

'Go on,' Eva said, still holding the radio that had now taken on the qualities of a talisman or holy relic, its value incalculable. It represented a link to others, a way to a new understanding of the world. 'Tell me everything. Leave nothing out.'

'I was captaining the *Alonsa*. We'd been at sea for four months. This was after the drowning. It happened so fast. We saw the waters rise while we were still in Southampton. The deaths came as quick as the water.

'We had communicated with the weather centre on and off for a few days before the first earthquake, as a storm had kept us in dock. That was during the first few days of the solar storms, before the big ones took out the satellites and the power grid.'

Eva remembered that well. She'd already said goodbye to her family a few days before when she headed off on a huge counter-smuggling raid on one of America's biggest drug importers. She and a dozen of her team had boarded a naval destroyer, ready to intercept a transatlantic cargo ship carrying one of the biggest shipments of cocaine in recent history. It was one of the first joint-agency operations she had got involved with. Her superiors thought it would be good experience for her to work closely on the opera-tion with the DEA and the coastguard. Along with the FBI's overall interest in that particular gang, each department had done its work and shared intel. This would be one of Eva's big breaks, a way for her to really make a name for herself.

Until the storms hit.

Within a day of the grid going down, they'd lost contact with their chiefs in Baltimore, and even the ship's radio didn't work because of the amount of EM interference from the storms. They ended up being pulled farther and farther out to sea and had finally completely lost control. Navigation was impossible due to the black cloud cover, destroyed GPS satellites and all radios down.

'People panicked,' Jim said, bringing Eva back to the present. 'Half the passengers got off the ship, and I watched them as the waves hit, killing them instantly. Every small vessel capsized. We broke away from the dock and drifted on the storm. Luckily we managed to steer away from land and head out down the English Channel before the worst came.

'Radio communication remained sporadic to non-existent dur-ing that first week. We heard reports of most of Europe drowning. With the winds and the constant electromagnetic interference, planes crashed out of the sky. We saw one go down in the Atlantic.

'I knew by then it was over.' Jim wiped his face and took another breath.

Tears were dripping down Eva's face as she reflected on a similar experience.

'After the seas finished rising,' Jim continued, 'we had already lost ninety percent of our passengers. Many people took to the life rafts, thinking they could make it back to land, not understanding that land was not a concept anymore.

'Others just couldn't go on. Those who'd left their families behind joined them in going over. I'll never forget that. The sea was still warm as it came up from the Earth's crust. We drifted down past Argentina towards the Western Peninsula of Antarctica. For a while we got stuck on drifting ice as the ice-shelf had completely come away from the main part of the continent. But within days it melted – the released water, huge oceans of it trapped in the planet's interior, came up, bringing the higher temperatures.

'That's what drowned the world – not the melting ice. There wouldn't be enough water. It came from within the rock. Probably still more of it under there. Before our very eyes we watched an entire continent sink into the sea.

'We used the last of the fuel to head north up the west coast of the Americas. Our navigator relied on manual navigation, but with the near-constant storms and the difficulty of spotting stars, we drifted off course.

'Eventually we ran aground here. The *Bravo* was already here. We managed to link the boats, using them as a safety barrier to bring other vessels in. During those early days we had nearly six hundred survivors.

'A year later, when you arrived, it was less than a quarter of that. But I'm getting ahead of myself. In those early days, radio communications were spotty. Some days we'd get through, most of the time not. I found that radio,' Jim pointed to the one in Eva's hand, 'on the *Bravo*.

'Over the course of a week I spoke with a doctor on a science vessel. Angelina, her name was.'

'Was?'

'I'll get to that.'

Jim broke off, thinking about the science woman, how he had read affection in her notes to him. It seemed crazy to have feelings for someone when their communications had been so sparse, but it wasn't beyond the realms of possibility. He'd heard about people falling in love over Twitter.

'Jim?' Eva prompted, bringing him out of his wandering thoughts.

'Angelina started to explain what her group of ships was doing and the dire state of things. Before the event, she'd worked as a lead virologist for the CDC. She and a group of researchers were tasked with investigating a new kind of marine-based bacterium. This was just a few weeks before the event.

'Angelina told me she believed it was manmade, specifically by the government. The full details of its origin were classified, but then the world drowned, and there was no longer anyone to report to.'

Jim stopped and gazed out of the porthole. Black clouds raced past the moon, casting the waters in stripes of black and silver, making it seem as though it moved in jitters and jolts.

'What happened to her and her team?' Eva asked, leaning forward. A distant memory came to her mind of her sitting at the feet of her grandfather one Christmas while he told a story.

'She continued to study the infection. Here on the flotilla we noticed people getting sick from the rainwater, which is why we try to only ever use desalinated water. Angelina believed that the water that evaporated off the sea's surface and mingled with the atmosphere created an incubation medium for this bacterium. By desalinating seawater and drinking it relatively quickly, we ensure that the spores don't have time to develop.'

Although Eva was starting to understand, she remembered her training not to rely on instincts, never to guess. She needed facts. And this confession from Jim was the best time to get them. 'Tell me more about Angelina and her team. Where were they? And why the secrecy?'

Jim closed his eyes for a brief moment and rubbed his face. He dropped his head as though in mourning.

'Jim?'

He lifted his head again, opened his eyes. 'Sorry. Yes. Angelina . . . It was a small flotilla of four boats, north of the Orizaba. The idea was they would intercept the survivors we sent out. One of the reasons I had to send them was to deliver resources to the scientists over there. Unlike us, they didn't have the vessels or the manpower to fish. Nor did they have the fuel we did. So every month we would send them extra resources to help them to keep doing research.'

'So they were doing all that for us?'

'Yes. And for anyone else who might have survived this. I sent them information about the spread of the infection here, how it was speeding up. Angelina believed it was adapting and mutating. That's why I sent Mike when we had the chance.'

Eva thought through his words while she looked out of the porthole, looking north past the mountain peak, wondering what they were like, Angelina and the scientists. Wondering what they had learned.

'Wait,' Eva said. 'No one came back. You were sending them to be tested on, weren't you?'

Jim's silence confirmed it. As did the guilty expression on his face. His eyes were glossy in the moonlight. Eva had often seen grown men, tough men, break down in the interrogation room.

Not because of the punishment they were facing, but because of the release of confessing what they had done.

'Is Mike the only one that survived?' Eva asked, trying to keep the tremble of anger from her voice. She had to try to understand, learn as much as possible. There still might be hope for Mike and everyone else on the flotilla, but she couldn't lose Jim's cooperation, not while he was in this mood of admission.

Jim shook his head.

'None were killed. The subjects were only ever used to test possible vaccinations. Up until yesterday Angelina had assured me they were being looked after. Some were looking promising. She thought she might have had a breakthrough in identifying a potential vaccine.'

'So what happened with Mike?'

'That's just it,' Jim said. 'I don't know. Since he returned I've not received any messages, and the messages I've sent haven't been acknowledged. Something catastrophic must have happened.'

'Why have you kept this a secret all this time?' Eva asked, though she had already guessed.

'It would destroy the flotilla. The science vessels would be overwhelmed.'

'Don't you think most residents would see the benefit of it?' Eva said, again already knowing what Jim's response would be.

He scoffed and shook his head. 'The way Faust's lot behave, thinking all this is God's way? Their anti-science stance . . . No, they would tear the place apart. And as for the residents, they'd ransack the place of resources. You know what they're like already with the food, even though with the fishing and farming we have enough.'

'I guess you're right,' she said, wanting to believe he wasn't right, that the members of the flotilla would rally round and see the best in the vessel, but she knew they wouldn't. Graves' lot, for one, would try to find an angle to exploit, let alone Faust's group.

Jim continued on as though he hadn't been interrupted. 'There was also the problem of the infection. It's still not entirely clear how it is transmitted from one person to another. They had to remain apart from us. By the time the lies had started, it was too late to do anything else. It would have split the flotilla apart. But I guess it's too late for that as well, now, isn't it?'

'So that's why you were so eager to talk with Mike. You didn't want him revealing your secret.'

'There's that, yes,' Jim admitted. 'But I also want to understand what happened out there. What went wrong? Is there anyone left?' He broke off, gathering his thoughts, then stared at her. 'Eva, now you know, you can't say anything about all this.' He pointed to the radio and the coded messages. 'You know what it's like out there at the moment with the water running out, the problems with the power, not to mention Graves and that bitch Faust jockeying for position.'

And there it was, exactly what she was afraid of: being made a part of the conspiracy. She hated the position it put her in. But she could understand it all from Jim's point of view.

In a bizarre way, despite his actions, he had proven to her that he was a good man and was doing all this, taking the huge amount of pressure on his shoulders, for the greater good.

She knew exactly what would happen if this got out.

The already strained relations between Jim and Faust's group, not to mention Graves always sniffing around in the shadows waiting for an opportunity, would erupt.

The power vacuum would create a lot of unnecessary division – division that could put the other vessel in trouble. If they were working on a cure, that couldn't be risked. The scientists needed to work in peace without angry, confused people potentially attacking them or, worse, refusing to supply them with resources as Jim had been doing.

With a killer and saboteurs on the loose, this wasn't the time to unleash a power struggle. As a group, they had to remain as united as possible.

There was still a chance she could use this to her advantage.

'Jim, I'll agree to keep your secrets safe, but you have to do something for me in return.'

He leaned forward, his eyebrows rising in hope. 'What is it? What do you want?'

'The working manifest you keep for the engineering department. I believe it will be crucial in narrowing down suspects for the murders.'

'Of course. It's in the bridge office safe; it's yours.'

'But there's something else, too,' Eva said. 'In the morning, I want you to let Faust go. Show them kindness and forgiveness and take some of the wind out of their sails. You might just buy enough time to sort all this out before they revolt further.'

'To be honest, I had considered that, but the woman's a cancer.'

'Not all of her followers are, though; many of them are just confused and scared. While you have her locked up, you're giving their fears focus. If they do continue to revolt, who knows what might happen? Other people of the flotilla might start to feel sympathy for her and be swayed to support her. You're risking making her a martyr, and we both know how that usually works out.'

'But what about the principle of justice? If we just start letting people like her off, where does it end?'

'We don't have that kind of set-up here, though. There's no justice department or jury here. We're all just trying to survive day to day. I don't think the principle matters anymore, Jim. Look around you: we could be all that there is left of our species – is it really worth the hassle over a principle?'

'If we don't stand for principles, is there any reason to go on? What if we're doomed and this is just the end? At least we can die out knowing we did the best we could.'

'I can't live this life thinking like that. Let her go, or I'll explain to everyone what you've done. And don't think I won't.'

Jim shook his head. His face took on a pinched, pained expression. Eva knew there was no real choice for him.

'Fine, but I won't be held responsible for her actions. It'll all be on you.'

'So be it. You have to make this right somehow, Jim. Keeping her locked away is only going to delay the inevitable and make things worse. Let her out, and we can work with the other residents to keep an eye on her. I'm sure I could persuade Graves to use his network of spies to watch what she is up to. Let her hang herself in front of the residents. Don't let this be about your word against hers.'

Jim just nodded slowly, breathing shallow breaths. She could see he wanted to do the right thing, but she had to admit that if she were in his shoes, she might not know what the right thing was, either.

Jim showed her where to hide the radio and how to decode the messages using the encryption key from his notebook. She left him snoring on his bunk and took the notebook with her. She realised it might help her decode the information taken from the sub. It was a long shot, but even if it just gave them some clue as to how to go about dealing with the indecipherable text, it was worth it.

On her way down the corridor, Eva stopped by Danny's cabin. Duncan was standing outside the open door. Eva looked inside and noticed Danny was fast asleep, clearly feeling the effects of his day working with the crew. Eva backed out and stood with Duncan.

'How's the wound?' he asked.

'Sore, but not fatal. I wanted to thank you, you know, for saving my arse. I really appreciate it.'

'I didn't get a chance to ask you – what was in the files you found? Graves took them off me when I dragged you out of the water before I had a chance to look. Was it worth Ade's death?'

'No,' Eva said. 'Nothing was worth that. But it's a lead to the killer. I think it's the object, or at least the information contained within it, that he wants. But right now I can't tell you any more.'

'Can't?' Duncan said, folding his arms across his chest. 'Or won't?'

'What's that supposed to mean? You think I'm keeping something from you?'

'I don't know. Are you?'

'No, and I resent that you think I would lie to you. For your information, we don't know what's in the files, as they're all encrypted. All we know is that the killer wants them desperately.'

'And Graves no doubt realises it has value in some way.'

She stopped herself from defending Marcus Graves, even though, so far, he was proving to be a useful ally in the mission to find whoever this killer was.

'Listen,' Eva said, softening her voice, trying to defuse the tension. 'I've got a lead. Jim's given me access to the working manifest. We've narrowed it down to an American male who has at some point worked in engineering and used their equipment to make key copies. It's also someone who has had access to your dad's keys.'

'By my reckoning, that's got to be at least one of twenty potential suspects,' Duncan said.

'It's something,' Eva said with a shrug. 'There's something else. About your dad.'

'I know. He's getting on everyone's case at the moment. He's just tense about Mike. Has he had a go at you too?'

'Not quite. Let's just say he got a bit upset with Susan Faust. We've had a chat about it. He drank too much rum. He feels terrible about it, but I've left him to sleep it off. He's going to release Susan in the morning. You might want to get some crew up with you to make sure there's no trouble when he hands her over. You know what her people are like.'

'Damn it, I should have been here to deal with this. This shouldn't be your responsibility.'

'It's fine; don't worry about it. Just look out for him, okay? He's having a rough time of it at the moment. We all are, but the pressure of being the figurehead can drive men and women to do things they normally wouldn't do.'

'Thanks, Eva. I will. I wonder, will things ever get any easier here?'

'I don't know, Dunc. But we've got to keep going, right?'

Duncan nodded, running his hand through his beard. His shoulders tensed.

'Eva, where are you staying? You're welcome to bunk here. Safety in numbers.'

She shook her head and watched his shoulders relax again. 'It's Danny,' she said. 'I promised to look out for him, but being on this case is dangerous. If I stay here, I'm making things more dangerous for him. The killer has already tried to finish me once. What's to say he's not waiting for another opportunity? I appreciate the offer, really, but it's better if I stay away.'

'It's Graves, isn't it? You're staying with him.'

Duncan's voice took on a jealous, accusatory tone, reminding her of her ex, Emily's biological father. She thought back to those strained days.

Saul, the ex, had tried to control her, possess her. It was only with the support of her work colleagues and her mother that she had managed to make the break. Ever since then, she had been determined to live an independent life.

Any attraction Duncan might have held for her died in that instant, and she felt herself become defensive because of it.

'Where I'm staying is none of your business. I'll check in on Danny in the morning. Look after your father.' She brushed past him. He turned and looked as though he was going to say something, or perhaps stop her, but didn't. She felt his glare on her back as she headed out onto the deck.

The cold hit her; the wind blew in her face. She knew she had been too harsh, but it was too late now. A low rumble of thunder came from somewhere off in the distance, beyond the peak of the Orizaba. She looked across the water, watching as the calm tide undulated beneath the thin slice of the moon and the wispy, dark clouds headed north.

Were they still out there, Angelina and her crew, stuck on their boats, waiting for someone, some help?

She considered taking a boat out, once all the troubles were over, and investigating. Maybe she would return like Mike had, but what if they did have a cure there? *What if . . .* Two of the most dangerous words in a situation like this.

Eva heard footsteps approaching.

She spun round, wincing with the pain of the sudden movement.

A man approached in the darkness. Eva stepped back, balanced and readied herself to hit out as the figure advanced.

'All right, love? Bit dangerous hanging about here on your own, ain't it?'

Eva exhaled in relief.

'You bastard, Graves. You scared me, creeping up on me like that.'

Stepping closer, she could make out his face. Pale light reflected off his pitted and scarred skin. He was smiling, satisfied with himself. Smug. That was Marcus Graves.

'Can't have you walking about on your lonesome at night, can we? I said I'd keep a watch. Never know who's stalking about in the shadows these days. Did you get the manifest?'

'Yeah.'

'The old goat just handed it over without a fuss?'

'Something like that.'

Marcus offered his arm to Eva like some Victorian lord. She batted it away and, clenching her jaw with pain, had the satisfaction of being the one to lead the way as they headed for Graves' yacht.

CHAPTER TWENTY-TWO

J im swallowed the last of his water. The cool liquid soothed his burning throat. Like others on the flotilla, he would have to start desalinating his personal stock of water. He'd done it before, using a piece of transparent plastic and the sun to speed evaporation.

Despite his throbbing headache and nausea, he remembered everything that had gone down the night before.

Remembered Eva's ultimatum.

Surprisingly, he found it a comfort that he'd get Susan Faust out of his hair. There was the chance that releasing her would appease her people, but he doubted it. His recent actions would have likely motivated Faust even further to seek revenge. A deal was a deal, though, and today he'd decided to be a better man than yesterday.

He never wanted to be that man again. The shredded photos of his wife and son, now collected in a small pile on a shelf, were a stark reminder of how easy it was to resort to destruction, how temporary life was.

His two-way radio chirped through the static and a voice came through, high-pitched, warbling on the edge of panic. 'Captain Jim, you there? It's Annette, Doctor Singh's assistant . . . there's been a . . . . Please, you need to come quick. Over.'

If he hadn't been sober before, he was now. 'Annette, this is Jim. What's happened?'

'They're dead. I just came in this morning, I don't know what I . . . Oh God, this is awful.'

'Hang on,' Jim said. 'I'll be there in five minutes. Don't touch a thing. Who else is with you?'

'No one. I didn't know what to do. Should I call someone else?'

'No, just wait for me. Over.'

Susan Faust would have to wait. Jim opened the cabin door and headed for the metal steps that led to the deck. On his way he passed a couple of his crew.

'Patrice, can you do me a favour?' Jim said, addressing a young Frenchman who had initially worked in the *Alonsa's* restaurant as a master sommelier, but now worked as one of the fifteen crew who kept the *Bravo* secure and maintained.

'Anything, Captain.'

'Let Duncan know I've gone to visit Doctor Singh, but I want him to wait here for my return, as I need to talk with him.'

'Of course.'

Jim nodded and rushed up to the main deck, heading for the *Alonsa.*

———◆———

Jim made his way towards Dr Singh's facility. His face stung from the cold wind outside. The rest of his body felt numb with the news. He stopped momentarily to catch his breath and to prepare himself for what he was going to find.

He'd known Kyra Singh for most of the time she had worked on the ship. She was one of the few constants and someone whom the flotilla had grown to rely on as their central medical expert. She was well liked, and as far as he knew, she had no enemies. Why anyone would want to harm her was beyond his imagination.

Jim scaled the steps to the first level and turned into the narrow corridor, where he walked into a group of people. Three of Faust's followers blocked his way.

'Just the man we were coming to see,' a short, squat man said. He wore a similar robe to Susan's – white, stained, made from sailcloth. The other two were similarly dressed.

Two men and a woman, all three of them agitators for Faust's cause.

Dietmar, the speaker, always reminded Jim of a Jack Russell terrier: small and yappy with a bad temperament.

'Now's not the time,' Jim said. He stepped forward, intending to ignore the situation, but Dietmar placed his hand on Jim's chest.

Heinrich backed him up, blocking Jim's route.

'You're here, we're here. I make that the best of times,' Dietmar said. 'We've been patient until now, Captain' – he emphasised 'Captain' with a sneer – 'but your time is up.' He took a step back and made to throw a punch, but Jim anticipated him, dodged to the side, unbalancing Heinrich, and landed a blow of his own, square on Dietmar's chin. The smaller man rocked back.

Heinrich and Monika were on Jim immediately, the latter clawing at his face as she screamed. Heinrich delivered two heavy fists to his ribs, knocking the wind from Jim's lungs, doubling him over.

Jim straightened up and pushed out his arms, throwing Monika from him.

She fell over Dietmar as he stumbled to his feet.

'Hey,' a voice shouted from behind the group. Stanic had come out of a side door. He held a wrench in his hand.

Heinrich turned to face him.

'I suggest you lot get lost,' Stanic said, his face promising violence.

Heinrich and Dietmar each took a step towards the engineer, but jumped back when he swung the heavy wrench their way, missing their heads by inches. Jim took the opportunity to grab Heinrich by the shoulders and pull him back, clearing a way through. The tall, blond German tripped as he fell back.

Monika broke ranks and dashed to Heinrich's aid, leaving Dietmar standing between Stanic and Jim.

'You still want to do this?' Jim said, making the small man spin round with surprise. He grabbed Dietmar by the robe and thrust him against the wall of the corridor, banging his head in the process. Through gritted teeth, he said, 'You dare try this shit again and you'll be joining Susan in the brig.' He tightened his grip on the robe, choking the man as the cloth tightened round his throat. Dietmar's face grew purple under the strain before he finally nodded. Jim let him collapse to the floor.

As soon as Dietmar regained his breath, he rose and staggered off, all the while swearing in German and promising various acts of retribution. Heinrich and Monika followed him.

'Thanks, Stan,' Jim said as he took a deep breath in an effort to calm down. 'I appreciate the backup. What happened to your hand?'

Stanic looked down in surprise. 'Oh, crap, I didn't even know. Must have caught it on something. I've been trying to get the desalinators running again. It's hard work without Ade. He knew those machines like the back of his hand. Ten times the engineer I'll ever be.'

'Nonsense. I've seen what you can do. I've all the faith in you. Though you should get that seen to.' It was then that he remembered why he was here.

The radio call.

Dr Singh. 'Shit. Sorry, Stan, I gotta go.'

Jim rushed past the engineer and dashed to the medical facility, crashing the door against the wall as he burst in. Ahead of him was the main desk where Kyla would often be doing paperwork or drinking coffee as she tried to work out some form of treatment for the quarantined citizens.

Much like Angelina and the others, he thought.

Loose papers littered the floor. A wastepaper bin lay on its side, the trash spilling out. A chair was tipped over, and fragments of a china mug lay scattered among the debris, leading Jim's eye through the obvious signs of struggle until he saw the first spots of blood.

Careful not to disturb the tableau, Jim made his way farther into the office until he saw Kyla Singh lying at Annette's feet.

Her body looked whole for the most part, save her neck. Her head was at the wrong angle. Broken, twisted, like a paper cup. A reddened gash split the skin and flesh below her chin. Blood surrounded her, covering the floor, turning it into a red lake, her head and neck a peninsula, and Annette's legs, shaking, behind the body like swaying reeds.

Annette was crying. She shouldn't have had to deal with this, Jim thought. Although she worked with Singh, had trained under her, she wasn't actually a medical student. She hadn't been exposed to situations like this before. Her main role was in triage and assisting Singh in gathering and analysing samples.

Her face was red and puffy. She wiped her nose with her sleeve and looked at Jim with glassy blue eyes. 'Why would anyone do this?' she said. 'Why?'

'I don't know, Annette, but we'll find out.'

'I can't believe she's gone . . . One moment she was here, and now . . .' She hid her face in her hands. Her shoulders bucked with sobs.

Jim remained in his place, paralysed, scared he'd ruin any evidence. He tried to think of the right words to console the girl, but all he could see was his wife in her hospital bed, the pillows stained red where she'd taken her own life, unable to go on fighting the cancer. He didn't blame her, of course; her condition had been terminal. She had often spoken of her wish to end her suffering sooner, but Jim hadn't been able to let her go.

'Annette, I know this is hard, but you've got to tell me what you know. What did you see when you came in? Was there anyone leaving the facility? Anything at all out of the ordinary?'

Annette took a deep breath and composed herself. Closing her eyes, she recounted what she had seen. 'I didn't see anyone when I approached. The place was empty. I opened the door, expecting to see Doctor Singh at her desk like she is most mornings. I was due to help her with the weekly samples—' She broke off, swallowing a sob.

Jim remained quiet, gave her room to gather her thoughts.

'It was the smell that I noticed first.'

'The blood?' Jim asked.

Annette shook her head, wrinkling her nose as though she were experiencing the scent again. 'No, it was some kind of chemical perhaps, or burnt rubber. I can't really describe it. If anything, it was kind of acidic, maybe. I don't really know. I thought it was strange, and that's when I noticed the mess in the office and . . . Doctor Singh's body.'

Jim remembered what Annette had said earlier on the radio. All this time he'd focused on Singh's death. 'You said "they" on the radio. Who else?'

She turned her head towards the door to the quarantine. 'Mike,' Annette said, almost with a reverential whisper.

He needed to go look for himself, to find out if it was true.

Being careful not to step in blood, he tiptoed through the office and opened the door. Bloody footprints stained the floor tiles, leading through to Mike's room. The plastic hung to one side where it had been cut open.

Not wanting to breach Mike's individual quarantine by opening the door, Jim stepped forward and peered through the small glass window. Mike's body was slumped on the ground, his face pressed against the floor, his arms beneath his chest and his legs spread out behind him.

There was less blood around him than around Singh's body, but Mike's head was caved in on one side, indicating he had been bludgeoned to death.

'Is it bad?' a voice said. Jim spun round to see Stanic standing on the threshold of the quarantine, his hand now bandaged, presumably by Annette. 'Anything I can do?'

'No, Stan, just give us some space, if you don't mind. We have to avoid contaminating the crime scene. I'll call Eva, see what she can find out.'

'Want me to fetch her? Probably not safe for her to walk about on her own given the circumstances, and with Faust's lot all het up.'

'It's okay. She's got company. Could you radio Duncan for me? Tell him Faust's lot are probably on their way to the *Bravo*. Tell him I'll be back once I've spoken with Eva.'

'I'll do one better,' Stanic said. 'I'll head there myself. I need to chat with some of your crew anyway about breaking up some of those small fishing vessels for parts.'

'Fine,' Jim said. 'Be careful.'

'Aye, Captain.' Stan gave him a casual salute and left the medical facility, thanking Annette for his bandage.

Jim left the facility behind Stanic and watched the engineer leave the ship. He reached for his two-way radio and dialled in Eva's channel.

'Eva, this is Jim. Are you there? Over.'

Static.

'Eva, do you copy? Over.'

'Jim? I'm here. What's up? Did you deal with the . . . what we spoke about last night?'

'I think you should come to the medical facility right away. There's been . . .' Jim took a deep breath, steadying his voice. 'Two murders. Come quickly, and bring Graves with you, just in case.'

'Who?'

'Doctor Singh and . . .'

Jim didn't need to finish the sentence: Eva knew.

'I'll be right there,' she said, her voice shaking.

The radio went dead. Jim went back inside and comforted Annette. 'It's okay. Eva will know what to do. She'll find out who did this.'

He just hoped that was true. Even though just this morning he'd promised himself he would be a better man than he was yesterday, he already felt the need to find a stash of rum and drink himself into oblivion.

CHAPTER TWENTY-THREE

Eva wiped the sea spray from her face, squinting against the low-hanging sun. The bright light glinted off the ocean, creating a dazzling panorama. She and Marcus Graves made their way from his yacht across boards and planks, from boat to boat, through narrow passages and up ladders to taller ships until they reached the edge of the main flotilla and made their way across to the *Alonsa*.

Tons of trash had floated in on the previous night's tide.

It always seemed odd to Eva that one of the most enduring remnants of humanity were tennis balls. Every tide that brought the tangle of plastic, wreckage and myriad other bits of human detritus to gather at the edges of the flotilla and the Orizaba peak invariably included dozens or sometimes hundreds of tennis balls, footballs and basketballs.

But mostly tennis balls.

The one thing they and the sheer amount of plastic brought into sharp focus was just how much time, energy and resources had gone into making pointless crap. Fitting that the pointless crap was what had outlasted humanity.

The flotilla's group of teenagers, some twenty in all, had woken, bleary-eyed, to their duties: cleaning off the trash. They chatted lazily as they took up their positions. Using fishing nets and hand-winches they brought it all in and separated it, filling the containers on the Chinese container ship with the organised materials.

Burnables were placed in one, plastic and other non-usable items in another. In the time Eva had been in the flotilla, they'd filled nearly ten large containers with plastics. A group of them smiled and waved at her as they headed to the far east of the flotilla to start their work. Eva nodded her head, but found it difficult to return a smile.

The pain in her ribs, although considerably better for her night's rest, still provided the proverbial thorn in the lion's paw. And with Jim's news . . . well, that was never good to receive. She didn't feel like she had woken and hoped this was just a nightmare. She thought that every morning when she woke to the sounds of lapping waves, creaking boat hulls and the distinct lack of Emily.

'Gotta be the same geezer, right?' Graves said. He helped her across the divide, watching that she didn't slip or crack her head on the edges of the opening. 'I mean, it's not likely we'd have a copycat.'

'Can't rule anything out yet. Got to keep an open mind, see the crime scene first.'

Eva let go of his arm when she had successfully traversed the gap. She walked past Graves, farther into the cruise liner, hiding her sudden feeling of grief. Thinking of Mike's death as a crime scene brought tears to her eyes.

Despite the bright sun outside, the level at which they entered remained dark and cold. The once gloriously decorated hallways and rooms were now ramshackle and barren, having been stripped for materials. Ducting, wiring, pipework and elements of the boat's infrastructure showed through the panelled walls like the arteries and bones of some great, long-dead beast.

After descending the central staircase to the level below, they passed a pair of old-timers. Marlene and Chad, the oldest left on the flotilla. They were both in their seventies, and every morning they came down to this level, which used to be a dining room and dance hall.

After their breakfast of fish and seaweed, they'd take to the dusty, water-damaged ballroom dance floor and tango, reliving their honeymoon night.

The last night before the world drowned.

Chad, bald and dressed in his tatty suit, gave Eva a wink as he led Marlene around the dance floor with a grace and agility that defied his age. Eva managed a smile for him and nodded back, despite finding the scene profoundly sad.

At least they had each other, she thought. This brought her back to Mike. At one time she had thought she had loved him. Well, that wasn't true. She *knew* she had loved him, but since he had returned, she had wondered whether those feelings were honest or whether they were some hopeful attempt at connecting with someone.

She felt like a magpie stealing from someone's nest.

If you were to face the end of the world, it would be easier to handle if you had a loved one to be with. Like Jean and Mike, or Marlene and Chad. Now the first two were gone, taking Eva's chance with them. She thought of Danny, wondered how she would tell him.

'How do they do it?' Graves said as they left the dining hall and entered the corridor that led towards the medical facility. 'Every damned morning.'

'I guess they do it to survive, to keep going. By remembering their night before the event, reliving it, they can remain hopeful. A few hours of happiness to offset reality.'

Graves shrugged. 'I'd rather sleep in.'

'The last of the romantics, eh?'

'I don't go in for sentimentality. I survive by staying focused.'

'Well, I hope the cynicism keeps you warm and comforted when you're the last one left.'

Eva didn't say any more until she entered the medical facility and found Jim comforting Dr Singh's young assistant, Annette. They were standing to the side of the room. Behind them, between the overturned desk and chair, was Dr Singh's body. Her arms were outstretched; the blood, now drying to a dark crimson, surrounded her. Her head lay at an angle.

Graves and Jim muttered something about a job, but Eva wasn't listening; she was analysing the tableau. There were distinctive and recognisable footprints where someone had walked in Dr Singh's blood. Though some were smudged, they got clearer as they left the body and headed towards the quarantine section.

Eva turned to Annette. 'How many people have come through here?'

'Just me, Jim and Stanic.'

Eva looked at her shoes, and then at Jim's. Neither were the large, heavy boots that had made the prints. She recognised them as the same messy prints from Jean's murder scene.

The killer certainly wasn't a careful craftsman. A man of rage, she thought. Someone who killed with fury and anger. She instinctively moved her hand to her ribs, knowing she had felt that fury firsthand.

'Where is Stanic? I'll need to rule him out.'

'He's on the *Bravo*,' Jim said.

'Good. I've got to see Danny. I'll catch up with him then.'

'I'm going there now,' Graves said. 'I'll let him know you want to see him.'

'You think this could have been Stanic?' Annette said. 'He was in engineering this morning; it couldn't have been him.'

'I doubt it was,' Eva said. Stanic had been nothing but exemplary, but if he was there, he might have seen someone or something.

'Some of Faust's lot was here when I arrived,' Jim said.

Eva thought about it for a moment. It just didn't make sense.

As far as she knew, none of them had any issue with Jean or Mike, let alone Dr Singh. It also didn't match with the evidence currently leading to an American male with engineering experience. After assessing the scene, she'd have to go through the manifest and narrow down her list of suspects.

The scene itself was fairly straightforward. Eva had seen it a dozen times before while working in homicide.

Singh had taken several blows to the head before having her throat cut. The wound looked rough, ragged. Wasn't likely to be a particularly fine knife.

Possibly a gutting knife or a hook.

Given the prints leading down the length of the office and their spacing – Eva stepped next to each one, making her walk with long strides – the killer had likely rushed forward, probably run.

Being careful not to disturb anything, she pushed the door open with the tip of her foot. The prints carried on, fading as they went, until they reached the door to Mike's room. The plastic flapped in the sudden movement of air.

As she passed the other rooms, most of the people inside were either asleep or drifting in and out of fever-induced unconsciousness.

A terrible thought came to her as she wondered why they kept them alive. The bacterial infection was a slow but efficient killer. It seemed cruel to keep these people locked away while they slowly approached death. But it seemed the idea of euthanasia still remained unsettling for most, despite the lack of any need, now, for governmental regulation.

Eva decided to question the ones who might have been awake at the time of the attack in case anyone had seen anything, but of the three who weren't in a fever state, two didn't have the strength to answer questions and were too far gone to really be able to articulate anything, and the other one, Nolberto's daughter, said she had seen nothing but the movement of shadows and had thought it was just Dr Singh doing her rounds.

With no help there, Eva approached Mike's containment room.

She looked through the window to see Mike slumped forward, his head clearly caved in.

It seemed the killer had had two weapons: one for cutting, and another for bludgeoning.

The same prints were evident on the tiles of Mike's room, just in front of the bunk on which he'd once sat. The room was still well tidied: the bunk was unruffled, the nightstand still had a glass of water and a book upon its surface.

The only thing that had been disturbed was Mike.

Eva's throat closed up as tears obscured her vision. She blinked to clear them, but more came. She reached her hand out, pressed her palm against the window, and let out a sob. She collapsed, then clenched her fists and struck the door, letting out a scream of anger mixed with grief.

This was far worse than when he'd left. Then, she had had hope that perhaps, despite the odds, he'd return. And he had. But now this.

Eva sat back on her heels and tried to compose herself. Tried to remember who she was and what she was. Eva Morgan, detective. Of course, back then she'd never had to investigate the death of a loved one. Now her best friend and the man she had grown to love were gone, there would always be that involvement.

Was it her fault? Had she not paid enough attention?

'Eva, are you . . . okay?'

A shadow enveloped her. She looked up. Jim stood behind her with his hand held out. She took it and stood.

'No, Jim. I'm not.'

Jim brought her in close, wrapping his arms around her.

At first she resisted, wanting to be the strong one, especially after finding Jim last night, but she realised none of them were the strong ones anymore. Everyone was just as broken. She hugged him back, allowing herself to be consoled.

Minutes ticked by, and memories of Mike came and went. The good times faded. Replaced with the image of his body slumped over.

She heard his weird mutterings, remembered what Jim had said last night about the other group of boats, and wondered just what the hell Mike had seen and whether it related to the documents he had, and whether it was ultimately the reason for his death.

Releasing Jim, Eva stepped back and wiped her face with her sleeve. 'Whoever it was,' she said, 'must have the infection too, or at least knows something about it. You wouldn't go in there with Mike in the condition he was in if you weren't already ill. Why risk it?'

'Maybe they just don't care?' Jim said. 'Do psychopaths think about those kinds of things?'

'We might not be dealing with a psychopath. As brutal as these murders are, they could have been done like this for a reason. Either way, we need to test everyone on the manifest.'

Eva and Jim left the quarantine and joined Annette at the front of Singh's office. Eva noticed Graves had left without saying a word. Just typical of him.

'Can you take samples from everyone on this list?' Eva said, handing Annette a copy of the manifest with all the main names she had identified as possible suspects.

'I'll have some of my crew come with you,' Jim added. 'Just to make sure you're safe. And in the meantime, you're welcome to come and stay with us on the *Bravo*.'

'Thanks, I'll do that. What should I do here, though?'

Jim looked to Eva. 'We could take the supplies and move to a different location.'

'Probably wise,' Eva said. 'What about the bodies?'

'I'll have them looked after,' Jim said. 'I'll get some of my crew to come back for them. We'll give them a proper sea burial, unless you need to examine them further?'

Although Eva had worked in homicide, she wasn't a coroner or medical examiner and knew only the basics when it came to biology. From the looks of the bodies and the way the blood had clotted, she had a good idea that they had been killed in the early hours of the morning. The wounds and causes of death were entirely obvious.

'I'm good,' Eva said. 'Better to deal with them now.' She hated how cold that sounded, especially with regards to Mike. But if she dared to show her feelings, she'd be no good at finding his killer. She had to remain distant. Or as much as was possible.

'Annette, if you come with me, I'll have you escorted back and accompanied while you take the samples. Have the other patients been taken care of?' Jim said.

'Yes,' Annette said. 'I kind of did it all in a panic, like autopilot, I suppose. After I saw Doctor Singh, I freaked out, but the routine took over.'

'What do we do with them now?' Eva asked. 'With no Doctor Singh to analyse them, isn't it cruel to just wait for them to die?'

A hush descended between them as they considered the thought of euthanasia.

'We could move them somewhere else, but we can think about it more later,' Jim said. 'Let's just get the bodies moved and the samples taken first. There's no need to make any rash decisions. We treat them as human beings, as usual, until we can decide on how to proceed.'

'What about their families?' Annette said. 'They usually come by in the afternoon.'

'I'll put out a bulletin to the families and have someone stationed on the door to make sure they're safe.'

'I don't think we should move them,' Annette said. 'And, well, I'd like to carry on Doctor Singh's work. I don't think there's any risk to me. It seems like whoever did this wanted to get to Mike, and well, Doctor Singh got in the way, I suppose.'

'That's how it looks,' Eva added, impressed by the girl's stoic attitude and ability to think. There was certainly no motive to kill Dr Singh other than she had blocked any access to the quarantine. 'I think she's right, Jim. It would be too much upheaval to move the patients somewhere else. We don't have another place as well set up as this. Can't you get some of your people to guard it until all this blows over? Let Annette here carry on her work?'

Jim thought for a moment, looking from one to the other. 'I guess you two know best here. I'll speak with my crew when I get back. I'm sure someone will volunteer.'

'Okay,' Eva said. 'While you go back, I'm going to go pay a visit to engineering and see if anyone saw anything.'

Before Eva left the room, she noticed a legal pad sticking out of a drawer within the overturned desk. It had Dr Singh's handwriting on it, the words unintelligible. She realised Dr Singh had written out more of what Mike had been saying, or a close approximation. She tore the single sheet from the pad and pocketed it.

Outside, in the corridor, while Annette locked the medical facility, Jim turned to Eva. 'Do you want me to come with you?'

'No, it's okay. It's only a minute away, and don't worry, I won't be asking any difficult questions. If the killer is there, he's not going to do something stupid and attack me in front of the others. Either way, it'll be a useful trip.'

'Where's all this going to stop?'

'I don't know, Jim. I just don't know.'

Jim shook his head and left, accompanying Annette.

When they had turned out of the corridor, Eva took out her two-way radio and called Duncan.

'Duncan, it's Eva. Are you there?'

The radio signal was weak, the static rising and dropping like waves. She tried again.

'Duncan, it's Eva. Do you copy? Over.'

A few seconds passed, but then his voice came over the speaker.

'I'm here. What's up, Eva? Are you okay? I heard the news.'

'Yeah. Can you come and meet me at engineering?'

'Sure. Give me five minutes.'

In the background when Duncan spoke, Eva heard raised voices, sounds of a struggle.

'What's going on?' she asked.

'I'll explain later. Got to go. See you shortly. Over.'

She didn't like the sound of that. It clearly sounded like something was going down, but she couldn't worry about that now. She needed to keep a clear head.

Securing the radio to her belt, Eva set off.

Halfway to her destination she heard footsteps behind her, matching her pace.

CHAPTER TWENTY-FOUR

Jim climbed the ladder to the main deck of the *Bravo*, then turned and helped Annette up. The poor girl had sobbed all the way there. Although he would have preferred to wait, her state naturally drew questions from the various flotilla residents. The news had already got out via Heinrich, Monika and Dietmar, and he felt it best to tell the truth to avoid any rumours and the distortion of facts they often brought.

On the main deck he saw Graves, along with Frank, Tyson and Shaley, and five members of Jim's crew, including Duncan, armed with fire axes, clubs and, in the case of Graves' lot, makeshift machetes.

They formed a line in front of the main gun turret. A group of five of Faust's supporters, dressed in their robes, backed away, all the while screaming expletives and threatening to burn everyone.

Jim pulled Annette to the port side and edged away from the group, as Graves' and Jim's crew continued to face them down, pushing them farther away from the bridge and closer to the edge.

'Dad, over here,' Duncan called, breaking away from the group. He pulled Jim and Annette behind him and turned to face the noisy group of zealots.

'What the hell's going on?' Jim asked.

Marcus stepped back from the group and faced Jim. 'It's done,' he said. 'Consider this a favour. One day, I'll need to call it in.'

At first Jim wondered what he'd meant by, 'It's done,' but soon caught on. He left Graves and his crew to deal with Faust's people and dashed to the bridge, taking Annette with him. Once he'd ducked inside, he pointed to his office. 'Go in there. I'll be right back. Don't go anywhere, okay?'

Annette took a breath and focused, gathering an air of calm about her.

'It's fine. It's my office. You'll be safe in there. I just need to check something. I'll be no more than a few minutes.'

'Okay,' Annette said. 'But don't be long. I don't want to be on my own.'

'Just a couple of minutes, I promise.'

She shuffled into his office and closed the door behind her.

He stood there for a few brief seconds, feeling sorry for her. She had no family on the flotilla, her parents having died of the fever six months previously. Dr Singh had taken her under her wing and trained her up. Annette had felt she could make a difference, perhaps out of guilt for not being able to save her parents. He could understand that, and it was good the flotilla had someone like her, someone with genuine compassion.

They were few and far between these days. The harsh realities of survival brought out the baser instincts in people. Much like the fracas outside, he thought. Seeing the hate in the eyes of Faust's people never ceased to surprise him. When there were so few of them left, why they still felt the need to divide the group and make things difficult didn't make any sense to him.

Jim dashed through the narrow passages of the destroyer, sliding down the stairs, his feet echoing as they clapped against the steel deck. He passed the main quarters area and descended to the brig.

'Danny?' Jim said with surprise. He halted as he reached the cells. The boy had his back to Jim and was staring into Susan Faust's cell. He didn't move or react to Jim's voice.

Jim approached and saw what Danny saw.

Susan Faust was hanging by her neck. It had snapped, and her head was at an obtuse angle to the rest of her body. The makeshift noose was made from a belt, and its buckle dug into the side of her neck. She was still swinging, the leather of the belt creaking under the tension. Her face had turned a greyish-red colour. A trickle of blood, now dry, came from one nostril. It had dripped down onto her robe.

Jim swept Danny up and carried him out of the brig section.

When they reached the next level up, Jim took Danny into his cabin. A couple of his comics were still on the kid's bunk.

Jim sat Danny down and knelt in front of him, looking him in the eyes.

'What you saw back there,' Jim said, reaching for the words, 'must never leave this room. Do you understand, Danny?'

Of course the kid didn't – how could he? He just looked back at Jim with tears in his eyes. Eyes that could well have been Mike's, such was the similarity. And every time Jim looked at him, he saw Mike on the small fishing boat, leaving the flotilla because of Jim. And then the madness in his eyes when he had returned.

'Susan was a very troubled lady,' Jim said. 'And when troubled people can't deal with their problems anymore, they seek other ways of dealing with it.'

'She's dead, isn't she?' Danny said, stating it more as a fact than a question.

'Yes, but she's with her God now. It's what she always wanted.'

'Is Mommy with God too?'

Jim gripped Danny's shoulder. 'I'm sure she's somewhere safe, just waiting to meet up with you in the future. You've got nothing to worry about there, lad.'

Danny wiped a tear away with his sleeve.

'When can I see my dad?'

'Will you wait here for me? I'll just be a minute.'

Danny nodded and picked up one of his comics.

Jim left the room and went two cabins down until he reached Duncan's quarters. He found his son's flask of grog in the night-stand and brought it back to Danny's room. Similar to how Jim often shared a cup of grog with Duncan, he laid out the cups on the nightstand and poured a finger of the watered-down rum into each cup. He handed one to Danny, downing his own in a single gulp before pouring himself another.

'Have you had grog before, lad?'

Danny nodded. 'A little. Dad used to warm it for me when I got a cold.'

'Here. It's not warm, but it'll warm you up and help settle your nerves.'

The boy took the cup with both hands, cradled it like a bowl, and sipped from its edge, scrunching his face with each mouthful. Jim finished his second measure and poured a third, wanting to feel that burn.

Danny's nerves weren't the only ones that needed settling.

Once Danny had finished his cup, Jim put his hand on the boy's shoulder and said, 'About your dad . . .'

***

Jim closed the cabin door behind him. Danny had quieted down after the news of his father. Jim's hand shook. It was still wet with his own tears. He had been an emotional wreck as he told Danny what had happened to Mike. He'd spared the boy the details, but it was never an easy thing to explain to a young boy that he had, through no fault of his own, become an orphan.

It took another cup of grog and fifteen minutes, but eventually Danny had tired himself out crying and fallen asleep. Jim left him to sleep while he made sure Annette was okay. On his way back to the bridge office, he came across Patrice.

'Captain,' Patrice said, 'I delivered your message to Duncan as you requested.'

'Message?'

'*Oui*, you asked me to let him know you wanted to speak with him on your return.'

'Oh, right, yeah. Sorry, it escaped me. I can't even remember what it was about now.'

'Are you okay, Captain? You look upset.'

'It's just been a difficult morning, Patrice. Listen, I've got some tasks for you if you're free.'

'*Oui*. Anything, Captain.'

Jim had always liked Patrice. One of the few good guys who just wanted to help and make a difference. Even though his new role on the flotilla didn't have the same status as his previous job, he didn't have any pretensions. Anything that needed doing, no matter how 'lowly', Patrice would be the first there, ready to get his hands dirty and do his duty.

'Can you get some of the crew to remove Susan Faust's body and put her over for the sharks?'

Patrice blinked once as he processed the request. Jim thought he'd baulk at this. He wouldn't have blamed him; it wasn't exactly an everyday request. But, with a short nod and a bow, as befitted his former role as a sommelier, the Frenchman took it in his stride.

'Of course. It's a sad bit of business, but I understand.'

'Thank you, Patrice. I appreciate your help and support.'

The Frenchman grasped Jim's arm and gave it a squeeze. 'I know things are difficult,' Patrice said, 'with the murders and the power struggles. But you can count on me, Jim.'

'Thanks. That means a lot to me.'

Patrice gave him a quick smile and a nod and headed off to the crew's quarters.

Jim wondered why everyone couldn't be more like Patrice. If more people were willing to drop their ego, the flotilla would be a much better place. They'd at least stand a better chance of surviving if everyone pulled in the same direction. It was a sad commentary on humanity that even when faced with extinction, people let their own issues get in the way of survival.

With those thoughts in mind, he remembered Annette, still in his office, and set off to get her settled in one of the crew cabins. And then he'd send her out with Patrice to take samples from everyone on the manifest. He hoped that would at least help Eva find the killer. Now that Mike and Faust were gone – and not by his hand – the killer remained the last major issue to deal with.

Unless Graves stepped up, of course. Who knew what game he was playing. Jim felt a wave of anxiety and depression sweep over him. There was too much going on for him to control. No matter how much he wanted to keep this place together, he had failed them.

He had failed Duncan, Mike, Jean, everyone.

Both Danny and Annette had become orphans under his watch, Angelina and her fellow researchers were seemingly lost, or worse . . .

He thought about leaving, just taking a boat and heading north so that he wouldn't keep screwing up. If Graves or someone else wanted to run the show, why not let them? He supposed they'd do a better job.

Jim sighed and headed to his cabin by way of the galley. He knew they kept some flasks of rum there to add some zing to the food. He'd drink, try to forget, pass out into sweet oblivion. It came to him then that, no, he couldn't be a better man than he was yesterday. Yesterday was *him*; he couldn't hide from it, pretend he was something better. Today, he was still what he'd always been.

CHAPTER TWENTY-FIVE

The footsteps kept up even as Eva increased her speed. She desperately wanted to turn around, but every fibre of her being told her to keep going, get to engineering. She could almost feel the person behind her now. She clenched her fist, ignored the ache in her ribs and readied to spin round to confront her stalker.

'Hey, Eva?'

She spun round. 'Brad? Shit, you scared the hell out of me.' It was one of the younger men who worked in engineering. Brad Dempsey was a former oil-rig engineer and brought some much needed experience to the crew. He stood there smiling at her.

'Oh crap, I'm sorry. I didn't mean to. It seems we're going the same way. Heading to see someone in engineering?'

'You've not heard the news?' she asked.

He shook his head. 'No, I had to get some parts for Stanic. What's happened?'

Eva waited for a moment to analyse his reaction. He seemed sincere, which wasn't surprising considering he'd been one of the few people to have worked here pretty much the entire time alongside Stanic and the others. Which of course made him a suspect if she was containing the investigations to the engineering department. It seemed unlikely, but she couldn't rule anything out.

'I'll fill you in on the details a bit later, but to answer your question, yeah, I'm here to see Stanic.'

'I'll let him know you're here.'

'Thanks. I'll wait here. I don't want to interrupt anyone's work.'

'Right, okay.' Brad smiled, passed her and went inside.

Eva watched him as he approached Stanic and then got to work at a workbench. Her inquisitive nature took over as she looked through the windows into the engineering department. The sound of metal and industry vibrated against the panes of glass. Inside, she saw Stanic, with his bandaged hand, going from station to station, inspecting the work of his various engineers – five in all, three men and two women. She noticed a close bond among the workers; they seemed happy in their jobs, laughing and joking with Stanic.

She waited for a few moments, wanting to have Duncan's backup, but she couldn't wait any longer as her desire to question Stanic overwhelmed her sense of caution.

As she walked towards the door, she had a look at their footwear. None seemed to wear anything but steel-toed boots. Not the kind of boot that had left the prints – that had been more of a fishing boot. Though that didn't mean a lot. Anyone could have changed their boots when they arrived to do their work.

She opened the door and went inside, feeling like an outsider entering some secret domain. The sound of metal on metal, saws and chatter assailed her. She wondered how they could work with such noise all day.

Stanic turned to see her enter, gave her a warm smile and a wave. He was near the middle of the room, with a young woman on a stationary bicycle set up to provide power to some of the machines. Although she'd seen it a few times before, this was the first time up close. It never ceased to grab her imagination.

A middle-aged man with grey hair stood over an electronic circuit board a few metres to the left of the bicycle. It was hooked up to the battery that the young woman was powering. The ingenuity brought a smile to Eva's face. It was like something out of a Victorian steampunk story, only with less steam and more bicycles.

The remaining staff seemed to be two men, one a teenager, the other at least in his late sixties, and an older woman who Eva knew was the older man's wife. It would be evident even to a stranger, given the looks they shared as they worked together on a large drumlike device.

'One of the desalinators,' Stanic said as he approached Eva. 'We've identified the issue caused by the sabotage and are finding replacement parts. Some of Jim's crew are breaking up a small fishing boat that we're hoping to salvage the electrics and hardware from.'

'You guys seem very busy at the moment,' Eva said as she scanned the room. Long workbenches were full of half-broken machinery and hardware. A rack of batteries, recharged by human power, were stationed at the end of each bench, providing power for soldering irons, multimeters and other various tools.

On one of the long benches, running along the back wall, lay a number of pieces of sheet metal shaped into what looked like aeroplane propellers. Stanic must have seen her confusion.

'New parts for a wind turbine. The other was so badly damaged we've had to essentially create one from scratch and use whatever we could salvage from the old one. If you ever find out who did this, I'd like permission to send them over.'

'Not if I find them first,' Eva said, giving him a grim smile. Although she meant it as banter, she felt a burning anger inside at the thought of someone purposely jeopardising the two essentials that helped the flotilla survive: power and bacteria-free water.

'Come into my office. We can chat better in there.' Stanic led Eva around a collection of large machines that she couldn't identify, like giant snails with their iron shells. The office was much quieter once the door was closed. Inside, Stanic had a desk littered with drawings and plans. A two-way radio transceiver sat alongside a pair of chipped mugs.

An old calendar hung on the wall, the dates changed to reflect the new year. Duct tape held the pages together. Stanic sat behind the desk, facing a window that looked out on the workshop. He gestured to an empty chair on the other side.

She sat down and noticed a pair of shoes – oil-stained sneakers – in the corner. Again, not the kind the killer had been wearing.

'I'm really sorry about Doctor Singh and Mike,' Stanic said. 'I know you were close. It's a terrible business after Jean and Ade. This place has been like a morgue lately, despite the veneer of a good mood out there. Selene was in pieces this morning as she took over Ade's role.' Stanic gestured to the girl on the bike. 'We all miss him greatly. Such a wonderful man, a true loss to this community.'

'How you holding up?' Eva asked, thinking it rude to expect him to handle all this without any feelings of his own. 'What happened to your hand?' she added.

The engineer shrugged, holding his hand up. 'I'll live. Of course, it's not easy to lose someone I worked with for so long. As for the hand, I cut it on a sharp edge of that fin over there. I was shaping it for a turbine, and I slipped and cut my palm. As for the other stuff, I don't know. I feel like I'm numb to it, you know?'

Although she didn't, it was a common reaction. Often, while she was on a case, the victim's relations retreated to a numb state, burying their emotions. It was as good a coping mechanism as any, she thought. Better than getting angry about it and doing something stupid like seeking immediate retribution. Murder begets murder. That was why it had to be nipped in the bud: so that it didn't grow and entangle more and more victims. It could spread like a disease. And there were no winners on either side.

'I don't really have an easy way of putting this,' Eva said. She knew she should probably have waited until she had backup, but in her experience, she knew that going right to the issue often shook things out of the cobwebs.

Stanic leaned forward on his elbows, looking serious. 'What is it?'

'I think the killer – and there is only one, I'm sure of it – either works here or has worked here in the past.'

His eyes widened. 'Are you sure? I don't mean to doubt you, but I know everyone in this department, and I just can't see how anyone would resort to killing other members of the flotilla. I don't mean to sound like a dick, but do you have evidence?'

Eva passed him the handmade key. 'In your opinion, would you say this was created here?'

Stanic held the key up to the porthole. Weak yellow light reflected off the key, detailing the tooling marks. He turned it over in his fingers, rubbing his thumb across the grooves.

'I think it was. This metal is likely from a piece we salvaged from one of the transport ships. You can tell by the mix of colours, the blue and white on the edge. And the way the teeth and grooves have been cut – that looks like the tooling marks made from our drills and bandsaws. That was when we still had the fuel to run the generators.' He indicated the snail-like machines out on the shop floor.

'When did you stop using the generators?'

'Last year . . .' Stanic stood, retrieved the calendar from the wall and flipped back through the pages. Running his finger across the days, he came to a date eleven months ago. 'Right there. I marked it, because I remember I argued with Jim about it. He was right, of course; we had to severely ration the fuel for more important things. At that time, we moved to human power with the batteries. If this was made here, it would have been back then.'

'How many of those out there were working here back then?'

'All of them, including me and Ade.'

'If I give you a list of names, can you let me know which ones worked here during that period?'

'Of course. Anything I can do to help.'

Eva took a copy of the manifest and handed it to him. Stanic took a pair of battered glasses from the top pocket of his oil-stained shirt and put them on. Using a pencil sharpened with a penknife, he ran down the list of names, his lips moving as he read, checking off those who had and hadn't worked in engineering during that time.

While Stanic continued with the list, Eva turned to watch the work on the shop floor. The guts of the desalination unit were spilled out on the workbench like the intestines of a beast. The workers were hunched over the parts like vultures, prodding and picking at the flesh and muscle of the machine.

Duncan, accompanied by Annette, passed the long windows on the corridor side.

'I'll be right back,' Eva said as she got up and opened the office door. A twinge from her ribs made her slow down only slightly as she moved over to the door that led out of the workshop. It was surprising how easily she'd got used to the near-constant pain in her side.

Duncan opened the door before she could reach it, and Eva stepped out, closing it behind her. Annette looked as though she had recovered a little from her discovery earlier that morning. Her face wasn't as red anymore, though Eva could still see the sadness in her eyes.

'Hey,' Eva said. 'You took your time. Problems?'

'Just some business with Faust's people causing trouble again. Nothing that wasn't handled. Annette's brought the samples. Have you spoken with Stanic about your theory?'

'Yeah, he's been pretty helpful. Confirmed that the key was likely made here. Even narrowed it down to a potential date. He's helping me identify which workers on the manifest were around then.'

'How's he taking it? I know he's proud of this place. Must be a shock to know that the killer was working right under his nose.'

'He's not happy about it, but who would be? At least he's cooperating.'

'Must make a change from dealing with Marcus Graves,' Duncan added venomously. Eva ignored it, not wanting to give him the satisfaction. Although she had a great deal of respect and admiration for Duncan, she didn't like how he seemed to be trying to make her feel bad for associating with Graves. It wasn't as if she were making a deal with the devil. And even if she were, at least it was proving fruitful.

'Sorry,' Duncan said, reading Eva's expression. 'Are you ready, Annette?'

'Sure. It won't take long.'

'How exactly do you want to do this?' Eva asked.

'I'll take a swab from each person, and when the medical facility is relocated, or at least the supplies, I'll run some tests.'

'How long will it take?'

'Depends on how long it takes to get everything from the facility moved over, but the tests themselves take about a day. I'll do them as quick as I can, though. I want you to nail the bastard that did this.'

She held the door open for them and followed them to Stanic's office.

'Hey, Duncan, Annette,' Stanic said, looking up from the sheet of paper. 'How you doing, Annette?'

'I'll be fine. It's just such a shock still. I don't really know what to feel.'

214

'That's understandable,' Stanic said. 'To what do I owe the pleasure of your visit?'

'Sorry, Stanic,' Duncan said. 'This seems like we're all descending on you here, but we need to take screening samples from everyone here.'

'It's just for elimination purposes,' Eva added.

He handed her the paper. 'There's a list of everyone I know of from that period. Some are no longer with us, unfortunately.'

'Thank you.' Eva counted eight potential suspects from the list. She folded the paper neatly and placed it in her jacket pocket. 'We won't take up much more of your time. We just need to take the samples and we'll be out of your way.'

'Is it really necessary?' Stanic asked. 'Everyone here was working with me since late last night. We've been working around the clock.'

'I know it seems unnecessary,' Eva said, 'but it'll make my job a lot easier by ruling everyone out.'

'Okay. I can't stop you, I suppose, and if it does help, then why not, but I don't think they'll like it. We're a tight group, and they'll feel persecuted.'

Duncan clapped Stanic on the shoulder. 'I know, mate. I get it. I'm sure I'd feel the same way if the *Bravo*'s crew were under suspicion too. But we won't be long.'

'Fine. You want to start with me?'

Annette stepped forward and took a swab out of a plastic tube container. 'I just need you to rub this on the inside of your mouth and place it in the tube.' Stanic took the swab and did as he was asked, handed the tube back to Annette. She smiled nervously at him and wrote his name on the side with a marker pen. 'Thanks,' she said.

Stanic called each person into his office individually to take the swab, not wanting to let the workshop potentially pollute the sample. Everyone gave a sample without too much bother except Brad Dempsey.

'I don't see why I should,' he said. 'I've not done anything. Stan, you've been with me all night and day. How could I have possibly gone over there and killed Mike and Doctor Singh? And why would I? Mike was one of my best buddies here. You can vouch for that.'

Eva kept her demeanour calm. She was fully expecting at least one person to get upset with this. People always did, even those with an alibi. There was a fear of corruption when it came to the police, unfortunately. Especially those in her district. They had a problem with some rogue cops fitting people up to cover for their scams. It hurt everyone: the public and the police. She couldn't do her job properly when the public didn't trust her, when they considered the police as potential enemies.

'I get that, Brad. I really do,' Eva said. 'But think of Mike. Your cooperation will help lead us to the killer faster. No one here is a suspect, so help us make sure it stays that way. Even aside from this, you're getting an extra infection screen.'

'I ain't got no infection,' Brad said, his face reddening with frustration. 'This is crazy. I've done nothing wrong. One of my friends and another colleague of mine are dead, and you think it could be me. That's a fucking joke.'

Eva checked his shoes: flat-soled work shoes. Not the right type.

'Calm down, Brad,' Stanic said. 'No one is saying you're the killer, dammit. Just give the sample, and you can go about your work.'

Annette stepped away from Brad as he clenched a fist and leaned forward closer to Stanic. 'You're on their damned side? I thought you were one of us, Stan. How could you betray us like this? People are dropping like flies around here. We should be looking out for each other.'

'Okay,' Duncan said, stepping in front of Brad and placing his palms on the engineer's chest. 'Just calm it down a bit. Right now, you're looking pretty guilty. You realise the situation we're in, right? Everything so far points to this place, and of everyone here, you're the only one refusing to help. Have a think about how that makes you look.'

'Fuck you, Reynolds.' Brad pushed Duncan back, making him knock into Annette. She slipped and fell against the desk, banging her head on the way down with a scream. She rolled on the floor, grabbing the side of her face.

'You goddamned fool,' Stanic said as he bent to help Annette.

Duncan grabbed Brad by the lapels of his shirt and slammed him up against the wall. 'Seems like you've got something to hide. Want to tell us something, Brad?'

Eva went to Annette and checked on her. No cut, just the beginnings of a swelling. 'Are you okay?' Eva asked, helping her to her feet. The sample tubes lay on the ground. Stanic picked them up and handed them to the girl.

Annette stared at Brad, fear in her eyes. 'I want to go,' she said.

Eva turned to Brad. It was all she could do not to take her anger out on him for scaring the poor girl. 'Just wait a moment,' Eva said to Annette. 'We'll be done in a minute.'

'Brad,' Stanic said, 'just calm down and cooperate before this gets any more out of hand.'

The young engineer squirmed under Duncan's grip. He kicked out, catching Duncan in the crotch. Duncan loosened his grip as he doubled over and staggered back. Brad pushed him farther and, before storming out of the engineering department, gave Stanic a look of disgust. He slammed the doors as he went, catching his colleagues' attention.

'What the hell was that about?' Eva said as she helped Duncan up. His face had turned red, and he breathed heavily.

'I don't know,' Stanic said, 'but despite all that, I can vouch for him. He's been here with us all night. You can confirm that with everyone else. We've all been working around the clock to get the desalinators back up and running.'

Eva knew it would be no good. With such a close group, even if one of them had left the workshop to commit the crimes, the others would provide suitable alibis. It was common pack mentality. She'd seen it a thousand times with gang members and business colleagues.

Annette handed Stanic a fresh sample tube. 'If or when he comes back, please try again. It's important to me.' Her face was already bruising on the side where she had caught the edge of the desk. Her voice fluttered with barely controlled emotion.

'Of course. I'll do my best to get it back to you by the end of the day. Brad's a fiery character, but he'll calm down and return and do the right thing, I'm sure.' He turned to Duncan, who sat on the desk getting his breath back. 'Are you okay, Dunc?'

'Aye, I'll be all right soon enough.'

'Don't take it out on him, though. He's as upset as anyone with all these deaths. He and Mike worked closely with each other for quite some time. Never been the same since he left.'

'All the more reason to let us eliminate him from the investigation,' Eva said. 'His lack of cooperation will only make this process more difficult.'

'I know. I'll talk with him later today. You have my word.'

With that, Eva left it in Stanic's hands. She wasn't convinced Brad was guilty, but she had learned that her first impressions weren't always right. People had a million ways to screw with that instinct. Evidence was what mattered, not feelings.

Eva and Duncan escorted Annette back to the medical facility so she could run the samples. Jim's crew should have removed the bodies by now, and at least there she'd be under guard in case anyone decided to come back, though Eva seriously doubted it.

It seemed to her that the killer was tying up loose ends, killing anyone with connections to the information he sought to recover.

She didn't feel better at that thought, wondering if she were the next target. She felt guilty about having Duncan or even Graves looking out for her.

What if one of them becomes the target?

Too many people close to her had already been taken away; she couldn't cope with another.

CHAPTER TWENTY-SIX

J im sat back against his bunk and closed his eyes. He dropped the empty rum bottle onto the blankets; the dregs spilled out. With his head against the hull, he could feel the vibrations of the waves and the other ships and boats lashed to the destroyer.

Together, they created a percussive language of struggle.

The waves tugged at the boats, wanting to dislodge them from the mountain's edge and take them out on a tide that ran from one edge of the world to the other. He thought about what that would look like from space.

The entire planet now blue with no landmass.

A smooth marble of purest cyan. A tiny, ugly dot stuck over the drowned remnants of Mexico. A rusting, decaying blight on an otherwise perfect surface.

He wondered how the flotilla would exist without him.

He saw Duncan and Eva potentially getting closer now that Mike was out of the picture; Duncan always did hold a candle for her. He'd never said as much, but he didn't need to. Jim saw the way Duncan looked at Eva and the way he casually brought her up in conversation.

He wasn't entirely against the idea. She was a fine woman, strong, determined, had her heart in the right place. If things were ending, Duncan couldn't hope for a better partner than Eva.

Then there was Marcus Graves and his obscure plans. Jim could never get a real grip on his motivations. Graves was like a shadow: indistinct, unreadable, silent. Jim had often watched Graves watch everyone else, moving chess pieces in his mind, working out an advantage, planning five steps ahead.

What his ultimate end game was, Jim didn't know.

Now that he and his goons had dealt with Susan Faust, Graves would have a clear run at taking over. Jim was too tired to fight anymore.

Without Angelina and the hope she had brought, Jim had nothing left.

Not feeling drunk enough to embrace unconsciousness, Jim got up from his bunk, the messages from Angelina falling around him like the remains of his photographs, and headed to his storage locker. He wanted to go to the bottom of the ocean, see what was down there. Stay there as long as the air would last and then . . .

He didn't know what then. Didn't care.

Jim put on his best 'tired but happy' face as he passed numerous members of the crew on the way to the storage lockers. The room was empty. He approached his locker and fumbled with his keys. He dropped them to the floor with a clank and swayed forward as he bent down to retrieve them. After a few failed attempts, he finally managed to find the right key and open the door, to discover there was only one set of scuba gear from the three available, and his wetsuit wasn't there.

He knew there was only one place for anyone to go with scuba gear: the sub. He checked his collection of keys and noticed he still had the key for the lock that he and Stanic had installed on the escape hatch.

But why would anyone go there?

The reactor was damaged. Jim remembered the day the sub had arrived: there was a lot of excitement as everyone thought they were being saved by the US military, but when they realised the sub was coasting and didn't respond to radio, the excitement had turned to anxiety. Inside, Jim had found the bodies of the crew.

Every single one dead.

Dr Singh, bless her soul, had inspected the corpses. Most had been killed by a knife to the heart or had had their throats cut. But there were a number who didn't display any physical wounds. At the time, Singh had postulated it was the infection.

The bodies were burned and set adrift in the style of the Vikings. Mostly to honour them, but also to reduce any potential spread of infection. It had already been amongst the flotilla when the sub arrived, but Jim had always suspected that its arrival was a portent. The victims had increased in frequency since then. He was no scientist, but it seemed pretty conclusive to him that there was a definite correlation and probably causation.

So why would someone visit the sub now? It was just full of ghosts.

Only one way to find out.

He grabbed the scuba gear and made his way up onto the main deck. The wind had died down earlier, and the usual blanket of black clouds had thinned, allowing the red early evening sun to bathe the world in a rare warm glow.

Jim felt none of the warmth. Not even the rum could keep him warm. He had died too much inside for that. Taking off his trousers and jacket, he hefted the scuba tanks onto his back and tightened the straps around his chest and shoulders.

The tanks had enough to get him to the sub and back if he was economical. But that didn't concern him. He didn't plan to come back. With the tanks in place, facemask on and regulator in hand, Jim descended a rope ladder hanging off the stern of the destroyer until his feet touched the cold water. He kept going down until he was treading water.

Regulator in mouth, he took one last look up at the *Bravo* and said a brief goodbye before ducking his head under the water and diving into the darkness beneath the flotilla.

CHAPTER TWENTY-SEVEN

E va was grateful to Annette for managing to run the samples, even in the chaos of the medical facility. Jim's crew had done a good job in removing the bodies and had cleaned the place up so as not to frighten any visitors for the other quarantined patients.

On their way out, Eva and Duncan thanked the husband and wife who stood guard. They were good, honest people who had come in on a wrecked sailboat and had always remained loyal to Jim.

'They'll do a good job,' Duncan said as they headed out of the *Alonsa*.

'I'm sure they will.'

'Eva, I'm sorry about Mike. Really.'

'Thanks,' she said. Unsure of what else to say, she adjusted her mask and continued on.

They walked back to the *Bravo* in near silence. Duncan tried to start a few conversations about the weather and the work Stanic and his engineers were doing to help keep the flotilla going. She nodded, affirmed, tried not to be rude.

Her rib continued to pulse with new waves of discomfort. It helped that the wind wasn't blowing a gale as usual. Even the sun was shining. It seemed completely at odds with the events of the day. Where were the black clouds to mourn Mike's and Dr Singh's passing? Where was the rain to wash away the grief?

Even the Orizaba looked resplendent, the golden light bathing the rocks that jutted out from the calm sea around it. There wasn't much trash on the surface, either. Most of it gathered at the flotilla's edges or had been cleaned up by the eager teens wanting to do their bit.

As they passed through the various districts of the flotilla, walking across the makeshift sidewalks of driftwood and rope, stepping from one stationary vessel to the next, one thing remained common with every person they encountered: the rumours.

Jim had put out a bulletin announcing the deaths.

The speculation was wild; Eva and Duncan were bombarded with questions about who was likely to have done such a thing, when the killing would end and why she hadn't found them yet. And all this bubbled under the rumours that Susan Faust had killed herself.

Unusually, her people weren't present out on the flotilla, spreading their hate from boat to boat. Even when Eva and Duncan passed their container homes on the container ship, they found them empty.

Duncan tried to distract them both from the attentions of the flotilla citizens with his nervous, infrequent words of encouragement. It was the worst of all polite conversations, loaded with unsaid thoughts and unclear intentions.

Although she had always felt an attraction to Duncan, Eva couldn't help but feel like a terrible human being for even contemplating a relationship with him, considering Mike had been gone for just a few hours.

No, whatever feelings might have been there from before Mike would have to stay buried.

'I want to check in on Danny,' Eva said.

'Of course. I'll come with you.'

Another awkward silence, and as she predicted, Duncan the Quiet didn't fill it, leaving it to her. At first she wasn't going to say anything, but something inside rose to the surface.

'It was weird,' Eva finally said as they ascended the ladder to the front deck, passing the main gun and heading for the door to the interior.

'What was?'

'What I had with Mike.'

Duncan didn't prompt her, just waited for her to continue.

She wanted him to say something to stop her from talking, prevent her from spilling out an essence of her real self. But it was too late; her mouth was betraying her, the words tumbling out. 'It was like there was this invisible barrier. At first I thought it was Jean, but he admitted his love for her had changed. He loved her as a friend and a mother to their son, but he didn't feel any real closeness to her anymore. They had grown apart, he said, become different people.'

'The flotilla does that to everyone in some way,' Duncan said as he opened the door to the bridge, holding it open for her to pass through.

She stepped inside; her mouth continued to run. 'It made me doubt my feelings. I wondered if they were illusions, if I was clinging to something that was never truly there. And to make matters worse, when he came back, I was unable to confirm it one way or another. If I could have just spoken with him one last time . . .'

'Love is distorted by life on the flotilla. It's like it has this force field that drags things away from people, makes them think things that aren't there, or wish for things that were.'

'And what do you wish for?' Eva said, wincing as she took a heavy step through the narrow confines of the ship. The pain wasn't just from her ribs; it was linked to the blatant question she knew would bring yet more raw insight.

A clanging noise came from the door. Duncan spun and tried the handle, but it wouldn't open. 'Someone's locked us in,' he said before shouting, 'Hey! What are you doing?' A glass bottle rattled down one of the narrow steel chimneys that they had opened up to allow for better airflow. It smashed on the floor before them in the narrow corridor. Horrified, they saw that it contained a flaming rag and gasoline.

Eva screamed and fanned her hands in front of her face as the heat pricked her skin.

Flames spread out, rode up the narrow walls packed with varied cardboard boxes of supplies, sucking the oxygen from the confined space. Eva and Duncan turned away from the door and headed towards the officers' quarters, on the second level towards the centre of the ship. When they reached the ladders that led down to the next level, Patrice and a group of six others were at the bottom, blocking the way.

Behind them, his face smudged black with smoke, stood Danny holding a comic.

'What the hell's going on?' Duncan asked.

'Faust's people . . .' Patrice said, climbing up to meet them. 'They're attacking. There are fires all over the ship. I'm trying to evacuate, but they've locked us inside – we were coming this way to see if we could get out.'

'No luck there,' Duncan said. 'Locked too. The rear hangar door?' Duncan asked.

'Blocked, welded – I don't know. Can't get it open.'

'What about the missile silo on the front deck?' Eva asked. 'We could get up the gantry and out the silo doors.' She knew the gantry itself was empty of missiles, the ship having emptied its full load of ammunition in some conflict before it crashed into the Orizaba.

'We tried,' Patrice said. 'Those bastards thought of everything.'

'Why didn't you radio us?' Eva said, not even hiding her irritation. 'You could have warned us before we got here. And why didn't you just go out of the front door?'

Patrice sighed. 'We were dealing with a minor scuffle on the rear deck with some of Faust's people and Nolberto. When we had that settled we came back down to return to our duties when we discovered they'd locked the exits and trapped us inside. There's only seven of us. It's not like we could have patrolled the entire ship! And there's no damned signal down here; they're blocking the frequencies. Don't you think we would have called for help if we could?'

Another crash and a roar of flames came from behind them. Another bottle smashed near Jim's office where they had another of the narrow chimneys – a piece of tube mast from another ship used for extracting the smoke of small burners.

'Okay, that's enough,' Duncan said. 'Let's try to work this out.'

Eva gritted her teeth as she climbed down the ladder and pushed through the crew to grab Danny's hand. She pulled him close. 'Danny, you okay?'

The boy just nodded. *Of course he's not okay*, she told herself. *He's lost both his parents and now this.* 'Patrice, are there any extinguishers left?' Eva asked.

The Frenchman shook his head. 'All gone, used months and months ago.'

'Any other way out of this damned ship?'

No reply.

She could see flames flickering up from the end of the corridor that led to the recreation area and brig. That access would be blocked now.

Farther up, towards the ops room and the bridge, smoke billowed.

Faust's people had them trapped.

Danny started to cough as the air grew thick with smoke.

Eva stepped into the first cabin to her left and grabbed a pillow. She took off the pillowcase and ripped it in rough sections. She wadded up one of the pieces and handed it to Danny. 'Hold this over your mouth and nose. It'll help with the smoke.' She handed pieces out to the rest of the crew and Duncan and kept one for herself.

'We need to shut the doors and hatches,' Duncan said. 'Keep it contained.'

Patrice nodded. 'Already done on the higher levels. There's nothing more we can do unless we can somehow get through the doors. I don't know how they've blocked them, but they're not budging.'

'Let's get out of here, head for the lower decks,' Eva said. 'If we close this hatch, it will buy us some time. We should be able to get under the galley and head to the aft machinery room.'

She led Danny through the low doorway and waited as everyone else came through. She closed the door behind them, turning the wheel to lock it in place. The thick steel should hold the fire at bay for a while, she thought, and if anything, it should die down, as there wasn't much to burn. It'd soon consume the oxygen in that part of the ship. But then she remembered Jim's secret radio in his cabin.

'Danny, everyone, wait here for a moment. I'll be right back.'

She reopened the door, choking on the smoke as she rushed to Jim's room, recovered the radio and zipped it inside her jacket. She didn't know if it would ever work, or whether there'd be anyone to receive the signal, but she didn't see the point of leaving it behind if there was still that small chance.

The flames had come down into the corridor now, feeding on the fabrics in the cabins. She joined the others on the other side and closed the door once more.

'Where's my dad?' Duncan said as they made their way through a passageway leading to the galley.

Patrice shrugged. 'No one's seen him since this afternoon when he came back from the medical facility. I don't think he's on the ship.'

'But you can't be certain,' Duncan added.

'*Non*, I guess not.'

'I should look for him.'

'But where?' Eva said. 'The upper decks are already done for. He's not there; someone would have heard or seen him. We should stick together, find a way out.'

'If all the doors on the top deck are blocked, along with the maintenance hangar and the missile silo, that doesn't leave any other options.'

'So what do we do?' Patrice said, looking at Eva as though she were in charge. Even Danny looked up at her, his eyes full of expectation.

In other parts of the ship she heard more bottles smashing and fresh fires erupting. Soon the deck would be completely on fire. With the upper decks sealed off, that didn't leave them any other choice than to head lower.

'We keep moving, get to the machinery room. Perhaps there's something we can use.'

Eva had no idea if that was true or not.

She fought to control herself, remain calm and clear-headed, which was easier said than done. Being trapped under all the metal and heat, with no exit points available to them . . .

God help us, she thought, as she gripped Danny's hand and led him through the narrow passageway, looking longingly at the empty fire extinguishers and the hosepipes that were useless without power.

CHAPTER TWENTY-EIGHT

J im's head swam with the alcohol and the need to breathe shallowly. He leaned against the sub's control panel as the water was pumped out of the lockout. The way the chains were locked over the hatch confirmed his thought that someone had been here relatively recently, within the last few days even.

Once the water had dropped to below his ankles, he opened the main hatch to the sub and clambered inside. The air was stale on his tongue; he tasted it like a snake. He had an absurd desire to call out, speak to the ghosts of the submariners who had died in this shell. Would they hear him and reply, or would they stay silent, unable to tell him what had happened to them? Or more accurately, he thought, *who* had happened to them. But he resisted the temptation to speak, not wanting to hear the truth even if it was to be found.

He made his way through the tight confines of the submarine to the bridge section. Inside, he sat in the navigator's chair, its yoke covered in a fine dust and mildew.

Jim sat in the chair for a moment, resting against the tanks on his back. A control panel lay in front of him, displaying an array of buttons switches and long-dead information screens. Just for the hell of it, he flicked the switches, pressed the buttons.

He stood up, waited a few seconds for the dizziness to disappear, turned away from the control panel and was about to leave the bridge when he heard a thrumming noise coming from somewhere in the sub. It vibrated against the hull beneath his feet.

Two lights, red, began to flash on the control panel.

'Holy shit,' he said under his breath, spinning round to see the bridge come alive with power. Lights coming online, information screens blinking on, their displays malformed and waterlogged, but alive.

Power, he thought. Somehow there was still power.

When Jim, Stanic and his crew of engineers had first come aboard, they had declared the sub dead. The nuclear reactor was offline, damaged by some unknown collision. They had abandoned any idea of using it to power the flotilla for fear of it breaking down and leaking radiation everywhere. Even the small radiation monitors on the hull wall had indicated an almost dangerous level of radiation, suggesting the core was indeed damaged.

Jim surmised that the power might be coming from an auxiliary battery, but he was certain they had checked for one when they first brought the sub into the flotilla. Scared he might be making any damage worse, he flicked the switches back to their original positions until the thrumming stopped and the lights went out, one by one, and the console returned to its slumber.

Curious about what might have gone on here and who else might have visited the sub, he decided to investigate the cabins, starting with the officers' quarters. The alcohol still swam in his blood, making him stumble over unseen obstacles in the ankle-deep water.

The officers' room already looked as though it had been ransacked. The drawers of the desk unit hung open, empty. On the bunk, however, Jim found a single sheet of paper with random, incoherent scribblings scrawled across its surface. He placed the paper inside a plastic bag attached to the belt of his scuba gear and carried on searching the cabins for something; he didn't really know what.

Floating about the sub like a ghost himself, aimless and wandering, seeking for something he knew not what, he conceded to the compulsion to search. The other cabins turned up nothing beyond a few personal effects. Pictures of loved ones, children and mothers and sisters and fathers. Even some pets.

He gathered up the photos, letters and badges and placed them all together on a single bunk as a memorial.

He thought back to his tattered photographs.

A deep sob welled up in his chest and burst out of him as he leaned against the bunk, burying his face into the damp mattress, letting out all the pain and frustration. He stood there for ten minutes or so crying, letting his tears soak into the fabric, wishing the pain would go away, wishing he could be a better man, a stronger man.

But he was neither.

Unable to look at the impromptu memorial any longer, Jim turned from the cabins and headed for the rear of the sub and the nuclear core. He decided that, like the submariners who had lost their lives here, he too would make it his grave, but not before he had seen the damage to the core for himself, radiation or not – it didn't matter anymore. The hatch to the nuclear reactor waited ahead. A radiation detection device, like a scarab beetle stuck to the bulkhead next to the hatch, glowed with a dull, red light, indicating the high levels of radiation inside.

Ignoring it, Jim reached out and turned the wheel, unlocking the hatch. He took a breath and stretched his right leg over the breach until his foot touched the floor. There was no water in the reactor room. He eased the rest of his body through the doorway until he stood entirely inside. It was too late to turn back now.

The light was low, but he could make out the core's structure hiding in the gloom like some ancient monolith.

Jim began to slowly move around the room, getting his bearings. Water from his clothes dripped onto the floor, making it slippery. He stepped forward and lost his balance. His head struck a low pipe, sending him falling backwards.

He lay with his face against the metal floor, his head swimming, the pain throbbing, the darkness coming to consume him. Whether it was death or merely unconsciousness he wasn't entirely sure. He just waited and let it take him.

CHAPTER TWENTY-NINE

Eva could smell the smoke with every breath now. Her throat seemed to tighten, and her lungs were straining with the diminishing oxygen. She led the others through a passageway and into the galley. She held Danny close to her as she approached a door at the end of the room.

'I've an idea,' Duncan said. 'I don't know why I didn't think of it before. Beyond the door is the galley fan extraction room. It sits between the galley and the junior ratings' cabins.'

'How big are the fans and ducting?' Eva asked.

'Never really thought of it,' Duncan said. 'Let's find out.'

The giant of a man stepped around Eva and Danny, who still held the cloth to his face to help filter out the smoke, and pulled the door open. Taking a flashlight from his belt, Duncan shone the torch round the room, following the contours of the ducting.

Eva stepped forward and looked inside. The huge fans stood almost as tall as her, with great tubes spiralling off and heading up to the top deck. She saw no easy way into the ducting, and couldn't really get a sense of how wide they were from their position.

Turning back to Patrice and the others, she looked them over to ascertain who was the smallest. None was particularly small, she thought, including herself.

'I'll open up one of the pipes,' Duncan said. 'At the very worst, we should be able to get some fresh air down in here.' He stepped into the room, navigating around the fan extractors, and headed for the machinery room opposite.

'What's going on?' Marcel asked.

'Duncan's getting something to open the ducting. One of us might be able to scramble through. They lead up to the top deck. I doubt those bastards will have thought of everything,' Eva said.

Marcel and the group huddled together, doubt written all over their faces. From behind them, smoke filtered down from the deck above. Whatever Faust's people were doing, they seemed to be damned good at it. Eva felt like she and the others were rats being smoked out of their nest.

'Eva, your help, please?' Duncan stood inside the extraction room, holding a fire axe.

'What do you want me to do?'

'When I hit the ducting, I want you to pull on it, see if we can rip it out completely.' Duncan indicated the wide-diameter ducting pipe that ran out from the back of the extraction unit and headed directly up to the baffles that would lead out onto the main deck. On the ceiling of the extraction room, a square frame held the pipe in place.

'Everyone else stay back,' Duncan said. 'Especially you, Dan.'

Marcel pulled Danny away from the room, out of swinging range.

'Ready when you are,' Eva said, gripping the ducting as though she were hugging it.

Duncan looked up and performed a practice swing of the axe, aiming for the very top, just below the holding frame. Eva gave the ducting a quick pull and realised how sturdy and heavy it was. The pipes were aluminium, and not so thick that they couldn't be shifted, but they still felt solid and were held by chunky bolts. Eva had a sudden thought. 'What if they hear?'

'We'll wait after. If they're gonna drop another Molotov, it'll go straight into the extraction unit. But given the noise from the rest of the ship, I think we'll be okay. We should only need a few blows to clear this from the mountings.'

Eva wasn't entirely convinced, but given how thick the smoke was now, she didn't see many other options. 'Okay, swing away. Let's see if we can get this thing free.'

Duncan bent his body back, the axe over his shoulder. Springing forward, he crashed the axe head against the top of the ducting, sending vibrations down through to Eva's arms. She yanked it back, but it didn't budge.

'Again,' she said.

Duncan complied, striking again, grunting as he hit the axe against the pipe once more. This time it shifted, twisting within the mounting frame. Eva pulled on it, and it shifted still farther, creating a gap between the top of the pipe and the rest of the ducting that led up into the top decks.

'One more should do it,' Duncan said as he pulled the axe back and struck against the pipe with all his strength. Eva timed the pull with his strike. As she hefted it backward, the pipe came away completely from its mountings. She had to hold on to prevent herself from falling to the floor.

'Good job,' Marcel said as he entered the room with Danny in front of him.

Duncan shone his flashlight up to the ceiling where the ducting headed off.

'Give me a boost,' Eva said. 'Let me take a look up there.'

Duncan handed her the flashlight and knelt, cupping his hand to make a platform for her foot. She stepped into his hands and hopped up as Duncan lifted her up to the ceiling.

She grabbed the edge with her free hand and put her head up into the extraction ducting, now nothing more than a black hole. Shining the light inside, she could see that the sides of it were charred. Squinting, she could make out a baffle at the top of the ducting. That must be the top deck, she thought. As her eyes adjusted to the light, she noticed movement.

At first she thought it was someone moving by, but soon realised the movement was from the clouds. She took a deep breath and tasted fresh air mixed with the reek of soot and old cooking grease.

The ducting was ridged in intervals where it had been welded in place. She brought her arm up and rested her elbow on the first ridge before pulling her head and shoulders farther up, but as she tried to bring her other arm in, the duct's narrow diameter prevented her from getting it up and above her shoulders.

'Let me down,' she said, lowering her chin.

Duncan guided her back down until her feet were back on the floor. She looked at the others. They regarded her with hope. 'It does go all the way up,' she said.

'But?' Marcel prompted.

'I'm the smallest here, and even I can't fit. It's just too narrow.'

Duncan kicked the extraction unit and dropped the axe to the floor. 'Great. Back to square one.' He leaned back against the wall, shaking his head.

His frustration was clear to see and reflected Eva's own growing anxiety.

'There's something we've not thought of,' said Ellie Stimson, one of the five crew members outside in the galley. She was a young girl, broad-shouldered, quiet. She looked sheepish as she spoke up, her Texas drawl evident. Everyone turned to face her. Eva noticed her almost shrink away as they did. 'Go on,' Eva urged. 'What is it?'

Ellie stepped forward, wringing her hands nervously. 'The hull breach. It's near the bow, but if we go down into the maintenance tunnel, we can get there by crawling beneath this deck. If someone took the scuba gear, they might be able to squeeze out between the rocks.'

She was, of course, talking about the Pico de Orizaba. One of its peaks had pierced the hull of the ship, grounding it in place, much like the *Alonsa*. But there was one key difference: they had managed to move the liner away from the Orizaba, creating a hole with which to get in and out. The *Bravo* had never been moved, and the rock was likely to have made a secure plug against the hull.

'Sorry,' Stimson said. 'I know that was a stupid suggestion. I just thought . . .' She ran a hand through her light blonde hair and stared at the floor in embarrassment.

'No,' Duncan said. 'It's not stupid at all. One of us should have thought of it before. It's a possibility that's worth checking out. I can get to the storage room from the side exit of the machinery store.'

'Even if there was enough space to get out,' Eva said, 'you'd be on the Orizaba. If you wanted to get back to the rest of the flotilla, you'd have to swim in open water.'

They all knew what that meant, and with Jean and Ade as recent reminders, Eva didn't think anyone would want to face that possibility.

'Let me at least check to see if it's an option,' Duncan said. 'I'll be five minutes.'

Marcel, Stimson, Danny and the other four crew members stared at Eva, waiting for her decision. Again, that feeling of being given responsibility without ever asking for it engulfed her.

'Okay, fine. We'll check it out. Stimson, go with Duncan as you seem to know your way around here.'

The girl gave a quick nod and a smile before following Duncan out of the extraction room and into the machinery store. Before Duncan could shut the door behind him, Eva moved up to him. 'Be careful,' she said. 'Don't do anything stupid.'

'I will . . . be careful, that is. I'll be back before you know it.'

He turned and closed the door behind him, shutting Eva in with the others. At least in there they were getting clean air from the ducting. With the galley closed off, they'd be okay for a while, but for how long, Eva didn't know.

She sat down with her back against the extraction fan unit. Danny sat next to her, holding her hand. 'It'll be okay,' he said.

What had it come to when it took the children to comfort the adults? 'Yeah, we'll get out, Dan. Get everything back to normal.'

What that normal was, she hadn't a clue. There certainly hadn't been any normal during the time she had spent on the flotilla, and she didn't expect it to start now.

While they waited in the silence, Eva could hear footsteps and voices coming from up top. Occasionally a shadow would fall over the ducting hole. She knew those weren't clouds; she could recognise the voices and accents of Faust's followers.

She moved everyone to the edges of the room and kept them quiet. If one of the thugs up there heard or saw them, they'd drop in one of their firebombs.

Eva wondered where Jim was. She pictured him beaten up, possibly dead in one of the upper-deck rooms. Or, if he had been lucky enough not to be on the ship when Faust's lot attacked, perhaps floating on the sea, having been thrown over. Although when she considered his mood lately and the near-constant bad news, she didn't rule out the possibility that he might have gone over himself. She felt the weight of his secret radio within her jacket and wondered if she should try to find someone out there. Their regular radios were jammed somehow, but would this one work, being on a different system?

She knew there was at least one place that it had communicated with – the scientists. But Jim hadn't heard back from them. In addition, considering the state Mike had been in when he returned, she had a feeling there'd be no one there capable of answering if they, too, had suffered the same fate.

After a long stretch of tense silence – twenty minutes? Thirty? She couldn't tell anymore – Eva heard the door between the extractor room and the machinery store open. Duncan stood there with Stimson. Eva put her finger to her lips as she approached them.

'Well?' she whispered. 'What did you find? Keep your voices down.' She indicated the ducting hole by way of explanation. 'We don't want to be overheard.'

'It's gone,' Duncan said.

'What is?'

'The scuba gear.'

'For fuck's sake. Is this Faust's lot, you think?'

Duncan shook his head, flailing his wild mane. 'Only one person has the key to that locker: my dad. And there's worse news.'

Eva waited.

'The locker rooms are ablaze,' he continued. 'I've closed off the store, but I don't know how much longer we've got. We can't get down to the lower decks; they've been sealed off.'

Eva looked at Stimson, who seemed to wilt under her gaze. 'Stimson, when was the last time you knew for sure the access to the lower levels was still open?'

'I don't know exactly, Miss Morgan, but it was at least two weeks ago.'

'So someone must have been planning this since then. A coordinated attack. This isn't good.'

242

Danny appeared by her side, tugging at her arm.

'What is it, Dan?' Eva asked, keeping her voice soft, trying to hide her general annoyance.

'There's smoke coming through,' he said before placing the fabric over his mouth.

Eva looked round, and sure enough, it was coming through gaps around the door where the frame had distorted over time, snaking up through the ducting. It wouldn't be long before someone spotted it, she thought.

Seemingly hearing her thoughts, Danny whispered, 'I can climb up there. Let me go. I've climbed higher places than that. Me and Xi used to go exploring in the *Alonsa*. I'm good at that kind of thing.'

She initially dismissed the idea of sending Danny up there. What if one of Faust's group caught him? Would they be so callous, so evil as to harm an innocent boy? It seemed too much of a risk to take. She couldn't let the poor kid shoulder the responsibility for their survival. 'I can't let you do that,' Eva said. 'It's too dangerous.'

'It's dangerous here anyway,' Danny said. 'What if the fire comes through?'

Kid logic. She couldn't refute it. But still, he was just six years old. She had promised Jean she would take care of him. Eva looked up at the ducting hole and knew Danny probably wouldn't have any problems in scaling it. His slim shoulders would get through the baffles too. He could get out, perhaps gather help.

She hated herself for thinking it.

Hated herself for not finding another way out.

Despite that, a plan was already falling into place in her mind. The cogs fitting together to present their only real option: Danny would climb up and out onto the main deck. From there he could go over the side and onto the exterior row of fishing boats via one of the rope ladders. As long as he kept hidden, he could climb across the boats until he reached the end and joined the flotilla on the northern edge, where he could either go into the *Alonsa* or carry on to Graves' quarter and fetch help. Or, once on deck, try to free one of the main doors, but they'd still have to negotiate corridors full of smoke and flame.

'Please,' Danny said, 'let me try. I want to help.'

Sweat dripped from her forehead, the pressure and heat getting to her. She looked at Duncan; he stared back at her with the same haunted expression she suspected that she wore, herself, at the thought of sending a child out there as their last hope.

'You'll just take a quick look first, okay?' Eva said, her guts churning with anxiety.

Danny turned and started to scale the ducting pipe like a spider monkey. Before Eva could reach him, he leapt off the top and caught the edge of the mounting frame, effortlessly pulling himself into the main ducting.

'Just a look,' Eva whispered up to him. The boy nodded and continued to climb, placing his feet on either side of the slim cylinder, using the ridges as rungs.

CHAPTER THIRTY

Jim woke with a blinding pain in his head. The sub felt like it was rocking violently to the side, but he knew it was coming from within, the rum sloshing around inside him, the alcohol in his blood. He leaned over and coughed, spittle splashing against the dark floor. He touched his head and felt a bump swelling on the side, near his right temple.

He got up on unsteady legs, using the overhead pipework to stop himself from falling. A few deep breaths later he started to regain a semblance of balance. The tanks on his back clanked against the reactor as he turned to grope for the door.

The memory of striking his head and knocking himself out came to him.

Was he contaminated with radiation? Was that the source of his illness rather than the booze? He doubted it; he didn't feel that much different from how he'd felt when he arrived on the sub. Drunk is drunk, and he knew all too well what that felt like. He opened the door and stepped out into the passageway, sloshing through the stagnant water.

He turned to regard the glowing red radiation beetle next to the door.

There was something about it that had bothered him before he went inside.

Taking it off the wall, he turned it over and saw that it had been tampered with. Prising the back off with his fingers, he saw that someone had twisted a pair of wires together, shorting the circuit.

Now why would someone do that? It appeared to him that having a nuclear reactor intact would be quite the asset to the flotilla. He knew that they were designed to last thirty-plus years and could easily provide all the power it would ever need.

Too late now, though, he thought. The flotilla was self-destructing, and he was at the centre of it.

He considered his next move. He could either stay on the sub until he starved or died of thirst – not a pleasant way to go – or perhaps he could go out and dive to the base of the mountain and let the ocean drown him.

But as he weighed up his various options, he realised he couldn't go without seeing Duncan one more time. He needed to tell him about the reactor. Even if Jim wasn't going to stick around, he could give his son a final gift and at least tell Duncan how he felt. How proud he was of him, how much better a man he was than Jim.

With his decision made, Jim staggered to the lockout hatch. From the controls on the outside, he initiated pressurisation and waited for the water to be expelled so he could climb inside. Once inside, he hit the button to let the water back in. The process took a while, allowing him to breathe and calm and let the effects of his bump ease.

He shook with cold as the water climbed up his legs, waist and chest. Biting down on the regulator, Jim took small breaths until the lockout had completed its procedure and the hatch opened.

Shivering with the cold, his limbs feeling like rubber, he pushed off, out through the hatch, not bothering to replace the chains and lock. The water was so dark it felt to Jim that he was swimming through crude oil. His arms were barely visible in front of his face. But he kept kicking and driving upwards, becoming ever more desperate to break the surface.

He didn't know how deep he was when he took the last breath through the regulator, a shallow inhalation that stopped halfway, his lungs expecting more. He spat out the regulator and tried not to panic but to keep swimming upwards with graceful movements, nothing too extreme, so that his oxygen would last a little longer.

An orange light undulated on the surface some distance to his left. Directly above him, the silver kiss of the moon marked his destination. He was close now.

What was that orange light?

It seemed to flicker independently of the ocean's tidal dance.

As he pondered and kicked his legs slowly and steadily, trying to ignore the fact that his lungs wanted to burst from his chest and steal what little oxygen they could from the water, he noticed a shadow tracking him from below. He stopped kicking, letting himself float upwards as he looked down into the inky depths.

Something nudged Jim's hip, knocking him about. He pulled his legs up and spun around, trying to see what it was. He just caught a glimpse of a tail fin flicking away, the moonlight shining on its tip.

Sharks.

Nearing the surface, where the cloud cover had blown away to reveal a full moon whose light penetrated the first few metres of the water, Jim saw a pack of them, at least a dozen, tracking his movements from below and from the sides. They had him surrounded even as he breached the surface and replenished his straining lungs with air. He began coughing immediately, choking on the smoke.

He looked to his left and saw the flames rising in the sky, the smoke dancing away like the spectres of the dead, heading up and up. All around him, he saw fins approaching.

Another nudge against his leg. Much harder this time.

They were getting nearer.

The flotilla's edge remained at least twenty metres away.

Jim screamed for help and kicked out, catching one of the sharks with his heel. He doubted he would last long, but by God, he would try.

As he frantically kicked and clawed his way closer to the flotilla, he reached down and grabbed the fishing knife from his belt. He spun around to see one of the fins coming closer, the great dark skin of the shark's body rising up in the water.

Jim struck out with the knife, skimming it across the surface, scraping the blade against the shark's hide. It darted away, crashing its tail fin against Jim's chest, making him drop the knife. The shark's blood looked like crimson oil.

The other fins drew closer before disappearing beneath the water.

CHAPTER THIRTY-ONE

Eva looked up at Danny as he climbed to the top of the ducting shaft, his small, agile body quickly scaling the cylinder, blocking out the light from above. When he reached the top, he slowed, pressing his face against the baffles, turning left and right.

'Well?' Eva said, fighting the urge to try to climb up there and bring him back.

He tilted his head down against his chest. 'No one's here,' he said, his quiet voice echoing down the ducting.

'Okay, good work, Dan. Come back down. Be careful, though.'

'I can get up,' he said as he pushed his shoulders against the fan baffles, shifting the unit up and clear. 'I'll get help.' He stepped up onto the next ridge, clearing the baffle completely and pushing his head above the deck.

'No, Dan, come back down. It's too dangerous.' Eva stepped across to stand directly beneath the hole and watched in horror as Danny lifted his legs out of the ducting and rolled away out of sight. 'Dan! Goddamnit.' Eva kicked the extractor unit. 'He's going to do something stupid, and it'll be my damned fault.'

Patrice, Duncan and the others gathered round and looked up into the night sky, waiting for Danny's face to peer back down, but they saw nothing. Heard nothing.

Eva stayed in place until her neck started to cramp.

'Come away,' Duncan said, gently turning her away by her shoulders. 'Someone might see us. We should move into the machinery store, just in case.'

'How can we just let him go? What if Faust's people are out there right now? . . . What if . . . ?' She pushed Duncan with frustration and barged her way through Patrice and the others until she reached the door leading to the galley. She placed her hands on the handle to open it but immediately recoiled, the heat singeing her skin. 'Fuck it!' She kicked out again, striking the door.

'He's a smart kid,' Duncan said. 'I'm sure he'll be fine. Let's all just calm down, think rationally.'

She spun and faced him then. 'Rational? Calm? We're trapped here and a young kid is out there on his own with a bunch of fucking psychos. What's there to be calm about? I'm fucking mad as hell, and I don't want to stand around doing nothing.'

'There's nothing else we can do,' Patrice said. 'We're blocked at all levels; we can't go lower, and these are the last two rooms. We just have to wait and hope that Danny can bring help.'

'And all the while we just stand by and burn to death?'

'Look,' Duncan said, raising his voice and adding a bit of grit. 'I get that you're stressed and worried. We all are. I don't even know where my dad is. But you know yourself, from your previous career, that doing dumb shit is what gets people killed.'

He had a damned good point. Eva clenched her jaw and yelled inwardly, releasing her frustration. Closing her eyes and taking a few deep breaths, she remembered her father trying to show her how to fish. His gnarled farm-worker's hands had gripped hers around the rod as he showed her how to cast. The float, thin and long with a bright yellow tip, splashed into the water until it bobbed upright, shifting on the river's current. For three hours she'd sat on the boat while he snoozed, all the while concentrating on the float.

She never did get a bite, but it taught her a lesson in patience and focus.

'You're correct,' she eventually said, her heart rate having dropped to a comfortable level. 'Dumb shit is what gets people killed. That's why I'm so worried. Kids aren't exactly the clearest of thinkers in dangerous situations. But as we don't have another option right now, I agree that we should wait.'

Waiting had never appealed to her, despite her lesson. Even when she was on a job, following or monitoring some perp, she always had to fight that desire to bust them there and then. She would just have to fight the urge now, do the sensible thing and wait it out.

Sitting down in a dark corner of the room, she joined the others in a tense, pregnant wait. A wait that she had hoped would be rewarded not just with their rescue but with Danny safe and in one piece. Patrice and the rest of his crew sat in the other corners, staying out of direct sight of the ducting, just in case one of Faust's people happened by.

Duncan joined her, moving his great bulk next to hers, making her feel like a child.

'I'm sorry,' Eva said, keeping her voice low. 'I understand it must be tough not knowing where Jim is. But like Danny, he's smart and would no doubt have got himself somewhere safe.'

'I don't know. He's been in a bad way lately, making tough decisions, taking a load of flak from everyone. It can't be easy for him. Then there's the trouble with Frank and Susan . . . the sabotaging. I don't know how he holds it all together.'

Eva wanted to say that he didn't, that he relied on the bottle and that he'd had external support, although the key term there was 'had'. Eva touched the radio through her jacket pocket and thought about confessing what she knew to Duncan. Dismissed it, not even knowing how to start the conversation or what good it would do.

Knowing his father had lied to him all this time would break Duncan.

Duncan and Jim, more like brothers than father and son. They were the twin backbones of the flotilla. She couldn't be the one to break that – not now, anyway.

'He's got a strong will, Dunc. It's why we've all survived for as long as we have. Without his commitment to organise and facilitate things, we'd have descended into chaos long ago.'

'But that's what's happening now, though, isn't it? The chaos. It's seeping through the cracks, finding a way to get into people's minds. And not just Faust's people either; we've never had this many killings in such a short space of time.'

'I'm working on that,' she said. 'We're getting closer.'

'Any ideas on what happened to Mike before he came back like he did?' Patrice said, leaning over into the conversation.

'I'm afraid not,' Eva said, not wanting to give too much away. 'I've got to go through Doctor Singh's notes to see if there's any hint, but even she didn't really understand what might have happened to him.'

Patrice nodded as he sat back against the wall.

Eva noticed Stimson and some of the younger members of the crew starting to yawn and wipe their eyes. Eva's eyes were tearing up too. The smoke had found a way into the room, and even with the open duct, it was affecting them.

From outside the ducting, a flicker of shadow caught her eye. Someone walked past, obscuring the scant light afforded them by the moon. She heard a man's voice. She recognised the German accent immediately – Faust's Jack Russell of an agitator, Dietmar.

It was just three words. 'Drop it now.'

A glass bottle fell from the ducting, spinning, turning.

The flaming cloth hung out of the opening, the flame licking at the oily sides of the extraction duct. Eva rose to her feet, opening her mouth to warn the others.

Duncan's eyes grew wide. He launched away from the corner, his arms outstretched like a wide receiver trying to catch a football.

Patrice helped Stimson and the others up and headed for the door to the machinery room. He opened it and ushered everyone inside as Eva grabbed Duncan's arm, pulling him away and around the large extraction units, towards the other side of the room where Patrice stood, holding the door open, waving at them to hurry up.

The bottle hit the top of the extraction fan casing, toppled over to its side, the fuel inside sloshing up its sides.

Eva and Duncan reached the door. Eva pushed Duncan and Patrice inside before grabbing the handle and backing into the machinery store. As she closed the door, she saw the bottle flip over and crash to the floor; the glass shattered and the fuel spilled out into a puddle.

The flaming cloth ignited the fuel, sending a blast wave of heat towards Eva as she slammed the door shut. But it wouldn't close completely. The hinges had worn and slipped, leaving a quarter-inch gap up the side of the metal jamb.

Smoke and heat bled into the machinery store, fouling the air with old grease and cooking oil, making Eva cough and choke. She tried to heave the door up to shut it completely. It wouldn't budge. The gap wouldn't close.

Patrice switched on a flashlight and inspected the gap while holding his shirt over his mouth. 'We'll need a crowbar or a hammer.' He turned and cast his light on the metal shelving units. They were bare, having been long since emptied of any tools and resources.

'What are we going to do?' Stimson said, coughing.

'Get back,' Eva said, ushering everyone away from the door. She took off her jacket, exposing the wound dressing on her ribs. All the movement had seemingly opened the stitches; blood spotted the white fabric. Her adrenalin had so far masked most of the pain, but as she reached up to try to squeeze her jacket into the gap, she winced with the effort.

Duncan's hand covered hers. 'Let me,' he said, staring at her wound. 'You should rest. You don't want to irritate it further.' He handed her back her jacket and took off his thick sweater.

'Thanks,' Eva said, covering herself back up and standing back. Patrice shone the light to give Duncan something to work with.

Even with his sweater pushed into the gap, the smoke still found a way in, filling the room, making them struggle for breath.

Eva joined the others in the far corner of the dark room. The flames flickering outside cast the briefest of lights, creating a shifting shadow theatre on the wall. At their backs, beyond the locked door, Eva could hear the fire roaring in the corridor.

No way out. Fire on all sides.

She thought about Emily.

CHAPTER THIRTY-TWO

S weat and salt stung Jim's eyes as he grabbed on to part of the hull of an old boat. A piece of fibreglass had come loose from some part of the flotilla to bob about on the surface. He hauled himself onto it. Kneeling, he began to paddle towards the safety of the flotilla.

Movement and splashing would give his position away, but it didn't matter at that point. The sharks might already have him in their sights, but at least he had a barrier between him and them, albeit a thin one easily destroyed.

'Help,' he screamed as he neared the floating city's edge. He could just make out movement on the edge. Three people were clambering among the small wooden rowboats that lined the city. One of them looked up.

'Over here,' Jim shouted, his throat hoarse. 'Help me, please.'

His flimsy boat lurched to one side, but he gripped on to the edges and stopped it from capsizing. The bulk of the shark swam underneath him; fear propelled him forward. He pulled his hands away from the edges of the fibreglass.

The people on the edge shouted back, their voices barely audible. He waved his hands over his head, hoping they'd spot him.

'It's Jim,' he screamed. 'I need your help.'

He heard the words, 'Hold on, I'm coming. It's Stanic.'

The sound of his friend's voice calmed him. He could make out the shapes of Stanic and two others hurrying into one of the rowboats. A rope was untied and flung onto the makeshift dock, and then they were approaching, the oars splashing into the sea. A pair of fins rose out of the water and circled the boat as it came closer.

Taking a chance, Jim thrust himself forward, paddling for a few seconds with his hands, eager to meet the boat. Another nudge, much harder this time, made him nearly lose his balance and fall into the water.

'Hold on, Jim, nearly there,' Stanic said. He sat at the front of the boat, shining a flashlight on the water. Jim could see in his other hand one of the many makeshift harpoon guns the engineering group had made. Almost every boat and ship on the exterior of the flotilla had one aboard for emergency defence.

Not wanting to aggravate the sharks any more, Jim made sure to remain still, keeping his hands out of the water and flat against the board's surface to help his balance.

A few tense seconds later, Stanic and his two colleagues had pulled the boat alongside him. Stanic held out his hand. 'Come straight over. Make it quick.'

Jim did just that: he gripped Stanic's hand and leapt off the thin fibreglass to tumble into the rowboat, knocking into Ahmed and Brad, two of Stanic's fellow engineers. Brad grabbed Jim's tanks and helped him onto a narrow wooden bench.

Stanic surveyed the water with his large flashlight.

'Thanks, guys' Jim said, his heart still racing and his breath coming in gasps. 'I thought that was it . . .'

Ahmed gave him a polite smile. He had never spoken much in all the time Jim had known him. One of the few people to have arrived in the last six months, he wore a haunted look behind his dark eyes. No one ever asked what had happened to him, afraid of what he might share.

The boat rocked violently to one side. Brad swore as the oar slipped from his grasp. Jim flashed out his hand and grabbed it before it could slip into the ocean.

'Fuck, nearly lost it,' Brad said. 'Thanks, Jim. What the hell are you doing out here at this time of night anyway?'

'Long story,' he said, fully sober now, his head throbbing with an early hangover and stress, his adrenalin and energy drastically draining away. 'Want me to take that?' Jim said, pointing to the harpoon in Stanic's left hand.

The engineer handed it over as Ahmed and Brad turned the boat and headed back to the flotilla. Only once did a shark seem brave enough to try to take a bite, its large mouth crashing against the hull, but it was a half-hearted attempt.

'We're not weak enough,' Stanic said with a wry smile. 'They only like the easy kills.'

'Which was me a few minutes ago,' Jim said, knowing it to be the truth. He was the weak one, the easy kill. 'What are you guys doing out tonight?'

'Getting weapons,' Stanic said. 'There's a war going down.'

'A war?' Jim turned to look at the flames at the far end of the flotilla. 'On the *Bravo*?'

'Yep,' Brad said. 'Faust's people have gone crazy. They've trapped people inside and set it alight.'

'Who's inside?'

Brad and Stanic didn't say anything. They didn't have to. Their expressions of sympathy told Jim Duncan was on there. Even Ahmed's eternally haunted look was now infused with genuine pity. Jim slapped his hand against the bench seat, frustrated that he'd been so selfish in his own pain and anguish that he'd let this happen. 'What's the situation?'

'Half the flotilla is doing nothing. Hiding, as usual,' Stanic said. 'The rest of us are trying to mount a defence. Problem is someone among them has a pistol. We can't get near without getting shot at. We don't know how much ammo they've got, and they've made makeshift barriers at the stern and bow. We came to get the harpoons, see if we could pick some off.'

As Brad and Ahmed carefully brought the boat into the dock and pulled them in by the rope, Jim watched out for any last-minute shark attack.

When they secured the boat, they moved onto the dock, Stanic constantly scanning the waters until they were safe. Jim breathed a sigh of relief when he saw the fins moving away. They knew they'd lost this one, but they must have recently fed; otherwise he doubted he'd have got away with just a couple of half-hearted nudges.

Not wanting to be in any doubt, Jim asked, 'Is Duncan in there? Trapped?'

'Yeah,' Brad said. 'The bastards have jammed the radios, but as far as we can tell, Eva's inside too, along with Patrice, Stimson and some other crew members.'

'What about Danny?'

'We've not found him, so we have to assume so,' Stanic said.

'We're going to need more than harpoons.'

'It's all we've got,' Stanic replied, passing one each to Brad and Ahmed, having recovered them from the other boats tied to the dock. Crude metal shafts with tensioned rope, they were more like crossbows than real harpoons, but they would at least serve as a second option.

'I've got a better idea,' Jim said, shrugging the scuba gear off his back. 'Someone helped us get into this situation, and they'll help us out of it.'

'Who?' Stanic asked.

'Graves.'

CHAPTER THIRTY-THREE

Eva shook Duncan's shoulder. He'd already slumped against the wall, unconscious. Stimson and Patrice had followed. She wanted to join them, just close her eyes and let the darkness take her. Every breath was filled with smoke. Her lungs felt like they were on fire; they were quickly becoming starved of oxygen, filling with carbon monoxide.

Duncan's sweater had fallen away from the door. Black, greasy smoke filled the machinery room, obscuring everything. Eva gave up trying to wake him. Her energy had all but died out as she laboured for breath. Somewhere outside, above them, she could make out the sounds of struggle. Dull thuds pounded against the hull before there was quiet. Another glass bottle smashed, adding more fuel to the existing inferno.

The door behind her, leading out into a passageway to the lower decks, was hot against her back. She stumbled forward, trying to drag Duncan's body away, but he was too heavy for her. She slumped against the floor, her muscles sore and screaming with the effort.

She mouthed the word 'help' as she closed her eyes and laid her head against the metal flooring, all the while picturing Emily in her blue dress, the one with the white tulips on it, dancing around in the garden, trying to catch the monarch butterflies. But each time she reached up for them, only wanting to get a closer look, they evaded her grasp, making her laugh with delight and wonder.

If only Eva could have known then what she knew now, understand how much she'd lost when she had left Emily behind. Even on that day, despite being at home on the farm with her parents, Eva had still been absent for most of it, dealing with calls at work.

But Emily hadn't minded. She had just been happy that Eva was there for once. That's why she'd worn her special dress that her grandmother had made for her. It had broken Eva's heart that Emily felt like seeing her mommy was such a rare and special occasion that she had to dress up for it.

Her eyelids succumbed, blocking out the smoke and the flickering light. Her mind reeled. The darkness shrouded her, took her away, and she no longer fought it, wanting the end to come.

CHAPTER THIRTY-FOUR

Jim approached Marcus Graves' yacht. Stanic, Brad and Ahmed had headed back towards the *Bravo* with the aim of scouting out the situation, perhaps to find a way onto it, to outflank the Faust group.

Jim approached the cabin door. Candlelight glowed from inside. From the movement of shadows, he knew Marcus and his family were in there. The door opened before he could reach it. Frank's face peered up at Jim, first confused, then smiling, then grimacing as he quickly realised something was up.

The knife in Jim's hand and the fact he wore nothing but a sodden T-shirt and shorts were clues that all was not well. Frank opened his mouth to speak but Marcus pulled him back inside and took his place at the door.

'What the hell are you doing here?' Marcus said.

'You not heard what's going on with Faust's people?'

Marcus's shoulders tensed and he stepped out onto the deck, closing the cabin door behind him, all the time watching the knife in Jim's hand. 'I heard. I just didn't want any part of it. It's your problem, Jim. You wanted her dead, remember? We had a deal. Part of that agreement was to keep your trap shut. Why should I risk my life and my family's lives clearing up your mess?'

'Give it a rest, Graves. I'm not here about what you did to Faust. She deserved it. I have no intention of reneging on our deal. I'm here for your help. My son, Danny and some of the crew are stuck in the ship. Those crazy bastards have trapped them inside and set fire to the damned thing.'

Marcus took a step back, rubbing his chin. 'Those fuckers are out of control. This, Jim, is what happens when you don't keep charge of things. You let one thing slip, and people take advantage.'

'That's a joke, coming from you. Since you arrived, taking advantage has been your number one strategy.'

'Exactly, which means I know what I'm talking about. So, what do you want from me? Why should I care what goes on over there?'

'Because, Graves, if they take over, you won't have me and my crew keeping the peace. Besides, they're armed.' That got Graves' attention.

Marcus leaned forward as though he hadn't quite heard correctly. 'Armed as in firearms?'

'That's what Stanic said.'

'You know what that means, don't you? The murderer is likely to be among them. Which means we can kill two birds with one stone.'

'You want to bargain at a time like this?' Jim said, shaking his head. His hands shook with the cold. His fingers cramped around the knife.

'We'll help you,' Marcus said, 'but when this is over, you step down and give me the destroyer.'

'As long as my boy and my crew are safe, you can have the damned ship.'

Holding out his hand, Marcus smiled. Jim transferred the knife to his other hand and reluctantly shook with Graves. 'There's one more thing,' Jim added. 'I want some of your clothes. I'm fucking freezing here.'

Marcus turned and opened the cabin door, bowing and holding out his arm. 'Go inside. Be my guest.' And to Frank, Tyson and Shaley, he added, 'Make Jim welcome, lads, and someone fetch the poor bastard some clothes from my wardrobe. While you're at it, get tooled up. We've got ourselves a ship to claim.'

Jim stepped inside and was greeted by sneers and smirks. At one time it would have got right to the marrow of his bones, but all he could think of was getting those bastards off the *Bravo* and recovering his son and crew.

Jim hurried across the flotilla, eager to deal with the situation. He ignored the questions from the other citizens, just told them to get back into their cabins and not get involved. He didn't want any more collateral damage on his conscience.

'You don't own us, Jim!' McCoy, a former yacht sailor said from a group of five residents. 'We can go as we please.'

'I can do without more people getting involved. I don't have time for this.'

'But you have time for cutting the power, though!' McCoy's Chinese wife said, before hurling more abuse him. He just let them cry into the wind as he pushed his way through the crowd towards the *Bravo*.

The smoke rose into the night, adding a darker shade to the already inky blueness of the evening sky. Clouds had gathered, obscuring the stars and moon. Jim used a flashlight to find his way. Four other beams stretched ahead, belonging to Graves' crew, lighting up their latest prize: a burning ship.

That was how far they had come, Jim thought as he jumped across onto the container ship.

Where once a prize had been something worth fighting for, they now fought over scraps and wrecks. Despite everything, there were still men and women who couldn't see beyond the gathering of physical possessions as a worthy concern. Capitalism had indoctrinated some so deep it was present in their very being.

Navigating through the containers, Jim heard voices and the crackling of flames reverberating around the metal-skinned boxes. Someone was crying; others shouted.

'Remember our deal,' Jim said as he approached the final container before the deck leading directly to the bow of the *Bravo*. Graves, Tyson, Shaley and even Frank huddled in behind him.

Graves' voice whispered into Jim's ear. 'Don't you worry, old son. I remember everything.' No matter what Marcus said, it sounded like a threat – a pattern of speech honed over the years to suggest some form of violence. Jim suspected that all Graves' followers had picked up the habit, used it to scare their ways to the top of their particular rat's nest. But it didn't work on Jim. A man who had wanted and courted death no longer feared another man. He saw Graves for what he truly was: a scared little boy fighting over broken toys.

Poking his head around the container, Jim saw fifteen of Faust's group on the bow of the ship. They had erected makeshift barriers against the railings with pieces of sheet metal, broken hull sections and driftwood. A crowd of onlookers had gathered at the base. Some were just watching the spectacle, others demanding they stop the madness. Stanic, Brad, Ahmed and two others from engineering had their harpoons trained in the direction of the ship.

One person, someone he couldn't identify, lay dead, face-down on a ship beside the *Bravo*.

Illuminated by the flames, Jim saw Danny in the clutches of Heinrich and Monika. A fishing net was wrapped around his neck, trapping his arms behind his back. He tried to kick out, but Heinrich's large frame seemed to swallow him like a storm.

'We go now,' Jim said, urging his uneasy allies to the front.

As he came forward, someone within the group of twenty or so onlookers spotted him. Everyone, including Stanic and the engineers, turned to him. A hush descended on the situation. Even the flames seemed to quieten as Jim approached.

Stanic stepped forward. 'They've been asking for you, Jim. Said they'll call all this nonsense off if you'll talk with them. They've got Danny . . . We couldn't attack, not with him . . .'

'It's fine,' Jim said, gripping Stanic's shoulder. 'I just appreciate your backing me up. Who specifically wanted to talk with me?'

'Dietmar.'

'It had to be that little rat, didn't it?'

Graves and his firm filtered into the crowd. Jim watched them take up positions around the ladders, ready to storm the deck as soon as the opportunity presented itself. He doubted that it would be an opportunity to suit him. They'd only get involved when it benefitted them, but still: something was better than nothing.

Amid the hush of the crowd and the crackling of the fire, Jim was suddenly aware that the longer things went on, the worse it would be for whoever was trapped. He stepped away from Stanic and headed to the ladder.

Before he put his hands on it, a voice called from above: Dietmar, using a megaphone.

'Stay where you are, Jim, unless you wish for young Danny to feed the sharks tonight.'

Heinrich lifted Danny with one arm as though he were a cardboard cutout and approached the port side facing the Orizaba. The big German lowered Danny over the edge, out of sight.

'Leave the boy alone,' Jim shouted up. 'He's nothing to do with this. Have some compassion!'

Dietmar grimaced, exposing his dirty teeth 'The same compassion you showed Susan when you hanged her? We're beyond that now, Jim. There's only one way out of this now for you, for Danny and Eva and your precious son. It might already be too late for them.' He indicated with his left hand the burning bridge section.

Smoke billowed up and out of the windows.

Jim grabbed the ladder and heaved himself up a few steps until Dietmar stopped him, pointing a pistol from between two sections of the makeshift barrier. 'Now, now, Jim. Don't do anything foolish. One word from me and the boy follows his mother.'

'What do you want?' Jim said through gritted teeth, keeping his eye on Heinrich and Monika. 'Just name it. This shit has gone on for too long.' He hated himself for giving in so easily, but at that point he didn't care about anything else other than getting his son and the others out safely and making sure Danny still had a future.

The look in Dietmar's eyes told Jim they'd crossed a threshold.

To them, killing a child would be justified. This was what he had feared from this group: that their views were so distorted that the lives of others meant nothing to them anymore.

'Confess your sins to me,' Dietmar said. 'Confess them all to the flotilla. Show the world what you really are, Jim Reynolds. And then we will judge you. Do this, and you may save your people. If not, we stay here until everything burns.'

Jim knew he was telling the truth. Faust's death had sent them over the edge. He looked down from the ladder and saw Marcus Graves staring at him.

'I'll confess,' Jim said. 'I fucking killed your precious Susan. I hanged her until she was dead. And I'd do it again if I had the chance. I'd hang the lot of you. That enough truth for you?'

Dietmar stood back from the edge of the ship, then pulled away a piece of the barrier. 'Get up here,' he said, still training the pistol on him.

Once on the deck, Jim faced Dietmar, wondering if he could disarm the small German and retaliate, but that was crazy thinking. He was surrounded, and Danny was screaming as they hung him over the side. 'Bring him up,' Jim said. 'I've done what you wanted; now leave the kid alone.'

Dietmar stepped backwards until he was close to his fellow cultist. He said something in German, and Heinrich hefted Danny up with his great arms and dumped the boy onto the deck. Danny's face was contorted, tears flowing down his cheeks. His body shook with fear.

'You evil bastards! He's just a boy!'

'We were all boys once, Jim. We all had to lose our innocence one way or another. I bet even your son had that transition.'

'I've confessed. Now let me get my son and the others out. They've done no harm to you.'

'Your task isn't finished,' Dietmar said, handing Jim the megaphone. 'Confess your sins to the flotilla citizens, and then we'll let you find them . . . if they're still alive.'

Jim snatched the megaphone, turned to face the watching crowd and admitted he had killed Susan Faust. Admitted that he had failed them. They looked up at him with expressions of sorrow, disbelief and hate. They hated him for what he had allowed to happen. He knew he had let them down. Jim handed the megaphone back and stood there, numb to the events around him.

Graves' and Stanic's people scaled the ship as Dietmar kept his pistol on Danny. 'Get your people out, but we keep the kid until you've done one more thing,' he said.

Jim waited silently for his next judgement. The words seemed to come from far off as he watched the men and women of the flotilla rush past him with tools and buckets of water. Dietmar's people had gathered around Danny's shaking form, using him as their protection. He didn't doubt for one moment that Dietmar was not beyond shooting a child.

'I want you to leave,' Dietmar finally said. 'In the morning you will be given the same send-off that you have given so many times before to those who never returned. Only you will never be welcomed back, and you will not take any resources with you. Once you are gone, we'll release the boy.'

With that, Dietmar and the group lifted Danny up and disappeared into the dark passageways of the flotilla, back to wherever they had set up camp.

When they were no longer in sight, Jim seemed to come alive as the fear and adrenalin hit his system. He heard the sound of panicked voices from the members of the flotilla, who were unbarring the doors and dousing the flames that came out of the ship.

He ran into the fray, determined to save as many as he could.

If this was to be his last day, he'd at least go out trying to undo the hell he had wrought.

CHAPTER THIRTY-FIVE

In her dream existence, Eva could sense movement and sound, a sudden rushing of activity somewhere beyond, in another world. An ever-present sense of suffocation gripped her. Limbs like stone, hanging uselessly from her prone body, refused to do as she commanded. Ignored her pleas to gather themselves and lift her off the floor. She felt it was important, but couldn't quite understand why.

The voices grew louder, urgent; she recognised her name, pictured her parents standing on the porch of their old wooden farmhouse, hands to their foreheads to cut the glare from the setting evening sun, calling her in from the cornfield.

She'd always pretended not to hear. For a while, anyway, and only to the point when Dad stepped off the porch and hitched up his dungarees. That was the sign she had pushed her luck as far as she could and would have to magically appear out of the cornfield, her dolls in hand, before Dad had to come out to collect her.

She remembered the day she stayed out too long and spent the night nursing a sore backside.

Light came now. Not the flickering light of the flames but a persistent white beam, searching ahead of her, the semicircular shape dancing about her head, occasionally kissing her skin. Her dream-memory faded. Her mom and dad went into the field, their heads dipping below the tall crop as the sun set below the horizon, bathing the sky in a salmon-pink light.

They never got those kinds of skies anymore, just a monochrome vista from a black-and-white photograph. From day to day, very little changed. Like the black smoke within the room, the dark clouds encompassed the air, trapping them against the Orizaba, imprisoning them.

'We've found them,' a voice called out. Male, familiar . . .

A shadow stood in front of the white beam, briefly cutting out the light. A hand touched her. With the dream world fading, Eva felt her body and mind return to the waking realm, the land of physicality and burning lungs.

Words wouldn't come despite her lips moving, shaping to form the words. 'I'm here, alive,' she wanted to say, but all that came out was a pitiful dry rasp.

'Don't try to talk,' the voice said. The speaker put his hands on her shoulders, pulling her up off the floor. 'We're getting you out.'

Through squinting eyes she could make out the rough visage of Marcus Graves as he lifted her off the floor and into a fireman's carry. Ahead of them, beyond the door, more white beams came. The smoke here was different – lighter, pale grey. She heard splashing.

More people passed them as Marcus brought Eva out into the night. She felt the breeze on her face. Her ribs were aching now as she regained full consciousness. Each step Marcus took jarred her wound. It was good pain, she thought. *At least I'm alive. I can feel it.*

Marcus brought her down from his shoulders and seated her on the deck of the ship, her back against one of the radar towers. All around her, the flotilla citizens buzzed like worker bees. They carried buckets and wet blankets, fighting and dousing the fires.

Stanic and Brad carried Duncan out between them. They laid him next to Eva and returned inside to get the others. Marcus stayed where he was, looking at Eva. 'Are you okay, love?' he said, with more sincerity than she'd ever heard from him before. He handed her a cup of water and touched it to her lips. The cold liquid stung her chapped lips, but she was grateful for it.

She continued to sip the water, letting each drop slide down her throat, hydrating the parched lands of her body like the welcome rains in the desert, bringing with them life and vitality.

When Eva had drunk half the cup, she took a long, slow breath, exhaling the smoke and particles before coughing up blackened sputum. Wiping her mouth with the back of her sleeve, she finished the rest of the water and turned to Duncan's prone form, resting her hands on his chest. She felt it rise and fall weakly, his breath shallow.

But at least he was still alive.

'Thank you,' Eva eventually said, wincing a little at the soreness of her throat. 'We would have died in there.'

Marcus patted her on the shoulder. 'Least we could do.'

'Is Duncan going to be okay?'

As if using his name conjured some spirit within, Duncan opened his eyes and coughed. 'I'm still breathing,' he said, his voice hoarse with the smoke. He inched himself up onto his elbows and then farther up until, like Eva, he sat with his back against the radar tower. 'You?' Duncan said, looking at Graves.

'Not just me. Everyone pitched in.'

'Did everyone else make it out alive?' Eva asked, thinking of Patrice and Stimson and the others. Then she remembered . . . 'Danny? Where's Danny? And Jim?' The words fell out of her mouth in an untidy tumble.

'My dad,' Duncan added. 'Did you find him?'

Marcus turned his head towards the bow of the ship. Duncan and Eva followed his gaze. Jim was standing there, watching over them. He raised his head in greeting. Either side of him, Dietmar and Heinrich stood. Jim's arms were tied with ropes. Danny was likewise bound by his side.

'Dad?' Duncan said, not understanding what he was seeing.

Eva sat up, tried to get to her feet, but the dizziness made her slip back onto her arse. She groaned as she hit the floor, jarring her ribs again.

'What the fuck's going on?' she asked.

'There's been a bit of trouble while you lot decided to have a nap,' Marcus said. 'Faust's dead. Her groupies decided to take revenge and' – he looked to Duncan with a brief glance of sympathy – 'hold your old man responsible.'

'He didn't kill anyone,' Duncan said.

A few of the rescuers around him gave him a pitying look.

'This doesn't make sense,' Eva said. 'And why have they got Danny? Is he okay?'

'The kid's fine. Just a bit scared. I'll explain everything shortly. It's not good news.'

'Tell me now,' Duncan said, leaning over, coughing into his hand. 'What's happening?'

Marcus looked Duncan in the eyes. 'Your old man admitted it. He's going to be exiled in the morning, in exchange for the kid. I'm sorry.'

Eva couldn't believe what she was hearing, but nothing about Marcus's face told her he was lying. Jim . . . exiled. A pit of anxiety opened up inside, threatening to swallow her whole. It seemed everything was happening too fast, too chaotic.

'What's to happen with Faust's lot?' Eva asked.

'I'll send every one of them over if I get the chance,' Duncan said, his voice getting louder with every broken word. 'They could have killed us all today, and they're just standing there as if nothing happened. Why is no one doing anything about it?'

The various flotilla citizens shied away from his glare and carried on transferring buckets to various parts of the ship. Patrice and Stimson walked out of the door with the help of some of Stanic's engineering staff. Eva was surprised that Brad was there after his recent blow-up.

'It's all settled,' Marcus eventually said. 'They're leaving tomorrow, once your old man has gone. I'm sorry, Duncan.' Marcus stood and headed back towards his family, who had gathered around the door leading into the bridge. 'The other residents were just scared is all. No one knows how they'll react when faced with a life or death situation.

One by one they went inside, and Eva knew something drastic had happened to the flotilla's society today.

It would never be the same again.

CHAPTER THIRTY-SIX

Amid the rain and gales, Jim embraced Duncan for the last time. It lashed against them as they stood by the rope ladder, swaying off the port side of the *Bravo* in the wind. The morning sun had retreated behind thick cloud cover.

Below them, bobbing on the waves, was a single rowboat with the most meagre of supplies: barely a few days' water and food for a few small meals. It wasn't so much exile as a death sentence.

But then, he deserved it. Even though Susan Faust hadn't died at his hand, he had wished it, conspired for it to happen, and now it was he who had to pay the price to ensure Danny's safety. He knew his time would come eventually – everyone's would here on the flotilla – but knowing it was never adequate preparation. Just yesterday he had prepared for death – at his own hands – and so had come to terms with the situation. At the very least, he had brokered a peaceful situation, and no one else had to die for his mistakes.

Duncan's strong arms gripped around Jim's back. 'I don't want you to go,' he said, reminding Jim of when he was a small boy and Jim had to leave for weeks at a time working in the merchant navy. It wasn't easy then, and it hadn't changed in the intervening years.

'You'll be fine,' Jim said. 'I brought all this on myself. I have to do this, for all of us.'

'We'll find another way, Dad. Don't do this.'

'It's already done. Listen to me, son. I need you to be strong, okay? I need you to keep this place together. God knows Marcus isn't up to it, and with Faust's lot leaving, there's going to be a need for someone to help reorganise. You help these people survive, you hear me?'

Duncan's arms loosened as Jim stepped back to look at his son. His beard still had smoke stains at the edges, and his eyes were red and sore, but he was still standing, still breathing, and twice the man Jim had ever been.

'You'll do great,' Jim said, smiling through the tears. 'Just lay off the rum . . . trust me.'

Jim squeezed Duncan's shoulder and turned, holding back the lump in his throat as he approached the rope ladder. The wind whipped at his waterproof coat, making it flap against his legs and face. Only a few citizens had gathered on the deck to see him off, a diminished version of the usual send-off ritual.

It was a bitter irony, Jim thought. Over a dozen times, he had been there with the others, on the deck, as they waved away the volunteers, all the while knowing they were never supposed to come back. Only this time, Jim knew he wouldn't be coming back. Couldn't come back, even if he wanted to.

Eva stood behind Duncan, her hand now on his shoulder. Graves' lot were outside the bridge door, having spent the night clearing out the damage, making themselves a new base of operations. Marcus wouldn't make eye contact, probably scared people would realise that it was he, in fact, who had killed Susan Faust. How long would he be able to enjoy the comforts of the *Bravo* before the truth came out, Jim wondered.

With Eva on the flotilla, he doubted it'd take long. She was a canny one and would soon see through the lies. Earlier, Jim had told her and Duncan what he found on the sub, that the core appeared intact, and that the radiation monitor had been tampered with.

He didn't doubt Eva's sharp mind would figure out the truth, and with Stanic's help, he hoped they'd be able to use the sub's core to power the flotilla.

It would make life generally a lot easier for everyone.

They would soon forget him and what he had done.

'Are you sure you have to do this?' Duncan pleaded as Jim turned his back to the horizon, gripped the rope ladder and placed his feet on the first rung.

'I'm sure. One day you'll understand . . . I hope. And forgive me for everything I've done. Just know that everything I did came from a place of wanting to help us all. Look after Danny and Eva, won't you, son? They'll need someone on their side.'

Like old-fashioned Brits with a stiff upper lip and all that nonsense, they shook hands, gripping each other firmly. Jim nodded once and added, 'I love you, son.' With that, he released Duncan's hand and descended down the side until he located the small rowboat tethered to the line of fishing vessels.

Once inside, he picked up the oars and set off, not wanting to delay any further.

These people had a new life ahead of them, and he wanted to make sure they could do that with as little fuss as possible.

The tide took him out, sparing him the effort of rowing.

He watched as Dietmar and Monika brought Danny up to the deck. Heinrich stood at the head of the twenty-strong group. He held the pistol in hand, presumably to ensure their safety.

'Let the boy go,' Jim yelled while he could still be heard.

Heinrich looked at Jim and sneered. But they were true to their word, and they let Danny go. The boy ran across the deck into Eva's arms. She'd barely said a word all morning.

Jim didn't blame her. It was a lot to deal with, a lot to take in.

And she had her own problems with the killer still on the loose, although it wasn't lost on her that Heinrich had a pistol. Though he could hardly be mistaken for someone with an American accent. Which meant either that Frank was lying about that, purposely diverting the investigation, and had been in on it with Faust all along, or that Heinrich was indeed innocent of the murders and his having a pistol was just a coincidence. None of it mattered anymore. It wasn't his problem to worry about any longer.

He raised his hand to wave goodbye for the last time. Only Eva and Duncan returned the gesture. The oar slipped through the broken oarlock and floated away. He slumped on the wooden bench, clutching the remaining oar as rain lashed against his face. He pulled his hood up to keep dry, not wanting to be too exposed to any potential bacteria, although, he thought, that was a case of locking the stable door after the horse had bolted. He had no real supplies and nowhere to go, just enough food and water to last a couple of days.

Bacterial infection or not, his time was now out of his hands and in the lap of whatever truly ruled the world.

Despite the waves, the tide was receding and dragging him away from the flotilla. A fleet of garbage that had washed in over-night followed him. Plastic, old pieces of wreckage,and thick lumps of seaweed.

It took an hour. The *Bravo* slipped beneath the horizon. He could just make out a few of the masts, but within minutes the Pico de Orizaba had obscured them. Duncan stood on the rail until the very last, like a queen's guard doing his duty.

Jim was confident he had left behind a better man.

Duncan would be good for the flotilla's future.

He took out the torn pictures. He had pieced them back together with sticky tape. Only the thought of seeing Morag again in whatever afterlife awaited him gave him any comfort. He wasn't scared of dying; he was afraid of what he might find on the other side. He knew he hadn't been a good man and knew also how he would be judged if such a system existed.

With the rain and wind refusing to let up, Jim hunkered down in the exposed boat, crossing his arms and tucking his chin into his chest, letting his hood hang down to provide some protection from the elements. He continued to clutch the picture in his fist, waiting . . . for whatever might come.

Jim guessed he must have huddled there for at least a few hours. At one point he had dozed off, passing in and out of a light, fractured sleep.

The sun had found a gap between the clouds, warming his back now that the rain had stopped. He turned to appreciate the rare glimpse of golden light, noting it was coming to early evening, probably around five or six. It would be a further few hours to sundown yet.

In the distance, forty degrees to his left on the horizon, he saw the glint of something made from glass or metal. Shading his eyes with his hand and squinting, he could make out the upright sections of a number of masts. Other ships . . .

The science flotilla, he thought. *It must be them!* Without a chart to check, he decided to head that way, knowing that if these were his last days, he might as well find out what had happened . . . and perhaps find Angelina.

He used his single oar to propel himself towards the ships, his curiosity urging him on, giving him a new lease on life, or at least a short extension. Considering how Mike had returned, he might not want to find out what had actually happened.

Whatever was there, he had to see, at least once. He rowed harder, feeling his muscles protest. It wasn't like there was anywhere else to go, he thought; just keep rowing . . . The truth is not far away.

CHAPTER THIRTY-SEVEN

Eva gripped Danny close, ignoring the pain in her side. 'I'm so glad you're safe,' she said. 'I . . .' She trailed off, not wanting to give the poor kid a lecture. He had left to try to save them and didn't deserve any kind of reprimand. 'Are you okay?' she asked, releasing him from the hug. Danny nodded but didn't speak. Eva didn't push him, knowing how much of a traumatic experience he must have had at the hands of Dietmar and his people. Dietmar seemed like the de facto leader now that Susan was gone. She still couldn't believe it was Jim who had killed her, despite his confession.

She remembered how Jim had been with her and how he had lost control, but despite everything, she knew Jim. Knew he was a good man and wouldn't have killed Susan. There was something else behind that. She didn't discount that it could have been Dietmar. Although equally as devout as Susan, he seemed to have come to the fore since her arrest. Perhaps he could taste the power of leading the group and had decided to take it for himself.

'Are you hungry? Thirsty?' Eva asked.

'Hungry,' Danny said.

'We'll just wait a few moments for Duncan, and then we'll go fix us some breakfast, okay?'

Danny didn't speak. He just nodded once, slowly.

Duncan stood alone against the ship's edge, staring off into the horizon. Jim had long since disappeared, carried away by the tidal forces. Taking Danny with her, Eva joined Duncan.

'He'll be okay,' she said, knowing it to be a lame line. 'Somehow . . . He's like you: strong, a survivor.'

'Only person to come back was Mike, and look what a state he was in,' Duncan said.

Eva looked away, feeling the sting of grief come back after trying so hard to hide it over the last day. Things had happened so fast and the case had taken up so much of her time that she hadn't let everything really sink in. With one sentence, Duncan had managed to dig up that terrible, hollow pain.

'I'm sorry,' Duncan said, turning to face her, placing his hand on her upper arm. 'That was thoughtless of me. I didn't mean to say it so coldly. I know you both must miss him a great deal.' He addressed Danny now. The boy just stared away beyond the mountain, trying his best to hold in the tears.

'Look at us three,' Eva said, forcing a smile, 'trying not to cry. But come on, let's not dwell on things. We've got work to do, and they wouldn't want us to just mope around, would they? They'd want us to get this place back straight again.'

'We can't stay here,' Duncan said. 'The cabins were all burnt out. The bridge and ops room likewise. Dietmar and his lot did a real number on it.'

'Patrice and the others have set up in the *Alonsa*,' Eva said. 'We could always—'

'No,' Danny said, speaking up strongly. 'Please don't make us go back there.'

She didn't blame him; there would be too many reminders of his parents there, and truth be told, she didn't fancy it either. Not with the killer still aboard somewhere. She had considered it to be Dietmar, but there was a lack of strong evidence to really point in his direction.

Like most of Faust's group, he hadn't arrived on the flotilla until quite late and had had no involvement with engineering. None of them had displayed any natural talent for work or helping out Stanic and his people.

'There's one place we could go for the time being,' Eva said.

Duncan's shoulders dropped. 'You're not seriously suggesting Graves' yacht? I know you've stayed there recently, but seriously? After all this . . .' He held his arms wide, indicating the fact that Marcus and his family appeared to be taking over.

'He saved our lives,' Eva said, keeping her tone even, not wanting to get into an argument about it. 'Don't you think this is as good a time as any to call a truce, build some bridges? Dietmar and the others will be gone by the end of the day; this is a chance for you to unite the flotilla.'

Eva could already see the splinter group of ships being untethered from the flotilla. Five in total: three larger trawlers, a small catamaran and a sailing yacht. A group of residents, featuring McCoy and half a dozen others, had gathered to confront Dietmar during their loading of stockpiled resources, but with the gun in hand, the German kept the others at bay: they realised he was prepared to shoot if necessary.

Eva didn't blame the residents for stepping back and having nothing else to do with Dietmar and his group. Resources or not, with them gone, the rest of the flotilla would be in a better shape to perhaps reunite.

Marcus stepped out of the door to the bridge and approached them. Duncan tensed, his body language becoming less friendly but stopping short of outwardly hostile.

'Hey, Danny boy,' Marcus said, ruffling his hair, 'how you doing?'

'Okay,' he said.

'Good lad. Eva, Dunc . . . Listen, I'm really sorry about how things went down. I know we don't always see eye to eye, and I know I caused your old man a few headaches along the way, but I did respect him, and I have to be honest, I'll miss him. Faust's lot are fucking off this evening, and I wanted to invite you three over to mine to discuss how we can all go forward. A single group, like. None of this tribal bullshit. Let's do this properly.'

He held out his hand. 'What do you say, Dunc?'

Duncan stared down at Marcus; his thick beard and wild hair, swept about his pale, strong face, making it hard to gauge his mood.

But then that was Duncan: impossible to read.

'Come on,' Eva said after a few moments, unable to stand the tension. 'It's an olive branch.'

A few more seconds stretched out, and as Marcus was about to pull his hand back, Duncan reached out and shook it. 'Fine,' he said.

It was done.

Eva exhaled a silent breath of relief. Maybe now they could return the place to some kind of order and she could return to her case. She wouldn't be entirely at ease until she had found the killer.

'My lads have recovered a few of your things,' Marcus said to Duncan. 'And your comic books, Danny boy. I'll get them to bring them over once they've finished the clean-up. What say we head back and get some tea down us before we rebuild this place?'

Eva turned up her nose. 'Seaweed tea is the last thing I need after all this.'

Marcus gave her a sly smile and a wink. 'Let's just say I've got a little stash of the real thing.'

Eva smiled at the thought of real tea. The first since she'd been on the damned flotilla. 'Okay,' she said, 'count me in. I want to get back to the case as soon as possible anyway.'

'You three go ahead,' Duncan said, turning away. 'I need to meet with Stanic, thank him for his help and discuss something my dad asked me to look into. I'll be with you later on.'

'I'll save you a cup,' Eva said.

'Thanks.' Duncan walked to the edge and nimbly climbed down the ladder to land on the small network of fishing boats. His large frame squeezed through the makeshift passages. The other citizens quickly got out of his way, giving him nervous looks.

With Jim's confession, it would take the flotilla a while to trust Duncan. Some would pity him, while others would no doubt believe he had had a hand in Faust's murder too, given his close relationship with Jim.

He was strong enough, though, she thought. He'd shoulder his father's burden.

'Right, let's get you two sorted, shall we?' Marcus held out his arm for Eva in order to help reduce the problem with her ribs. She declined, wanting to prove she was still capable.

During the night, while recovering from the smoke inhalation, she had cleaned the wound and applied a fresh bandage made from old T-shirts. The skin was starting to heal over.

As Eva followed Marcus to his yacht, she paid attention to the pain, used it to focus her mind on the person who had done this to her, and vowed she would, one way or another, find out who it was.

─────◆─────

Eva took a seat at the table inside Marcus's yacht. Shaley and Frank were there, trying to decipher the files. Caff and Marcus stood by the narrow kitchen counter, preparing tea.

'Here, love. Get that down ya.' Caff handed Eva a cup of real tea. The steam tickled her nose, bringing with it the much-missed smell. She sipped at the hot liquid, enjoying the taste.

'Thanks,' Eva said, 'I appreciate it.' Though she had to remind herself that she was only drinking the tea because Graves' firm had stolen it from the container ship in the first place. But then property was a tricky thing to decide on the flotilla. Especially now things were breaking down.

'Things should settle down once Dietmar and the others go,' Eva said, trying to make conversation.

Marcus turned to face her, leaning against the kitchen counter and cradling his own mug of tea. 'You know,' he said, 'I think you ought to drop the case, Eva. Given that Dietmar's lot had a pistol, and given what they did to you and the others, it's probably one of those that's the killer. And they'll be gone by the end of the day.'

'Well, we can't be sure. It doesn't explain Frank's suggestion that the killer spoke with an American accent.'

'Frank could have been mistaken.'

Frank looked up. 'No. I was not mistaken. I might not be a brain doctor, but I ain't so thick I can't tell the difference.'

Marcus shrugged it off. 'Whatever, Frank, but it's not like this investigation is going anywhere, is it? I mean, without the USB drive, we ain't decoding that stuff any time soon.'

'What about Brad?' Eva asked. 'Surely his reaction back in engineering is worth keeping in mind?'

Throughout all of this, Danny sat in the corner, dozing in and out of sleep. The poor kid had had way too much trauma to deal with of late. Eva couldn't drop the case. Danny at least deserved to have some closure and justice.

Eva finished her tea and left the cabin. The dark clouds were gathering as usual, bringing with them the cold winds. She embraced the cold, wanting the chill to wake her up, jolt her into action or bring with it some epiphany.

Sometimes, back in her day job, she'd just walk through the streets in the rain, letting the natural rhythms of life drum out insights into the particular case she was stalled on. It hadn't failed then. No matter whether she got stuck or faced a brick wall, going out into the city and just tuning into life had always brought her clarity and a spark of an idea that often led to a breakthrough, or at least a new way of thinking about things.

Watching out of the porthole, she saw that to her left, facing south, Dietmar's group were finishing loading their stolen supplies onto their small fleet. A group of other residents approached the craft, gesticulated at the boxes. A Russian fellow made to step down into the craft when Dietmar raised his pistol at the man.

Two women, both wearing their masks and wet-weather jackets, pulled the Russian away. She couldn't hear what they were saying, but she guessed it was something to the tune of how it wasn't worth it. Sure, they were losing fresh water and food, but with Faust's group leaving, there'd be fewer people to feed and care for. With Stanic and his fellow engineers working on the machinery, she was sure they'd get back to some kind of normality soon.

And without Dietmar and the others poisoning the atmosphere, there was a hope the flotilla could be reunited.

'Hey, Eva, you okay?'

Eva jumped at the sudden voice. She spun round.

Annette stood in the doorway to Marcus's yacht.

'I will be, eventually,' Eva said. She got up from her seat, put on her waterproof jacket and mask and joined Annette outside where they could talk with a degree of privacy. She closed the door behind her and leaned against a jetty bollard.

'I heard what happened,' Annette said, through her mask. 'I'm sorry; that must have been awful. How are your lungs doing?'

'Every breath is a little sore, but I'm still breathing, so I can't complain too much. What's up?'

'I finished running the bacteria tests from the guys in the lab and thought you should know right away.'

Was this it? Was this the epiphany to break the case? Eva leaned forward. 'And?'

'Negative,' Annette said. 'None of them showed any signs of the infection.'

Eva slumped her shoulders. That was not what she wanted to hear at all. 'Are you really sure? There could be no mistake? I don't mean to suggest you don't know what you're doing, but is there any possibility the tests could be inaccurate?'

'I'm afraid not. I ran them twice. Both times, each sample came up negative for the infection. I'm sorry. I know this isn't the result you wanted.'

So much for the epiphany. If anything, this set them back even further.

The killer was out of reach, and nothing was helping them to get any closer. Annette's face was tight with tension.

'It's okay, Annette. I know it's not your fault. I really appreciate you turning the results around so quickly, and it has helped; at least we can eliminate those in engineering from the investigation.'

Stepping closer like a conspirator, Annette whispered, 'So who else do you think it might be?'

Given the way she was looking past her shoulder, Eva thought the girl was considering it could have been one of Graves' firm. 'I don't know yet,' Eva said, genuinely unsure who could be a suspect now. She'd have to go through her notes again and see if she could see any new patterns, any reason to suspect someone else.

'Well, if I can be of any more help, just let me know,' Annette said. 'And come by later today and I'll check on your wound.'

'Thanks, Annette. I appreciate that. Be careful over there,' she said, referring to the medical facility.

'It's okay,' Annette said as she turned to walk away. 'Stanic and Ahmed have been coming by often, making sure I'm all right.'

Eva stayed in place, leaning her weight on the bollard.

She rested her head on her hands and closed her eyes. Her ribs and lungs hurt. She was tired and hungry, and just wanted to curl into a ball and sleep for eternity. She thought back to her idea of finding Emily in the afterlife, or whatever there was in death.

That seemed increasingly appealing.

For the first time since she'd arrived, she could relate to those who had thrown themselves overboard. The burden of surviving was growing too heavy.

And the results of surviving were not necessarily outweighing the cost of doing so.

When she opened her eyes, she focused on the wooden boards of Marcus's yacht. A wet, dirty footprint caught her attention. She stepped back and noticed another print. Turning around, she saw, against the low raking sunlight, the prints heading into the cabin.

Without any shadow of a doubt, she knew these to be the prints from the fishing boat where Jean had been thrown over and, of course, from the medical facility.

The chunky grip pattern was unmistakable – she had imprinted every little detail into her mind since she first saw it.

Like a bloodhound on a trail, Eva followed the prints, which became fainter now, through the cabin door, down the steps, and . . . they led to Marcus, still standing against the counter. She looked at his feet: boots.

How had she not noticed before?

Marcus was joking with Shaley when he looked up at Eva.

His smile dropped.

CHAPTER THIRTY-EIGHT

With tired arms, Jim pulled his boat up to the second flotilla.

A ship, similar to a cruise liner, the name *Excelsior* adorning its port side, formed the centre of the group. Painted in white and navy blue, it was an elegant sight, almost out of place when compared to the general bad condition of most of the boats on what he used to call his flotilla. Ten smaller vessels lined its perimeter. He recognised them as those he had sent away. Each one brought back the images of those volunteers heading off.

It hadn't been easy for him to send any of them, despite what the others thought, but his correspondence with Angelina had given him the strength to do it. Each volunteer was to help with the cause, the search for the cure for the infection. He never knew exactly what happened to them when they arrived at her ship, but he had been assured they were treated humanely and with respect.

That had always reminded Jim of old news reports talking about how cattle were slaughtered humanely. A cold chill slithered down his neck and back as he tied off his boat and turned to face the ship.

How many dead would be on it?

If anyone were alive, would they be like Mike? Or worse?

Jim stood and for a moment considered taking one of the fishing boats and heading as far north as he could, leaving all this behind. But the need to know was too strong. Curiosity was a powerful force; it had been making people do stupid things for thousands of years, and he knew that, like them, he couldn't resist. The desire to see the truth for himself was greater than the desire to flee, to save himself.

If these were indeed his last days, he'd be damned if he wasn't going to go out with the full knowledge of what his complicity and actions had wrought.

Clambering from boat to boat, Jim approached the *Excelsior*.

A steel ladder hung down from the deck. He gripped the handrail and gave it a yank to see if it would take his weight. It seemed solid. He placed his first weary leg on the rung and lifted his weight up. With each step up, he left the relative safety of the known world behind.

He reached the top and noticed he was holding his breath. He was expecting the deck to be littered with bodies. There were none. Just the sound of the wind making the ship's mast lines whistle and hum and a ship's bell tolling ominously.

The ship was well made, expensive. It had a generous-sized bridge with large, open windows. He pressed his hands to the glass but couldn't make anything out within the gloom. The bow had a crane and winch and a platform that he knew would have once carried a number of life rafts.

He made his way down the side until he found an entrance.

Placing his hand on the handle, Jim hesitated, bracing himself for what might be on the other side. He rued not stopping on one of the fishing boats to find a knife or some other weapon, but one didn't need a weapon against the dead, so he opened the door.

He gagged. The stench of rot made him vomit, each subsequent breath reactivating his gag reflex. He had to step back outside to get some fresh air. Sweat from the sudden exertion covered his face.

Although the place was in darkness, he had caught a brief glimpse of unmoving shadows. Once he had recovered, he decided to return, this time leaving the door open to let in the sun and fresh air.

With his shirt over his mouth and nose, Jim waited for his vision to adapt. Every passing second brought more clarity, and he wished it wouldn't.

The bridge section of the ship looked as if there had been a fire. All the computer monitors, navigation screens and various control panels were charred. Beneath the sweet, putrid, rotting smell, he could detect smoke and sulphur. It couldn't have been long ago. When he approached a desk, he could still feel a degree of warmth from its melted plastic chair.

Turning away, following the sunbeam, he saw five dark lumps in the middle of the open space of the bridge. Although knowing they were at a fundamental level, the curiosity that had gripped him made him move forward, carrying him closer. He didn't want to see them, but he knew he had to.

Using a plastic arm broken off one of the chairs, he prodded the nearest lump. Meaty. Nothing moved. He pushed against it, turning the body over. The face stared back at him with a tight grimace. Jim spun away, unable to bear it. A tide of grief threatened to drown him as he considered the others there. Whatever had killed them had done so with extreme pain and terror.

Jim didn't really know why, but he felt compelled to explore further as though seeing everything would dispel the horror, even though he doubted it would. Still, he carried on, walking through the passageways, inspecting the ship's various cabins and rooms.

Most of them appeared to be laboratories with white furniture, desks and racks of equipment: glass flasks, test tubes, slides and electronic equipment that he presumed were used in testing and analysis.

Other rooms were clearly quarantine zones. Only these weren't like the temporary ones set up on the *Alonsa*; these had thick, multi-glazed plastic doors, more white furniture and proper beds for the sick to live out the remainder of their lives in some semblance of comfort and dignity. Though the first few he encountered were empty, the next nine were not.

He recognised every single one of them, each flotilla volunteer that he had sent over during the year. Each one dead.

This time, though, he knew the cause of death.

The quarantine doors were closed but unlocked. He didn't go inside, but through the clear doors he could see that each person had either been sitting on the bed or sleeping. Dark red blood, not dry and clotted, was sprayed across the wall behind their heads. The entry wounds were all in the same place: their foreheads.

They had been executed, Jim thought, though whether by the same person who had killed the bridge officers he couldn't tell.

Jim shook his head and said a silent prayer for them, and then pressed on, going down farther into the ship via a hatch and a ladder. He guessed he was in the lowest or second lowest deck, as it started to resemble the *Bravo* with its exposed ducting and pipework. The galley came next, through a steel door, and a communal mess beyond that.

It felt strange for it to be empty.

The place was as tidy as if it had never been inhabited.

A desire bubbled up inside him to shout out, to call for anyone, in that most British of ways, 'Hello there.' No words came forth, however.

He walked through the mess hall and came to a wide storage room where a number of tall fridges stood across the rear wall. In front of them was a bench that extended almost the full width of the room, around which were a dozen stools, and on those stools, slumped over the desk, were a dozen men and women in white lab coats.

Something told him these were the others he'd suspected were here.

One woman in particular sat in the middle with her back to him, her long, curly brown hair spread out on the desk.

It was her; he knew it.

She had once described herself in very brief terms, during one of their communications. Angelina . . . As though acting on their own behalf, his legs brought him closer, and his arms reached out to pull her hair back, wanting to expose her face. But as he felt her hair against the palms of his hands, he heard a rush of footsteps behind him.

Before Jim could turn, a thick arm wrapped around his neck, constricting his throat. Jim struggled, trying to throw off his attacker, but he was too quick and pulled Jim backwards until he lost balance.

Jim felt the arms tighten still further.

A mix of anger and fear filled his mind as he was dragged back out of the room. He kicked his legs, trying to get purchase on something to stop his progress, but it was useless; his attacker was too strong.

A door slammed open, bouncing against the side of the passageway. Jim's attacker dragged him into a darkened room. His vision had started to fail, the lack of oxygen bringing with it a nebula of colours and flashing lights.

With a thud, Jim landed on the floor, the back of his head bouncing off what felt like tiles, hard and cold. A shadow covered him as a light suddenly blazed. Gasping for breath, Jim looked up, squinting against the light. He couldn't make out the face of the person standing over him, but saw they were wielding a claw hammer.

CHAPTER THIRTY-NINE

E va and Marcus stared at each other like gunslingers in an old western.

'What?' Marcus said, breaking the tense silence. Frank and Shaley had turned their attention from the files to watch Eva and Marcus. 'Well?' Marcus added. 'What's the problem? Why are you looking at me like that?'

'You fucking liar,' Eva said, keeping her voice low, not wanting to wake Danny, who was now lying on the settee, his head on a cushion. She took a step closer, looking at Graves' boots again. There was no mistaking them; they were the ones that had made the footprints. 'It was you all along, wasn't it? Pulling the strings, obscuring the truth? You set Frank up for the attack on Jim! There was no American, was there?'

Frank stood up from the table to intercept her as she jabbed a finger into Marcus's chest. The fury was building inside her. How could she have trusted him? She knew what he was like, but she'd let him manipulate her all along.

Taking a step back, Marcus held out his hand to Frank, signalling him to sit back. 'Look, love, I don't know what's going on here. Where's all this coming from?'

Eva grabbed a kitchen knife lying on the counter and held it out in front of her, keeping an eye on Frank and Shaley, who sat at the table facing her. She wouldn't be able to take all three of them, and she'd have to somehow get Danny out. Caff had gone, probably into a berth or the bathroom. She swung the knife in a slow arc encompassing all three of them.

'The boots,' she finally said. 'They're the same prints I found at the two murder scenes. You can't deny that; they're right there.' She pointed to the deck and the steps where the muddy prints were clearly visible.

'You stupid bitch,' Marcus said. 'These aren't even my boots.'

'And I suppose you're telling me that you're not wearing them either? Don't take me for a fool, Graves.' She noticed Frank edging closer to the edge of his seat as though ready to pounce. Eva took a step back so that she could bolt out of the cabin if necessary.

'Listen to me,' Marcus said, inching forward and pointing to the boots. 'I traded these yesterday. I needed to do some mucky jobs this morning, and my other pair had long since worn out.'

'He's telling the truth,' Shaley said. 'I was there when he got 'em. I borrowed a pair too.' Shaley held out a foot, showing a work boot of a similar style, but slightly different.

'I haven't lied to you, Eva. On my dear old ma's body. I can even prove it if you aren't convinced.'

'How?'

'We'll take a trip to engineering right now and you can ask Stanic. I traded some tobacco for them. Who's got tobacco on the flotilla anymore? I don't smoke, so I gave him some for the work boots. We'll go there now and prove it.'

'Shut up!' Eva said, holding the knife out. She had to think. It didn't make any sense. She hadn't found any of those kinds of boots when she and Duncan had visited engineering before. It wasn't beyond possibility that they had been hidden or in some other place, but why trade them? Perhaps there were multiple pairs, and the killer just happened to have the same ones. Or perhaps Marcus was being fitted up . . .

'Okay,' Eva said, 'someone needs to stay here with Danny. The rest of you are coming with me to speak with Stanic. We're getting to the bottom of this, one way or another.'

'Frank? You and Caff do the honours?'

'Sure, we'll keep an eye on the lad.'

'And find somewhere safe for those files,' Eva said. 'I don't want to put Danny in any more danger if possible.'

'We'll go to the *Bravo* – Jim's old crew are there patching up the damage. I'll get them to keep on eye on us.'

With the plan set, Eva made sure Shaley and Marcus walked in front of her while she kept the knife. She didn't want to rule anything out right now.

As they headed for engineering, she wished she had Duncan with her.

She remembered him saying he was going to see Stanic. Hopefully he'd be there when she arrived. She wanted someone to back her up. She felt this was the critical moment. Something would shake out and give her the lead she needed.

CHAPTER FORTY

Jim sat up and snapped open his eyes, expecting the claw end of the hammer to crash into his face.

The attacker, however, had stood back out of the light. With no silhouette to disrupt Jim's view, he saw that it was a man – mid to late thirties, crazy wide eyes, unkempt beard. His body looked gaunt, wasted away, yet he was incredibly strong. Jim worried for a moment that he might have been someone who had escaped from one of the empty quarantine rooms he'd seen earlier, but unlike the others, he wasn't wearing a pale blue gown.

Jim tried to speak, ask who the man was, but his throat was still painful and he only managed to croak out a few unintelligible syllables. The claw hammer hit the floor with a sharp clang.

'You're not one of them,' the man said, kneeling down on his haunches, inspecting Jim, looking him over like a predator assessing a meal. The man touched Jim's jacket, running his fingers over the brass buttons and the embroidered badges.

Badges and medals awarded to Jim for his performance as a captain.

'You're from the other place. You shouldn't be here.'

Jim backed away from the man, whose breath reeked of bad eggs.

The man stood up and turned his back. There was a sound like he was opening a cupboard. When he returned, he held a scalpel in his left hand. The blade caught the light. Jim pictured it slicing through his skin. His heart thumped, the fear driving him to back up, get some distance between them, but he drew up short against a wall, his back pressing against it.

'No,' Jim croaked out as the man stepped closer, bringing the razor-sharp blade down to Jim's face. With his free hand, the man pushed Jim's head against the cold, tiled wall.

'Stay still,' he said.

Before Jim could react, the blade had struck, cutting him across the cheek. The sharp pain burned for a few seconds. The man rubbed something against the wound. Within seconds the cut felt like nothing more than the merest of scratches. The man held a piece of cotton wool to Jim's cheek. 'Hold it,' he said. 'It'll stop bleeding shortly.'

With that, he stepped back and placed a swab into a plastic container of clear liquid. He held it up to the light, flicking the bottom of the tube with his free hand. The liquid turned a dark purple colour, and the man turned to face Jim with a smile on his face.

'Lucky for you,' the man said. 'You're not one of them.'

Jim didn't know if that was a good or bad thing and just stayed sitting against the wall waiting for his pulse to slow, for rational thought to take over.

'Call me Tom.' The man held out his right hand.

For a moment, Jim said nothing and just stayed where he was, his arms by his sides. Was this some kind of cruel joke, a madman's game? Tom thrust his hand closer. 'I'm sorry,' he said. 'Please, let me help you up. You'll have questions.'

Reluctantly, but knowing he hadn't much choice, Jim reached out and took the man's hand. He briefly considered trying to overpower him, to reach for the hammer that lay on the floor by the small white cupboard, but given Tom's strength, Jim didn't rate his chances.

With a swift tug, Tom lifted Jim onto his unsteady feet. Jim felt sick, dizzy. Tom steadied him, gripping his shoulder. 'Here,' Tom said, directing him to the side of the room. 'Take a seat; get your breath back. How's the neck?'

'Fucking painful,' Jim said, speaking the truth as he massaged his windpipe.

'I'm sorry about that. I didn't know who you were . . . or what you wanted. What are you doing here?'

'Isn't it me that should be asking the questions?' Jim said, managing to speak through the soreness. 'Who the fuck are you, and what happened here? What were you testing me for?'

'The infection,' Tom said, bringing a stool from across the room to sit opposite Jim. 'It's mutated, taking the others.' He shook his head, exhaling a long, soulful sigh. 'It was human error. It's always human error.'

'Let's go back,' Jim said, closing his eyes for a moment. 'What exactly happened here? Where's Angelina?'

Tom's eyes were wide, staring, as though looking back to the past. 'It ended so quickly. One day I was taking the vaccine, recovering. The next, the outbreak happened, and within an hour everyone died.'

'Wait, there's an outbreak? Shouldn't we leave this place right now?'

Tom shook his head. 'I've got the vaccine. No one else to spread it. I've contained the fungi samples.'

'You're confusing me,' Jim said, rubbing his face, trying to make sense of things. 'Tell me from the start how this happened.'

Tom fidgeted on his stool and took a moment as though he were organising the events in his memory. He leaned in and made eye contact. 'Angelina and her researchers found a cure for the infection a few days ago. They had tested it on one of the flotilla volunteers, but needed to confirm it. The others had developed too far.'

'That's why I sent Mike,' Jim added.

'And you communicated with Angelina?'

'Yes, I was the one in contact with her for the last few years. She asked for another volunteer after I had sent Mike, but he came back . . . Something had happened to him. It was then that I couldn't get in touch with anyone.'

'It was the mutation,' Tom said, his voice grave. 'Mike was patient zero. The vaccine was created with a combination of fungal spores and antibacterials. Once in the system, it would compete with the infection, killing it.'

'And this fungal spore is what killed everyone?'

'No, no, it's what kept us alive. There's no harm to humans from the fungal spores. Once it destroys the infection, it stays in the body, inert, like many of the bacteria we carry around inside us.'

Jim stood up and stretched his legs, wanting to burn off some of the nervous anxiety. 'So how did this mutation happen? I don't understand.'

'I don't have all the answers,' Tom said. 'But when Mike arrived, Angelina injected him with the vaccine. Within hours he went crazy, killing two of the researchers. There was something within Mike that didn't react well to the infection and the vaccine. It spread so fast . . . It should have been contained, but one of the researchers . . .'

'What did they do?'

'It's so stupid. Something so small. They dropped a vial of blood from Mike after his reaction. The mutated spores became airborne.

I watched it all happen in less than an hour. Those who weren't cata-tonic were killed by the other scientists and workers who reacted badly – it was terrible. People I had come to know turned into indiscriminate killers.'

'How did Mike get off the ship? He came back to the flotilla. And why hasn't it spread from him?'

'It has a really short half-life. By the next morning, I saw one of the infected researchers recover from the mutation. As for Mike . . . well, something within him that started the mutation must have been the difference. It's hard to tell without doing more research.'

'Where is this other researcher now? Can I speak with them?'

Tom looked away then, his face growing pale. 'He couldn't cope with what had happened. He . . . drowned himself. I'm the only one left.'

'Why you?' Jim asked. 'Sorry, I didn't mean that to sound that way. I just mean, how come you survived? Who are you?'

Tom stood up from the stool and moved over to stand right in front of Jim. Looking right into his eyes, Tom said, 'You really don't know? You don't recognise me?'

Jim racked his brain, analysing Tom's face. Nothing came to him. 'I'm sorry,' Jim said. 'I don't.'

Tom's face twisted with pain. 'I'm not entirely surprised. I was the first, after all. It was a long time ago.'

'The first?'

'The first volunteer that you sent from the flotilla. Have I really changed that much since you sent me away?'

Jim rocked back on his heels before slumping back down onto the chair. He dropped his head into his hands before looking back up at Tom. He still didn't recognise him, but he didn't suspect Tom had any reason to lie. The first volunteer had, indeed, been a man.

'I'm so sorry,' Jim said, unable to say any more.

Tom shrugged it off. 'I'm still alive, probably wouldn't be if you hadn't sent me away. I volunteered anyway. I wanted to go. I just didn't expect I'd be coming here.'

'Did they . . . treat you and the others well?'

'Yeah. At times I felt like a lab monkey, being jabbed with various vaccines and monitored, but I felt like I was helping. Angelina especially was kind. She was the one to make the breakthrough, to discover the fungal response to the infection. I'm going to miss her and her team.'

'Me too,' Jim said, 'and I didn't even get a chance to meet her.'

'You want to see her now?'

The first reaction was to say yes. But did he really? Did he really want his first proper introduction to the woman he had grown so fond of to be with her corpse? It seemed crazy, but that rogue curiosity took over again and made Jim nod his head. 'Yes, I would.'

Tom led Jim out of the small medical room and into the passageway. While they headed for the rear of the ship, to the room where the various specialists were slumped over the tables, Tom explained how he had survived by hiding in the ducting of the ship, and how when the fire broke out he had managed to put it out, but not until it was too late.

'When the calm descended and the shooter – one of the infected researchers – had finally succumbed to the infection, I came out and saw the damage. I couldn't believe it. It was then I met one of the other researchers, called Claudia, but she went over the side before I could help her. I tried . . . I . . .'

'When was all this?' Jim asked.

Tom's explanation coincided with the lack of responses to Jim's messages. So this whole mess had happened over a couple of days. It shocked Jim to think that while he and the others were struggling on their flotilla, Angelina and her crew were having the same struggles. It had a dread kind of symmetry to it that he didn't appreciate one bit.

'It got ugly real fast,' Tom said. 'As soon as the infection spread, it was just a few hours before everyone was at each other's throats. Mike got away later that day, after one of the researchers went crazy and let everyone out of their rooms.'

'You too?'

'Yeah, but I didn't hang around. I managed to escape into the ducting above my room and stayed there while the craziness went on. When I no longer heard any more shooting or voices, I waited a while longer – that's when the fire broke out. I'm not sure what happened, but I couldn't stop it. It had spread too far.'

'It's okay,' Jim said. 'You don't need to justify anything. It sounds like an impossible situation.'

Tom opened the door to the room from where he had first dragged Jim. 'This was the conference room,' Tom added. 'It's also where they stored the fungal samples and vaccines. There's a batch still in the fridges.' One of the fridges was open, empty, spilling cold air into the room.

Jim went over to the body of the woman whom he had approached before. 'Is this her?' he asked, his voice trembling.

'It is.'

So Jim's intuition had been correct. He wished it wasn't. He wished he had been completely mistaken and that somehow, somewhere, she was still alive. For the next ten minutes, Tom told Jim what she had been like and 'introduced' him to her colleagues around the table.

Tom moved to the side of the room and, from a filing cabinet, took a number of manila folders. He handed them to Jim. 'Here's all of their research. Everything charted back to before the drowning. They knew about this infection four months before the Earth's crusts burst open. They think the bacteria came from the Antarctic ice shelf. As the ice melted, it released it into the seas. Argentina was the first country to discover it. It quickly spread after that in the water system.'

'Why didn't we know about this?' Jim asked.

'Governments covered it up. They had too much else to worry about, with infrastructure being overwhelmed and low-lying countries flooding. But Angelina's team was set up to research it. They just didn't realise they wouldn't have the time.'

'We need to deal with the bodies and leave,' Jim said, slipping back into his leadership role. It was the only thing he could do now. He had to honour the dead here and then get back to the flotilla, taking the vaccine with him. He didn't care about Dietmar's threats now. He'd deal with him when he got back. The most important thing was making sure Angelina's discoveries were used.

'We can send the bodies off on one of the smaller boats,' Tom said.

'Aye. How much of the vaccine is there?'

Tom opened one of the fridges. There were at least two hundred stoppered vials in racks. 'We can make more,' Tom said. 'The formula is all in those files. We just need to take the fungal samples. They're slow growing, but we should be able to harvest enough in time.'

'What about the mutation?'

'That's what this is for.' Tom held up the tube of dark purple liquid. 'Before the mutation spread, Angelina's team developed a test to determine if patients would react to the vaccine.'

'And what if they test positive? Then what?'

'Nothing we can do for them. They'll have to be quarantined until they no longer pose a threat. We can't afford the mutation to spread. What happened when he went back?'

'We quarantined him as soon as he arrived. He was already catatonic by then. But . . . he didn't make it.'

'The infection killed him?'

'Not quite.'

Jim filled Tom in on the details of the killer and the murders on the flotilla as they moved the bodies from the *Excelsior* into a sacrificial boat. It took a couple of hours, but eventually all twenty-three bodies were laid out, covered in sheets and tarps, on the deck of a boat called the *Jezebel*.

The sun had nearly set when they roped off the wheel and throttle of the craft. Standing on the deck of the *Excelsior*, they stood in silence as Jim pulled the rope that activated the throttle. He dropped the rope and they watched the boat head out to the horizon.

Tom muttered a prayer.

When the boat's meagre stock of diesel had run out, it drifted on the tide until it disappeared over the horizon. Jim wiped a tear from his face. The wind was whipping up, bringing with it a cold snap. Rain started to patter softly against the sea's surface.

Once back inside the bridge, now devoid of bodies, Tom fussed with a control panel. He pulled out a wiring loom and fiddled with the wiring. A spark came from a nearby panel, and a couple of the overhead lights flickered on, bathing the bridge in a cold, white light.

'The ship still has its own power?' Jim asked.

'The supplies you sent with the volunteers were stockpiled. The ship has hydro and solar. They rationed it throughout the day to make sure the inverters were always topped up.'

'Is there enough fuel to get back to the flotilla?'

'This vessel hasn't moved in two years, so there should still be adequate diesel supplies. But, before we do go back, there's something I should probably tell you. I've not been entirely honest with you, when I was on the flotilla and here today. And I suspect there's one other person on the flotilla who has also been lying to you.'

Jim found an unmelted chair to sit on. 'Okay,' Jim said. 'Tell me. What is it?' He disguised the nervousness in his voice and waited for Tom to start.

'When you first brought the sub into the flotilla, you found all the crew dead.'

'That's right . . .'

'You missed one.'

Jim stood up then. 'That's impossible! I checked every body and every square foot of the sub.'

'I know,' Tom said. 'I watched you. My name is Thomas Martinez, and I was the first mate of the sub. I made it out alive. I hid.'

'What? That makes no sense. Why would you hide? And how did you get on the flotilla? Why are you telling me this?'

Tom placed the panel back into place and started to press a number of buttons and flick a series of switches. The ship rumbled as the engines started up. 'I didn't know who you were,' Tom said, his back to Jim as he manipulated the ship's controls without the help of a working monitor. 'The captain had killed the entire crew, except me. I hid beneath the bodies of my two cabin mates. When you arrived and began to investigate, I stayed out of the way. I swam out of the torpedo tube and joined the flotilla later that night and pretended I'd drifted in on a wreck.'

'That can be done when a sub is underwater? Through the torpedo tube?'

'Sure, and you can return inside if the tube is flooded and the breach is open.'

'I don't understand the need for the subterfuge.'

'I knew too much.' Tom turned to face Jim. 'I had discovered the encrypted files. Orders from the government. When I volunteered, I thought I'd get away, but I ended up here . . .'

Jim instantly knew what he meant by the encrypted files. He thought of Eva and her case, and how it was all tied together. 'These files,' Jim said. 'The decryption key is held on a USB drive, isn't it?'

Tom lowered his head. 'I'm assuming they've been discovered, then?'

'We believe it's what the killer is looking for and why Mike was targeted. It was why he volunteered. He came to me, said he wanted to leave as it was too dangerous for him to stay. This is all connected, isn't it? What's in those files? And more importantly, who's killing people in order to recover them?'

When Tom told him and described the person, Jim knew immediately.

'We need to go. Now,' Jim said.

CHAPTER FORTY-ONE

Eva, Marcus and Shaley entered the corridor leading to the engineering section. Black fabric blinds covered the windows. Eva got that bad feeling again as they approached the door.

'Open it,' she ordered Marcus.

He reached for the handle, but it wouldn't open. 'Locked,' he said. 'They must have finished up for the night. Or maybe doing repairs.'

'Knock,' Eva said.

Marcus dropped his shoulders and sighed. 'Fine.' He rapped twice against the window of the door. Waited. Rapped twice more. He turned to face her. 'See? No one's in. We'll have to come back.'

Shaley pressed his face against the window, trying to see inside.

A sudden eruption made Eva jump. She dropped the knife to the floor, just missing her foot. Marcus spun round. Shaley collapsed against the door, his face catching on broken glass as he slid down, the back of his head blown out.

'Shit,' Marcus said. 'Duck.'

It was too late for him. Another gunshot fired through the black fabric and one of the windows, catching him in the shoulder, spinning him round as he collapsed to the floor, grimacing in a silent scream.

Eva ducked and spun round as she rolled to the side, her instincts kicking in at the sound of the gun. The door swung inwards. Stanic stepped over Shaley's body, holding a pistol with both hands. He aimed at Eva's head as she looked up into his face.

'Do as I say and you might just live. Get in here. Now,' he said.

His arms were dead still, his face a picture of calm, but those eyes . . . They were the eyes of the unhinged. Eva thought about going for her knife, but she'd never be quick enough. Stanic had already proved to be a good shot. She clenched her teeth, furious that she hadn't seen it sooner. Stanic – one of the backbones of the flotilla. It didn't make sense. Why put in all the effort he had only to split it apart?

'Why?' she asked aloud, unable to understand.

'Get inside. I won't ask you again.'

Stanic stepped out farther into the corridor, clearing the way. He waved her into the workshop. She looked at Shaley and Marcus. The latter was breathing but still. She had to step over Shaley's body. Despite her feelings about him, it wasn't a good way to go. At least it had been quick. 'Grab his arms. Drag him inside.'

'Do I look like Wonder Woman? It's not like I'm in good shape. Remember how you knifed me, tried to leave me for dead?'

'That was admittedly a mistake. Don't expect me to make another. Drag him in or die where you stand.'

She didn't fancy testing his patience. Gritting her teeth, Eva pulled Shaley into the room. Her ribs screamed with the effort. As the body slid, Stanic lifted his legs and pushed him all the way inside.

Once inside, Eva dropped the body and used the opportunity to look for a weapon. When she turned her head to search the workshop, she saw that the place had been cleaned. There was nothing on the worktables; the tool racks were empty. It seemed as if Stanic had prepared the room.

She heard a muffled noise coming from the back of the room, behind one of the huge generators. She saw Duncan tied to the steel legs of a workbench, a gag in his mouth, his wrists and ankles bound. Blood dripped from a cut above his eye.

'Duncan!' Eva readied to go towards him, but before she could move her feet, Stanic slammed the butt of the gun against her temple, knocking her to the ground. Her vision blurred. A burning pain spread through her head. She tried to crawl away. Stanic grabbed her hair and pulled her head up, stretching her neck backwards, cutting off her scream.

He kicked her in the ribs, making her yelp and curl into a ball. He pressed her face to the ground as he wrapped something around her ankles. A plastic tie came next, binding her wrists behind her back. Then came a gag. The piece of fabric cut into the corners of her mouth.

'You had to make it difficult, didn't you?' Stanic said. 'If you'd just kept your nose out of things, none of this would have had to happen. No one else would have needed to be hurt.'

Eva shook with rage. She tried to pull her wrists free but knew it was futile. He'd used the same kind of ties she had once used in the line of duty.

With no tools or sharp surfaces anywhere, she knew she'd be stuck there until someone arrived. How long would it take before Frank realised something was up and brought help? Probably too long. She knew she had to remain calm, wait for an opportunity and be ready to take it if it came.

She heard a moan from farther back in the workshop. Not Duncan this time – Marcus. Stanic had brought him in. The sound of the 'zip' from the plastic tie told her he was facing a similar fate.

———◆———

Stanic had bound her to the leg of the workbench opposite the one where Duncan was tied. With her hands behind her back, she felt around the floor with her fingertips, trying to find anything useful, any piece of metal she could attempt to use to free her from the plastic tie. There was a trick to opening the clasp within the catch. But she found nothing beyond the rusted bolts that kept the workbench firmly in place.

Her head rested against the cool steel of the leg. She breathed slowly, keeping her pulse under control. Now was not the time to panic. Although she hadn't specifically trained to deal with interrogations, she had read up on the subject a great deal on her own time. That was when she'd thought she'd join the CIA: she'd felt it to be a good idea to swot up on the job in order to impress any potential employer.

That opportunity never came, though. She had ended up in narcotics instead. Ironically, although she'd thought at the time it was the end of her life as she'd known it, it had actually saved her life: if she hadn't been on that ship during the bust, she doubted she would have survived.

Right now, though, bound and gagged, she had to wonder if that was a good thing after all.

A metal cart trundled down the length of the workshop, its wheels rattling and wobbling against the floor. It stopped a few feet to her right. Her vision was still blurry from Stanic's attack. Her head felt like an overripe melon, as though her brain was pushing against the inside of her skull.

Stanic stood in front of her and lifted her chin with a piece of cold metal. She jerked away, fearing he would strike her again. He held a large wrench in his right hand. He knelt, the wrench resting across his thighs.

'You've left me no real option, Eva,' he said, shaking his head as if he was disapproving of the behaviour of an infant. 'I liked you. More than most, in fact. I regret that it's had to come to this, but if only you had left well enough alone, if you had taken your flesh wound as a warning and dropped the case, we wouldn't have had to do this.'

She tried to speak, but the gag stopped her.

'No, no, no. There's no need now,' Stanic said. 'You just be quiet while I tell you a little story. After I'm done, you'll have the chance to speak. Your response, however, will determine both your fate and Duncan's.'

Stanic stood up and placed the wrench on the top of the cart. When he pulled his hand back, he held a pair of long-nosed pliers. 'One day,' he began, 'a submarine captain was ordered to deliver a president to a secure underground facility. On this day, the world was drowning. The president was on a foreign visit and got stranded.'

As he spoke, he paced back and forth like a college lecturer.

'It was this submarine captain's duty to make sure the president was delivered safely, and in that, the captain did a fine job. Do you know how the captain was rewarded? No? He was rewarded with a death sentence. He was left to drift on the seas with a crippled vessel and a set of final orders. There was no sanctuary for him as promised.'

Stanic's face contorted. He continued to pace back and forth, gesticulating with the pliers to punctuate his sentences. 'There could be no survivors, they said. None. I had learned too much.

In exchange for my life, I had to take those of my crew. Now don't think I found that decision easy. It took me months to come to terms with it, but I eventually realised they were right. No one could know. It was too risky . . . The infection couldn't be allowed to get to them. We were pawns.'

Despite his clear tone of voice, his wide-eyed stare as he ranted told her that he had likely gone insane over the years with that kind of truth lurking in the back of his mind. It wasn't a massive shock that he could have survived this long pretending to be the Stanic everyone knew and loved: sociopaths could be completely fine and fully functioning on the outside, and entirely mad inside.

That he had multiple identities made her think she could perhaps reason with one of them. She had some training on how to deal with these types and so she remained quiet for now, not wanting to talk into him a further rage. She hoped he would calm a little to the point where she could start a dialogue – reach the more rational side of him.

He knelt down in front of Eva, the pliers close to her face. 'I thought we could start again. I thought we could make a go of things here, but you had to stick your nose in, didn't you? You and Mike had to bring it out of the shadows when I had already sacrificed so much to keep it hidden. To give us all a chance.'

He stood and turned away, pointing to Duncan and Marcus. 'How many more of you know about the files? Think on that very carefully. I'll offer you the same deal I was offered: you tell me who else is involved and you'll live. Spare your own life by condemning theirs.'

Eva shook her head. She tried to somehow shift the workbench, find a way free, but it wouldn't budge. Stanic leant over her again, the pliers in his right hand. He loosened the gag, dragging it down her chin.

She briefly considered screaming to get attention, but forced herself to remain calm and tried to get a dialogue going, buy some time. 'What's so important about the files anyway?' she said, trying to keep the tremble in her voice under control, show him she wasn't scared.

'No. You answer my questions. Who else knows?'

He jabbed the pliers into her ribs as spittle foamed around his mouth and Eva knew then that he was too far gone. He actually smiled as she screamed with pain.

'Go fuck yourself,' Eva said. 'You're insane. To think we trusted you all this time. How could you live a lie for this long, huh? How could you murder your friends, the sub's crew?'

'Because I fucking care!' Stanic shouted in her face.

She felt his hot breath blast her skin.

'I always cared – that's why I had to do what I did. You'll never understand the pressure. If I couldn't go back, then no one could. The time was over, you understand? We were cast off, exiled, left for dead. This is all we have. This is our entire world right here. I couldn't stand by and watch it split apart. I couldn't watch these people return to *them*, only to be refused and eliminated.'

The veins in his temple throbbed as he continued to work himself into a frenzy. He stepped away, faced Duncan, then Marcus, and shook his head before returning to Eva.

'They were my friends. Even Ade, Mike and Jean. But like all of us, they were just pawns. I had to do it. Mike had let the genie out of the bottle, and there was only one way of stopping it. Stopping everyone from learning about . . . them.'

'Who? What are you talking about?'

'You don't get the answers. You don't have the luxury of asking questions here. The files, Eva. Tell me who else knows. Your life or theirs? I'll find out eventually. I already know Frank and Caff know. I saw you all poring over the files, trying to understand the words. But you'll never decrypt them, not without the USB drive.'

Eva thought of Danny. He was with them. She couldn't let him get embroiled in this.

'I don't understand,' she said. 'Why all of this for some files? There must have been another way.'

Stanic thrust the pliers into her ribs again, driving the hard metal tips into the wound, splitting the stitches apart, making her gasp for air. The pain gripped her, and she clenched her jaw so hard she thought her teeth would break. Tears streamed from her eyes. Her back arched in an attempt to lean away, relieve the pain, but he kept up the pressure, kept driving and twisting until she cried out for him to stop.

'Don't make me do this,' Stanic said, withdrawing the pliers. 'Tell me everything.'

Eva sobbed with the agony and thrashed her legs against the floor, bucking back and forth, knocking her head against the workbench leg, but it held firm. Should she tell him a lie just to get him to stop? But what could she say that wouldn't eventually lead him to Frank and Danny?

She remembered her oath to Jean. She couldn't give in . . . If he was going to kill her, then she knew she would take the truth of the files with her.

Stanic waited in silence for a minute. The tips of the pliers dripped with blood, and she felt the warm, wet sensation of blood oozing from her wound. When she looked up at him, she saw the beginnings of a fresh smile on his face and knew then, without any shadow of a doubt, that he was completely crazy. It went beyond whatever conspiracy he was embroiled in: he enjoyed this at some unnatural level.

She needed to break him out of his current thought pattern. Reason wouldn't work so she decided to push him, to see if she could break his cycle of calm and chaos. Get him to make a mistake.

'You're screwed in the head,' she said, spitting in his face, trying to get more of a reaction from him, push him over the edge. 'You failed once before, and you're failing again! Why can't you control anything, eh? Are the voices in your head telling you to kill me now? Is that it? You won't get the truth then, will you? You can keep on killing, but it won't get you any closer. It won't erase what you've done – what you've been made to do.'

At first, she didn't think he would bite, but his neck and cheeks reddened and the whites of his knuckles showed as he gripped the pliers even tighter. He crouched down to her, but as he did so, Eva saw a shadow move behind him, something by the door. She refocused on his face, not wanting to give away what she had seen. Stanic just stared at her. The pain in her ribs subsided enough for her to catch her breath and get herself under control.

'I enjoyed what I did to Jean,' he said now, his voice low and throaty. 'And some nights, when I think about what I did to my crew on the sub, I enjoy it too. But you . . . You're the one I'm going to enjoy the most. I'm going to take my time with you. Eventually, when I'm done, you'll be telling me everything I want to know and more. You're going to beg!'

'Okay, okay,' she said, stalling for time. 'I'll answer your questions. I'll tell you everything, but you have to meet me halfway. Before you kill the others, and me, I want to know more. I want to know what's in the files. Who was it that made you do these terrible things? I can see how hard it must have been for you—'

Her right cheek erupted with a sharp pain as her head was thrust to the side by the force of a blow that made her skin burn. She closed her eyes and waited for the bloom of agony to pass.

'No,' he said, quietly and simply. 'We've covered this already.' While Stanic looked over at Duncan, she caught a glimpse over his shoulder of someone approaching the door. Someone poked their head through the blown-out window. Jim! Her heart leapt, and it was all she could do not to shout out to him.

Her eyes grew wide as she made eye contact. How could he be here? Jim must have seen Duncan because his face twisted and twitched. Then he saw Stanic and placed his finger over his lips to indicate for her to be quiet – as if she was going to give him away!

'I'm sorry,' Eva said, getting Stanic's attention. 'You're right. I just wanted to try to understand. You've been with us so long. You've been such a solid foundation of this community. I can't imagine why these people, whoever they are, would want you to do these things.'

Another slap rocked her head violently to the side once more. She tasted blood in her mouth and spat it out on the floor. She turned her face back to him. Stanic's nostrils flared and his lips curled at the edges. He grabbed her chin with his left hand and squeezed, forcing her mouth open. With his other hand, he gripped her tongue between the pliers, applying enough pressure to make her choke and thrash. His hands were too strong; he continued to pull on her tongue, squeezing the pliers closed.

Eva clenched her eyes shut in response to the pain, fully expecting Stanic to pull her tongue right out of her body. She could feel it stretching all the way down, tensing against the ligaments and muscle fibres that held it in place.

She heard a loud crash and then Jim screaming, bellowing like a wounded beast.

The pliers were no longer crunching down on her tongue.

When she opened her eyes, she saw Jim beating Stanic's head into the floor with the large wrench.

The cart had collapsed, spilling out tools and the fragments of the USB drive. A large, heavy-looking gear had fallen onto the drive, smashing the flimsy plastic case.

Holding the wrench with both hands, Jim raised it above his head and brought it back down with a sickening thud, cracking Stanic's skull.

A dozen more times, Jim struck down. Eva had to look away from the mess. Blood spattered over her with each blow.

'Stop,' she managed to eventually say, finding it difficult to speak with a swollen tongue. Everything hurt, and she turned away, not wanting to see the mess that Jim had made of his former friend. She had seen many terrible things, but this was the worst of all. 'Stop,' she whispered again. She leaned over and closed her eyes, breathing through her nose, and waited for Jim to release her.

She could hear him sobbing over Stanic's body.

They had been solid friends for years; she didn't blame him.

But he had done what he'd had to do.

'Dad?' Duncan said. He sounded groggy, as though he had just awakened from an aeons-long sleep. 'Is that you?'

'You're safe now, son,' Jim said between heavy breaths. 'We're all safe now.'

CHAPTER FORTY-TWO

Eva nursed a headache. She sipped the steaming mug of tea and swallowed three codeine pills. They were officially out of date, but she no longer cared. Her body needed something, anything to dull the aches and pains. She looked out of the *Bravo*'s bridge windows and watched with satisfaction as the horizon remained empty, with no signs of Dietmar's vessel. It appeared that they had gone for good.

Once the truth had got out about Stanic and what Jim had done, he had been quickly accepted back into the fold and reinstated as captain. Tom, having created a distraction for Jim to get onto the *Alonsa*, had recovered the broken USB drive and taken it with him back to the *Excelsior* to try to recover the data.

No one would miss the fanatics now. And with Marcus agreeing not to take over as leader, although still claiming the *Bravo* for his own, the flotilla once more felt united – to a degree. It would take a while to restore peace and get the other residents back on side after all the tragedy, but now Jim had returned with the vaccine that would help revive their faith in him. They didn't have the full story or fully understand Stanic's actions, but, like Eva, they were just glad it was all over. She winced as she spun on her chair to face the others sitting around the bridge. They had set up a temporary medical bay there, since no one wanted to stay at the *Alonsa*, given what had gone on. Shaley's body had been sent off to sea, like the others, earlier that morning with Frank, Caff, Tyson and Marcus himself in attendance.

At the moment, Annette was checking on Marcus. A bandage and dressing covered his shoulder. Despite his grumbling, he was okay. Luckily, he hadn't lost a lot of blood, and his unconsciousness had been brought about by shock more than by any lasting wound.

'You'll be fine if you keep it clean,' Annette said when she had finished with him.

'I'm sorry,' Eva said, catching his eye.

Marcus gave her a nod of gratitude.

Duncan came in with Danny by his side. The boy rushed to Eva and hugged her. She grunted with the impact but didn't mind. 'I'm glad you're safe,' Danny said.

'Me too, Dan,' Eva replied. 'Couldn't let you down, now, could I?'

Eva looked up at Duncan. 'How you feeling this morning, Dunc?'

'Like hammered shit, but I'll live. It could have been a lot worse. You?'

'Just a bit banged up. Jim still with Tom?'

Duncan thumbed towards the *Excelsior*, which was now tied up next to the *Bravo*. 'Yeah, he's going over some stuff. Hopefully he'll have some positive news. I for one would love to know what was on those files that drove Stanic to do what he did. Oh, here they come now.'

Eva saw Jim pat Tom on the shoulder as the two men walked across the makeshift bridge between the two ships. A minute later, amid fevered conversation, they joined everyone else in the bridge.

The crew had done a decent job of cleaning it up after the fire, although smoke stains still covered parts of the grey walls.

Marcus stood with the help of Annette. He approached Jim and held out his hand. 'I just want to say thanks for what you did, and, well, sorry about . . . everything.'

Jim shook his hand. 'Likewise, Marcus. I'm sorry about Shaley. I know we didn't get on, but still, you've got my condolences.'

'So?' Marcus said, looking at Tom. 'Long time no see. Do you have the key to this mystery?'

'There's good and bad news on that front,' Tom said, addressing everyone as they looked to him for information. 'The good news is I managed to recover some of the data. The bad news is I can't decrypt the documents fully.'

'Show Eva the files,' Jim said with excitement in his voice. Tom took a set of papers from inside his jacket and placed them on a console in front of Eva. Duncan and the others, including Marcus, gathered around as Eva read the first piece of paper.

It only contained five short paragraphs.

After she'd read them, she turned to face Jim and Tom.

'Is this legit?'

'Yes. Thomas was Stanic's first mate,' Jim said.

Tom continued. 'You see, I didn't know he'd survived. I was hiding for my life when Jim and the others brought the sub in. After I came aboard, bringing the files and various other items with me – I didn't know what they were at the time; I just recognised the seal on top – I decided to leave, not knowing Benedict had infiltrated the community.'

'Benedict?' Eva asked.

'That's Stanic's real name,' Tom said. 'Stanic is his mother's maiden name. His full title was Captain Benedict Montgomery. He was one of the best sub captains of the navy. It's how we got the mission to get the president.'

'He was going on about that,' Eva said. 'I didn't understand. He kept talking about a "them" and how they had used him as a pawn. But now . . . after reading this, it makes sense.'

The unencrypted text was partial orders from an executive committee. Montgomery had been ordered to slaughter his crew in return for safe passage to an underground facility.

'"They" are a group of world leaders,' Tom said. 'And on that second page are the coordinates for their facility. That is what Benedict was killing for.'

Eva rubbed her face, still feeling the bruise from Benedict's attack. 'That makes sense now,' she said, looking at the numbers on the sheet of paper. 'He kept saying how if he couldn't go there, no one could. He wanted to keep us independent and said this would split us apart.'

Jim looked out the window. 'He was probably right, a few days ago. But the flotilla is different now. With no Faust and her group, and with a united citizenship . . .'

Marcus turned to Jim. 'Are you suggesting what I think you are?'

'I don't know. What are you thinking?'

'You want to pay this committee a visit?'

Jim looked at each person, his eyebrow raised in an unspoken question. Eva fidgeted on her chair, looked again at the papers, read the kill orders. She hated the fact that a small part of her empathised with Benedict. A celebrated and capable captain who was dedicated to his country and his job had been put in a difficult situation; they knew he would find it impossible to break his commitment. They had manipulated him, and all those crewmen and flotilla citizens had become victims of a broken man.

'I want to go,' Eva said, voicing what she could tell the others were thinking. 'Whoever they are, and whatever the reasons, I want to hold them accountable. Hiding in their safe facility while the rest of us cling to life. I say we go.'

'Aye, I'm with Eva,' Duncan said. 'I'm sick of this place.'

'Count me in,' Marcus said. 'I'm always up for expanding one's possibilities.'

Annette and Danny also agreed.

'We taking the *Excelsior*?' Eva said.

'No, not enough fuel, unfortunately,' Thomas said. 'It's too far a journey. But there's a way we can do it. We won't be able to take everyone, though, so Benedict was right in that this would split the flotilla.'

'The sub?' Jim said.

'If what you said about the tampered-with meter was right, it seems Benedict had set it up such that we would stay here, in his vision of his own world. If the core isn't compromised, then I can get it up and running.'

'When do we leave?' Eva said.

'We'll need some time for Annette to identify any potential new patients before we hand out the vaccine,' Jim said.

'And I'll need to train some people in how to crew a submarine,' Tom said.

Annette added, 'I can do the tests in a few days, as Angelina and her team had developed an early detection solution. It'll take a few more days to run the regular infection identification tests, so I'd be ready within a few weeks.'

'That would be perfect,' Tom said. 'I only need five good men and women.'

'You'll have me,' Duncan said. 'I'm sure we could find other suitable people from the crew.'

For the next hour, the group planned their departure below deck in the ops room. Duncan came up with another pot of tea. They were finishing up the last of Marcus's personal supply. Eva had been reading comics with Danny, admiring how resolute he was. She could never truly know what effect all this trauma would have on him, but he seemed to be handling it well.

Duncan ruffled Danny's hair as he placed two mugs on the console.

'Eva, I just wanted to thank you,' Duncan said. 'For everything – for being brave, for investigating the case and for stalling Stan— I mean Benedict. If you hadn't, Dad might not have been able to get the jump on him.'

She reached out and gripped his hand. 'I'm glad we survived. There was a time when I . . . Well, let's say I'm glad I didn't get my wish.'

'When we find this place . . . deal with what we have to do, I wondered if . . . Well, I don't know how to say this, but it's something I've thought about for a while, but with—'

'He wants to ask you out,' Danny said, grinning from behind his comic. 'He hasn't stopped talking about you all the time I've been here.'

'Thanks, Dan,' Duncan said, blushing behind his beard.

Eva stood up and placed her arms on Duncan's shoulders. 'Let's see how things go, but in the meantime, I would like some company.'

'Hey, you two,' Jim said from below the hatch, 'no time for slacking. Get your arses down here. We've got a mission to plan.' He flashed them a smile and ducked back into the ops room.

'I guess we'd better do as the skipper says,' Duncan said, his arms around Eva's waist.

She shrugged. 'He can wait a few minutes longer.'

Eva reached out her right arm and pulled Danny into the hug. She sighed with a mix of relief and anxiety at what the future might hold, but right there, she knew they'd be okay if they stuck together.

As a group.

ACKNOWLEDGEMENTS

A big thanks to Krista Walsh, Jennifer Bender, Maureen Speller, Pauline Nolet, my grandad and my mum for all their help in creating this book. I'd also like to thank the Royal Navy and Simon Warren for their generous help with my ship-related questions.

I'd also like to thank everyone who has taken the time to review one of my books. It means a great deal to me, and I appreciate each and every one of you.

Thank you!

ABOUT THE AUTHOR

 Colin F. Barnes is a publisher and writer of science-fiction and techno thrillers and a member of both the British Fantasy Society and the British Science Fiction Association. He honed his craft at the London School of Journalism and the Open University, where he studied English. Colin has run a number of tech-based businesses, worked in rat-infested workshops, and scoured the back streets of London looking for characters and stories – which he found in abundance. His hobbies include building mechs, pondering the end of the world as we know it, and being manipulated by an evil black cat.

You can connect with Colin at www.colinfbarnes.com and www.facebook.com/colinfrancisbarnes, and you can also follow him on Twitter: @ColinFBarnes.